EATING THE LIVER OF THE EARTH
Mousedeer Tales

THERESA FULLER

Print ISBN: 978-1-925748-29-1

Contents

Section 1-The Trickster

Section 2-Menteri belukar = vizier of the underwood or brush

Section 3-Sheikh Rimba

Section 4-Sang Kancil the not so nice

Beginning of the end of the stories

Foreword

For as long as there have been storytellers, and listeners sitting spellbound at their feet, there have been stories of tricksters - Anansi, Brer Rabbit, Loki. They can be powerful, even frightening; or they can be cute. And when they are little, we're rapt to hear about their adventures, because they remind us that superpowers often come in small packages.

But forget meerkats! You'll love these stories about Sang Kancil - a mischievous little mousedeer, a chevrotain, from Southeast Asia. He may be small, but he can fool a huge elephant, skip across a bridge of crocodiles, and dodge the coconuts flung down at him by monkeys - then cheekily enjoy a drink from the shells they didn't mean to split open for him.

Theresa Fuller loved to listen to her grandfather telling her these stories when she was little and now she's brought together a wonderful collection from Malaysia, Indonesia, Sri Lanka, the Philippines - magical places of rainforests, tigers, leopards, pythons - with words that sound like the chiming and tinkling of music, or the whispering of wind in the bamboo.

Eating the Liver of the Earth opens up a whole world of unexpected treasure!

—Dr Mark MacLeod

Mark co-ordinated courses in Children's Literature and Australian Literature at Macquarie University and courses in Australian Literature and Film for Rollins College, Florida for many years before becoming Children's Publishing Director at Random House Australia.

He published books for young readers and for adults under his own name imprint at Hodder Headline and was Project Manager of 'My Favourite Book' for ABC TV.

Well known as a television and radio presenter, he also writes books for young readers. Mark has been president of the NSW branch of the Children's Book Council of Australia and national president in 2005-6.

He has won the CBCA Lady Cutler Award and the Australian Publishers Association Pixie O'Harris Award for distinguished services to children's literature.

Currently professor at Charles Sturt University, Tasmania

Introduction (Pendahuluan)

My *kun kun* (grandfather) was the Penglipur Lara (Soother of Care i.e., the storyteller) in my family. At bedtime, grandfather (kun kun), would tell me story after story.

As his first-born grandchild, his chu chu, I held a special place in his heart. Sadly, he died young, and I miss him dreadfully to this day. Kun kun nourished my love of folktales, starting with Sang Kancil the mousedeer.

Hence, the mousedeer (chevrotain) holds a very special place in my heart.

After becoming a mother, I searched for the tales I had grown up with and loved. Sadly, I couldn't find many. In fact, most people I asked could, on average, remember only two or three. This spurred me on to collecting all the folktales of the mousedeer that I could find. Each time I thought I was done, I found a few more.

I hope these precious folktales will never be forgotten, as they are a part of my heritage, indeed for everyone who has grown up in Southeast Asia. I found stories from as far away as ancient Ceylon, the Philippines, and even from the sea nomads known as the Moken.

I have always looked upon the folktales of Sang Kancil as pure childish fantasy, stories with morals, of an underdog defeating the villain, of good versus evil, and so I was shocked to discover that not all these folktales were innocent. Quite a few portrayed the mousedeer in rather an unfavourable light.

I have also learnt that folktales can be insidious and not the simple stories I had always presumed. However, what deeper political meaning these tales may originally have held has been lost through the years.

In some stories, I have played the role of the penglipur lara, telling the story in the oral tradition I hope the penglipur lara of old may have done with many repetitions of the same word or phrase or description. The audience of old expected such a style. In some stories, I lead in with my thoughts. These are always in italics to differentiate between the start of the story proper.

In many stories, the spelling of the animals or certain words is different depending on where they originate e.g. raksa, raksasa etc. I have tried to retain this, which is why the spelling appears at times inconsistent.

I hope you enjoy reading these stories as much as I have enjoyed writing them.

Theresa Fuller
12ᵗʰ of January 2024
Sydney

"Reason is a better paragon of virtue than a thousand stupid and foolish friends."
—Author of the Hikayat Sang Kancil.

List of Illustrations

Illustrations by Miriam Bestia
Beruang tossing Terkura out of the tree - Eating the liver of the earth
Pelanduk becomes King
Grandmaster and the Gergasi
Kantjil to the Rescue
The Victory of the Buffalo
Mousedeer and the Crocodile have a tug of war
The Monkeys and the Crocodiles

Illustrations by Lucas Panda
The White Mousedeer
The Leopard and the Mousedeer
The Tragic Tale of Tiptibau the Nighthawk
The Resident's Compound
Sucking the Pond
The Mock Funeral of the Great Commander Harimau
Harimau berdamai dengan kambing
The Celebration

Book Divisions

I have divided this book into 4 sections. My way of dividing made sense to me at the time I started this project but later I found that apparently, consciously, or unconsciously, I had separated the stories into clear divisions with which even the *Penglipur Lara* (Soother of Cares) of old were familiar.

This was a revelation to me and confirmed that these stories are part of my psyche.

Hence it only showed me how important this project is not just to myself but all who are Southeast Asian and perhaps to the world.

Section 1 – Sang Kancil the Trickster

Trickster stories are ubiquitous.

This animal was often weak and small but intelligent.

In Malaysia, Singapore, and Indonesia this was the Pelanduk or Kancil (mousedeer).

In Borneo it is Pelanduk (mousedeer).

In the Philippines it is Pilandok (mousedeer).

In Sri Lanka it is Mīminnī (female mousedeer).

In Sudanese stories, it is Kera the monkey.

In Sulawesi (among the Toraja people) it is the Tarsier monkey.

In Indochina, it is often the rabbit.

But even these tricksters can find themselves tricked by smaller creatures, thus showing that brains matter more than size.

In this first level, the mousedeer is vulnerable to all the dangers of the jungle. He survives only through his wits.

Here, you will find childhood stories: folktales such as Sang Kancil and the Farmer; Sang Kancil and the Buffalo; Sang Kancil and the monkey, etc.

To this day, these simple tales still delight.

Section 2 – Sang Kancil and King Solomon

In this level, the mousedeer now has rank – *pangkat*. He is the Chief Magistrate of King Solomon. His job is to bring peace, hence his title *Sheikh Salaam di Rimba* (Judge of the Jungle).

In this section is King Solomon or Raja Suleiman, as he was known in Malay.

And how a horned creature (Pelanduk) who played jokes (Jenaka) was able to become a leader, a king and more...

Section 3 – Sang Kancil as judge and as king

In this level, mousedeer is king. He rules well but will punish those who disobey. Here are stories from the Hikayat Pelanduk Jenaka (Humorous Tales of the Mousedeer).

I had always thought of Sang Kancil as the underdog. But in these tales, Sang Kancil is a figure of authority.

Section 4 – Sang Kancil the-not-so-nice

I have always loved Sang Kancil but as I researched, I found stories that cast the chevrotain in a rather unsavoury light, and these are featured in this section.

Sometimes Sang Kancil is referred to as Akal Pelanduk.

Those familiar with my book on folktales – *The Girl Sudan Painted Like a Gold Ring* – will remember that the Sea Dyaks referred to Sang Kancil as Akal Pelanduk.

These stories, like the ones in Section 4, present a more vicious mousedeer rather than the well-beloved Sang Kancil.

Here then, are the efforts of my labour.
Enjoy!

And maybe fall in love with Sang Kancil all over again.

Theresa Fuller
19th of April 2023

Geography

Most of these stories take place in the jungle, termed today the rainforest. In Nusantara.

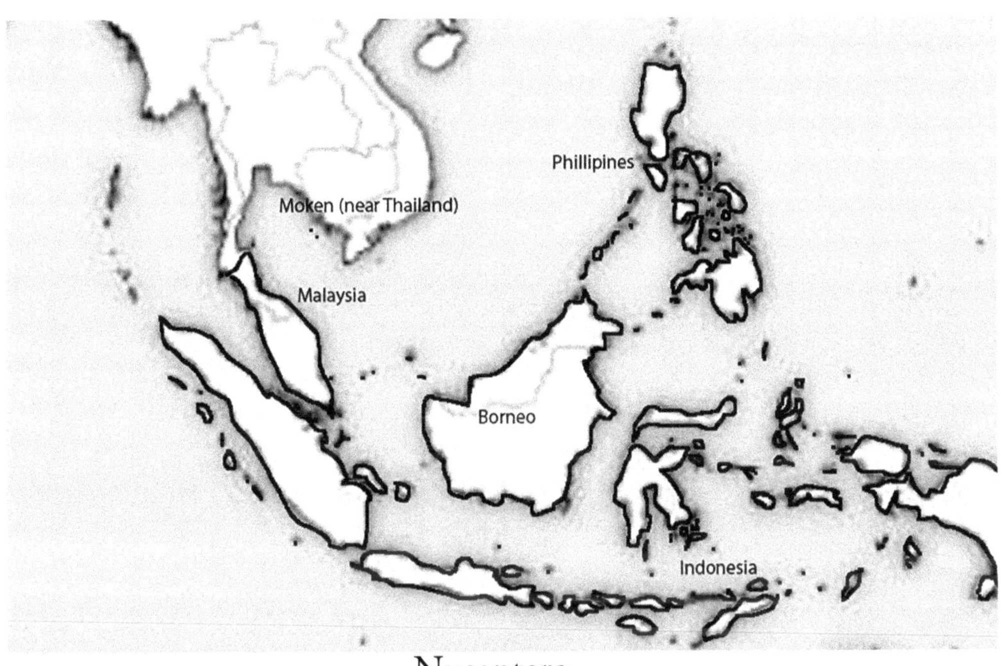

Nusantara

Nusantara is supposed to have originated from Old Javanese and means archipelago: a group of islands. In Malay, it means the Malay world.

The word was apparently taken from an oath by Gajah Mada in 1336, who swore to live an ascetic life by refraining from food containing spices until he conquered the Southeast Asian archipelago.

In Indonesian, it means Maritime Southeast Asia.

Today, it refers to the future capital city of Indonesia.

But the animals in the past had another name for it – The Country of the Gaping Mouth.

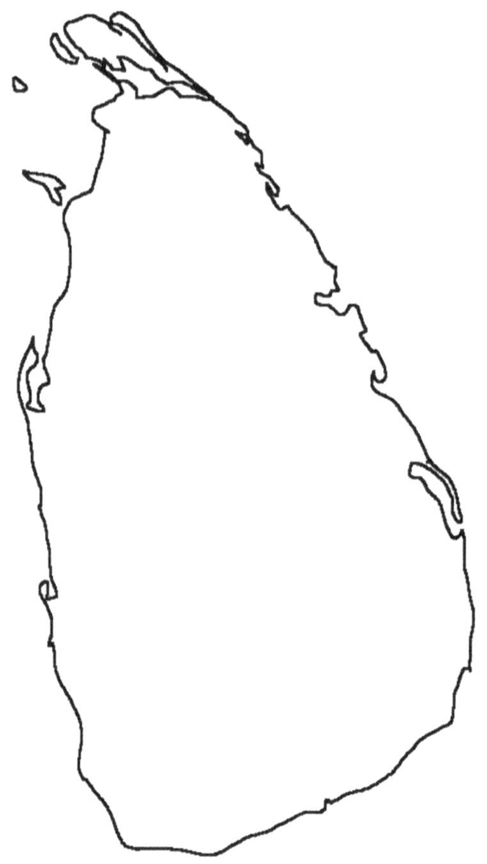

Sri Lanka

Countries from where the stories originate
Indonesia – Once called Nusantara or Dutch East Indies
Malaysia – Once called The Golden Chersonese by the Greeks.
Philippines – Probably 'Ma-I' by Chinese traders.
Singapore – Once called Temasek. (It had quite a few names).
Sri Lanka – Ceylon.
Thailand – Once called Siam.
In the 13th century the Majapahit empire ruled over modern-day Malaysia and Indonesia.

The many names of our Hero

The mousedeer hero of these stories goes by many names:
Sang Kancil – Malay
Kanchel – Baba Malay
Mīminnī – Ceylonese or Sri Lankan
Akal Pelanduk – Borneo, Malay, and Indonesian
Pilandok – Philippines

Europeans have also spelt his name as P'landok, Pelandok, or Kantchil, Kantjil, etc.

Further meanings
Sang = Revered
Akal = Timeless
Pelanduk = Mousedeer or Horn
There is a saying 'As clever as a Kancil.'

Section 1-The Trickster

Trickster tales feature a protagonist who is generally an animal who has been anthropomorphised. Sometimes they have magical powers and can have dual characteristics.

Trickster stories are told for amusement as the trickster creates order out of chaos. The trickster can also play the fool.

The first story shows Sang Kancil at his best as he strives to survive in the rainforest (the correct term nowadays for the jungle.)

The second tells us a little about his home.

This third story is special because it shows Kancil as a child. Pilandok is the Filipino term for mousedeer. Mousedeer fawns are weaned by 10-13 weeks and become adults at 6-8 months.

Enjoy!

Sang Kancil and the Old, Old Woman

I have been in the rainforest at night. I have stretched out my hands and not been able to see them.

Heart thumping, my friends and I stumbled about in the seemingly solid black, walking into tree trunks, praying hard, and all the while, insects screamed and crashed around our heads.

Thankfully, it was only a school trip and within minutes our instructors gave permission to turn our torches back on. Blink! And the jungle appeared before our eyes once more. Relieved to be able to see, we hurried back to camp and to our hard camp beds. And so, I can understand, why when Sang Kanchil saw a fire at night, he raced towards it.

AT FIRST, SANG Kancil thought it was the klips-klips (fireflies).

The orange glow danced before his eyes.

But no, too late did Sang Kancil discover that it was a real fire with a real man seated before it. The man was sharpening his real *parang* (knife). A real, big knife that shone and winked in the firelight.

Lekas! (Quick!) Sang Kancil shot into the hollow of a log.

"*Apa tu?* (What is that)?" said the man, whose name was Abdul Rahman bin Samsudin, which meant - for those of us who are interested – Abdul Rahman, the son of Samsudin.

But it was too dark inside the log for the man to be able to make out what had dashed in.

"*Takpa.* (Never mind)," sighed Abdul. But he knew he had heard something and so to Sang Kancil's shock, the man sat down, his back hard up against the opening of the log and fell asleep.

Sang Kancil would have run out the opposite end of the log if there had been an opening, but sadly, there was not.

So Sang Kancil waited, and perhaps all would have been well. The man would have eventually given up and gone away, only something else happened.

The man's family arrived. Wife, children and uncles.

Abdul's children milled around the fire, warming their hands, and looking around to see if their father had left any food, for they were hungry. Children are always hungry.

They picked up the golden Angsana blooms that lay on the ground and sniffed the Angsana pods, idly cracking open a few, but there was no food to be found.

Their mother was angry, for she had been forced to leave her comfortable house and journey out into the darkness of the night in order to find her husband.

And why had their defender not returned? What was he doing, sound asleep, in what appeared a rather uncomfortable position?

"Some creature rushed into the log, and I was waiting to see what it was," said Abdul sheepishly.

"I see," said the eldest uncle who had been busy judging the situation. "You are guarding by sleeping."

And the other uncles all exchanged a knowing look. They had been busy judging, too.

Abdul blushed and hung his head.

"But if there is something inside, then perhaps we can catch it and eat it," said the eldest uncle, throwing Abdul a lifeline.

And so, Abdul gratefully set about to make a trap. And when he had finished, he showed it to his uncles. "There! Now whatever comes out of that trap cannot help but put its paw in the rotan (flexible piece of bamboo) loop. That will spring the trigger and release the bent sapling."

And all the men smiled as they imagined their prey, perhaps it was a mousedeer, a great delicacy, dangling by one hoof in the air.

But already the children were rubbing their eyes.

"We will need the old, old woman," said the children's mother. "For it is late and they need their bed."

The family only had the one bed and they all shared it, sleeping lumped together in a heap.

And so, the old, old woman was summoned, and she took the place of Abdul while the rest of the family returned to their homes and to their beds.

But the old, old woman did not mind being out in the *hutan* (rainforest). She had a fire for protection, and there was nothing better than to sit idly by and do nothing.

If only she could do that - nothing - all day. But for a woman *something* always needed doing.

And so, she sat in a half stupor, remembering the days when she was young and beautiful. Of bathing in the river. Of meeting her lover. And of her babes.

Warmth washed her face. Her eyelids closed. Her breathing slowed. And the bright red fire spit and crackled.

Things would have gone on in this fashion were it not for the burnished blooms of the Angsana trees carpeting the ground gold, soaking the night air with their exquisite fragrance. A scent stunningly stronger than the creamy white flowers of the Durian.

Blooms drifted onto the old, old woman. With no one seated at the opening of the log, golden blossoms drifted inside.

The strong scent made the old, old woman sneeze.

The strong scent made someone other than the old woman sneeze.

"Eh, *siapa tu?* (Who is that?)" said the old, old, woman.

There was no answer.

The sneezes, however, continued…

As the old, old woman would not leave off asking, Sang Kancil eventually answered.

"It is I."

"Who is *I*?"

"Sang Kancil."

"Ah, I thought it might have been you, Sang Kancil! The wily Sang Kancil. Fastest of Raja Suleiman's creatures in the jungle. And I caught you!" The old, old woman chortled.

Sang Kancil said nothing. He was thinking too hard to speak.

"I shall tell everyone. And they will say there goes the mother of…"

The old, old woman was a grandmother. All grandmothers boast. And so, the old, old woman began. She crowed about her children. Bragged about her grandchildren.

But before the old, old woman could gloat about her *great*-grandchildren, Sang Kancil interrupted.

"I have heard about your handsome sons. So strong and mighty. And I have heard about your beautiful daughters. So well-taught and kind. But please gracious lady, let me come out of this hollow log so that I can listen clearly as you speak about your great-grandchildren, too."

The old, old woman was not having any of that. "Do you think I am stupid? Why, as you are such a fast runner, no sooner will your hooves touch the ground than you will spring away. And what will I be left? *Kosong*. (Nothing.) No, no. I am not as stupid as that." And she laughed, showing the black gaps in her mouth.

Inside the hollow log, Sang Kancil had grown hot and thirsty. He shook his head and blinked twice. But it was no good.

Seated in front of the roaring fire, the old, old woman had also grown hot and thirsty. She snuck her fingers inside the opening of her kebaya blouse and felt the sweat on her skin. She ran her hand up her throat and felt perspiration beading. Then she sighed. If only she could remove her kerosang brooch and spread the two ends of her kebaya apart for relief.

"If only I could stand under the waterfall," said the old, old woman.

"Quench my thirst from the river."

"A coconut, freshly cracked open."

"Durians, yellow and sweet."

"Mangoes! Orange and dripping with juice!"

The old, old woman and Sang Kancil sighed.

"Dukus!"

"Chikus!"

"Pineapples!"

"Limes!"

"*Sedap!* (Delicious!)"

"*Sedap sekali!* (Very delicious!)"

At the thought of freshly squeezed lime juice sweetened with sugar, the old, old, woman smacked her lips hungrily. It was almost morning, and soon the family would be back. One or two swings with the axe and the log would be open…

Sang Kancil swallowed hard. He knew what she was thinking. "Hey, gracious lady, would you like to earn a dollar?"

"*Satu ringgit?* (One dollar)"

"*Ya, saringgit.* (Yes, one dollar)"

"*Apa macham?* (How?)"

Sang Kancil smiled. "Besides me, there is another in this log. A long *ular* (snake)."

"Ah," said the old, old woman. "But what good is that to me?"

"I can drive the snake out. And when I do, catch it. Smack its head against the log and kill it. Then you can sell it at the *pasar* (market)."

"Why will you do that?"

"We have had such a pleasant conversation."

"That is true," said the old, old woman and she put her hands on the ground and slowly she pushed herself up to find that her legs had gone to sleep.

Grumbling, the old, old woman smacked her thighs then crouched in front of the opening. "I am ready."

"*Bagus.* (Good.)"

Sounds of scuffling emerged from the log.

Excited at the thought of earning a dollar, which was in those days a lot of money, the old, old woman stretched her hand out.

Sang Kancil stamped one hoof. "Ready?"

"Ya, ya!" The old, old woman flexed her hand in anticipation.

"Now!"

Something tiny and brown stuck out of the opening.

"Ah!" The old, old woman snatched at snake's head. Only-

"*Aiyoh! Alamat!* (Oh dear! Oh God!)" The old, old woman had forgotten about the trap.

Shooting her hand out at the prize, she had accidentally set off the trigger. Instantly, she was pulled up into the air.

"Aiyah!" And now the old, old woman swung, startled and silenced by her stupidity.

Soon the family would be back.

Sang Kancil trotted out of the log. He dropped the stick he had been holding in his mouth and stopped to admire his handiwork.

A human caught in a trap meant for him.

Swinging back and forth, the old woman was too dazed to even make out the trickster. She kicked her feet and flailed about desperately, but still she swayed, upside down. All she could do now was to wait.

Sang Kancil trotted off to find a drink. It had been hot inside the log.

Sang Kancil and the Elephant

S ANG KANCIL LIVED at the edge of the rainforest, where there was plenty of food, and where the dense undergrowth of creeping bamboo allowed many tunnels that led to resting and to feeding areas. One day, however, he awoke to find a great number of the familiar plants of his habitat had been torn down.

With the odour of raw earth strong in his lungs, the chevrotain picked his way about the terrible scene of destruction.

Whatever could have happened?

Trees had been pushed to one side, bushes had been trampled, and a broad path had been cleared, along with most of the undergrowth that had fed and protected the animals. Harsh white heat beat upon his face as he peered at the sun, for the sheltering canopy was gone.

The chevrotain stopped to examine a young kapok tree lying on its side. Buttress roots, torn from the ground, reached like straggly fingers for the sky, imploring help.

Too late, sadly, thought Sang Kancil, shaking his head.

From the size of the wreckage, the culprit was obvious.

As Sang Kancil blinked in the sudden daylight, the sounds of branches breaking, and trees being pushed aside reached his ears.

That can only be the perpetrator returning.

Sang Kancil waited patiently as the beast approached.

Leaves shook. Branches cracked. The ground rumbled. Then a long grey trunk poked out of the bushes.

"*Apa Khabar*, (What news. This is a form of greeting. Like saying 'Hello'), Sang Gajah?" said Sang Kancil politely, as elephant came into view.

Sang Gajah stopped his feeding for a moment to lift his head high and spread out his ears – the elephant form of greeting.

"Oh, Sang Kancil," said Sang Gajah, looking embarrassed. "I did not know you lived here."

"I have made this area of the jungle my home for some time now," said Sang Kancil, his big round eyes, pools of innocence. "It is very kind of you to come and visit. Is there anything that you want?"

"Well, you know how it is, Sang Kancil," said Sang Gajah, trumpeting effusively. "We all have our part to play. As the largest of the animals, mine is an important role. I trample the forests and the grasslands, and thus make paths for the smaller species. Even Sang Harimau the Tiger uses my paths, you know."

"*Sang Harimau?*" said Sang Kancil, cocking his head. "Do you truly expect us to be grateful that you allow a predator to move around the jungle easily?"

"Oh," said Sang Gajah, his grey ears flapping in embarrassment at his slip. "I also dig waterholes, you know. Very important that."

"Water is certainly important," said Sang Kancil. "I have no argument with you about water, but as you can see, my tunnels are all gon-"

"A great opportunity for new tunnels then. Well, if I were you, I would get started immediately."

Sang Kancil's big brown eyes rounded, for with the trees felled, much of the undergrowth had also been uprooted. He stared pointedly.

Elephant cleared his throat as he looked down at the chevrotain. "Umm, well, as I was saying, I am a *big* animal. I have a *big* role to play in the jungle. Now if you would excuse me, Sang Kancil, I would like to chat longer except that I have *big* things to do, *big* places to be. So, good day!"

And with a hurried trumpet farewell, Sang Gajah mowed down another section of the rainforest as he hurried off.

When the beast was finally gone, Sang Kancil stamped on the ground in anger. This is what mousedeer do when they are annoyed. Their four-toed hooves make quite a racket.

Big! Sang Kancil seethed. *Big indeed!*

He began to think of a plan.

It is true, the Crafty One thought after a while. *When the undergrowth was too thick, it was virtually impossible to move around the jungle. But this is my area. My food. My safety tunnels. My home.*

His deep brown eyes narrowed as an idea formed.

Oh ho, Sang Gajah, you say you make paths. Very important. You say that you dig waterholes? Very important. Ah, yes! Now I know now what I must do. Also, very important.

The next day, Sang Gajah was shearing down a new section when he heard a voice calling.

"Oh, oh!"

"Sang Kancil? Is that you?" said Sang Gajah frowning.

An elephant has a very keen sense of hearing, able to detect sounds from miles away. So Sang Gajah was able, not just to pick up the faint voice, but also its strange unearthly timbre.

Sang Gajah peered about, uneasy at the tone, but could not see the annoying mousedeer. He was about to sneak off when the voice rang out again, this time more urgently.

"I am so glad you have come, Sang Gajah."

Glad? After the confrontation yesterday, Sang Gajah was surprised at the choice of words. "Where are you, Sang Kancil?"

"Over here! Hurry, Sang Gajah," piped the voice. "Hurry before it is too late."

Too late? There was peril in those words.

Immediately, Sang Gajah sniffed the air.

Smell is an elephant's keenest sense to detect danger.

But after a few moments of deep inhaling, Sang Gajah had to admit he had perceived nothing suspicious. He trod forward a few paces in the direction of the mousedeer's voice, pushed aside leaves and vines, and unexpectedly, found himself in a clearing.

Leaves and fallen branches carpeted the ground.

The flat, *treeless* ground.

Elephant paused; he did not remember coming this way.

This was where Sang Kancil's voice had come, yet there was no sign of the chevrotain.

Frowning at the extraordinary development, Sang Gajah lifted his trunk, nostrils crinkling, just as a distinctive smell reached him.

Dank, musty, wet.

Recognising the familiar odour, relief flooded his whole being as finally, elephant understood. He knew *now* what to look for.

He found it.

There in the middle of the clearing.

Leaning his huge head forward, tiny eyes squinting as he searched, he had finally spotted the hole in the ground, partially covered by leaves.

An old disused well, probably abandoned some time ago when it had run out of water.

Gajah was congratulating himself on his cleverness that he had not walked into the well when Sang Kancil called again.

"Hurry, Sang Gajah! There is no time to waste. This is important."

Baffled, elephant took two steps forward and then leaned his huge head over the opening. "Are you in there, Sang Kancil?"

His big voice echoed down the well and elephant winced uneasily, not liking the ghostly reverberations. But now he understood why the quality of the mousedeer's tone had changed.

It was clear that the mousedeer was in the well. Deep down inside the well.

Elephant smirked. "Have you fallen in, and do you want me to pull you out?" said Sang Gajah, ready to laugh as soon as Sang Kancil confirmed that this was the case.

Instead, to Sang Gajah's utter consternation, his words were greeted with a peal of laughter. "Fallen? Nonsense! I jumped in."

Jumped? Gajah cocked his huge head. "I do not understand."

"Why Sang Gajah did you not know? The sky is falling!"

At those words, a frisson of fear took hold of Sang Gajah.

"The… the sky? What do you mean, Sang Kancil?" said elephant, feeling terribly exposed as he peered up at the great expanse of blue, now clearly visible after all the terrain he had torn down.

He imagined being hit on the head as the big blue beyond came suddenly tumbling down. He did not like to think of the consequences if that should happen. Elephant shivered from the slender tip of his grey trunk to his great grey toes.

"Why, exactly what I said. The sky is indeed about to fall. Why do you think I have found myself such a nice and snug shelter here, right at the bottom of this deep well?" said Sang Kancil, sounding very pleased with himself.

Elephant shivered uneasily, not liking how exposed he was to the elements.

"Well, now that you know the sky is falling, hurry and take shelter," said Sang Kancil, sounding wise and contented and snug. Safe.

"Oh, yes, of course," said elephant, wondering why he had not thought of that idea.

"You will need a large hole in the ground," said Sang Kancil helpfully. "Hurry!"

"Why yes, of course," said elephant looking around. "Just how soon is the sky about to fall? How much time do I have?"

"I am afraid I do not know the answers to your questions," said Sang Kancil. "You just need to find a spot like I have. That is the important thing. A *big* hole."

Sang Gajah drew himself up. "You know Sang Kancil. You have a lovely hiding place. A *big* hiding hole."

"That I do," said Sang Kancil, sounding very contented. "*Big.*"

"I am surprised you have not invited me to join you."

"Join me? Why, I would have, if only the well were bigger."

"Bigger?"

"Why, yes. *Bigger.* As you pointed out yesterday, you are the largest of the animals. As you can see, it would be a snug fit if you were down here with me. But you are right. This is a lovely spo- Oh Sang Gajah! Whatever are you- Ah!"

With a loud crash, Sang Gajah had jumped into the well.

Sang Kancil leaped onto the back of Sang Gajah, up onto its head and out of the well.

"What? What are you doing? Should you not be down here?"

Sang Kancil landed neatly on the ground. Then he trotted over to the edge of the well and looked down.

Deep down.

All was darkness.

Slowly, Sang Gajah reached out with his trunk, but so deep down was the well that only the grey tip of the trunk could be seen poking disconsolately around.

"I was thinking… I thought I knew that the sky was falling, but clearly, if such a big and important animal like you did not know about such a big and important event, then I must be wrong. Very wrong. For if the sky was really falling, you would know."

And laughing gaily, Sang Kancil made his way back to his home.

See Notes on Page 325

Pilandok and Sumusong sa Alongan

Animals in the wild leave their parents at an early age to learn to forage for themselves, and Pilandok is no exception.

The Philippines have six types of forest: mangrove, beach, molave, dipterocarp, pine, and the cloud forest. Here, the mousedeer is the Tragulus nigricans; Tragulus meaning 'little goat' so named because of the horizontal pupils of its eyes. Its coat is black and brown, and it has white stripes on its throat and chest. It is known as Pilandok.

EARLY ONE MORNING, Pilandok sets off in search of sustenance but after walking some distance and not finding anything, Pilandok decides to rest under a tree. It is hot work hunting for food. Instead of closing both eyes though, Pilandok only closes one. This is how he comes by the nickname – Close only One Eye.

Soon, Prince Sumusong sa Alongan comes riding along. Bags of gold and other treasure from his many conquests hang from his saddle, winking in the sunlight. He sees Pilandok and at once asks what he is doing.

Startled, Pilandok, still with only one eye open, looks around for the sound of the voice. His chest tightens when he spots the prince.

What am *I doing? How do I answer without getting into trouble?*

Then he notices the beehive and an idea comes. He does not want to appear idle, in case the prince decides to punish him for laziness. He opens his other eye and tells the prince that he is guarding the gong.

Now, gongs in Asia are status symbols. In some cultures, simply touching a gong can bestow wealth and good fortune on the individual. Gongs are often beaten to clear the way for important officials or for announcements, to summon help, or spirits, or even in some instances to initiate healing.

It is little wonder then that the prince is agog with this discovery. Of course, he wants to beat the gong. It is his birthright!

"Oh," says Pilandok. "Gongs should only be beaten by royalty. Not by ordinary men. I am only a humble servant-"

The prince stamps his foot. "That's right! Gongs should only be beaten by royalty, and I am a prince. I am no ordinary man. My father is a Sultan. I, therefore, have every right to beat this gong."

When Pilandok hesitates, Prince Sumusong sa Alongan offers him gold. A whole bag of gold.

Gold opens doors. Gold will buy food for Pilandok's family, and the mousedeer is tempted to accept. But there is no gong, only a beehive.

Even at this young age, mousedeer knows what will happen when Prince Sumusong sa Alongan beats *that* gong.

Pilandok swallows hard. "Your Highness, please understand that I am only a humble servant and that your servant does not wish to get into trouble." He bows.

"I am a prince." Prince Sumusong sa Alongan lifts his chin and rakes his long black hair.

What royalty wants royalty gets.

"Very well then, if you insist, but please before you do so, allow me to take the bag of gold and to be a respectful distance from your august person when the deed is done. For I do not wish to be around when my master discovers what I have done and decides to chop off my head."

"Do not worry," says Prince Sumusong sa Alongan graciously. "When your master discovers that it is I, all will be well."

So Pilandok takes the bag of gold and is leagues away when Prince Sumusong sa Alongan beats the golden gong.

Only it is not a gong at all as Pilandok has always known. And what Prince Sumusong sa Alongan is about to find out.

Bang! Bang-bang-boom-bang!

The hive collapses inward.

Enraged bees swarm out. Before the startled prince they form a hideous mass of moving black. Then they confront the invader who has attacked their home.

Prince Sumusong sa Alongan is bitten mercilessly and would have died, had not a troop of soldiers passing by come to his rescue. They push him into the river.

And save his life.

Pilandok returns in triumph to his parents and lives to trick again.

> Mousedeer Fact: Mummy mousedeer are pregnant from five to nine months. When born the foal can stand on its own within the hour. The young look like miniature adults when born. Parental care is limited, and the foal is weaned at three months of age. They reach sexual maturity between 5 to 10 months.

See Notes on Pages 325-326

Sang Kancil counts the crocodiles

In Malaysia, Singapore, and Indonesia, Sang Kancil is the Tragulus Javanicus. Or Tragulus Kanchil.

I T IS SAID that riverbanks are dangerous places. Fallen trees, slippery rocks, soil slippage, mosquitoes, and of course crocodiles. Thence, the rain forest animals go down to the riverbank only when they need water desperately.

Sang Kancil was trotting along the riverbank one day, where, in the green-brown water, resembling logs, floated the *buaya* (crocodiles).

"Eh, *kawan* (friends)! You look so big and so strong!" said Sang Kancil. "Strong enough to conquer any country if you so choose."

Emerald eyes blinked open. Black slits narrowing, the crocodiles watched the chevrotain hungrily. "*Ya*, (Yes), Sang Kancil. Even man is afraid of us. Look how well we are armed."

The crocodiles swam towards the bank where they showed Sang Kancil their great sharp claws and their great sharp teeth and slowly waved their great heavy tails. "A single swing can knock a man down."

"That I can believe."

The crocodiles preened.

A crocodile's tail is not only a tremendous source of power, but also a weapon. Enormous muscles attach a crocodile's tail to its hips and back legs. Combined with the tail's very shape — flattened on the sides with scales that stick up — enables the crocodile to not only shoot through the water but also to propel themselves out. It is a weapon that allows crocodiles, for short bursts, to move faster than humans on land. Fast enough to catch a mousedeer loitering on a riverbank.

Sang Kancil cocked his head. "Just for my sake, how many of you are there in the river?"

"Ah, many!" said the crocodiles and smiled their toothy smiles.

"Ah, but how many? I need to know. Would you mind if I counted you?

"Certainly, you may. Only how do you propose to do so?" Emerald eyes gleamed, knowing that they had all the time in the world.

Sang Kancil's dark brown eyes danced in response. "If you could please form a line across the river, then I can jump from back-to-back as I count. Why then I can tell all the others, what a great number you are!"

The conceited crocodiles did as Sang Kancil instructed. They formed a line from one riverbank to the other. Then they slitted their emerald eyes and waited.

Sang Kancil did not hesitate. He jumped ever so lightly onto the back of the first crocodile and began to *kira* (count). "*Satu* (One), *dua* (two), *tiga* (three), *empat* (four), *lima* (five)-"

In this manner, Sang Kanchil trotted along the crocodile *jambatan* (bridge) until he reached the other side. At once, he leapt onto the shore.

Scrambling safely out of reach, he turned back to address the excited crocodiles.

"How many? How many of us are there?" And they waited eagerly for the answer.

A hundred? A thousand?

"A number that is just enough to form a bridge from one side to the other!"

The crocodiles opened their mouths to object, but to their shock, already Sang Kancil had turned and trotted off. The chevrotain called out as he made his hurried way up the bank, "Thank you very much, Sang Buaya, for helping me to get to the other side! I really did not want to get my feet wet."

Wet?

The angry crocodiles hissed and snorted and lunged at the chevrotain when they realised that they had been duped.

Only it was to empty space. For already Sang Kancil had reached the top of the bank!

The enraged buaya thrashed the water with their mighty tails.

"Do not forget, Sang Kancil, that we live on land as well as on water!" Opening their mouths wide, the crocodiles roared. And roared.

But Sang Kancil was out of sight.

Kancil's goal is always food, but what food?

Peanut leaves are one such example. Air jambu, chadong fruit, rambai and lamah-lamah are others.

See Notes on Pages 326-327

Pilandok and Sabandar

P RINCE SUMUSONG-SA-ALONGAN had a relative named Sabandar.

And Sabandar wanted revenge.

Pilandok was resting under a tree when Sabandar found him.

"Are you Pilandok?" asked Sabandar.

"Yes, I am," said Pilandok. He stood and smiled politely but he was ready to shoot away if necessary.

"Good. I am going to kill you." And Sabandar drew his sword.

Pilandok thought quickly. Luckily, just above his head, wrapped around a branch hung the heavy coils of a python.

> Pythons are non-venomous snakes. Their colour patterns which include olive green, black, white, tan, yellow, gold and brown allow them to camouflage themselves. They constrict i.e., coil around their victims, squeezing tighter with each breath suffocating their victims, utilising the stretchy skin between their lower jaw to swallow prey six times their size. Including humans.

Pilandok smiled politely and pointed to his big bright eyes. "Wait, please. In this village are two Pilandoks. There is Pilandok-Upstream and Pilandok-Downstream. I am Pilandok-Downstream. You can tell that this is true because Pilandok-Upstream is blind in one eye. As you can see, I am not."

"Oh!" Sabandar dropped his arm. "I can see that you have two eyes so that must be true. Sumusong-sa-Alongan had mentioned that the mousedeer who tricked him had one eye closed. So, what are you doing here?"

"You see that black belt?" Pilandok indicated the sleeping snake with the tip of his snout.

Sabandar nodded.

"That is the belt of my queen." Pilandok bowed.

Queen. Sabandar's eyes widened. "Oh, please if that belt belongs to royalty, then please, I must try it on. You must let me try it on."

"No, of course not. You must not ask me. You cannot. Do you know how angry the queen will be if she finds out that someone has even touched her precious possessions, let alone tried them on? No, no, never ask me such a question. I am a good and honourable servant to the queen whom I love so much."

"Please," begged Sabandar. "Look, is it wealth that you want? I am a rich man. Just name your price."

"No, please, I beg of you. Do not ask. I will never betray my queen's trust." Tears appear in his brown eyes.

Sabandar was touched, but he really wanted that belt. "Here, please. Take this ruby ring for a start."

The red jewel sparkled and glimmered in the band of gold.

And Sabandar smiled as he saw how Pilandok's eyes rounded.

Pilandok swallowed. "No, no, please do not even bother to tempt me. My mistress will cut my head off."

"Here, then, is everything that I own."

"Oh!" Pilandok pretended to be shocked. He appeared to be considering. "I cannot just let any man touch her belt."

Sabdandar threw his chest out. "I am not just any man."

Pilandok sighed deeply. "Very well then. But it is true what I said. I do not wish my head separated from my body. You must give me plenty of time to get away."

"Take as much time as you need." Sandandar rubbed his hands, unable to believe his good luck. He waited until Pilandok had gathered up all his wealth and was a long, long way away before he strode up to the python.

Sabandar hummed merrily as he removed the belt from the branch.

"It must be worth a fortune. It is so heavy."

Sabandar held the belt this way and that, enjoying how the sunlight reflected off the skin, turning the black sheen almost iridescent.

His heart swooned at the belt's rich beauty.

"What beautiful colours!" Sabandar wrapped the belt carefully around his waist.

He was admiring the exquisite workmanship when the end that he was fastening suddenly reared up. "What?" His jaw dropped.

"Ah, lunch," said the python whose jaw dropped even lower. Then he proceeded to squeeze and constrict.

Pilandok, of course, was far, far away.

Mousedeer and the Crocodile
have a tug of war

> The common crocodile in Malaysia is *Crocodilus Porosus*. It varies in colour, being sometimes black and yellow, at other times completely black. According to the late H.N Ridley, the yellow variety is considered by Malays to be the most dangerous. As a tidal as well as a marine animal, this species seldom goes up beyond tidal waters and may be found far out at sea.

Sang Kancil was walking along the river one day when he spotted his enemy, Sang Buaya. The crocodile was sunning himself quietly on the banks.

Of course, the mousedeer would decide to go over and say hello. Only Sang Kancil is brave enough to do something like this. And this is why I love him so.

"APA KHABAR (WHAT NEWS I.E., HELLO), Sang Buaya," said Sang Kancil. "*Lu baik*? (Are you well?)"

Now Sang Kancil and Sang Buaya have an understanding.

Sang Kancil knows that Sang Buaya will eat him if he strays too close. And Sang Buaya knows that Sang Kancil is a trickster. There is no love lost between the two, just the plain and honest relationship of predator and prey.

Only who is who is sometimes unclear.

Snap!

Sang Kancil leapt into the air narrowly avoiding Sang Buaya's jaws.

"Ah, Sang Kancil," said Sang Buaya with a heavy sigh as the mousedeer landed safely and sadly out of his reach. "It would be a fine morning indeed if I could catch you. I am so hungry."

Sang Kancil laughed; he had no hard feelings. This was Sang Buaya after all. Kancil knew what to expect. "Lu? (You?) You cannot catch me because you are too weak."

Sang Kancil's words surprised Sang Buaya but then Sang Kancil cannot avoid saying such things.

Sang Kancil is Sang Kancil.

Sang Buaya's eyes rounded as he stared at his presumptuous prey and then the mighty predator laughed. "Ha, ha, ha! You joke!"

Sang Kancil puffed his chest out. "Eh, why are you laughing? It is true. I am strong and you are weak."

Sang Buaya laughed once more only this time the laughter was softer. He cocked his head uncertainly at the tiny creature. None had ever spoken to him in this manner.

His prey's eyes were large and luminous and brown. "Let us have a contest."

Contest?

This is Sang Kancil through and through.

When Sang Buaya hesitated, the cheeky one laughed heartily.

Now if there is one thing that Sang Buaya does not like, it is being laughed at. After all, is he not the king of the river?

Who dares laugh at a king?

But of course, the obvious answer is - Sang Kancil.

"Here is a length of rope. I will take hold of one end while you grasp the other. When we each have a good firm grip then we will have a tug of war. We shall both pull as hard as we can."

Sang Buaya shook his head impatiently. "I am too hungry to play stupid games." He readied himself to swim off.

"Stupid? If you can pull me into the water, then you can eat me."

Eat Sang Kancil?

Sang Buaya lifted his mighty head. He liked the sound of this contest. He liked his prospects. He liked to eat. Especially foolish, irritating creatures who toyed with him. And laughed at him.

Sang Kancil threw one end of the rope to Sang Buaya, who caught it in his powerful jaws.

"Now to be fair, move backwards a little, so I have a chance to flex my muscles," said the trickster. "As for me, I shall move back myself to be fair to you."

Ah, thought the cruel beast, the water is my environment. I can use all my brute strength. I will pull Sang Kancil into the river as quick as blinking.

For the Big One had a secret weapon. And it wasn't his tail.

But what he didn't know was that so did Sang Kancil.

So Sang Buaya moved good-naturedly down the bank until he was in the water. But while he was doing so, the trickster calmly tied his end of the rope to the sturdy trunk of a tree.

To anyone observing, it appeared he had gone behind the tree. Sang Buaya had no idea that the rope was tied to the tree.

When Sang Kancil was done, he plonked his rump down behind the tree, and called, "Ready, Sang Buaya? Then pull!"

He was completely out of sight.

All that could be seen was a rope going up to and around the tree trunk and then disappearing behind the tree.

Filled with thoughts of an easy victory, Sang Buaya clamped hard with his jaws and then to distribute the force throughout the mouth, he fastened down with his second jaw joint. That was Sang Buaya's secret weapon.

This second jaw joint is how crocodiles latch on to their prey and never let go. It is a sinister device.

The rope tightened with a loud *twang*!

The crocodile thrashed. Clouds of water sprayed the air.

But then the rope was tied to a tree, and as for the tree the rope was tied to, well, the tree bent. A bit.

The contest continued. After several tense moments when nothing happened, Sang Buaya released his grip and rose to the surface.

As he did so the rope relaxed, and the tree straightened. It really wasn't that bent.

Sang Buaya glanced along the line of the rope which led straight up the riverbank and disappeared behind the tree. The crocodile had no idea that hidden behind the massive trunk of the tree was the mousedeer simply sitting.

Sang Buaya assumed Sang Kancil was using the trunk of the tree for leverage.

"Are we having a rest?" called out the chevrotain. "Why, we have barely started!"

Sang Buaya went cold. He had used most of his strength in trying to pull Sang Kancil into the river. But he would never admit it.

Instead, the mighty crocodile hissed, a sign that an attack was imminent.

"I am ready." Sang Buaya lifted his great head with fierce determination, and then without warning, he yanked once more.

Head above the water, Sang Buaya saw how as he tugged, the tree bent. And yet there was no sign of the mousedeer.

At this, Sang Buaya grew afraid.

How strong was the creature?

He jumped as a tiny voice piped. "Do you wish another rest?"

"Yes, but only for a short while," said Sang Buaya in his most pleasant tone. "I believe I know now what to do."

To Sang Buaya's amazement Kancil did not even sound breathless.

The competition began again.

Once more, the two animals pulled.

And once more, the rope tensed until the mighty Sang Buaya did what all crocodiles do to subdue prey – he rolled.

The Death Roll.

And once more the tree bent. But only the teeniest bit more.

By now Sang Buaya was exhausted. The Death Roll had accomplished nothing.

The crocodile had tried his hardest, but no matter how much he thrashed and no matter how much he splashed, and no matter how much water washed against the bank, the monster was unable to pull the mousedeer into the water.

Finally, Sang Kancil popped his head round the tree. He saw the fear in Sang Buaya's green-slit eyes and smiled. "How about one last pull? You surely should have the gist of things by now?"

Sang Buaya quivered deep inside when he saw how calm Sang Kancil appeared.

He does not look tired at all. And if we pull one last time, there is no doubt that he will pull me out of the water. The thought made Sang Buaya's stomach roil.

But he was not the only one thinking that thought.

Kancil cocked his head at the giant predator. "You know, Sang Buaya, we agreed that if you pulled me into the water, then you could eat me. But what happens if I pull you out onto the land? What would you like to happen?"

Sang Kancil's eyes were limpid pools of innocence as he waited patiently for an answer.

The mighty predator had used all his power and strength, and to his shock he was still unable to pull the mousedeer into the water. So instead, he reminded himself that the silly mousedeer was only a tiny morsel. Not worth the effort. While he, he was technically the dominant predator.

"Oh, you know what, Sang Kancil? We don't need to decide that now. As I said before, I am hungry, and consequently I am not as strong as I could be. Let's have this competition some other day when I am not as famished. For now, I am happy to say that you are possibly as strong as me."

"For sure?" Sang Kancil tilted his head innocently.

"Have a good day, Sang Kancil," said Sang Buaya as he ducked off with one flick of his enormous tail.

And as Sang Kancil laughed merrily, Sang Buaya swam slowly down the river. And did not look back.

See Notes on Page 327

Tiger gets his deserts

*H*ARIMAU (TIGER) WAS caught in a trap one day.

As a man was passing, the desperate tiger pleaded to be released before the hunter arrived.

"If I set you free," said the man, scratching his chin as he pondered. "Will you promise not to attack me?"

"Of course," said the crafty Harimau, looking innocent.

The man decided he would do good and so opened the trap.

The tiger sprang out, but before the man could go on his way, the deceitful creature leapt upon the poor soul, pinning him to the ground.

"What are you doing?" cried the stunned rescuer. "You promised only a moment ago, to not do exactly the thing you are doing."

Harimau winced, a touch embarrassed. "When I was in the trap I was prepared to say and do whatever I must in order to obtain my release, but now that I am free, I am bound by nothing."

"But I did good," said the man. "Surely you cannot repay good with evil. That is what the *adat* decrees."

"*Adat?*"

"The Law of the Land. Can you not at least wait to see how the law stands with our contract?" said the desperate man.

"Let it not be said that I broke the law," said Harimau. "I can wait."

The man and the tiger set out together.

They came upon a road.

"Oh Road, tell us. Is it lawful to repay good with evil? Surely good for good only?" said the man, his eyes watering.

"I do good to man, but they repay my goodness with evil, for they defile my surface daily," the Road replied.

On hearing these words, Tiger prepared to devour the man, only the man begged that he be allowed to ask a second time.

"Let it not be said that I am unjust," said Harimau. "I can wait."

The man and the tiger set out once more and this time came upon a tree.

"Oh Tree, tell us. Is it lawful to repay good with evil? Surely good for good only?" said the man.

"I do good to man, but they repay my goodness with evil, for they lop off my branches, and in the end cut me down," the Tree replied.

On hearing these words, the tiger opened his mouth to devour the man only the man begged to ask, one final time.

"Let it not be said that I am unkind," said Harimau. "I can wait."

The third inhabitant of the jungle that the man and the tiger came upon last was Sang Kancil.

The chevrotain blinked his big dark eyes as the pair approached.

"Oh, Sang Kancil, tell us. Is it lawful to repay good with evil? Surely good for good only?" said the man, his voice shaking. For this was his final chance.

But to the trembling man's despair, the mousedeer's immediate reaction was to simply shake its head. "I really do not understand what you are asking."

By now, Harimau was ravenous. "Well then that is that. I shall now proceed to ea-"

"Wait!" said Sang Kancil. "I may not understand, but I know how you can solve my confusion. Let us return to the trap so you can explain how this situation came about."

"Let it not be said that I am unaccommodating," said Tiger. "I can wait."

The man and the tiger, along with the puzzled mousedeer, returned to the trap.

"This is the trap," said Tiger, indicating the structure with a toss of its head.

"And this is where I found Harimau," said the man, his face long with worry, for he sensed that his end was near. He had asked three inhabitants of the jungle, and none had been able to assist. How would a creature like a mousedeer be able to help?

Most likely the tiger would eat him, and then for dessert, the mousedeer.

Sang Kancil frowned as though thinking hard. "Is that so?" The mousedeer trotted up to the wooden structure and sniffed. After several long moments, he finally turned to the waiting pair. "I do not believe it."

Tiger's jaw dropped. "What? Do you doubt my word?" The words ended with a roar.

The man cowered with fright.

"It is just that you are so big…" said Sang Kancil cringing. "And the trap so…"

"Ah, is that all?" Harimau gloated smugly. "Easily solved."

The large cat strode up to the trap. "I will demonstrate."

Before their startled eyes, the impatient tiger entered. "See, and this is-"

"Shut the door!" shouted Sang Kancil.

The man wasted no time in drawing down the door of the trap, this time, shutting the astonished tiger within.

"Accursed creature, you have repaid good with evil," said the man.

"What! I was just demonstrating!" Harimau choked. "Let me out!"

"Let you out after you broke your promise?" The man gave a bitter laugh. "Never. And now you shall get your just rewards."

And so, the man called his neighbours, and together they killed the tiger.

See Notes on Pages 327-328

The Kinot

B*AHASA MELAYU DAN* Bahasa Inggeris
Malay and English

Dua pemotong rotan kena hilang dalam hutan rimba.
Two rotan cutters got lost in the Deep Forest.
Satu takut.
One afraid.
Satu berani.
One brave.
Buat apa?
What to do?
Mari kita tidor.
Come let us sleep.
Kepala takut antara paha berani.
The head of the frightened man between the thighs of the brave man.
Kepala berani antara paha takut.
The head of the brave man between the thighs of the frightened man.
Semua tidor.
They all slept.
Kemudian harimau tiba.
Then the tiger arrived.
Harimau terperanjat.
The tiger was surprised.
Apa binatang itu?
What animal is that?
Saya tak nampak sebelum hari ini.

I have never seen it before tonight.
Kemudian Sang Kancil tiba.
Then the mousedeer arrived.
Apa khabar, Sang Kancil?
Hello, Sang Kancil.
Khabar baik.
I am good.
Apa khabar, Sang Harimau?
Hello, Revered Tiger.
Khabar baik.
I am good.
Sang Kancil, awak tahu-kah, apa binatang itu?
Sang Kancil, do you know what that animal is?
Sang Kancil tak terperanjat.
Sang Kancil was not surprised.
Ya. Saya selalu ada nampak binatang ini.
Yes. I have always seen this creature.
Awak tidak tahu apa binatang ini?
Do you not know what animal this is?
Tidak. Saya tidak tahu apa binatang ini.
No. I do not know what animal this is.
Ini Kinot.
This is the Kinot.
Apa Kinot?
What is a Kinot?
Says tidak pernah melihat Kinot.
I have never seen a Kinot.
Saya tidak pernah mengdengar tentang Kinot.
I have never heard of the Kinot.
Ini-lah binatang yang membunoh awak punya ibu, bapak dan nenek datok.
This is the creature that killed your parents and grandparents.
Lari chepat-chepat!
Run quick!
Sebelum dia membunoh awak.
Before he kills you.
And this is why from that day forth, no tiger has ever been seen on the boundless isle of Borneo.

See Notes on Page 328

The Leopard and the Mousedeer

THERE WAS A leopard who lived in a cave in the middle of the rainforest in Ceylon. When the leopard went hunting one day, a female *Mīminnī* (mousedeer) who was lame, entered to give birth.

Now female mousedeer can generally give birth at any time of the year. In fact, they breed from 5-6 months on. A mousedeer being a hoofed animal means that the newborn fawns are precocial i.e., born in an advanced state and therefore able to feed themselves and move independently almost immediately. It can stand within 30 minutes of having been born and are weaned at around twelve weeks.

The doe had not one but two fawns, which is very rare. She began to worry.

The leopard will soon return.

And in fact, shortly after the birth it rained. So, the leopard would return even earlier.

Though the cave had provided precious protection for the act of birth, it might soon be their tomb.

When the doe heard sounds of the leopard returning, she beat her two fawns.

"Spoilt things! I have given you fresh leopard's meat. And now when I give you dried leopard's meat you cry and grumble for fresh!"

On hearing those words, Leopard was taken aback. "No doubt if I enter, I will be eaten." And so, Leopard sprang away in search of his preceptor.

His teacher was a jackal.

"Why are you running away, sir? You look to be much afraid. Why is that so?"

Leopard explained that a *Mīminnī* had entered the lair to give birth.

"And she feeds her fawns fresh leopard meat," finished the distraught Leopard.

The preceptor's cycs widened. Such a thing was unheard of!

"Why as I entered, she sprang at me and when I turned to flee, she chased me! I was lucky to escape with my life!" said Leopard, dramatizing a little.

His teacher rose to his feet. "Do not fear. I will come with you. I will enter the cave and drive her out. Young or no young."

Leopard was mightily afraid, but he agreed to follow the preceptor. When they neared the cave however, he hung back.

"I cannot go. I cannot."

Seeing his student in such a state, the wise teacher had a plan. "Let us rope ourselves together."

Leopard went off to gather some creepers and they tied one end of the creeper to Jackal's throat and the other end to Leopard's waist.

And so, in this manner, they proceeded.

As they neared, the mother mousedeer saw them. Once again, she beat her young ones. "Don't cry, don't cry my babies. See, here is the kind Jackal and look at what he is bringing! A leopard!"

Then she turned to Jackal. "I asked for seven yokes of leopards. Why do you only come with one? My babies will still cry with hunger."

When Leopard heard those words, he panicked.

And he shot off as fast as he could. But he forgot that the other end of the creeper was still attached to the startled Jackal, who took off in the opposite direction, so that the preceptor found himself dashed and slapped up against boulders and trees and bushes.

After a while, when Leopard felt he had covered a sufficient distance from the cave to feel safe, he stopped.

Although the creeper had loosened a little in the tumult, when Leopard turned and glanced over, he found himself still attached to Jackal.

Leopard cocked his head and stared aghast.

For Jackal's face was plastered in a grin.

"The laugh is on you," said Leopard, lifting his head in anger. "I am still breathing."

But when Leopard took a long hard look, he realised that Jackal's face was frozen in the caricature of death.

His preceptor was dead.

See Notes on Pages 329-330

How Beruang lost his tail or
Pickled Tiger's Eyeballs

*T*ULISKAN CHAKAPAN BABA *or* Baba Malay
Written in *Inggeris* or English

Amcham Beruang sua hilang dia mia ekor
How the Bear lost his tail.

Tempu sinjakala.

The time was twilight.

Sa-ekor kanchel dudok dalam lobang kat atair busut tengah makan buah terung, bila dia dengar arimo datang.

A mousedeer was sitting in a hole on top of a mound eating false eggplant, when he heard the tiger coming.

Sang Kanchel pikir dia mo main bangsat.

Sang Kancil thought he would play a trick.

Kanchel gasak bising-bising.

Kancil gobbled noisily.

"Kerab kerab kertub kertub. (Sounds of eating.)"

"Kerab kerab kertub kertub."

"Amboi! Saya makan achair mata-mata arimo ni yang sedap sekali!" kata Kanchel ampat ka lima kali.

"Hey! I am eating pickled tiger's eyes that are the most delicious," said Kancil four or five times.

"Kertab kertub kertab, kertub."

"Kertab kertub kertab kertub."

Arimo sedair ada binatang dalam lobang, tapi bila arimo dengair kata-kata binatang tu, dia terperanjat.

Tiger was aware that there was an animal in the hole, but when Tiger heard the animal's words, he was shocked.

Sua malam kat hutan rimba.

It was already night in the Deep Forest.

Pasair gelap, Arimo, Maharajah Belang, tak'leh nampak sapa makan achair mata-mata arimo.

Because it was dark, Tiger, the Striped Emperor, could not see who was eating pickled tiger's eyes.

Takot, Arimo chabot.

Frightened, Tiger fled.

Arimo bersua Beruang.

Tiger unexpectedly met Bear.

"Hei, Apa khabair, Sang Beruang?"

"Ho, what news, Revered Bear?"

"Khabhair baik, Arimo."

"I am well, Tiger."

"Sapa tu gasak achair mata-mata arimo kat situ?" tanya Arimo.

Who is that stuffing himself with pickled tigers' eyes far away over there?

"Saya tak tau." jawab Beruang.

"I do not know," answered Bear.

"Mari kita pi kat tempat tu tengok sapa makan achair mata arimo," bilang Arimo.

"Come let us go to that place to see who is eating pickled tiger's eyes," said Tiger.

"Gua takot," kata Beruang.

"I am scared," said Bear.

"Kita kawan baik bukan kawan biasa. Beruang yang brani sekali, mari kita bungkus kita mia ekor bersama-sama janji persahabatan. Pasair tu kita bolih tolong sama-sama kita."

"We are good friends, not ordinary friends. Bear, who is bravest of all, come, let us tie our tails together as a promise of friendship. Then we can help each other."

Abis, Arimo bungkus dia mia ekor sama Beruang mia ekor.

So, Tiger tied his tail with the tail of Bear.

Arimo balek kat tempat tak'ah pokok-pokok sama Beruang.

Tiger returned to the clearing with Bear.

Kanchel nampak Arimo balek sama Beruang.

Kancil saw Tiger return with Bear.

"Selamat Malam, Ng Ko Arimo!" kata Kanchel. "Kamsiah! Lu ada ati. Saya pikir lu malair, tapi saya salah. Lu tau adat. Lu bawak kasi tangan kasi saya."

"Good night, Elder Brother Tiger!" said Kancil. "Thank-you! You are thoughtful. I thought you were lazy, but I was wrong. You know the law. You have brought me a gift."

"Eh, Kanchel kata apa?" tanya Beruang.

"Eh, what is he saying?" asked Bear.

"Bohong!" jawab Arimo.

"Lies!" answered Tiger.

"Rajin! Panday! Brani! Lu kasih gua lu mia hutang. Tarok gua mia beruang bawah pokok ni," suroh Sang Kanchel.

"Diligent! Clever! Brave! You are returning your debt. Put my bear under this tree," instructed Sang Kancil.

"Gua suay!" pekek Beruang. "Lu mo hampus saya!"

"I am unlucky!" screamed Bear. "You want to get rid of me!"

Beruang chobak lari-kan diri, tapi dia mia ekor bungkus sama ekor arimo.

Bear tried to escape, but his tail was tied to the tail of Tiger.

"Jangan lari! Jangan takot! Dia chakap bohong," pekek Arimo.

"Don't run! Don't be frightened. He is telling lies," screamed Tiger.

"Lu chakap bohong," jawab Beruang. "Gua mo lari!"

"You are the one who is telling lies," answered Bear. "I must run away!"

Macham gila dua binatang begadoh-gadoh.

Like crazy, the two animals fought.

Abis-

Then-

Adoi! Beruang mia ekor koyak.

Oh dear! Bear's tail tore off.

"Tak pa. Ng Ko Arimo, lain kali beri saya beruang puteh," suroh Kanchel.

"Never mind. Elder Brother Tiger, next time bring me a white bear," instructed Kanchel.

Ni chrita amcham beruang tak'ah ekor.

This is the story of how the bear has no tail.

See Notes on Page 330

Sang Kancil and Sang Beruang

Sang Beruang (Revered Bear) was resting under a tembusu tree when Sang Gagak the crow found him.

> Tembusu trees are native to Southeast Asia. Their bark is a dark brown and deeply fissured; their leaves are light green and oval shaped, and their flowers are yellowish. Their red berries are bitter, and often eaten by fruit bats.

THE CROW LEANT over. "*Mana Sang Kancil?* (Where is Sang Kancil?)"

"*Tak'tau.* (Don't know,)" said Sang Beruang lazily.

"Ah, then you don't know the plans that Sang Kancil has for you."

"Plans? What plans?"

"He intends to kill you."

Sang Beruang jerked out of his stupor. "What? Why?"

"He has confided in me that he is tired of having to find food for you. That you are too lazy to do so on your own. So, he has made up his mind to kill you."

"What! Why that good-for-nothing!" Sang Beruang jumped up. He stamped his feet. "*Terima kasih* (Thank you) for telling me."

Sang Gagak bobbed his head. His mischief done; he flew off.

Sang Beruang sought out the mousedeer. To his surprise, Sang Kancil was limping.

"What happened to you?"

The mousedeer looked grateful for Sang Beruang's solicitude. "I have hurt my paw."

Was this true? Did it matter?

Beruang beamed. "No problem. I will take you to my friend. He will have medicine that will help."

Sang Kancil was delighted. He thanked Sang Beruang and together they went off in search of Sang Beruang's friend.

As Sang Beruang walked, he congratulated himself.

How clever am I? Not only does the mousedeer believe me, but he is also injured. It will be a simple task when he is not looking to pounce on him. I wonder what mousedeer meat tastes like.

Sang Beruang drooled. He towered over the mousedeer, so it was hard not to notice slimy saliva pouring from the bear's lower jaw.

Sang Kancil swallowed hard. But his slim legs never faltered.

Oh no! Sang Beruang wants to eat me. What shall I do?

At once a plan came to mind.

Kancil smiled sweetly. "Oh, Sang Beruang, what a good friend you are. You have no idea how grateful I am that you are helping me."

Sang Beruang blushed guiltily.

"I can see that it is early and that you have yet to breakfast. Let me show you where you can find a suitable repast."

"You can?" said Sang Beruang who was indeed ravenous. But bears are almost always hungry.

"Of course. Let it be my way of saying thanks." Sang Kancil showed the way to a nearby beehive.

"There." He pointed with his delicate snout. "There you will find the sweetest food available."

And that was so true.

Already, Sang Beruang could smell the honey. He wasted no time in climbing the tree and attacking the hive.

As the bear did so, Kancil stole away as fast and as far as he could. He knew what would happen.

As soon as the bees were aware of the black, hairy invader, they amassed in their hundreds and stung the silly bear.

Oh, Sang Beruang, when will you ever learn that few get the better of Sang Kancil.

See Notes on Page 330

The Golden Collar

S ANG KANCIL WAS still hot and thirsty, but the old, old woman had given him an idea and so he trotted along looking for coconut trees which are plentiful in Malaysia and Singapore. Indeed, in all Southeast Asia.

Mist clung to the ground. Faint golden light seeped down from the canopy as the jungle emerged from the gloom of night. *Pagi.* (Morning).

Soon he came upon a coconut tree. Coconuts lay scattered on the ground. Sang Kancil trotted over, eager to find a broken one so he could drink the cool coconut water inside.

Coconut water is not the same as coconut milk which is the result of squeezing the coconut flesh (copra). Young green coconuts are the best for this. The older a coconut gets, the less the water and the more the meat.

A man lay under the *kelapa* (coconut) tree. Quickly Sang Kancil stopped.

"*Dia tidor.* (He's asleep)." A monkey (*Berok* – coconut monkey, most likely a baboon) called out helpfully from the top of the tree.

Monyet had been clinging onto the trunk as he picked coconuts, tossing them for fun. He squealed with laughter each time he narrowly missed the slumbering man below.

But now that Sang Kancil had appeared, he dropped to the ground and ambled up excitedly.

Sang Kancil could not help but grin. "Another stupid human."

"Another?" said the monkey, and laughed when Sang Kancil told him about the episode with the old, old woman.

"Aren't I clever," said Sang Kancil.

"Aren't I clever, too!" Monyet stuck his chest out.

The chevrotain sniffed.

Monyet tossed his head. "Why, all I need now is a golden collar to show the world just how clever I am."

"I see," said Sang Kancil thoughtfully. "A golden collar, you say?"

"My heart's desire."

Sang Kancil smiled showing his front tusks. "If I get you one, will you admit that I am cleverer than you?"

Monyet snickered. "I do not see any golden collars on you, Sang Kancil. How will you be able to obtain one?"

Kancil's big brown eyes glistened. "Why, that man will provide one."

Monyet laughed even louder. "You barely escaped with your life from the old, old woman. How will you make a sleeping man do your bidding? Despite my throwing several coconuts at him, he sleeps on. It would be a miracle if you could even wake him."

"A miracle indeed," said Sang Kancil with a coy look. "Why do you think that none of your antics worked? Did you not know that the man is under my spell. Just as the old, old woman had no choice but to do my bidding?"

Spell? At the sound of magic, Monyet stared at Sang Kancil uncertainly. Was this true? He had tossed several coconuts down, some of which had landed uncomfortably close. But the man had slept on, not even shifting his position in sleep.

"Meet me here tomorrow," said Sang Kancil sounding sure. "Then I will give you your heart's desire."

"Why can't you do so now?" said the monkey, grumbling.

"Because then you will see my magic. Go now and meet me tomorrow in this very spot."

"Really?" Monyet's eyes grew large.

"Yes, really."

"What can I do to repay you?" said Monyet eagerly, for a golden collar had long been his dream.

The mousedeer appeared to consider. "What can you do?"

Monkey's shoulders drooped. "I- I can break open coconuts by throwing them down hard onto the ground."

Sang Kancil arched one brow as if to say, is that all. "Why don't you then open one for me now." And he smiled magnanimously. "That will be payment enough."

"*Terima Kasih*. (Thank you!)" Monkey scaled the coconut tree and before Sang Kancil could blink, a coconut newly split lay open before him.

The sweet aroma of coconut water filled the air and Sang Kancil salivated. But Monyet was watching...

"Go now," said the crafty chevrotain. And smiled as Monyet took off.

Alone, he sipped from the newly split coconut. As soon as his thirst was quenched, Sang Kancil went up to the sleeping man. He had a plan. But then he always has a plan.

The mousedeer bent and whispered in the man's ear, "Make a monkey sized collar in bright yellow leather. Then come back tomorrow to this place. A monkey will be here waiting for you. Slip the collar around the monkey's throat. Make sure to affix a long chain to the collar." Then Sang Kancil trotted off.

The man blinked, rubbed his eyes, and sat up. In awe, he stared at the tree under which he had slept. Everyone knew that spirits dwelt in trees. Some kind spirit had no doubt taken pity on him. For dreams were how the spirits communicated to humans. And everyone knew that dreams had to be obeyed.

The man took off to carry out the spirit's bidding and the next day, he returned.

As the spirit had promised, a monkey waited patiently under the tree.

The man needed no prompting. He fastened the collar around the neck of the monkey, but as soon as he did so, the monkey screamed and wept and yanked.

Too late did Monyet realise what had happened.

Sang Kancil had kept his word: Monyet had a beautiful yellow collar, but Monyet was now the slave of the man who held the chain.

No longer could Monyet roam freely around the jungle, lazing about and playing tricks.

From that day on, man learned to place collars around the necks of monkeys and to train them to pick coconuts. And so monkeys climb trees and hurl coconuts hard to the ground.

They are trying to hit Sang Kancil.

But Sang Kancil is too clever. He just drinks from the broken coconuts.

See Notes on Page 330

The Monkeys and the Crocodiles

T HE MONKEYS WERE not happy.

While they had been pleased to hear of the trick that Sang Kancil had played on the old, old woman, they were not glad to hear of the trick that Sang Kancil had played on one of them.

They decided to make their displeasure known.

They followed Sang Kancil around. Spread gossip, chattered and screamed. Invariably, they made pests of themselves. Soon the other jungle animals too, learnt of Sang Kancil's tricks.

The result was that all the animals were rude to the chevrotain.

Finally, Sang Kancil decided that it would be in his best interests to move closer to the riverbank. Few animals chose to dwell there, for the river was where the crocodiles lived.

But the daring monkeys followed.

"We are smart!" the monkeys chattered. "We know the river is dangerous, but we can climb trees!" And they snickered and laughed and cavorted. And to demonstrate that this was true they swung from branch to branch, as if to say, see! See!

Unlike Sang Kancil, they were able to stay on the tops of trees, high and out of reach of the crocodiles, while Sang Kancil remained on the ground.

After a while, Sang Kancil decided to approach Raja Buaya. "*Apa khabar*? (What news?)"

A log rose out of the water, water foaming and frothing around, within seconds becoming Raja Buaya – King of the Crocodiles.

The change was so swift from innocent log to lethal predator that even Sang Kancil could not help but give a little shudder: he bit his tongue and held his nerve.

"Ho! Sang Kancil! I have been hearing lots of news about you recently. What do you want?" said Raja Buaya, and he swam towards the shore.

"Nothing, at least nothing for myself," said Sang Kancil, taking a few cautious steps back up the bank. "I only wanted to say that I would like to give you a treat."

"Is that so, Sang Kancil? Like the treat you gave the old, old woman? Or the treat you gave

Monyet?" Raja Buaya crashed two massive legs onto the shore and lifted his great bulk out of the water.

Sang Kancil retreated further up the bank, his gaze squarely on the massive predator. "Raja Buaya, it is true that I played tricks on the others. But you are the King of the Crocodiles. You are wise and clever. I could never fool you."

"It is true that I am wise and clever," said Raja Buaya gloating. "Yet I cannot see why you would choose to provide me with a treat without any ulterior motive."

Sang Kancil's cheeks heated. "You see straight through me, Raja Buaya. I will not hold anything back from you."

Raja Buaya preened. "Tell me, what are you plotting?"

Sang Kancil lowered his eyes submissively, and took care to speak softly, for the monkeys were listening. "*They* follow me, everywhere I go now."

"This is why you have willingly come to my abode," said Raja Buaya and he laughed, showing all his great, nasty teeth. "Ho, ho! I understand. And I am particular to monkeys. Very particular indeed. But they are up there, and I am down here. Otherwise, I would help you. No thanks needed."

"It is true. They are up there, and you are down here. But it is also true what I said earlier. I wish to give you a treat. A treat of…" And Sang Kancil swept his eyes back and forth to indicate the monkeys in the trees above who had gone quiet.

The monkeys could see that Sang Kancil was speaking with Raja Buaya but being high up, they could not hear the gist of the conversation.

So, they whispered to each other like villagers do when they are trying to find out a piece of juicy gossip! "What is he saying? What did he say?"

"Who cares?" said another.

"That close to Raja Buaya, all it will take is a snap of his jaws, and no more Sang Kancil!"

And the monkeys all laughed nastily at the amusing thought. They were certain they were safe, so high up in the trees.

Only they wished they could hear the conversation. They had a dreadful suspicion that it might be about them.

Sadly, that was true.

"*Monyet*. (Monkeys)," said Sang Kancil.

"Monkeys?" said Raja Buaya. And he stared glassy-eyed at the monkeys swinging from vine to vine, safely out of his reach, before turning back to Sang Kancil. "Yum! Yum! And how do you propose to do that?"

"Easy. I am going to tell the monkeys about a big and wonderful party. Monkeys, as you know, love food. I am going to tell them about a wedding party on the other side of the river."

"On the other side? But how will they get there? And why were we crocodiles not invited?"

"How will they get there? Why, using the bridge that crocodiles will form with your tails and trunks. You do understand that there is no wedding."

"Oh, oh, of course."

"Listen carefully, then. For this is the most important part," said Sang Kancil.

"The most important part," said Raja Buaya, and craned his massive head forward.

"Form a line. In your mouth, take the tip of the tail of the crocodile in front of you. But do not move. Do not do anything until I give the order."

"But what will you do, Sang Kancil?"

"I will lead the monkeys onto the bridge. And you are to wait. *Wait* until I give the command before you snap your jaws shut and then you can catch all the monkeys you want."

At that, Raja Buaya laughed. He thumped his great and powerful tail that could sweep animals off their feet, lashing waves of water onto the bank.

Sang Kancil skipped to the top of the bank to avoid getting wet. "Remember. Wait." Then he turned and headed towards the monkeys for the next part of his plan.

Raja Buaya swam off at once to gather the rest of the crocodiles, so hungry was he.

"Ho, monkeys!"

The monkeys had been curious to see Sang Kancil conversing with Raja Buaya. At Sang Kancil's call, they leaped down to where he waited. They knew that they were still safe, high up on the top of the bank and far away from any of the predatory crocodiles in the river.

"Ho *kawan-kawan monyet*, (friend monkeys)," said Sang Kancil. "I would like to invite you to a wedding party."

"A wedding party! What wedding party?" The monkeys looked around eagerly, as if expecting to see a bridal pair go past.

The mousedeer patiently waited until the uproar subsided.

"Why did we not know?" The monkeys sniffed the air excitedly for everyone knew that a wedding meant food. Lots of food, and they were always ready for a feast.

"Why, the wedding that is to take place on the other side of the river. I have only just learnt the news myself and I thought that I would share it with my friends," said Sang Kancil.

"Friends? Are we friends?" said the monkeys dubiously.

"Well, neighbours at least," said Sang Kancil, undeterred, "for did you not relocate with me to this neighbourhood only recently?"

The monkeys blushed. "Yes, yes, neighbours! We are neighbours." At least until the wedding was over, thought the monkeys. But they said nothing of the sort to Sang Kancil.

"Well, then I am doing the neighbourly thing by inviting you to a wedding party."

"A wedding party!" And the monkeys danced and cartwheeled. They shaded their eyes and eagerly looked about to see if they could spot the wedding parade.

Again, Sang Kancil waited patiently.

Realisation soon dawned.

"But there is no bridge! How are we to get across?" The monkeys wept and punched the air. "And the river is full of crocodiles. Nasty crocodiles. Awful crocodiles!"

"I have taken care of everything. I have charmed the crocodiles away." Sang Kancil pointed with his dainty snout at the river.

As the monkeys looked, the surface of the water appeared clear. Not a single log floated.

The monkeys were astonished and delighted and chattered to each other at the miraculous sight. For it really looked as if the crocodiles had gone.

The crocodiles *had* gone. But not far.

As soon as Sang Kancil had explained what he was to do, Raja Buaya had gathered to him all the crocodiles in the river. As one they had submerged to listen to his instructions.

This was why, in the world above the water, when Sang Kancil had indicated the river, not one single crocodile could be seen.

The monkeys were astonished.

"It is what I do," said Sang Kancil modestly. "I know a little magic."

Magic…

"But how do we cross?" asked one monkey who was a little cleverer than the rest.

"*Eh bodoh,* (Oh, silly,) me. Have I forgotten to mention the bridge?"

"Bridge? What bridge?" And the monkeys scanned the river eagerly.

To their surprise, as they stared, a bridge rose slowly out of the river. Knobbly-looking, as if made of logs but to any onlooker - a bridge – glistening fresh and wet like a newly caught fish in the bright sunlight. Gleaming.

Magic!

The rabble would have rushed over at once except that Sang Kancil held them back.

"Take care! Take care! I have conjured up the bridge but if the bridge were to know that the lot of you wished to cross at once, why your combined weight might cause it to become unruly and it might take it upon itself to start to sag or worse, to break up."

The monkeys gasped. So enchanted were they by the disappearance of the crocodiles and the sudden appearance of the bridge that they now believed everything that Sang Kancil was saying. All except the one monkey who was a little cleverer than the rest.

"Ah but is it safe, Cil?"

"Safe? How can you doubt me? Especially since I will be leading the way," said Sang Kancil disdainfully.

Leading the way? Why, then, it had to be safe!

And at those convincing words the other monkeys pulled the tail of the monkey who was a little cleverer than the rest, so that it disappeared back up the trees in shame.

"We are ready! We are ready!" The remaining monkeys clamoured and leapt and danced. "We are ready."

"Yes, I can see that!" Sang Kancil laughed as if he, too were excited. "*Sambal* (Chilli), *udang* (prawns), *kambeng (goat)*! Even I cannot wait to attend. But. But. But."

"But, but, but what?" said the monkeys. "What? What? What? Have you changed your mind, Sang Kancil? Oh, please say that you have not changed your mind!"

Another monkey wailed. "Oh, I can smell the Ayam! Fried and crispy chicken flavoured with turmeric! The feast has already started." He plonked itself down on the bank and wept. "We are too late!"

And the horde of monkeys craned their necks as they peered across to the other side. "Where? I cannot see anything. Can you smell it? What is going on? Is the feast over?"

"I *can* smell it!" screamed the little monkey stubbornly.

"Plenty for everyone," said Sang Kancil. "I will take you, but before I do so, I must warn you."

"A warning, what warning?" And the monkeys ceased their chattering and listened, completely enthralled by the trickster, so charmed were they by Sang Kancil's words and by what they had seen.

"Remember, the bridge is new. Very new. And so, I will go first. You are to follow closely behind so that I can keep an eye on you. But no shoving. No noise. Nothing but your best behaviour. Remember this is a wedding!"

"Yes, yes, Sang Kancil. We will listen. We will obey." And at once the monkeys formed a solemn line behind Sang Kancil.

"Very well, then, let us cross," said Sang Kancil and he trotted down the bank, and straight up to the bridge, not pausing, not hesitating but moving in a steady rhythm. *Trip-trap, trip-trap*. Moved the well-behaved column of monkeys.

Down the bank, and up onto the bridge, they made their way across to the other side with Sang Kancil leading.

Trot-trot. Trip-trap!

As Sang Kancil approached the first crocodile, he dunked his head whispered, "Wait, wait for my signal."

And so, the ravenous crocodile waited, half sunk in the water as the ravenous troop of monkeys filed along steadily.

All solemn but quivering with excitement at the thought of the feast.

Sang Kancil approached the second crocodile, and again he whispered, "Wait, wait for my signal."

The crocodiles obeyed.

Solemn, but quivering with excitement at the thought of the feast.

The line of crocodiles, which was the bridge, held firm as slowly, slowly, they were loaded up with monkeys.

Wonderful monkeys! Glorious monkeys! Delicious monkeys! And one tasty mousedeer.

The troop was halfway across and still they came, with Sang Kancil just a little in front. And as he skipped, he bobbed and whispered, "Patience, patience. Almost there."

Only by now who was he talking to?

The monkeys or the crocodiles?

Did it even matter?

"Patience, patience. Almost there."

The monkeys began to lope a little faster. They could see that they were almost at the end, and the bulk of them were on the bridge.

The crocodiles began to fidget. It was not easy holding onto the tip of another's tail in your mouth for such a long time. Not easy smelling your food ambling along your backs. Not easy taking orders from your food. No, not easy at all. But they did it because they wanted the monkeys. Monkeys and more. A little more.

Sang Kancil continued to whisper, "Patience, patience."

Trot-trot. Trip-trap. Trot!

Soon mud was spotted up ahead.

The mousedeer trotted onto the last crocodile. Its tail. Its back. Its head.

"Wait!" Please wait. I am almost there!

And then almost unexpectedly, he *was* there. Right at the end of the bridge. No more crocodiles.

The monkeys stared about startled, their concentration broken. *What? No! Noooo!!! N-*

The crocodiles snapped.

Water turned bloody. Air filled with screams. Flailing arms. Falling arms.

But it wasn't just the monkeys screaming.

When Sang Kancil had given the order, the crocodiles had obeyed. Instantly.

They snapped their mighty jaws. Breaking the bridge. And something more.

Bridge broken, the horrified monkeys found themselves helpless in the water, and at the end of the jaws of very hungry crocodiles.

Sang Kancil had kept his promise. The monkeys did attend a feast - only they were the menu.

And as for the crocodiles, while they did get what they wanted which was monkey, lots of monkey, they also got something unexpected. A little something more.

A piece of the tail of the crocodile in front!

Except Raja Buaya who, at the end of the line, had his own tail resting safely on the bank.

Sang Kancil, of course, was nowhere in sight.

And only the monkey who was a little cleverer than the rest, who was safely up a tree back on the other side of the river, saw what had happened.

And he spread the news.

But all it did was increase the other animals' admiration for the cheeky chevrotain, for monkeys are liked by few, such a pest they are, stealing others' food and spreading gossip.

While crocodiles are detested by everyone.

And with the crocodiles well fed, the jungle was a little safer. At least for the next six months, for that is how long it takes for crocodiles to become hungry again.

Sang Kancil and the Deep Pit

THE GREAT GOA Rocks near the Thai border are composed of limestone. The formation is tremendously steep and full of holes and caves inhabited by creatures seldom encountered down in the steaming rainforest.

Sang Kancil was exploring these magnificent structures when unexpectedly, he came across Serau, the *Kambing Gurun* (Capricornis Sumatraensis).

Dark of coat, with a colossal head sporting dangerous horns it is rumoured that even man avoids these wild goats.

Sang Kancil turned and trotted off.

Serau stood stock still, glaring, contemptuous for every creature beneath him especially those who had no business being in this part of the world.

The chevrotain next explored the caves. Here, the pungent stink of guano almost overcame him.

"I do not like bats," said Sang Kancil in a huff and trotted off in haste.

"That's quite alright," said the bats. "We don't like chevrotains either." And they laughed before folding themselves back into their black leathery wings and falling asleep, for it was morning and they had just returned from a night of feasting and foraging.

The Great Goa Rocks are not just full of holes and caves and strange animals but also crags and waterfalls and deep chasms.

Sang Kancil quenched his thirst from a rockpool. He knew better than to drink from water that was not flowing because it might be poisonous.

Above his head, flying lizards soared, looking like miniature dragons, so it is no wonder that they are also called flying dragon lizards. Unlike common geckos, the flying structure of these creatures – patagium – attached to specialised ribs, enable them, when extended to glide.

For a while, the mousedeer watched the *naga* (dragons) fling their long bodies off trees. They whipped their tails as they extended their front legs and soared through the thin blue dappled light above his head, looking like orange and yellow discs zipping effortlessly through the air.

"I am glad I came," said Sang Kancil as he watched these wonders above his head.

But he was not so sure a moment later when he spotted Kabaragoya, the great monitor lizard, all seven metres of him.

Kabaragoya can swim, run on land, and even climb trees. And it would have been no trouble for Kabaragoya to catch a delicacy called Sang Kancil.

Thankfully, Kabaragoya was snoozing.

Just in case though, Sang Kancil trotted off.

The Great Goa Rocks near Tengku Lembu is dangerous. It is not the place to go running about.

Sang Kancil liked adventure. He liked seeing new things. He was racing along when the sky darkened.

A flock of green pigeons was flying overhead.

"Oh, how pretty," said Sang Kancil at the sight, just as his hooves trod onto a scattering of leaves and branches and twigs. Only…

It is a dreadful feeling to step on nothing. His stomach lifted.

"Oh, oh!"

The world spun, leaves and twigs and dust flew about. And when everything settled and Sang Kancil landed, he found himself at the bottom of a pit.

"No!" He ran at the sides, hoping to find a slope whereby he could scramble up.

But the pit was deep, and the sides were smooth slippery limestone.

There was nothing to be done. Sang Kancil had to get help. He waited.

Sometime later, a pig came along. It was surprised to hear a voice calling.

"Would you like to come down?"

The curious pig peered over the edge. "Why?"

Now, pigs are known to be highly intelligent.

"Come down because Raja Suleiman has announced that the sky is going to fall. Come down if you want to be safe."

"Is this why you are down there?" said the pig, thinking hard. This particular pig, being extremely intelligent, knew that Sang Kancil would not do anything stupid. There had to be a good reason why Sang Kancil was in a pit – a very deep pit. "Ah, I have it. You have chosen this pit because you need to get below the surface for it is only then that you will be safe?"

"You are wise. This is the case," said Sang Kancil, knowing that all pits are below the surface for that is what makes them pits in the first place.

Pig gloated.

"Come down at once."

And so, the clever pig, thinking even more highly of himself than usual, jumped into the pit. "It is good that there is plenty of room."

"We must be generous, though," said Sang Kancil, "and share our good fortune with others."

"Of course, of course," said Pig, smugly believing even more that he had made the correct decision, the wise decision, the big pig decision.

The next creature to come along was Kijang, or the Southern red muntjac, one of the oldest species of deer in the world.

It made sense to Pig for Sang Kancil to invite Kijang, for the deer was Sang Kancil's half-cousin.

Kijang, looking down into the pit and seeing the Pig, a highly intelligent creature, knew that Pig would have thought long and hard before jumping into such a deep pit. There had to be a good reason.

And so, in this fashion, more animals joined Sang Kancil, the pig and Kijang at the bottom of the pit.

There was Batang the Rhinoceros, a Tapir, and a bull buffalo known as Seladang who was famed for his wisdom.

Finally, *Raja Gajah* (King of Elephants) came along.

"What are you doing down there?" said Raja Gajah as he poked his trunk down the hole and sniffed.

All the animals started to explain, and the cacophony was deafening.

"Stop, wait. S'ladang, as you are the oldest and wisest, would you mind explaining the situation?" said Raja Gajah.

Seladang lifted his neck proudly. "Of course! Raja Suleiman has given instructions for our safety to gather here when the sky falls."

"The sky falls? That is indeed news," said Raja Gajah. "But if Raja Suleiman says a thing, then it must be so. Is there space though for me down there?"

"If we all form a circle, you could jump down in the middle. That way, the rest of us will not be squashed," said Sang Kancil.

"An excellent idea," said Rajah Gajah and he waited politely for the others to move to their positions before he jumped into the pit. Only…

"Oh, oh, but it is crowded down here," said Rajah Gajah, and so it was, with so many animals surrounding him.

"If I might speak once more, Rajah Gajah," said Sang Kancil. "I have an idea."

"Speak," said Rajah Gajah in a lordly tone.

"As you are the largest animal, might it be an idea if the others, in order of size, were to climb upon your back? That way, there will be more room in the pit. And if the rest of us, were to form such a structure, it would almost be as good as a set of steps."

"I can understand about making more room. But what good would be a set of steps?" said Rajah Gajah, frowning. It was very squashed in the pit and therefore difficult to think.

Difficult for everyone except one.

"Why, a set of steps would enable me to get to the very top of the pit where I could, for the briefest of moments, peer out just to see if the sky is falling. Then I could give warning, of course!" said Sang Kancil.

"What a good idea," said Rajah Gajah, and if Raja Gajah thinks something is a good idea, who is anyone to think otherwise? Especially if you are stuck in a pit with Raja Gajah, who is capable of stamping on you at any second.

The animals formed the set of steps as Sang Kancil directed, from the biggest to the smallest animal.

Sang Kancil climbed onto Raja Gajah, "Ah, I am not high enough."

Sang Kancil climbed onto Seladang, "Ah, I am not high enough."

Sang Kancil climbed onto Batang the rhinoceros, "Ah, I am not high enough."

Sang Kancil climbed onto the tapir, "Ah, I am not high enough."

Sang Kancil climbed onto the pig, "Ah, I am not high enough."

Sang Kancil climbed onto Kijang, "Ah, I am not high enough."

The animals gasped.

If Kancil was not high enough, then how was he to peer out to see if the sky is falling?

"But wait, I have an idea," said Sang Kancil.

The animals sighed and they waited.

Sang Kancil cocked his head as if thinking very hard. "Raja Gajah, if you would not mind stretching out your trunk, I think I could just make it to the top of the pit."

His words slowly filtered down to Raja Gajah who considered them. "Very well." Rajah Gajah stretched out his trunk, so that the tip of his trunk lay on the top of the pit.

Sang Kancil took a deep breath then he loped up the trunk and out of the pit. "Goodbye!" he called out as he trotted away.

Goodbye?

The animals at the bottom of the pit could not see what was happening on the ground above. All they could hear were tiny pitter-pats growing softer and softer. Then silence.

Could it be? Surely not?

When they realised what had happened, they were not happy.

"How could Sang Kancil do this?" said Raja Gajah. "And to his own cousin."

"Half," said Kijang.

Raja Gajah trumpeted and bellowed at the top of his voice.

Now Rajah Gajah is not King of the Elephants for nothing, and at his call, his subjects came racing to his aid. First, they used their trunks to help lift the other animals out of the pit, and with Raja Gajah shoving from below, one by one the animals were soon safe on the top once more.

All except Rajah Gajah, who, being the biggest and the heaviest, would take more effort, but then he had his herd there and they shoved and pulled, and it was not long before Raja Gajah was also out of the pit. But it had taken a lot of effort.

The animals were all angry at having been fooled and their pride injured as one they agreed that they would never believe Sang Kancil again.

And as for a particular chevrotain, he cared only that he was soon home.

See Notes on Pages 330-331

Anak-Beranak Arimo or Keluarga Harimau

It is said that there is never ending enmity between Harimau the Tiger and Sang Kancil.

The enmity is simply this:
Harimau wishes to eat Sang Kancil.
Sang Kancil does not wish to be eaten.

But there was a time when Sang Kancil was invited to live with Harimau and his family.
And Sang Kancil accepted.

Rimau – Part I

RIMAU THE TIGER caught Sang Kancil one day.

"It was only a matter of time," said Rimau, trying to speak in a lordly manner, which was hard to do as he had something in his mouth. But he preened and gloated: for the day he had been waiting for, for such a long time, had finally arrived.

Today, he had caught Sang Kancil!

Pride flooded through Rimau. He lifted his head high, enjoying the weight of the chevrotain in his jaws, savouring the glory for as long as possible, until the time when he would clamp his jaws together and gobble up the delicacy. Once gone, this moment could never be recaptured.

"I was waiting to speak with you," said Sang Kancil matter-of-factly, as he dangled from the tiger's jaws.

"Oh," said Rimau, deflated. He swallowed awkwardly. "Waiting you say?" Was that true? A moment later, he chortled. This was Sang Kancil's style. "Why not just admit that I caught you?"

"Whatever you wish," said Sang Kancil and sighed.

The fact that his catch was not making the slightest attempt to escape worried Rimau. He would have devoured Sang Kancil, but in true cat fashion, he was curious as to what the chevrotain had been planning to say.

"I will bring you back to my Lady Wife and my boys." And so, buying time, Rimau hurried back to his den.

His family were curious to see what he had brought.

Sang Kancil was released, however he made no move to escape. Instead, he bowed before Mrs Rimau as if awed.

"What a beautiful family you have, Mrs Rimau," said Sang Kancil in the politest of tones. "But of course, their mother is loveliness itself."

Mrs Rimau blushed. "That is very kind of you to say, Sang Kancil, but they are just boys," she said, yellow eyes flicking away in modesty as was the custom.

"There is no doubt, then, that they are as intelligent as their father."

"The truth is that they are lazy," said Rimau, deprecating as tradition warranted. "And far behind in their lessons."

"Fortunate then, that I am a renowned teacher of the Koran," said Sang Kancil.

Rimau and Mrs Rimau were impressed. It is not every day that one comes across a Koran teacher in the jungle. That's probably because Koran teachers know better than to wander about the jungle.

"Seems such a shame to eat you," said Rimau. "If I let you go, could you teach my sons? You may discipline them, of course."

It was customary in those times to discipline children using the rotan.

"Certainly," said Sang Kancil.

And so, the deal was struck. The mousedeer was to coach the two sons of Rimau in exchange for his life.

Now Sang Kancil to his credit did do his best. He really did try to teach the Koran to the two sons of Rimau, but what their father had said was true. The two boys were indeed *malas* (lazy).

"Silly Sang Kancil! Why would we want to learn from you? Perhaps if you were big and strong like Papa, we would accept your teaching. But you?" They laughed. "You are barely anything at all!" And they poked and prodded Sang Kancil.

"Stop that!" said Sang Kancil and to teach the boys some manners, he lashed out with one sharp hoof. However, the hoof caught the younger boy across the temple. He lay unmoving on the ground.

Dead?

Sang Kancil did not think it prudent to wait to find out.

"Oh, oh, Papa!" The elder cub screamed.

Sang Kancil tore across the clearing and into the rain forest, desperate to put as much space between himself and the enraged parents.

"Oh, oh!" wept Mrs Rimau, heartbroken.

Rimau plunged after Sang Kancil. This time he would not hesitate to rip the chevrotain to bits when he caught him.

And the mousedeer knew this.

Trees and bushes flew past as prey and predator plunged through the jungle, whipping round trunks, flinging themselves off rocks, crashing into startled animals.

The landscape blurred.

The smaller animals hid. They did not want to be a substitute for a certain chevrotain. But the larger animals stopped their foraging to watch. They were curious to see how this would end.

Today just might be the finish of Sang Kancil.

Sang Kancil was aware that he could not go on indefinitely. So, when he spotted a familiar sight up ahead, he swerved round some ferns, raced up to the gingko tree, and sat down. It took all his courage to face the enraged tiger. But the sound of the loud buzzing overhead reassured him.

Rimau had to stop suddenly to avoid crashing headfirst into the tree.

Careful. No doubt Sang Kancil is planning something.

"I am going to eat you, Sang Kancil! That is what I should have done from the beginning," said Rimau as he approached, padding silently on furred feet.

"It was an accident," said Sang Kancil truthfully. "And I am sorry. So sorry that I want to make up by giving you the best present that anyone can give."

Present?

Kancil indicated the tree.

Rimau gave the tree a cursory glance. The only thing obvious was the large hornets' nest at the top. Surely, Sang Kancil did not mean the nest? How stupid did the fool think he was?

The nest looked like any other hornets' nest. Made of chewed wood, and cylindrical in shape, the only difference was that this one appeared larger than normal.

"You! I will never believe another word *you* say! Never!" Panting hard, Rimau towered over the chevrotain.

It was all Sang Kancil could do not to bolt. He boldly locked eyes with Rimau. "Even if it is a present that will make you Lord of the Jungle?"

"What?"

"And lord of the creatures in the jungle forever?" added Sang Kancil. And when Rimau hesitated, he knew the battle was his.

"You speak lies, Sang Kancil," said Rimau, in a half roar. "Raja Suleiman is Lord of the Jungle and of the creatures forever."

"Of course, Raja Suleiman is, but can you not hear the drumming noise above our heads?"

"Hornets," said Rimau disdainfully.

Kancil gave a little laugh. "I can see why you would think this way. And that of course, is what Raja Suleiman would like everyone to think. But the truth is that this is his great Kendang Drum."

> A Kendang (or Gendang) Drum is a two-headed drum used to make music. It is also played before the beginning of a story by the Penglipur Lara. And at the start of a war.

"Kendang Drum?"

"Do you think you are the only creature who uses camouflage? Why who do you think invented it?"

Rimau's jaw dropped open.

The nest was the right size, shape, and colour. Was it really a Kendang Drum in disguise?

"It sounds like hornets only to fool you. But it is Raja Suleiman's Great Kendang Drum that he has hung up while he has a sleep. Did you not know that whoever beats the drum three times becomes Lord of the Jungle?"

Now there is some truth in this. For rulers always announce their arrival by sound.

Rimau snorted. "Well, then why do you not beat the drum yourself?"

"I would if I could reach it," said Kancil plaintively.

That sounded undeniably true.

Rimau stared down at the chevrotain then up at the drum. He hesitated.

"Beat the drum," said Sang Kancil softly.

"But…"

"Beat the drum and you will be Lord of the Jungle."

The delicious words swam around Rimau's head.

"I…"

"Beat the drum. This is your last chance before Raja Suleiman wakes." And at that the mousedeer sighed. His eyes were limpid pools as he stared covetously at the wonderful nest.

"I think I will," said Rimau, swallowing hard.

Kancil sighed heavily as if he expected no less an answer. "Just let me check to see if Raja Suleiman is still asleep."

And so Rimau obediently waited while Sang Kancil trotted around the trees to check. A moment later, he reappeared.

"All clear," said Sang Kancil. "You may beat the drum. Three times! All I ask is that you be generous to us mousedeer."

Rimau had no thought of being generous, but prudently kept silent.

I will devour every single mousedeer I come across. Starting with this one right here.

"Move aside," said Rimau, his disdain increasing as he enjoyed the sight of the mousedeer bowing and scraping.

"I shall be the ideal king," said Rimau, plans for his accession already forming in about his head.

The powerful tiger stood on his hind legs, then he stretched his powerful body to reach the nest.

This is the moment!

Lifting a powerful paw, he smashed the nest with all his strength.

Whump! The nest shook a moment, swayed, and then landed on the ground.

Bzzz BBBZZZZZZ!!!!

The shocked tiger leapt in the air as hundreds of enraged hornets flew out of their nest.

Thinking that the camouflage would end only when the nest was hit two more times, Rimau destroyed the nest. "Stop! I am your king! Your Lord and Master!"

But the hornets' only thoughts were of revenge.

They attacked the stunned tiger, stinging and biting and crawling all over his body.

Unable to see, unable to shout, for Rimau soon learnt quickly that opening his mouth only allowed the insects to enter, the enraged tiger bounded away, stumbling into tree trunks, rolling across shrubs, and finally, to his relief, finding a river where he could submerge himself and his shame.

It was a long time before the pain subsided.

When Rimau returned to the jungle his only consolation was that his younger son was not dead but only unconscious.

And as for Sang Kancil - he knew only too well that he had to keep out of the way of the tiger family.

And this he did, until one of them found him.

It was only a matter of time.

See Notes on Page 332

Sang Kancil and Siput the Water Snail

SIPUT THE WATER Snail lives under the white sand of the Dusun Tua River. Although Siput has never left the river, he knew what was happening in the land above, for he and his kin shared everything. They knew when a predator was near, when food was scarce, and they even knew when a certain mousedeer was visiting, for they communicated constantly.

The very next time Kancil came down to the river for a drink, all the snails knew.

> Snails have two pairs of stalks, also called tentacles, on the tops of their head with an eye on each of the taller stalks which enable them to see obstacles. They pivot their stalks without needing to turn their bodies, increasing their field of vision. The smaller stalks are used to feel around the snail, a useful method of detecting obstacles without vision.
>
> But although snails have eyes, they only see in black-and-white, and their vision is blurry. This is probably one of the reasons snails have light sensing cells covering their entire body as this allows them to know when a shadow falls on them – generally a sign that a predator is near.

Kancil was busy greeting a porcupine, very politely, because porcupines have the sharpest of quills, when Siput addressed him.

"How are you, Sang Kancil?" said Siput.

Sang Kancil peered into the water but saw only his own reflection. "*Khabar baik*, (Good) *Sang Siput*. (Revered Snail)."

"I heard that you have laid claim to the title of the fastest of Raja Suleiman's creatures in the jungle."

"That is true."

"Well, then, I want to challenge you to a race."

"You?"

"Why not? I have been known throughout my youth as a racer, after all.

Kancil sniggered.

"We will have a race," said Siput determinedly. "You on the bank. I in the water."

Sang Kancil's ear pricked. Was Siput serious?

"To make sure that I gain no advantage from the water, we will go upstream."

"But how will we know when one of us has won?" said Sang Kancil, unable to believe that a snail was challenging him.

"We will race until one of us calls out that they are tired. And if you win, I will pay you one bag of gold."

Sang Kancil's eyes lit. "I will pay you two bags of gold if you win."

"*Baiklah*. (Good)," Said Siput. "It is settled. Now go and ask the Raja of the Butterflies and the Raja of the Rhinoceroses if they can be our judges. Raja of the Butterflies can fly along the route while Raja of the Rhinoceroses can be the umpire. That way we know all will be fair."

"Very well," said Sang Kancil and would have dashed off except Siput called him back.

"One last thing. It has been a while since I raced. I need to practise. Give me one week to do so."

Seven days.

Sang Kancil agreed and set off to ask the two Rajas if they could assist.

Both Rajas agreed. They guessed Siput had a strategy. For how else could an animal as slow as a snail, even a water snail, expect to win a race?

Siput did indeed have a plan.

He spent the entire week communicating his idea to the other Water Snails. All the snails upstream understood what they had to do and so at the end of the week all was ready.

Sang Kancil turned up bright and early on Race Day and was pleased to see that the Raja of the Butterflies and the Raja of the Rhinoceroses had already arrived up and were ready to oversee the rules and to start the judging.

Other animals also having heard the news, had joined the spectators, each anxious to see who would win.

The excited creatures waited along the banks of the river for the race to begin.

The Raja of the Butterflies, Raja Brook, hoovered in the air as all held their breath. "Go!"

The animals cheered and shouted.

Sang Kancil dashed off, hooves clitter-clacking on the gravelly banks. At the first bend of the river, he turned to look back. As he expected, Siput was nowhere to be seen. "Well then," he huffed to himself. "This should not take long."

Siput, however, still at the starting line, simply settled himself into the white sand and went to sleep, confident that his plan would work.

Sang Kancil raced and raced. All he could hear were his hooves trip-trapping. He could see straight ahead was the next turn of the river and still no sign of Siput behind him. After a while, though, Sang Kancil grew tired. His pace slowed.

Where exactly was Siput?

Sang Kancil had been racing on the bank where everyone could see him. But Siput had said that he was racing under the water…

The reality was that no one could see what was happening below water.

"Eh, Siput, *lu mana*? (Where are you?)" asked Sang Kancil, convinced that he was way ahead.

He was stunned, therefore, to hear Siput's voice close by.

"Right here, Sang Kancil. Please do not stop to wait for me. As you can see, I am keeping up."

Sang Kancil snapped his jaw shut. "Oh of course, we have only just started. Now here we go again!" And once more, the mousedeer darted off, just not quite as fast as before.

After another bend or two, Sang Kancil was tiring. Surely Siput would not be able to catch up. Once more he called. "Eh Siput, *lu mana*? (Where are you?)"

"Why, right here. In fact, I think I am just ahead of you. I did mention that it was a long time ago when I was a racing snail. It appears that all my old tricks are coming back. Oh, this is wonderful. This looks like it is going to turn out into a nice long race. A very nice long race indeed"

Long!

Sang Kancil was indeed tiring. He had been running in the humid jungle and already his hooves were hurting but it would not do to let the other animals see him falter and so, he put on a brave face and called out in a merry voice, "Of course! Here we go again!"

Another bend or two and Sang Kancil could feel himself slowing dramatically. He was annoyed to find the Raja of the Rhinoceros easily keeping up. But the Raja had a distinct advantage compared to the two competitors. Sheer size. And longer legs.

"Eh, Siput?" said Sang Kancil, too out of puff to say much.

"Oh, Sang Kancil, I am really enjoying this race. I honestly believe that I have regained all my skills as a racing snail and that I can go on and on and on. Forever."

Sang Kancil's slender legs shook, sweat dampened his fur. How was this possible?

Now what Sang Kancil did not know was that one Water Snail's voice is very much like another and so while he had stopped each time and called out, he had assumed that the answering voice was that of the old Water Snail, Siput.

It was not.

Each time Sang Kancil had called out, it had been one of the other Water Snails who had replied. They did sound like each other.

"Sang Kancil, do you wish a rest?" asked the Raja of the Butterflies, itself struggling to keep up.

The Raja of the Rhinoceroses, able to take one step for about ten of Sang Kancil's steps, waited patiently.

Sang Kancil shook his head and raced on, but before long he was forced to stop. He trembled with exhaustion from head to foot.

"How about a rest?"

"No-" But before Sang Kancil could continue, his legs gave out and he fell to the ground, landing on his belly.

How the watching animals laughed!

"Never mind, you did your best," said the Raja of the Rhinoceroses.

"And that is all anyone can do," said the Raja of the Butterflies when he caught up.

Sang Kancil, breathing heavily, had no strength left to answer. He remained in a heap, his eyes closed tight.

After a while, when he was sure that the other animals had departed and that he was quite alone, he rose shakily and made his way back home.

The two judges had indeed left and gone home, knowing that neither Siput nor Sang Kancil had any gold to present.

The word was communicated right back to the starting line, where old Siput had remained the entire time while the race was on.

How old Siput laughed and laughed with his friends. Serve Sang Kancil right! He deserved to be put in his place. Maybe next time he might think twice about getting another animal in trouble. And the snails chuckled and snickered.

They were not alone. Many of the other animals, too, had heard as to how Sang Kancil had lost. They would have fun in the coming weeks reminding the cheeky chevrotain of his failure!

Sang Kancil trotted back to his den. He turned a couple of circles then lay down. He was incredibly tired. He had been running the whole day and now he just wanted to sleep.

But it was *sinjakala* (twilight). The dusk chorus was in full symphony.

This was something that Sang Kancil had heard every day when darkness fell. For the first time though, he really listened. And it was as if he heard it anew.

Fresh.

His head between his paws, he listened to every note. To every flutter and to every flap. He allowed the trilling sound to seep through his being, deep into his muscles and into his head, filling the void that was there. The emptiness that he felt right now. Revealing the significance of it entirely.

Darah (Blood) pounded in his head.

I matter! I do, I do. I d-

As the chorus died, a certain sound persisted. The voice grew louder and louder.

A frisson of excitement shivered across his skin. Sang Kancil knew what it was.

It was the call of the Tiptibau.

Toc-toc-toc. Toc-toc-toc-toc.

He sounds as miserable as I feel right now.

And so Sang Kancil did something he had never done before. He reached out to the sad bird. "Ho Tiptibau, how are you?" he called.

The tocking stopped instantly.

"Did- did someone speak?" said the Tiptibau after a long pause.

"Only I," said Sang Kancil in a little voice.

"Ah, it is you, Sang Kancil." And the Tiptibau heaved a tiny sigh. "It is not every day that someone speaks to me."

The bird sounded so miserable.

"You make it sound as if no one has ever listened to you."

"No one." Came the swift answer.

"That is not true. Does not the White Man listen?"

"Only to say to one another to watch out for the Brain Fever Bird."

"Well, I have heard it say that the Chinese listen ever so intently to you."

The Tiptibau snorted. "They never really listen. What they do is bet on the number of *tocs* that I make."

"Is that so," said Sang Kancil. "Well, I am here now. And I am ready to listen."

And so, although Sang Kancil was extremely weary, he asked the Tiptibau to narrate his story.

See Notes on Pages 332-333

The Tragic Tale of Tiptibau the Nighthawk

Or The Man who became a bird

The owl is commonly referred to as the Burung Hantu (the Devil Bird) in Malaysia.
Burung = Bird
Hantu = Devil or spirit

There are many owls from the Nightjar (Caprimulgus macrurus) whose tock-tock-tock call sounds like the skimming of a stone across ice. Malays call it the Burong Tukang Kayu or the Carpenter bird or Burong Malas the lazy bird because it makes no nest, merely lays its eggs on the ground beneath a bush. It can even be found sitting on the road sometimes.

During the day it hides on the ground in the bushes or ferns, coming out at dusk. In the big jungle, there is another owl – the Lyncornis temminckii. This is believed to be the owl of the story.

This is the story that the Tiptibau told:

THERE WAS ONCE a man who thought himself happy.

His name was Mat Saman, and he lived in Perak. Perak is a state of Malaysia, and it means silver.

Mat Saman had built his own house.

"You should be happy," said his relatives when they came to visit. "You have your own house."

"That is true," said Mat Saman. "I have a house of my own."

"Ah, but if only you had a wife."

"A wife?" said Mat Saman, scratching his head.

"A wife will cook your food for you."

"A wife will wash your clothes for you."

"A wife will plant a vegetable garden and raise fruit and vegetables, and you will be able to save a lot of money because you will no longer have to buy these things at the market."

"That is true," said Mat Saman. "Perhaps a wife is a good idea. I am happy now, but perhaps a wife might make me even happier."

And so Mat Saman's relatives got together, and they found a nice girl for Mat Saman. They paid her dowry, and they gave her to Mat Saman, and he married the nice girl and for a while they were happy.

But when his relatives came to visit, they found that Mat Saman was no longer happy.

His relatives were puzzled.

"Does your wife not cook for you?"

"Does your wife not wash your clothes for you?"

"Does your wife not plant a vegetable garden and raise fruit and vegetables, so that you are able to save a lot of money because you no longer have to buy these things at the market?"

"Yes, yes, yes," said Mat Saman, only he sounded quite miserable. "My wife does these things and more."

"More?"

"What more?"

Mat Saman sighed. "She talks. She talks day and night."

"Well, what is the problem? Just listen."

"But she doesn't talk about anything interesting," said Mat Saman.

"What does it matter? Just nod your head from time to time to keep her happy."

And so Mat Saman took his relatives' advice. He listened to his wife, or at least he tried to. He nodded his head from time to time.

But no matter what he did, she kept talking and talking and talking.

Talk. Talk. Talk.

"I like peace and quiet," said Mat Saman. "I had peace and quiet. I was happy once, but now I am unhappy."

At this point the Tiptibau hung its head and was silent.

"What did Mat Saman's relatives advise?" asked Sang Kancil, after he had waited a long while.

"They continued to tell him to listen. But Mat Saman had had enough. Tock-tock-tock-tock."

Sang Kancil sensed that the Tiptibau was very upset. "What happened then?"

"Mat Saman did an unwise thing. Tock-tock-tock!"

"What did he do?"

"He invited the girl's mother to come and live with them. Tock-tock-tock."

Sang Kancil sucked in his breath. Two women in the same kitchen. Trouble.

"The girl and her mother had arguments. They shouted at each other. They broke plates. Ripped up the vegetable patch and so - so finally came the day when Mat Saman could stand it no longer. Tock-tock-tock-tock!"

"What happened?"

"Tock-tock-tock! Mat Saman ran out of his house leaving the two women inside. Tock-

tock-tock. Mat Saman took his parang and destroyed his house. Chop. Chop. Chop. It was only held up by rattan. The whole structure fell upon the two women, who were so busy arguing that they never made it out of the house."

The Tiptibau fell silent as if recalling the dreadful scene.

"Raja Suleiman must have been furious."

"He was. He turned Mat Saman into a bird. A bird that goes Tock-tock-tock." The Tiptibau screeched. He flapped his black wings, lifting off a few feet and then clawed the air. "I was so happy. Why did they do it? Why could they not control their tongues? Look what they did to me. Look! I am a bird. A bird who goes Tock-tock-tock. A bird who drives everyone crazy."

"I see."

"I had my own house," squealed the Tiptibau.

"You had your own house."

"All she had to do was cook and wash and clean."

"All your wife had to do was cook and wash and clean."

"But all she did was talk and talk and talk!"

"Talk and talk and talk." The mousedeer's voice was soft.

"Yes, talk and-" The Tiptibau's eyes widened as a thought occurred. "Oh- oh!" The bird landed suddenly. Then it covered its face with its wings. "Oh…"

Sang Kancil waited.

Shaking hard, the Tiptibau's eyes were stricken with sudden realisation. How its black eyes gleamed!

Sang Kancil shot the poor bird a look of sympathy.

"Talk. Talk. Talk." The Tiptibau whispered heartbrokenly as it locked gazes with the mousedeer. "Tock. Tock. Tock. What a fool I was never to have seen it. Thank you, Sang Kancil. You are the first creature to have ever really listened." And so, saying the Tiptibau spread its ink black wings and flew into the night.

A sad bird, no doubt. But also, finally, a happier and a wiser bird.

See Notes on Page 333

Agas the Midge

KANCIL WAS ASLEEP when he was rudely awakened by a loud buzzing.

"It is no doubt Agas the midge," he grumbled.

"Apa khabar, Sang Kancil!" said Agas the midge.

> Midges generally appear in swarms. They often live near water. Unlike mosquitoes, they carry no diseases and live for only a few days. Their aim while alive is to breed. A nuisance, they however provide a source of food to the fishes and insectivores.

"*Khabar baik* (Good)," said Kancil and although he did not feel like it as he had been abruptly awakened, he had to be polite. This was the Asian way. "Would you mind flying a little more quietly?"

"I wish I could," said Agas politely. "It is my stomach that is the problem. While I was cleaning the hide of Sang Kerbau, a splinter pierced my stomach."

"A splinter," said Kancil squinting.

"Yes, a splinter. About a finger long."

At that Kancil laughed. "I cannot imagine how a splinter the length of a finger could possibly do so! Why you are so small I can barely see you. Go complain elsewhere! For I cannot believe such a story!"

The buzzing intensified. "Buzz! Buzz! I have always had a good opinion of you until now, Mister Know-it-all. Why can what I say not be true?"

"But-but-"

"You have a heart. I have a heart. The only difference is size. Everything is relative, is it not? Your heart is surely not the same size as Gajah's heart!"

Kancil's jaw dropped.

Twice in one day, he was being shown to be anything but the confident trickster that he believed himself to be.

He bowed his head. "You are right. I humbly beg your apology."

Agas buzzed a little louder for he was annoyed beyond words, but this was Kancil, after all, and now he had a story to tell. A story of how he bested the trickster of the jungle. That was worth something indeed.

And even Kancil realised it, as he respectively took his leave of Agas the Midge.

Mak Rimau (Part II)

I T IS SAID that Tiptibau repaid Sang Kancil's kindness one day. For the mousedeer had not only listened to his tocking without going mad with brain fever but had also listened to the time when he had been a man.

So, when Tiptibau spotted the tigress stalking, he knew what he had to do.

Mak Rimau (Mother Tiger or Mrs Rimau) had taken on the task of revenge ever since Rimau had come home complaining how hornets had attacked him and therefore stopped him from catching Sang Kancil.

Mrs Rimau had sniffed disdainfully at his version of events. While she had been very glad that her younger boy had recovered, Sang Kancil needed to be punished. And now she smelt mousedeer! She leapt! Only -

"Tock-tock-tock!" screamed Tiptibau, flapping his black wings. "Look out! Rimau! I mean- I mean Mrs Rimau! I mean Sang Kancil look out for Mrs Rimau! Oh-Mak-Rimau-I-mean!"

Kancil exploded out of the bushes. He plunged through the undergrowth, Mak Rimau in hot pursuit.

Darting left, then right, Mrs Rimau's breath heating his tail, Kancil spotted something shining in the sunlight.

At once he knew what he had to do. It would be dangerous, but he had little choice. He was desperate to throw the slavering tigress off his trail.

Sang Kancil skidded to a stop.

Oh, oh!

One minute the mousedeer was in front of her, the next, Mrs Rimau found herself tumbling head over heels as she, too, tried to come to a complete halt.

"*Berhenti!* (Stop), please, stop," said Sang Kancil.

"What are you playing at!" Mrs Rimau shook her head hard, as she picked herself up. "I am going to eat you up right now!"

"*Nanti*! (Wait), please, wait, kind Mrs Rimau. Polite Mrs Rimau. Gracious Mak Rimau. Beautiful Tigress."

The mousedeer's brown eyes gleamed dark and luminous. "Mrs Rimau, you know that I did my best to teach your two sons."

While Mrs Rimau was used to her food begging for its life, this was unexpected.

Mrs Rimau winced. She knew that her two boys were lazy. She had eavesdropped many times as the lessons were in progress and had been astonished at the patience Sang Kancil had displayed. She could not fault him.

When she hesitated, the mousedeer continued. "What happened was an accident. Pure and simple. And because you are the loveliest of creatures, I wish to bestow upon you the title of Queen."

At that, Mak Rimau snorted. *Sang Kancil is up to his old tricks.*

"You speak lies! *Bohong!* (Lies!) There is nothing to stop me from devouring you where you stand." And she expected the mousedeer to make one last attempt to flee.

But instead, Kancil turned his snout towards an object draped around a branch.

"Look before you! Can you not see the glorious colours?" said Sang Kancil.

Mrs Rimau hesitated. A tigress is a cat, albeit a large cat. And all cats are curious.

So focused had she been on her prey, that only now did Mrs Rimau notice the coils of the giant python. Twenty feet of sparkling scales. For the colours and scales belonged to Sang Ular, asleep in the sunshine.

"That is a snake. He kills by strangling his prey before swallowing them whole, crushing their bones as he does so. You, however, have a different fate." And she smiled nastily.

"Ah fate," said Sang Kancil. "Did you ever wonder what fate has in store for you, beautiful lady? And whether you, damsel, are destined to be more than a mother living day to day in the jungle with much more to look forward to than what life has to offer you now?" And so, saying, Kancil put a hoof forward. "Salaam Aleikam." And the chevrotain bowed low. So low that his forehead touched the ground.

Mrs Rimau gasped.

Why the gesture seemed… nice. Almost touching.

Obeisance.

Mrs Rimau swallowed hard. Being a tigress, she had a high opinion of herself. And being one of the dominant predators in the jungle she was already *pangkat* (ranked) highly. But to be a queen? To have everyone bowing like that each time she passed…

She sniffed regally. "You are a liar, Sang Kancil. For me to be queen is an impossibility." But she watched the mousedeer intently.

Just in case.

For she did not wish to lose. No one does.

Kancil beamed. "Do not say such things. Can you not see before you the answer to your prayers? Behold! The Belt of King Solomon! Whosoever dons this belt will become undisputed ruler of the jungle."

"But- but that is simply a python." She cocked her head uncertainly.

"Of course, it *looks* like a python. You surely know that Raja Solomon is not stupid enough to leave his belt lying around while he goes for a swim. He has *disguised* it to look like a python."

As Mrs Rimau stared, a shaft of sunlight lit up the scales of the python, so that they dazzled, glowing orange and brown like a cat's eyes.

Glittering.

She was mesmerised. "Well then, why did you not say so? Only…"

Kancil seeing the hesitation, nodded knowingly. "You need to put it on. Simply wrap that glorious belt three times around your tiny waist. And abracadabra! You will find yourself the queen of the jungle."

Mrs Rimau needed no further prompting.

She grabbed the python and began to wrap its heavy length around her torso.

Of course, what happened next was that Sang Ular woke up. He had gone to sleep after a particularly heavy meal, and he was not impressed to find himself being wrapped around the waist of a vain tigress.

He squeezed. And squeezed.

"Oh!" Mrs Rimau's eyes rounded in shock as the belt came to life. Before her astonished gaze, one end of the belt lifted and orange eyes, slitted black blinked open.

Mrs Rimau's jaw dropped.

Then Sang Ular opened his mouth, and a long red tongue shot out!

And Mak Rimau knew that she had been right all along.

Horrible, horrible mousedeer! I should never have trusted you!

Poor Mrs Rimau found herself fighting for her life.

Thankfully, Sang Ular had just eaten. He was half-asleep still, and so Mrs Rimau was lucky to escape. She was only the second to do so.

The first, of course, was Sang Kancil.

See Notes on Page 333

The Resident's Compound

Growing up in Singapore in the 20ᵗʰ Century, I was aware of such things as traps: a rope tied into a noose at one end with food in the circle and then the long wait until an animal came along, the pull of the rope and the subsequent capture of the animal.

Alternatively, a box could be used, propped up with a stick, food underneath, then CRASH!

While I knew of the existence of such things as traps, I had never made any. I had plenty of animals to play with: the family dogs and cats, along with the occasional chick, duckling, rabbit, and tortoise. All pets.

Maybe if I had lived on the edge of the jungle…

MANY YEARS AGO, before even I was born, a little boy caught Sang Kancil, using a trap baited with ludai leaves (Sapium baccatum). Mousedeer are apparently quite particular to ludai leaves. A fact the boy knew and used to his advantage. Thankfully, the boy was also kind-hearted. He did not wish the mousedeer eaten and so he took the animal to the Resident.

A Resident is a government servant and how the British used to rule the Malay states back in the days when Britain was a colonial power.

The Resident was kind-hearted, and he paid the boy a dollar.

Mousedeer meat is a particular delicacy with Malays, so Kancil was lucky. The Resident only wanted him as a pet. The Resident had many pets, and they all took turns to visit the newcomer.

Shut in a wire cage, Kancil watched enviously as the other animals strolled around the compound.

"Do not worry," said the mongoose as it stuck its pointed nose through the bars of the cage. "You will soon be free like us. The Resident just needs to get used to you."

"Thank you for your kindness," said Sang Kancil. He had heard of the legendary battles between the cobra and the mongoose.

Kancil soon became great friends with the mongoose, and a couple of days later, had the chance to observe the mongoose in action.

By then, Sang Kancil had grown so used to seeing the Resident's pets mingle freely – even natural enemies in the wild - that when he spotted the cobra, he thought nothing of it. He assumed it was another pet of the Resident's.

But the mongoose had also noticed the cobra.

On the dusty ground of the Residency, the cobra undulated, coming closer and closer to the bantam coop when a grey object shot suddenly into view.

It was the mongoose.

Interrupted in its pursuit of a meal, the cobra instantly reared and spread its hood in warning of the deadly attack.

Sang Kancil was mesmerised. All the animals in the compound stopped to watch.

For some time, the mongoose darted from side to side, unable to attempt an attack on the snake's swaying head.

As if tiring of the mongoose's futile efforts, the snake slid forward aggressively.

The mongoose retreated.

The snake pursued.

Back and back and back the mongoose stepped, short legs moving frantically.

The snake pressed its advantage while the frantic mongoose backstepped the snake's relentless onslaught.

Suddenly, the mongoose held its ground.

The snake lunged; fangs aimed at the mongoose.

But its poisonous jaws closed on air.

Sang Kancil dared not blink. It would take one tiny bite. A mere scratch.

But each time, amazingly, the mongoose whipped out of reach. This was the famous speed Sang Kancil had heard much about. But how long could the mongoose keep this up?

As if the snake, too, knew time was running out, it lowered its head to its body, to attack from below, when the mongoose exploded into action. It sprung.

Snap!

The mongoose bit down on the neck of the cobra. Released.

Kancil sucked in his breath. His eyes widened in admiration as the valiant mongoose burst forward again, this time seizing the head of the cobra between its powerful jaws.

CRUNCH!

The snake's skull was crushed. The deadly fight was over!

The mongoose had won. As life drained out of the snake's body, it thrashed one last time, then stilled.

Picking up the body of its enemy, the mongoose disappeared out of the compound.

Later that evening, when the mongoose came over to have its usual chat, the mousedeer congratulated him.

"Well done! I have heard much about your speed and ability, and I see that it is all true!"

The mongoose blushed modestly. "Not at all. Not at all."

"Do you eat them?"

The mongoose frowned at the question then smiled. "Oh! I took the carcass to my old master. Before I came to live in the Residency, I had a different master."

Kancil's brows shot up. This was news. "You can leave at any time?"

"Yes, I sneak out when no one is looking. But I always come back," said the mongoose proudly.

This made little sense to a creature born wild. "Why?"

"Here, I am safe and protected. Well-fed. All I do is kill the occasional snake. Life is good here," said the mongoose.

"Why did your old master sell you?"

The mongoose explained patiently. "He needed money to buy a bicycle."

"Why?"

"A bicycle would enable him to get to places faster. Which would enable him to work more. Which would enable him to earn money."

"Money?"

"Money buys things. And so, whenever I kill a snake, I take it to my old master. Then the government pays him money. If I could kill more snakes, then my old master could get his bicycle faster, but it is not often that snakes enter the compound." At this the mongoose sighed.

Kancil did not like to see his friend unhappy. "Is it only snakes for which the government pays money?"

"No. Baby crocodiles. Crocodile eggs. All earn money."

Kancil brightened. Crocodiles, he understood. "Well then, why doesn't your old master simply go and collect them?"

"Mother crocodiles hide their eggs too well."

"Ah, then I have an idea." And Kancil bent his head and whispered to the mongoose.

The result was that the mongoose dug a hole for Kancil to crawl through, and soon the two friends were on their way to see the crab-and-fish-eating mongoose, who knew intimately the location of the crocodiles' nests.

The crab-and-fish-eating mongoose welcomed the mousedeer. "About time we taught those *buaya* (crocodiles) a lesson. But there are too many eggs. We need more of us to carry them."

And so, on the way to *Kampung Buaya* (Village of the Crocodiles), they collected the mongoose's cousins. The mob were eager to learn how Sang Kancil planned to trick the crocodiles.

For Sang Kancil's tricks were legendary.

At *Kampung Buaya*, it did not take long for the crab-and-fish-eating mongoose to point out the nests hidden in the yellowy-brown mud. Kancil picked a particularly large one and when the mob were stationed nearby and ready, he put his plan into action.

He trotted out into the open and called out, "Adoi! Mrs Crocodile!"

Mrs Crocodile, who had been half-dozing in the afternoon sun, raised her heavy head out of the putrid mud.

"Oh, it is you, Kancil. What do you want?"

"Watch me!" said Sang Kancil, his dark eyes gleaming.

When your next meal invites you to watch them, it is always wise to accept.

And so, as Mrs Crocodile cocked her head, the mousedeer carried out his daring plan.

Before the startled mob, he stood up on his hind legs and-

Danced!

He pranced and cavorted.

Now deer can dance. Including mousedeer. At least in the folktales. They just don't do it very often. And certainly not within reach of the jaws of a crocodile.

It was a dance of life and death.

The crocodiles could not believe what was happening. Neither could the watching mongooses. Open-mouthed with disbelief.

At first, Kancil bobbed, then he trotted around in a tight circle which grew wider as Mrs Crocodile took playful nips. He leaped in the air with all fours and kicked merrily.

And when Mrs Buaya came even closer, he stood on his hind legs, balancing, almost falling.

Mrs Buaya salivated. But whenever she snapped her powerful jaws, he skipped daintily away.

"Why don't you come closer, Kancil," said Mrs Buaya, "Then my poor old eyes will be able to see you better."

Kancil panted hard. Sweat ran down his throat from his efforts, but he only smiled and swayed a little faster and always just out of reach of the cajoling Mrs Buaya.

And what were the others doing, while Kancil danced?

At first, the mob stood and watched.

But when Mrs Crocodile became more and more engrossed in the antics of the chevrotain, they nodded to each other and began, one by one, out-of-sight, to each pick an egg. These they carried carefully, hurrying along to finally deposit the precious cargo at the feet of the mongoose's old master.

Everyone in the village was most surprised to see a trail of mongooses, each carrying a creamy, oval egg. But the mongoose's old master soon put two and two together and realised what his old pet had been up to.

The master was overjoyed. He knew that his former pet wanted him to get his wish and purchase a bicycle. But there was still a dilemma.

Crocodile eggs only received ten cents each. Far from enough for a bicycle. But if the eggs hatched, baby crocodiles fetched one dollar.

The old master put his head between his hands and moaned and groaned, he was thinking that hard, but soon an idea came to him.

All he needed was heat, and in every village, there was a steady source of heat available that came not from a fire. The old master and his family gathered the crocodile eggs and put them in with the piles of unhusked rice, like settling a guava to ripen. Left with the heat, after two months of careful watching, the eggs hatched. Soon, baby crocodiles were crawling all over the rice stores.

The old master and his family celebrated. They sold each baby crocodile for a dollar.

The old master now had his bicycle.

He rode around the kampung on his new purchase. And as the mongoose smiled, Sang Kancil smiled, too.

"Thank you, my friend," said the mongoose, beaming from ear-to-ear.

Sang Kancil's cheeks heated. "Not at all. Not at all. Now that you have accomplished what you set out to do, what are your plans?" And eagerly he awaited his friend's reply.

"Plans?" The mongoose's smile faded. "My plan has always been to return to the compound of the Resident."

Kancil swallowed. "But your freedom..."

"I have always had my freedom."

The Resident's Compound is what the mongoose is particular to.

Unconsciously, Sang Kancil's head dipped as he recalled the weight of the Resident's hand on his head.

His eyes sought out the mongoose's eyes.

Olive green with horizontal pupils, thought Kancil.

The mongoose glanced away. Then he sat up straighter. "In the deep forest, there is the crocodile and the tiger."

The eternal dance of life and death.

Kancil and the mongoose stared at each other for a long time, gazes locked, before the mongoose blinked twice. Then the mongoose turned and darted off.

The last Sang Kancil ever saw of his friend was a small grey dot, bobbing rapidly out of sight.

Anak Rimau (Part III)

KANCIL STAYED IN the village for a while.

The villagers noticed the mousedeer standing on the edge of the kampung. Alone. Looking out as if waiting for something. Someone.

Because he had helped them, they left him alone.

On the third day, however, someone came.

But it was not for whom Kancil had been hoping…

Tigers generally conceal themselves in bushes or long grasses upwind when they hunt. Stalking their intended victim, they sneak forward gradually before pouncing on their target. But the young tiger prowled boldly into the kampong.

The villagers were busy about their work when they spotted the huge tiger making its way toward the village.

The women screamed and gathered up their children, while the men armed themselves.

Only one man did not make it back to his hut in time. He froze on the footpath when the tiger arrived.

Behind the safety of their walls, the villagers watched to see what would enfold.

"*Lari*! (Run!) *Chepat*! (Fast!) *Chepat*!"

But the last villager was riveted to the spot. Out in the open.

The sun turned cold.

Time froze.

Then, something brown shot between the man's legs. Kancil.

To the terrified villagers' gaze, the mousedeer did something surprising. He turned and faced the tiger.

Mouths dropped open.

Everyone watched as the powerful tiger padded on the orange clay towards the man and the mousedeer.

The panicking man looked down, and saw the mousedeer, then he looked up and saw the tiger approaching. A terrified grin spread across his face.

Now, when facing an attacker, the last thing anyone should do is display fear.

Unfortunately, at that very moment, the fear-stricken man's whole body began to quiver.

The villagers shook their heads. They knew what would happen next.

Out in the open, the only thing that moved, slowly, step by step, was the enormous tiger as it made its way towards the mousedeer and the man.

Mothers covered the eyes of their children.

Pad. Pad. Pad. On the orange clay.

Swallowing every sound.

The wife of the man shoved her fist in her mouth and bent her head. She could not bear to look.

Finally, within striking distance, the great predator halted.

All in the village heard the low rasp emitted from the mouth of the tiger.

Only one man, however, heard the high-pitched reply.

The man caught out in the open. The man standing and shaking. That man.

To his infinite astonishment, he heard a scratchy sound that, as it came out of the mouth of the tiger, melted into a single word.

But of course, that was not possible, he reasoned, persuading himself that he must be close to death to be able to imagine that the tiger was talking.

For how could animals talk, even to each other? And even if that was possible, humans could not understand. Or could they?

It is a dream, thought the terrified man.

But he had heard it.

A single word.

"Chegu."

That word made no sense to the man.

But it did make sense to a certain mousedeer.

Teacher? That single word dropped like a stone into the mousedeer's being. At once Kancil knew who confronted him.

Young Rimau.

Grown into adulthood. Bigger. Even more powerful than his father. And thirsting for revenge.

It had been a while since he had seen the cub.

> Now most people do not know this, but the word 'chegu' is a composite of two words: 'Che' which is short for 'Inche' or 'Enche', meaning 'Mister'. And 'Gu' which is an abbreviation for 'guru' meaning 'teacher'. So 'Chegu' means 'Mister Teacher' which is a term of respect and what I used to address my Malay teachers.

But that simple word immediately told Kancil who the tiger was.

Young Rimau may have been thirsting for revenge, but the *adat* (law) had been drummed into him, and once someone is your teacher, there will always be respect for them. Even if you are like Young Rimau and out for blood.

Of course, Kancil took advantage of the situation.

"Oh, Young Rimau is it? How are you? Did you finally end up learning the Koran?"

Teachers always ask how their students are doing.

In an instant, the tables had turned.

Young Rimau squirmed visibly. He lowered his broad head just for a second. But it was enough.

At once, Kancil pushed his advantage. "What a shame. Never mind. Maybe you might be able to-"

But Young Rimau, seeing his superiority slipping away, roared.

The watching villagers shook and trembled at the earth-shattering roar. They covered their ears and gripped their weapons.

How was it that the tiger had not attacked?

"Enough of that! I am not here to *makan angin* (take the air) or to ask about niceties, or the news. I am here only for one thing, and that is to take my vengeance."

"Vengeance? I would not speak so loudly or so boldly if I were you," said Kancil quietly.

This was not the reaction that Young Rimau was expecting. He was still not fully tutored in the ways of world. And so, it was natural that he fumbled. Most animals usually fumble when dealing with a certain chevrotain.

"What do you mean?"

"As I am your ex-tutor, I have an obligation to you to see that you are protected."

Young Rimau snorted. "Protected? Is this how you explain your behaviour? You knocked my brother unconscious. Attacked my father with a hornets' nest. And as for my poor mother! You- you deserve what is coming to you!"

"I did my best to teach. You cannot deny that. If you did not learn, then that was your choice. You and your brother made fun of me."

Young Rimau hesitated.

He and his brother *had* been teasing the mousedeer at the time of the incident.

"My brother is now deaf in one ear. And it is all your fault. I am going to carry out my revenge. Do not think that I am afraid of you!"

"Afraid of me? No, it is not me you should be afraid of but this man." The mousedeer's words dripped with regret.

Baffled, Young Rimau cast a glance at the villager. "Ha! Why should I be afraid of him! He is so petrified of me that he, *he* is shaking!"

At those words, the mousedeer laughed. "Oh, poor Rimau. You mistake his laughing at you for fear. Be thankful that I am your teacher therefore and can offer you this advice: run. Run far away before the man draws his kris and kills you!"

Kris!

A kris is an asymmetrical dagger with a distinct wavy blade. Although there are some that have straight blades. It is a mythical weapon, a piece of art as well as a spiritual object. Some possess legendary power, but all are supposed to contain an essence or a presence.

A magical blade.

And even Rimau knew it.

"You lie, Sang Kancil!" Young Rimau hissed.

"Look at his face. Can you not see his smile?"

Young Rimau looked up to see the grin splitting the man's face in half.

Was it true what the mousedeer was saying?

"But if he wishes to slay me, then why does he not do so?"

"Ah, that is because he wishes to kill you in front of an audience. Unfortunately, all his friends have hidden inside their houses. If you can wait, he will fetch them only… only…"

Because the kris was such a powerful weapon, the mousedeer's words rang with truth.

"Only what?"

"Only he is worried that when he goes to fetch them you will run away."

Young Rimau roared with laughter. "Is that so! Well, I can tell you that I am so strong and so powerful and so in command of the situation that I will gladly wait while this man goes and fetches his friends."

"You will? That would be most kind of you, only… if you allowed the man to bind you, then we would be assured that you would not fun away."

So politely put was the request, that, of course, Young Rimau had to acquiesce.

The terrified man could only listen as the two conversed.

"Well then, what are you waiting for? Go and get your ropes and bind the tiger," said Kancil.

Unable to believe what he was hearing, the man looked from one animal to the other.

"Well, what are you waiting for?" chided the chevrotain. Then winked.

The man did not need to be asked again.

He darted off to get some rope, and when he returned, he quickly bound the great tiger.

"You know that the ropes aren't quite strong enough," said Kancil as he studied the man's knots.

"Too true. I could most easily break out of these," said Young Rimau with a sneer.

"Would you mind if the man fetched more ropes?"

"Certainly. Hey you, hurry up!"

The man, still believing that he was dreaming, rushed off and returned with even more rope.

How often after all does a tiger ask to be bound?

Again, Kancil examined the man's efforts and again the man had to run off to fetch more rope.

Finally at the fourth attempt, when Young Rimau tested the ropes, did both animals deem the ropes strong enough to withstand the tiger's strength.

"Now we are ready," said Kancil.

"Yes, we are most ready," said Young Rimau. "Go and fetch your audience."

The man ran off. It took him a while to convince the villagers that it was safe but as they had all watched in utter astonishment as the man bound and rebound Young Rimau, the rest of the village eventually gathered around the tiger.

"Quick," said the man, who with his friends now around him, had found his tongue. "The silly fool is unable to escape. "Now gather him and we can sell him for a great deal of money to the zoo!"

"Wait! What?" stormed Young Rimau.

But all the villagers ever heard was a roar.

They covered their ears with their hands, and their knees shook, but when they removed their hands, they found to their enormous delight and gratitude that the tiger was indeed bound and unable to escape.

So, they did as the lone villager suggested and put the mighty predator onto a cart and took him away to the town where they sold Young Rimau to the zoo. And there he is to this day, or at least his progeny. And do not feel too sorry for him, because tigers are now very rare in Malaysia.

So, in a way, Kancil did him a favour.

Sang Kancil and the Buffalo

ALTHOUGH IT IS dangerous, *Kerbau* (Buffalo) loves eating the grass near the riverbank, for it is fresh and succulent.

Pada suatu hari (On one day), *Kerbau* was feasting on a particularly tasty green patch when he heard screams.

"Help me! Please, help me!"

The buffalo raced off to see what the matter was.

To his surprise, the voice seemed to come from way down the riverbank. Now if there was one thing that Kerbau knew, it was that *buaya* (crocodiles) lived in the river.

To stay safe, *Kerbau* understood that he had to remain several paces back from the water's edge, for crocodiles were renown for snatching creatures from the edge. And a crocodile on land is almost as fast as in the water.

To *Kerbau's* surprise, not only was the voice coming from near the water, but from under a fallen tree.

Some poor creature appeared to be pinned under the massive trunk, he thought. But that was not the worst of it.

As *Kerbau* drew closer, he could see that the caller itself was a *buaya*.

"Oh, save me! Save me!" *Buaya* blinked in pain as *Kerbau* approached. "This tree trunk fell on me and is pinning me to the spot."

To his credit, the kind buffalo did not hesitate. "I am coming!"

"Thank you! Thank you!"

Buaya sounded so grateful that Kerbau hurried to the trapped animal, and using his mighty horns, attempted to lift the massive tree off the poor crocodile.

The task was not easy for the tree was huge. But Kerbau dug his hooves into the ground and heaved and pushed and did not give up until finally, after a tremendous amount of effort, he rolled the tree off Buaya.

"Oh, thank you, thank you, thank you, kind Kerbau. You have no idea what your kindness means to me," said Buaya, weeping tears of gratitude."

"I am pleased that I could help," said Kerbau, huffing from exhaustion. "Now I shall be on my way." And he swung around, only-

Snap!

Pain exploded along Kerbau's leg. Stunned, the buffalo whipped round to find his right leg caught in the jaws of the crocodile that he had just rescued.

A look of disbelief washed over Sang Kerbau's broad face. "What are you doing? Are you mad? Is this the manner to which my kindness is being repaid?

"Oh, kind sir, please forgive me. You see, I was stuck under that log for so long that I grew very hungry. If you would not mind, I would now like to gnaw on your leg," said the greedy crocodile.

"*Gila!* (Mad) Let me go at once!"

"I cannot, for I am ravenous," said the crocodile and was about to start his meal when a tiny voice piped up.

"*Apa khabar?* (What news? Hello?)"

It was Sang Kancil.

"*Khabar baik,* (Good news), Sang Kancil," said the crocodile beaming, for after all, had he not poor Kerbau's leg in his mouth.

"Oh, Sang Kancil," wept the unfortunate buffalo. "Help me, please! I saved Sang Buaya's life by removing that log. But despite my good deed, I find myself totally betrayed for now I am to be Sang Buaya's meal."

"Is what Sang Kerbau saying true, Sang Buaya?" said the mousedeer.

"It is indeed," said Sang Buaya, not in the least embarrassed. "And this here is the log."

Sang Kancil trotted up to the log. He sniffed the wood then tapped the trunk with his hoof. "Hmmm, the tree is large." He turned to look at Sang Buaya. "Sang Buaya is big and strong. It is impossible for anyone of Sang Buaya's stature to possibly have been trapped by this log. Therefore, I cannot believe that this was the case."

"What!" said Sang Buaya. "Are you calling me a liar?"

"Not at all. But look," said the mousedeer, knocking on the mighty trunk of the tree with his tiny hooves and only managing to elicit a muffled *thunk*. "This tree is solid. No one, not even a creature of Sang Kerbau's stature, would be able to lift this."

"Well," said Sang Kerbau with a weary shake of his head. "It is true what you say. The log is indeed big and solid. But the fact is that I did it. I did it!" Tears poured down his wide face. "And now I regret it." Buffalo's whole body shuddered in grief for he believed that his end was near.

Sang Kancil arched his dainty neck. "I do not believe that Sang Kerbau has the strength to lift that log. And if it was true that the log fell on Sang Buaya, then I believe that Sang Buaya by himself would have had the strength to lift the log off. Therefore, I will need to see the situation for myself before we can proceed."

"It is as Sang Kerbau said. But if you wish, we can revisit the incident. I am huge and strong after all. You are free, Sang Kerbau," said Sang Buaya, gloating at the praise, and he opened his mouth.

The astonished buffalo immediately pulled his leg out.

Sang Kancil nodded. "Thank you for your assistance, Sang Buaya. I am sure we can solve this problem in a very short time. Now Sang Kerbau, if, indeed you are capable, can you play your part by pushing this log onto Sang Buaya's back?"

Although Sang Kerbau's leg ached, and although he was exhausted, Sang Kerbau lost little time replacing the mighty log on Sang Buaya's back.

"There," huffed Sang Kerbau as the log settled with a thump. "This is exactly how I found Sang Buaya."

"So, you say," said Sang Kancil with a frown. "I can see that you did speak the truth when you said that you lifted the log off Sang Buaya. You have proven that much, only…" The chevrotain waggled its head.

"Do you still not believe us?" said the exasperated Sang Buaya, struggling to speak for the log on top of him was indeed massive. "Well, what more do you want us to do?" Then he groaned, pain was throbbing through his body.

Sang Kancil trotted up to Sang Buaya. "Well, you are Sang Buaya, and you are so mighty and so strong, and you did say that you would have no problem rolling the log off?"

Had he said that? Crocodile could not remember. Pain swallowed up all his energy. "Get it off!" screamed Sang Buaya, unable to stand another moment of the agony. "I lied. I abused Sang Kerbau's kindness."

"You did?" said Sang Kancil, affecting shock.

"There!" said Sang Kerbau. "Sang Buaya tricked me."

Sang Kancil turned to Sang Buaya with a smile. "And so, the truth finally comes out."

"Please! Let me go and I will never be mean to you again!" wept Sang Buaya.

"Now you know what Sang Kerbau felt when you bit his leg," said Sang Kancil.

"I do, I do. And I promise, I promise never to be mean again."

"Sang Kerbau, you have been kindness itself. I know this is a lot to ask of you, but would you mind?" said Sang Kancil. "I will understand if you choose not to."

Sang Kerbau was exhausted, but he was a kind-hearted creature and so with the last of his strength, he rolled the heavy trunk off Sang Buaya's back.

"Thank you, thank you, thank you," wept Sang Buaya. "I have learned my lesson."

But there was no answer for Sang Kancil had bounded away, followed swiftly by Sang Kerbau.

The two knew that there was a chance that Sang Buaya may indeed have been speaking the truth, but everyone knew the sincerity of crocodile tears.

See Notes on Pages 333-334

The Elephant has a bet with the Tiger

DULU-DULU (ONCE UPON A TIME), *Gajah* (Elephant) and *Harimau* (Tiger) were the best of friends.

One day the two friends came upon a clearing where they saw *Lotong* (the long-tailed Spectacle Monkey) in a tree.

"Let us make a wager," said Gajah. "For Lotong is far too noisy. If I can shake him off his tree, then I shall eat you. But if instead you can shake him off his tree, then you shall eat me."

"Done!" said Harimau.

And so, the foolish wager was made.

Gajah had the first go. "Au. Au. Au," he trumpeted, only instead of scaring the monkey out of the branches, Lotong fled from branch to branch.

"Well, *Kawan Gajah*, (Friend Elephant) do you wish a second try?" asked *Kawan Harimau* (Friend Tiger).

"No, thank you," said Kawan Gajah confidently. "You may have a go and if you can really make him fall then you shall eat me."

So Harimau had his turn. He roared his longest and his loudest. He crouched as if to spring and then growled thrice. The mighty Tiger so terrified the monkey that the creature's hands and feet, paralysed with fear, knuckled over and it fell at the tiger's feet.

And so Harimau won the contest.

"Well, Kawan Gajah, as the rules declare, I should eat you now," said Kawan Harimau with a polite smile. They were friends after all. *Dear* friends.

Kawan Gajah shook his big grey ears as the enormous consequences of his foolish dare became clear to him. Somehow, he still managed to speak calmly, "You have won, it is obvious, and I will not dispute. But I beg leave to allow me to return to my home for seven days where I shall take farewell of my family. I would so like to see my dear wife and children one last time."

Harimau granted Gajah's request and so Elephant went on his way home, bellowing and sobbing as he shoved his way through the rain forest. So loud was he that his wife heard him from far away.

"Whatever can be the matter," said the Elephant's wife to their children.

"It is Dear Father," said the elephant children. "Whatever can be the reason for his sorrow?"

Presently Gajah returned to his family. At once his wife asked him what the matter was, and Gajah told her.

"I made a wager with Kawan Harimau. Lotong was being a nuisance and so, I declared that if I could shake Lotong out of the tree then I would win the wager."

"And what was the prize?" asked the Elephant wife, unable to believe the stupidity of the dare.

"That I would eat Kawan Harimau."

The Elephant's wife only shook her head. She could guess where this was leading. "And what was the prize should Harimau win?"

"That he would eat me," said Gajah, his sobs beginning afresh. "I was beaten and so Harimau was to eat me only I begged him to allow me to say my goodbyes to my family."

And so, for seven days, Gajah wept and sobbed. Neither did he eat or sleep.

The matter finally came to the attention of Sang Kancil.

"What is wrong, Kawan Gajah. The rains are almost upon us, and yet I hear you bellowing and bellowing without ceasing," said Sang Kancil.

"It is no empty noise for I have gotten myself into a dreadful dilemma," said Gajah. "You see, I have made a wager with Kawan Harimau. It was about shaking down a monkey. Whoever won the wager would eat the other."

"I see," said Sang Kancil.

"I lost so Kawan Harimau was to have eaten me only I begged leave to return to say my goodbyes to my family and to write my will."

"I should not like to hear of Harimau eating you. Let me see what I can do," said Sang Kancil.

"Help me and I and my descendants shall be your devoted slaves forever," said Gajah.

"Very well," said Sang Kancil. "I will assist."

Gajah dried his tears at once.

"Go find a jar of molasses," said Sang Kancil.

Gajah went off to the house of the toddy-maker (maker of palm wine). However, when the toddy maker saw the enormous elephant at his door, he fled for his life.

Undeterred, Gajah pushed down the walls of the house, found what he was looking for and gave the jar to the mousedeer.

"When does Harimau expect you?" said Sang Kancil.

"Tomorrow," said Gajah.

"Very well. Now this is what you must do," said Sang Kancil and proceeded to explain.

The next morning, Gajah did as Sang Kancil had instructed. He poured the molasses over his back, allowing the sticky mess to spread as it ran down his legs.

When the elephant was done, Sang Kancil jumped onto the elephant's back. "Now remember. As soon as I start to lick, you are to bellow as loudly as you can. Do not forget to wriggle and moan, and to make believe that you are dying. Really dying."

"Do not worry," said Gajah. "I shall do exactly as you instruct."

Sang Kancil bent and proceeded to lick.

Immediately, Gajah writhed and squirmed and pretended to be mortally wounded.

Continuing in this fashion, the pair made a tremendous noise as they trampled through the rainforest on their way to Harimau and all the while Gajah trumpeted and groaned and acted as if he was dying.

Now sound in the jungle is the forerunner of some event. And it tends to be that the louder the sound, the more momentous the event.

The animals listened, eyes wide with terror.

What could it be?

Harimau heard them coming from a long way away. "Whatever can be making that terrible ruckus? It appears that whosoever is guilty of that disturbance is coming towards me." And Harimau watched in great perturbation as trees were smashed aside and branches ripped off.

As the commotion came closer and closer, Harimau's heart began to beat more and more rapidly, and his throat grew drier and drier. Soon he was able to make out his friend Gajah as the elephant burst through the tangled mess of jungle.

"Surely that is Kawan Gajah, but why is he trumpeting as if he is in great pain? And what is that sticky mess upon his back? Blood? Why it is almost as if dear Kawan is bleeding to death." And at that Harimau grew mightily afraid.

When the elephant came within earshot, it halted. It did not appear to notice the tiger, so great was its misery.

The concerned Sang Harimau was about to call out in greeting when the tiger suddenly spotted something atop the elephant's broad back.

Small and smeared with the dark liquid, the *thing* was vigorously chewing.

Tiger stilled, unable to believe the sight of the *thing* atop the huge colossus of the elephant. Why it almost looked as if it had been licking up the blood. But surely that was not poss-ible?

But then the *thing* spoke and when Tiger heard the *thing's* words, his blood ran cold.

"Why, a single elephant large as he is, is not going to fill my belly." Almost before the *thing* finished speaking, it lifted its misshapen head and peered about.

When his gaze stopped at Harimau, the creature's eyes grew large and luminous. "Now, if only I could lay my fangs on that fat tiger. What a juicy accompaniment it would be to this tough old elephant."

When Tiger heard the *thing's* words, he quaked.

No doubt this lethal predator has the better of my poor Kawan Gajah. And I have little doubt that if he catches me that my fate would be that of my friend.

Without wasting a moment, Harimau took off. He did not wish to remain to meet the *thing*.

Leaping over bushes, twisting round trees, Sang Harimau hurtled through the rain forest, attempting to put as much ground between him and that thing.

As Tiger raced off, he soon encountered a Black Ape.

"What ails you Kawan Harimau, that you run so fast?" said the Black Ape. "The rains are almost upon us. Now is not the time for noise."

"Noise? Noise? Did you not see the *thing* upon poor Kawan Gajah's back devouring him with great gusto? Why Kawan Gajah was wriggling and writhing as if in the throes of death. And the blood, the great gobs of it, all congealed and gooey down his back. Furthermore, the *thing* that was on his back announced that it would love to catch a fat tiger such as myself, for then its hunger would be appeased."

The Black Ape listened and scratched its chin. It would not do to show fear in front of Sang Harimau. Whatever the situation, the Black Ape understood that he had to appear the dominant predator. So, he made what he believed was a wise assumption. "What was that thing? Could it be Sang Kancil?"

A tiny sliver of doubt grew in Harimau's brain. But to admit that the *thing* was Sang Kancil, was to admit that he – the king of the jungle – had made a grievous error. "Certainly not!" snorted Tiger. "For why would Kanchil say that he wanted to catch and devour me? Me! A tiger. Whatever it was upon Kawan Gajah's back was feasting upon meat. Flesh! It was not Sang Kancil!"

"It may be as you say," said the Black Ape, perturbed at Sang Harimau's words. "But I would like to check it out."

And so, the Black Ape persuaded Harimau to return.

Harimau and the Black Ape, both pretending to be sure of the situation, each raced to be at the fore, so that at one instance Harimau was in front and in another it was the Black Ape. In this noisy fashion the pair soon came upon the *thing*, and Gajah.

The astute Sang Kancil heard the curious pair approach before he saw them and as Tiger and the Black Ape neared, the mousedeer had a plan.

Sang Kancil always has a plan.

"This will not do, Father Ape," said Sang Kancil, slowly shaking his head. "You promised me two tigers and instead you bring only one. I refuse to accept it."

On hearing those words, Tiger paled. He swung round, glared at his betrayer, and ran off as fast as he could for his life.

"Wait, stop," called the Black Ape. "Do not believe the trickster!"

"You are a fool if you think you can trick me again," roared the terrified tiger.

And no matter what the Black Ape spoke, Tiger did not believe him.

"Do not venture onto the ground, for I shall grant you the death that you plotted against me."

This is why from that day forth; apes have always kept to the trees.

See Notes on Pages 334-335

Monkey and the Kueh

In the past, it was believed that many animals lived together peacefully co-existing in the jungle (hutan) now termed rainforest. All with their own lives and families and various pursuits. Some were cunning, others intelligent, and quite a few quick: however, only one was all three.

*M*ONYET (MONKEY) FOUND a round, yellow cake one day. He climbed the branches of a tree and would have gone higher except that he was anxious to eat the unexpected treat.

Trembling with anticipation, the monkey lifted the fluffy steamed cake to his nostrils and inhaled the fresh aroma of eggs. And sugar. Sweet, sweet sugar.

Saliva filled his mouth.

Oh, how cunning he was to have spotted the kueh (cake*) cooling on the table.*

Oh, how intelligent he was to know how he could duck in and out of the kampung (village)*.*

And oh, how swift he was to lift and make off with the cake while the terrified child screamed for its mother.

Monyet quivered with delight to the point of swooning. He could almost taste the sugar on his tongue. Opening his mouth wide, he prepared to devour the kueh in one enormous gulp, when the bushes below rustled.

Harimau! (Tiger.) Had that dreaded predator found him? Harimau was well known throughout the rainforest for his love of eating monkeys.

Monkey leapt to a higher branch and peered down, rebuking himself that he had not gone higher. But he had been so hungry.

To Monyet's relief, it wasn't the vicious predator. But it was someone almost as bad - Sang Kancil.

The chevrotain trotted into sight. "Oh, Sang Monyet," called out Sang Kancil gaily.

Sang... Monyet winced. Once again, he wished he had climbed higher. Or at least high enough to be hidden. But nothing could have hidden the tantalizing aroma of freshly steamed cake in the early morning air.

Eggs! Sugar!

The delectable fragrance was probably how the pest had found him in the first place.

Monyet gazed down to the bottom of the tree where the mousedeer waited. He found it hard to ignore the stare of the chevrotain.

For one long moment, the two animals stood simply regarding each other then-

Slurp!

Sang Kanchil's thin, pink tongue shot out. He did look unbearably hungry.

Monyet sighed and lowered the piece of cake. "Sang Kancil, *apa khabar* (what news)?"

"You have cake, Nyet," said Sang Kancil, his eyes big and round and dark as he stated the obvious. "Oh, Nyet, please give me some."

Nyet… Monyet sighed. Custom demanded that if a friend came to visit that one must offer refreshments. Not only had Sang Kancil referred to him as '*Sang*' (Revered) but also his nickname 'Nyet.'

The correct protocol took precedence, and reluctantly Nyet descended to Sang Kancil's level.

Why was it that Sang Kanchil was always around when Monyet had food, and why was Monyet never around when Sang Kancil had food? That was an eternal mystery.

"It is only a tiny, tiny kueh," said Monyet cunningly, now at eye level with the chevrotain.

In response, Sang Kancil nosed forward.

Panicking, Monyet pushed the kueh behind his back.

If Monyet had thought that by removing the treat from Sang Kancil's sight, it would also remove it from Sang Kancil's thoughts, he was gravely mistaken.

Sang Kancil simply trotted round to Monyet's back. Unable to see what he was up to, Monyet whipped his arm back, protectively pressing the yellow kueh against its chest, like a mother cradling her newborn.

"Oh Nyet! Nyet! I am so hungry, surely you will share your piece with your friend?"

Friend…

Monyet snapped his mouth shut. "I have such a tiny portion," said Monkey. *Two could play this game.* "*Chil,*" he added.

"You have something. I have nothing. If I had something I would share with you."

Monkey knew he would never be able to test this proposition. "I am hungry."

"All I am asking is to share."

Share… Monyet considered. Well, perhaps the situation was salvageable. It didn't sound as if he was going to lose his entire cake. Perhaps he could break off a bit. A teeny bit. A crumb.

As if aware of Monyet's thoughts, Sang Kancil clamoured, "Half. Half. That is what friends would do. Good friends."

How Monyet longed to say that he was not Sang Kancil's friend. Let alone a *good* friend. Instead, Monkey broke off a piece and handed it to Sang Kancil. Best to get this over and done with. Then he could settle himself down to enjoy his treat.

Better half a kueh than no kueh at all.

"Thank you, Nyet!" said Sang Kancil gratefully.

Monyet nodded, his tummy rumbling. Now he had divided his cake in half, he assumed he had gotten rid of that pest.

But he was dealing with Sang Kancil.

"I knew you cared," said Sang Kancil appearing genuinely grateful.

Monyet blushed at his earlier ungenerous thoughts. But at least he had cake. He opened his mouth-

"Oh Nyet, look!"

Groaning inwardly, Monkey lowered his arm.

"Oh Nyet, *tengok* (look)! You were in such a hurry that you have not divided the cake equally."

Equally?

Monyet stared at Sang Kancil's half and his. Surely the two were identical! "They look-"

But Monyet wasn't quick enough.

"Do not worry, I know what to do." Without hesitation, Sang Kancil took a chomp out of Monyet's slice.

"Adoi!" called out Monkey in anguish.

"I know that you wouldn't want to be unfair," said Sang Kancil chewing hastily.

"But now your slice is larger!" screamed Monyet.

And it was true. Sang Kancil's slice did look larger.

"Oh, Nyet, I am sorry. It looks like I took too big a bite out of your slice and now my slice looks larger. Do not worry. I know what to do."

And before Monyet could say another word, Sang Kancil took another swift bite. This time out of his own slice.

"There! Now the two are even, I mean just look at them, I mean oh. Oh! Oh, yours is the larger one again."

And so, as Monyet stared again in disbelief at the audacity of Sang Kancil, the cheeky creature took yet another bite. Out of Monyet's slice.

Crumbs remained in Monyet's paw.

"Oh!" snorted Monkey unable to believe what had happened. As the rattled Monyet stared, Sang Kancil popped the rest of his piece into his mouth, nodded his thanks and trotted off.

"That was lovely, thank you so much! And don't worry. You keep yours. You are my friend, and I want you to be happy."

Monyet screamed in silent anguish. He knew that if he made too much of a ruckus that he would attract the attention of the other inhabitants of the rainforest. How they would laugh when they learned that Sang Kancil got the better of him. Again.

Monyet stuffed the remains of the yellow kueh into his mouth and swung away. As far away as he could. Far, far away.

Since that day, Monyet has always hated Sang Kancil and dreams of getting the best of him.

But this will never happen, as Sang Kancil is Sang Kancil.

And that is why we love him so much.

See Notes on Page 335

Sang Kancil and the Farmer

All farmers the world over work hard. In Malaysia, farmers grow paddy, and their farms can be large with their homes anywhere from one to five kilometres away from their fields. Besides paddy, many also produce vegetables and fruits to supplement their diet.

Although the soil is fertile, these farmers have many pests to deal with and unfortunately, one of them is a notorious chevrotain.

Mousedeer eat leaves, buds, shrubs and fallen fruit that is until they are bored.

A T THE EDGE of the jungle where man had made his home, Sang Kancil lifted his snout.

Ahhh…

Timun. (Cucumbers.)

Sang Kancil's nostrils quivered as he inhaled the delightful scent. Unlike the wild cucumbers, these vines were cultivated. Hence, he was less likely to be stabbed by thorns.

(Yes, cucumbers have thorns. The ones that we buy have their thorns already rubbed off.) Kancil didn't like thorns.

The watery landscape of the farm spread to the mountains on the horizon; the vast blue of the sky reflected in silvered squares. Butting up to the farmer's house was the vegetable patch.

Sang Kancil drooled.

Tall papaya and mango trees lay in one corner with the juicy green cucumbers in the middle of the garden, right after the leafy dark green Choy Sum.

Baik. (Good.) *Tak ada orang.* (No one about.) No doubt the farmer was elsewhere on his large farm, which meant that this was the perfect time for a meal of cucumbers.

Mousedeer eat leaves, buds, shrubs and fallen fruit. And sometimes cucumbers.

Sang Kancil ate. He pulled down crunchy cucumber after crunchy cucumber and was just about to attack the last one when the scent reached him.

Man.

No problem. Sang Kancil coolly vanished into the jungle.

It was only later in the evening when the farmer's wife went to gather some cucumbers to have with their meal that the theft was discovered.

The farmer and his wife ate the last cucumber along with kangkong fried with chili that night with their rice.

"All that hard work, pinning up the vines," said the farmer.

"All that hard work, weeding around the vines," said the farmer's wife.

They sighed.

The next day, the farmer set traps around his farm.

And all was well for a few days.

The sun shone.

The tropical rains fell each afternoon.

And the vegetables and fruits grew and grew. Luscious, plump, and fresh.

Until Sang Kancil grew bored of his diet once more.

Mousedeer eat leaves, buds, shrubs and fallen fruit. And sometimes cucumbers and jackfruit.

The jackfruit is the largest of all fruits and grows to around 18 kg in weight – the mass of a dog.

At the edge of the farm, the tempting treat taunted.

Even better, an enormous fruit had fallen and conveniently split open where it had hit the ground. This meant that all Sang Kancil had to do was to stick his head into the opening and enjoy the luscious golden fruit.

No wondering how to rip the tough skin open.

No wondering how to extract the inside bulbs.

No wondering how to avoid the sticky sap.

Just a golden gift, laid out, waiting to be devoured...

One last sniff and Sang Kancil trotted up to the vegetable patch.

Trot-trot-trot.

Smell of farmer's wife.

But Sang Kancil was not worried.

She daily tended the garden. But he had seen her down at the river with a load of clothes. She would be gone a while.

Trot-trot-trot.

Smell of farmer.

But Sang Kancil was not worried.

He had seen the farmer set off, changkol over one shoulder, his faithful dog following at his heels. The farmer would be gone a while.

Trot. Trot. Trot.

Smell of bamboo, vines, and wood. Traps!

But again, Sang Kancil was not worried.

Even though the traps had been set up specifically for him, all Sang Kancil had to do was avoid them. Which he cunningly did.

Stupid farmer!

Soon, Sang Kancil was standing at the bottom of the jackfruit tree and there before his unbelieving eyes was a newly fallen green speckled jackfruit as large as a fat spotted piglet.

Sang Kancil ate and ate and ate. He managed to avoid the sticky sap. But soon, he had gobbled up all the fruit within reach.

Now the problem with jackfruit is that once you start it is difficult to stop. Very difficult indeed. The luscious golden fruit has a delicious tang that makes you want to eat and eat and eat. And you do not have to be a certain chevrotain to want to keep on gobbling.

Stupid farmer is far away. When I hear him, I will just pull my head out. Easy!

So Sang Kancil stuck his head in deeper to get at the rest of the precious fruit.

But what he did not know was that the farmer was already returning for his midday meal.

Sticky white sap coated Sang Kancil's ears and head but still he ate and ate and ate. He kept an ear out though for the return of the farmer and so when he heard noises, knew his time was up.

He pulled his head out-

Oh! He pulled his head out-

Oh! Oh! He pulled his head out-

Oh…!

Sang Kancil was stuck.

While Mousedeer eat leaves, buds, shrubs and fallen fruit and sometimes cucumbers and jackfruit, the farmer eats rice and vegetables. And meat. Any meat. And sometimes mousedeer, which is a delicacy, if they can get their hands on it.

The farmer smiled. Even from across a great distance, he had spotted the tiny brown body in the vegetable patch.

"*Jangan,*" he instructed his *anjing* (dog). For the dog had recognized the mousedeer and would have run off to investigate, only the famer held the animal back.

He did not want his dinner torn to pieces.

The farmer's smile broadened.

The wooden traps were untouched. But here was the fallen jackfruit.

The farmer bent to examine the body, but as he did so, his smile died. Filled with unease, he poked at the body of the mousedeer. At the limp legs. "Stiff already."

Stupid thing must have suffocated when it stuck its head into the opening of the jackfruit. Should have made the hole bigger.

"You are a fool," said the farmer. "And had I been quicker, I might have had mousedeer for my meal tonight."

For a dead animal on a farm is seen as a curse, and no one eats an animal that has already died, for who knew how long its body had lain decomposing under the tropical sun.

The disappointed farmer picked up the carcass of Sang Kancil and hurled it as far away as he could into the rainforest.

Imagine his disgust when a moment later, he heard rustling and saw the supposedly dead creature bounding away.

"You will not trick me ever again," said the farmer roaring with anger.

And that might have been the case, except that after a while Sang Kancil grew bored.

Mousedeer eat leaves, buds, shrubs and fallen fruit. And sometimes cucumbers, jackfruit and rambutan. Red and juicy.

Rambutans are a favourite.

The last time Sang Kancil visited, he had noticed the rambutan tree along with the other fruit trees in the corner of the vegetable patch. Once more, he wanted to try his luck. He knew it was impossible to scale the trunks of the papaya and mango trees but a rambutan tree with low lying branches was a potential feast.

When Sang Kancil arrived at the vegetable garden, this time however, he found a figure standing in the middle of the patch. A curious figure with yellow straw protruding from under a woven hat. More straw drooped from the ends of sleeves and even more curious, there appeared to be no legs.

Intriguing.

A pole thrust into the ground supported the figure, and when the wind blew, its clothes wavered in the breeze lifting the scent of the farmer to the chevrotain who had not seen anything like this before.

Sang Kancil pondered; he could hear the farmer's wife pounding spices in her kitchen.

Chilli! Red and hot! Already his eyes watered. Nosing its way forward, Sang Kancil inhaled deeply.

This figure smelt like the farmer only it did not quite look like the farmer, and it made no sense as to why the farmer was not tending to his fields.

Only standing still. In the middle of the vegetable patch. With the hot Malaysian sun pouring down on him. Steam rose from the ground as the day heated.

Sang Kancil licked his upper lip with his long pink tongue. Even he was hot, and *he* was lying in the shade. But still he sat and stared, remaining to see if the farmer would move, preferably leave but no matter how long he persisted, the farmer continued to be still. Unmoving.

Long past midmorning, Sang Kanchil finally rose to his feet.

Trot. Trot. Trot.

Smell of farmer's wife.

Trot. Trot. Trot.

Smell of farmer.

Trot. Trot. Trot.

Smell of bamboo and straw.

He came closer. To his perplexity, the farmer neither turned his head nor shouted for his dog.

Sang Kancil trotted right up to the figure. All around dancing in the air were the distracting fragrances of papaya, mango, rambutan, jackfruit… all the fruits that were in the vegetable patch.

Come and eat! Feast! Makan! (Eat!) *Chepat!* (Quick!)

Sang Kancil was ravenous, but forced himself to investigate further before he could feast. His persistence was rewarded. Finally, Sang Kancil understood what was happening.

This was the farmer and not the farmer.

This was simply a bamboo pole.

A bamboo pole dressed up in the farmer's own clothes, which was why the farmer's scent was intense.

And when the breeze stirred and the clothes flapped limply, Sang Kancil knew he was correct.

"There is no substance to this apparition of a farmer. Only clothes hanging from a pole, swaying in the wind," Sang Kancil said to the wind.

The wind said nothing.

But now anger filled Sang Kancil for the figure had kept him from his meal.

You think you are so smart, ha! And Sang Kancil kicked at the figure.

His legs struck empty air.

Frustrated, Sang Kancil thrust once more, and he was pleased to hear a satisfying *thunk* as his hooves contacted the bamboo pole.

He kicked again, feeling satisfied and self-assured and extremely clever with himself to have figured out what was going on.

Thunk!

Thunk!

Thun- Oof! Sang Kancil almost went down headfirst. What had happened?

Sang Kancil turned in shock to find one back hoof stuck to the figure.

Annoyed, Sang Kancil lashed out to free itself.

Only…

Only now not one but *two* hooves were stuck.

Oh! Oh! Adoi!

Both back hooves were fixed fast to the figure, for the pole was smeared with the sticky sap from the jackfruit tree.

Oh, how Sang Kancil remembered the curse of that horrid white juice. Days it had taken to finally remove all traces from his hide. And now once more he was smeared with the nasty muck!

Sang Kancil jerked and kicked and twisted. But no matter how much he struggled, instead of freeing himself, his two back legs remained glued to the pole!

Let me go!

But a pole is only a pole. It could not hear his desperate pleas. Or respond.

The wind picked up. The clothes flapped violently, warning the frantic one that the farmer was on his way back. But there was nothing Sang Kancil could do except wait.

The wind howled, billowing. Leaves and twigs flew smack bang into the desperate one who was digging his remaining hooves into the ground, doing everything he could not to get bowled over.

The wind screamed. Shrieked. Implored! Get away!

Suddenly, a monstrous bulk towered over Sang Kancil. The reek of pungent sweat almost overcame him. The pupils of the creature's eyes bored into him: merciless.

The farmer.

The farmer was triumphant to see that his trap had worked. He examined his prize; it was all the trapped mousedeer could do not to cower.

Sang Kancil may be a pest and a thief, but he is also a hero. In the face of impossible danger, he did the only thing he could do. He stretched his neck tall and looked straight into the farmer's monstrous face.

But there was no mercy to be had in those black flashing eyes.

"So, you think you are so clever! But you have not gotten the best of me!" The farmer ripped Sang Kancil cruelly from the scarecrow and stuffed him into a cage.

"Look after it well. Tomorrow, we shall feast," said the farmer to his wife and then sauntered off to the river to bath.

"Look after it well." The farmer's wife chewed her lower lip thoughtfully. Then she went off to pluck succulent Choy Sum. She placed the fresh green vegetables inside the cage and carefully lowered a bowl of water.

"Goodnight, I have carried out my husband's instructions and looked after you well," she said and left.

Sang Kancil stared at her retreating figure. Thinking very hard, he mustered all his courage. It had to be done.

And when the farmer's dog raced up to the cage, he carried out his bold plan.

"Hahaha!" said the farmer's dog as he lifted his great brown snout to the cage and showed off great white fangs. "I will feast on you, too." And it gave a great big bark.

"Hahaha, yourself," said Sang Kancil, and sighed with feigned boredom.

"Hahaha," said Anjing once more, but not as loudly this time.

Sang Kancil waited patiently.

"Why are you not upset?" said Anjing finally.

"Why should I be upset?" said Sang Kancil, cocking a brow.

Baffled, Anjing stared at the surprising creature in the cage, unable to believe what he was hearing. "What? Did you not hear? You will be our meal tomorrow."

"A meal there most certainly will be only I will be the guest," said Sang Kancil calmly.

"Hahaha," said Anjing, his laughter now anything but convincing.

"Remember the farmer's words. 'Look after it well. Tomorrow, we shall feast'," said Sang Kancil. "And what did his wife say and do?"

Anjing recalled his mistress's word.

I have carried out my husband's instructions and looked after you well.

Sang Kancil tilted his head at the pile of fresh Choy sum and the bowl of water. Proof.

Anjing wrinkled its brow. "But- but"

"How many years have you served your master?" said Sang Kancil kindly.

No one had ever asked Anjing that question before. It was almost as if the mousedeer genuinely cared. To the dog's surprise, its eyes grew moist.

"Ten," Anjing said. Strange how a few gentle words so easily turns away wrath.

Sang Kancil's dark eyes grew limpid with emotion. "You poor thing. Your master is right. There will be a feast tomorrow. Only I will be the Guest of Honour at the feast. And you, you who have served your master loyally for ten years will be left with scraps."

And that part was true. For the farmer had only ever fed his dog scraps.

"Do you not agree that it is most unfair?"

Anjing could only nod.

"But I wonder… I wonder if there is a way. If we can right this wrong. If… after all, you have always served your master faithfully. Should you not be the guest, rather than I? There must be a way." Sang Kancil appeared thoughtful.

Anjing hung its massive brown head. "But what can be done?" For his master was a hard man, bent down by too much hard work and not enough reward to show for it. Perhaps had life been kinder, he might have been fashioned kinder. But life is anything but kind to farmers.

Sang Kancil narrowed his eyes. "Do you believe me when I say that there is a way, I can help you? Make things right."

Anjing thumped his white and brown tail eagerly on the ground. "Oh, please. Tell me what it is that I must do, and I will do it. Then I will be your servant forever."

"You must take my place," said Sang Kancil simply.

"Take your place?"

Sang Kancil nodded. "Once, your master sees you in here, he will understand that it is you he should be honouring for all your years of service rather than me."

"You will sacrifice your honour for me?" said Anjing awed.

"You should be Guest of Honour, not me."

"You are right," said Anjing, and began to pant with excitement.

"I am right. Open the door. We will swap places."

"At once." Overjoyed, Anjing unlatched the cage. The two animals exchanged places.

"I shall go and tell your master what we have decided."

"Thank you so much!" said Anjing, tearfully. "I shall never forget what you have done for me."

"Oh, I am sure you will not. Now be a good dog and finish all those vegetables that the farmer's wife left for me."

Obediently, Anjing bent his head. Vegetables were not his favourite, but he did as Sang Kancil ordered, wanting the farmer to see what a good and faithful servant he was. Finally, when the vegetables were all gone, he looked up.

But Sang Kancil was also all gone.

See Notes on Pages 335-336

The Stork and the Mousedeer

THE MOUSEDEER AND the stork were friends.

Once the two friends found a large crust of cooked rice.

They were enjoying nibbling off bits of rice off when Sang Kancil decided that he wanted the entire rice crust to himself.

"You know Kawan Upeh," said Kawan Kancil, shivering with excitement, "it might be safer to finish this this rice on the other side of the river just in case the humans who left this crust behind come back."

"You are wise, Kawan Kancil," said the stork, nodding. "Let us do as you say."

And so, the two friends set off to cross the river, using the rice crust as their boat.

At first the journey went well until the mousedeer decided that he would continue nibbling. Oh, that rice crust was so delicious!

"Stop, stop," said the stork in a panic. "You must stop, or you will end up devouring the boat and we will drown."

"Nonsense, it is such a large crust. That will never happen."

And so, he continued to nibble.

"Stop," said the stork getting angry.

"But I am hungry."

Soon water began to lap at the edges of the rice crust.

"Did I not warn you about the consequences of your action?" said the stork before it flew away.

"Nonsense," said Sang Kancil but soon he had time to regret his greed.

"Oh, it is sinking. And I along with it."

And indeed, the rice crust filled with water and disintegrated leaving the greedy mousedeer to the watery elements.

Thankfully, mousedeer can swim, and the river was not deep.

See Notes on Page 336

Pilandok and the Falling Sky

Bombola, which means 'hairy' in the Philippines, is another trickster and the mortal enemy of Pilandok. The two are continually tricking each other.

The story goes on to say that both characters were poor, and that the rivalry started when Bombola wrapped a dirty old mat up and pretended that it was a thing of value, while Pilandok wrapped three cooking stones.

The two swapped parcels and were bitterly disappointed with the results.

ONE SUNNY DAY, Bombola was on the lookout for opportunity. Bombola is always on the lookout for opportunity just like another character we know and love.

Instead, to his surprise he found Pilandok tied to a tree.

"What are you doing, Pilandok?" said Bombola with a sneer. "Has someone finally managed to get the better of you? Hahaha!"

"You would not say that if you knew what was really happening," said Pilandok calmly.

Bombola rubbed his hands. "Just admit that you have lost."

"Do you want me to tell you the real reason why I am tied up? Or do you prefer to make bad jokes? Go ahead and decide. Time is running out."

Bombola snapped his mouth shut. *Time is running out…* "What do you mean?"

Pilandok cocked one eye. "You have obviously not heard the news."

"News, what news?"

"The sky is falling."

"The sky? Why? Impossible," said Bombola, but he stared nervously at the bright blue above.

"I knew you would say that." Pilandok shook his head sadly.

Just at that moment, the wind picked up, and the sky had been solid blue now had clouds clogging a corner.

It just seemed too coincidental. Did Pilandok know something that he didn't?

"Well, if the sky was really falling, wouldn't you be running around looking for a place to hide?" said Bombola, his voice to his annoyance a touch higher.

"Precisely." Pilandok smiled smugly. "I have tied myself up, to avoid running around in a panic."

Bombola studied the tree.

It is tall and mighty, and the shade it provides is deep and dark. It does look safe underneath.

He looked up.

Just at that moment, the sky darkened. The clouds clotting one corner now crowded in masses overhead, blotting out the sun. The air chilled.

Bombola's face tightened. He inhaled deeply and smelled rain.

Was it true what the mousedeer said?

"But it only looks like a storm." The last thing Bombola wanted to do was to trust Pilandok.

"That is the beginning."

Bombola waited for more, but Pilandok simply closed his eyes. Almost as if he had dropped off to sleep. He looked so content and calm, unlike Bombola whose heart was beating nervously.

The clouds darkened.

"Wait, what else is to happen?" Bombola rasped. He could not hide the streak of terror in his voice.

"I have told you," said Pilandok patiently, eyes still closed. "The sky is about to fall. This is why I have tied myself to this tree."

That trunk looks so thick and strong…

"Oh Pilandok," said Bombola. "I know we have never been the best of friends, but surely, as one living creature to another, surely you can help me in this time of need?"

Pilandok opened one eye. "Why should I?"

"Why not?"

"Would you do the same for me?"

"Nev- I mean, of course I would," said Bombola so staunchly that even he believed his own words. Then he willed Pilandok to agree.

For the storm was almost overhead.

The wind had picked up and was blowing twigs, leaves, dirt, and everything that was not tied down up into the wild sky. Bombola's face was plastered with dirt.

A large branch came bouncing wildly in his direction and he had to duck. "Pilandok, please! Help me!"

Pilandok opened both eyes. "What? What did you say?" Then he yawned.

Bombola cursed. By now the trees all around them were bending from the violence of the wind. The only tree standing staunchly upright was the tree that Pilandok was tied to. "Please. Help." He raised his voice. "Me."

"What? I didn't catch that! The wind is too noisy," said Pilandok.

Bombola punched the air. "Please help me."

Pilandok feigned surprise. "You want me. Me? To help you?"

Bombola gritted his teeth. "Yes…"

"Hmmm…" Pilandok appeared to be thinking. "Well, that would mean that I would have to untie myself. And that would mean that I would be in danger. And that would mean that-"

"Yes, yes, yes!" said Bombola, distraught.

"Well, why didn't you say so?"

Bombola hissed in anger. But before his eyes, Pilandok swiftly untied himself.

"Wait here."

Where was Bombola planning to go? If he had any thoughts of lashing himself to the very same tree, he had barely begun to look around for rope when Pilandok returned. The mousedeer brought lashings of rotan with him.

"Stand with your back to the tree." Pilandok waved one paw impatiently.

Bombola complied without a word of complaint.

Pilandok did what he had promised. Within minutes, Bombola was strapped to the same tree that Pilandok had been tied to.

"Thank you so much, Pilandok," said Bombola, relief on his face. "I will never forget this."

"Before you thank me, just for safety's sake, check: can you wriggle?"

"Why do you ask such a thing?"

"I just want to make sure that when the storm increases you will stay safe and secure, bound to this tree."

That made complete sense. So Bombola wriggled. "Just a little more, please. Just in case the wind strengthens even further. Please hurry, before the sky falls."

"Very well," said Pilandok and tied Bombola even more tightly. "There. How about now?"

"Just a teeny bit more," said Bombola. "Just to be safe when the sky falls."

"Hurry up! I want to be safe, too," said Pilandok then he looked around. "Oh dear."

"What?"

"I think I have used up all the rotan."

"Oh, what a shame," said Bombola. *I am safe and he is not.*

"I might be able to find some more."

"Oh. I mean, oh good."

"Wait here, while I go and look."

"Of course," said Bombola pleasantly.

Now I know why Pilandok was so happy strapped to this tree. Yes, yes, I certainly feel happy and secure. Why I could even go to sleep.

"Take your time. I am going nowhere." Bombola laughed.

Pilandok did not laugh. Instead, he disappeared into the bushes.

Bombola closed his eyes. Tried to relax as the storm lashed its fury.

He waited, his eyes clammed shut. Whether Pilandok returned or not, he did not know.

Lighting streaked across the sky. Thunder cracked! Again, and again. Rain lashed Bombola, tied to the tree. Unable to move. Unable to even wipe his face. Wind viciously whipped his head like a coconut one way then the other. Rain poured unceasingly in rivulets down his cheeks.

The storm took a long time to wreak its havoc, but Bombola was safe under the tree. Finally, after several hours had passed, the wind died and the rain lessened, the storm eventually coming to an end.

Soon the sun was out again and Bombola felt its pleasant warmth on his face. Soaked and drenched completely, he shivered a little. But he was glad.

I am alive.

He blinked open his eyes and looked around.

Utter destruction met his gaze.

The smell of raw earth.

Soaked greenery.

"Pilandok!" Bombola croaked. But no one was strapped to the tree except him.

He wondered if Pilandok had managed to make it make to the tree at all.

But the sky did not fall. Hooray! I am alive and the sky did not fall.

Bombola made to push away from the tree only-

Only to his horror he was stuck, like a bug on a board.

He was strapped to the tree and unable to escape.

"Pilandok! Pilandok?"

Slowly, Bombola realised that he had been tricked. His eyes watered.

The sky was never going to fall.

Hours passed as Bombola yelled. He screamed and shouted and ranted. He called Pilandok every dirty name he can think of. But Pilandok was long gone.

Days passed.

"Please," he begged before he died. "Pilandok. Someone. Anyone. Save me."

But no one came.

And the sky never fell.

Pilandok in the Kingdom of the Maranaw Sea or Si Pilandok sa Kharian ng Dagat Maranaw

DATU USMAN WAS an evil ruler.

And like all evil rulers, he plotted to rid his kingdom of any threat. Little wonder that top of his list was Pilandok.

Sadly, it didn't take long for Datu Usman's men to capture Pilandok, but so powerful was Pilandok's reputation that instead of simply doing away with him immediately, the men were ordered to let the waters of the Maranaw Sea do the job.

No one wanted Pilandok's blood on their hands. The blood of an innocent, no way.

The men imprisoned Pilandok in a cage and set off at once to the shore.

> The Maranaw Sea is most likely Lake Lanow, one of the fifteen ancient lakes in the world. The lake encompasses 340 square kilometres and is so wide that the other side is barely visible. Waves continuously caress its surface, and its waters contain many fish.

When the men reach the Maranaw Sea, they decide to stop for a rest. It was a hot day and capturing prisoners was hot work. They sat the cage containing Pilandok on the warm sand while they lay under a coconut tree.

The sun beats down, the wind blows, and soon the men are lulled by the sound of gentle waves into a slumber.

As soon as the men are asleep though, Pilandok executes his escape plan. Now he knows that if he simply called for help, that no one would come. So, he did the opposite. He called out instead, "I don't want to marry the princess."

A merchant who was passing by heard and immediately went to investigate.

Now merchants are always on the lookout for opportunity. This is what makes them merchants in the first place. They buy cheap in one spot then travel to another spot where there is demand and sell their goods. This is how they make their profit. They love opportunity.

The curious merchant came up to Pilandok. "What is going on?"

"What is going on? Why, simply this. I do not wish to marry the princess! That is what is going on," said Pilandok sounding most indignant.

"But is it not a good thing to marry a princess," said the puzzled merchant. "Why wouldn't anyone want to marry a princess? Is it Datu Usman's daughter? You can tell me, you know."

"Well, for a start I am a mousedeer," said Pilandok.

"That is true," said the merchant looking Pilandok up and down. "I could not help but notice that."

"And two, I am already married. With Dame Pilandok and two newborns."

"Ah, that is a pity," said the merchant, commiserating. "I wonder why then that you were even chosen for such an honour."

"Is it not obvious?" said Pilandok. "I am Pilandok."

"Ah, yes," said the merchant. "I thought I recognised you."

"Well now you know," said Pilandok. "And you have come at the most opportune time. For I have an idea that will benefit both of us."

The merchant rubbed his hands. All merchants love to hear of opportunities that benefit them. Never mind anyone else.

"What is it? You know you can trust me."

"Firstly, are you married?"

The merchant's eyes lit. He could see where this was going. "Married? Why of course not!" he lied.

"Why then, you can take my place."

"But I am not a mousedeer," said the merchant, frowning. "Won't anyone notice if we swap?"

"Pilandok cocked his head as if thinking hard. "You have a point."

The merchant waited patiently. He didn't have to wait long.

"I know!"

The merchant looked up eagerly. "What? Tell me quickly!"

"Why don't we swap places? No one will notice. Especially not if we swap clothes. Of course, you will need to take my place in the cage."

The merchant didn't need much persuading. "Of course!" He unlocked the cage and clambered inside as soon as Pilandok stepped out.

The merchant tore his clothes off and put on Pilandok's while Pilandok donned the merchant's apparel.

"One last thing, you must shout, 'I agree to marry the princess,' but do so only after I am long gone, or else the men will see me and know what we have done."

"Of course," said the merchant gratefully. He waited until Pilandok was no longer in sight before he shouted in his loudest voice, "I agree to marry the princess!"

The sleeping men woke up and discovered what had happened. Of course, the disappointed merchant doesn't get to marry the princess, any princess, because there was no princess in the first place. Let alone Datu Usman's daughter.

In fact, the greedy merchant ended up getting thrown into the Maranaw Sea.

Datu Usman's men said nothing of what had happened when they returned, only that they threw the cage and its contents into the sea as ordered. So, Datu Usman thought that he had rid himself of a pest. He was therefore extremely surprised when he came across Pilandok alive and well and still wandering around freely.

"Did you not get tossed into the Maranaw Sea?"

"Why yes, I did," said Pilandok nonchalantly. As if it was an everyday occurrence with him to escape with his life, which technically it was.

"Why then are you not drowned?"

"Drowned? Why when your men tossed me into the ocean, the cage sank to the bottom. And there I found a long-lost cousin of mine. Did you know that I have a cousin who is also the ruler of the underwater kingdom of the Maranaw Sea?"

Datu Usman was shocked. "Your cousin a ruler?"

"Why yes, why do you act so surprised? In fact, he was so glad to see me that he feasted me for days and before I left, he rewarded me with many treasures."

"Where are they then, these so-called treasures?" said Datu, suspicious.

"Why, you know me. I distributed all the gold and pearls to the poor."

Datu Usman frowned. If that was true, then his position as a ruler was a precarious one. He imagined his people revolting against him and his heavy taxes. He had to do something.

Datu Usman smiled benevolently as he patted Pilandok on the head. "There, there, what a lovely story!"

"Ah, but it doesn't end there. You see my cousin would like you to visit him. As a ruler himself, no doubt he has many stories he would like to share."

"A state visit," said Datu Usman, thinking only of the treasures to be shared. "Why that sounds wonderful! A state visit is in order then."

Pilandok took Datu Usman to the shores of the Maranaw Sea.

"Where is the kingdom?" said Datu Usman, shading his eyes, seeing nothing but bright sunlight glittering like diamonds sprinkled on the surface of the deep blue waters.

"Underneath the surface, of course," said Pilandok nodding at the waves. "I did say it was an *underwater* kingdom."

"But- but how am I to get there?"

"Why, the same way that I did. In a cage."

Datu Usman looked dubiously at the deep depths.

"Here, let me show you. Now that I have been down before, I know what to do." Pilandok dived into the water. Before long, he popped back up to the surface. He was carrying something large and round.

When Pilandok reached the shore, everyone saw what he had – a lustrous pearl the size of a man's fist.

The pearl glistened in the yellow sunlight, flashing as Pilandok rolled it on the sand.

Datu Usman swallowed hard. He needed no more persuasion; he clambered into the cage and ordered his men to lower the cage into the water. "But haul me up as soon as I yank on the rope."

The men nod.

The cage is lowered.

Down and down, it goes, as the men let out the rope.

Down, down, down. Finally, the rope goes slack.

The cage has reached the bottom of the sea.

Everyone watched and waited.

Then there was a tug.

The men were about to haul the cage up, when Pilandok stopped them.

"Wait, that is just my cousin opening the door. You must give him time to greet Datu Usman."

"But the yank."

Pilandok shrugged. "Well, if you really want to pull the cage up, you may. I just don't want to be on the receiving end of Datu Usman's anger when he says that my cousin was about to present him with a giant pearl only you pulled the cage up too soon."

The men looked at each other. How well they all knew Datu Usman's temper.

"Just wait a moment longer."

The men wait a moment longer, then two, then three.

But the tugs on the rope became more and more frantic.

Finally, the men dared wait no longer.

They pulled the cage up as fast as they could.

Up, up, and up.

Then all at once, the cage landed, tumbling over and over on the shore. The men rushed to open the door and Datu Usman fell out, half-drowned.

His face was green, and his belly swollen from all the water he had swallowed.

The men looked around in anger for Pilandok, but as usual Pilandok was long gone.

Along with the pearl.

See Notes on Page 336

The Mousedeer's Shipwreck

I T IS SAID that one day Sang Kancil decided to sail to Java. The Mousedeer loved having adventures, exploring, and learning new things. So, he invited his *kawan baik* (good friend), the Stump-tailed Heron.

Kawan Mousedeer held the tiller while Kawan Heron made sail. With the sail spread wide the boat got underway. As the monsoon blew, the boat skipped lightly across the waves as the two friends headed to the island of Java.

With the luxurious breeze blowing in Sang Kancil's face, his lids grew heavy. Soon his head nodded, and the tiller fell out of his hands. And the small boat fell out of the wind.

Kawan Heron noticed the change in rhythm at once and grew alarmed. "Why does the boat slacken so? It has fallen off the wind. Why have you not the helm, Kawan Kancil?"

"I was only resting my eyes," said Sang Kancil.

"Get us back on track at once."

And so Sang Kancil brought the boat up to the wind once more.

However, soon the mousedeer dropped off again.

Kawan Heron huffed. "If that is to be the way of things, then I am done with you. I shall peck a hole in the bottom of our boat, and you can go down with it."

At those words Sang Kancil's eyes snapped open. "Oh please, don't do that. I promise I shall stay awake this time. And besides, I am a poor swimmer."

So, Kawan Heron stayed his hand.

But when Sang Kancil drifted off for the third time, Kawan Heron made good on his promise.

"Chelaka, Kawan Kancil!" In a rage, Kawan Heron pecked a hole in the bottom of the boat. Water flowed in as Kawan Heron flew away.

Sang Kancil woke in a fright when he felt his toes wet.

"Kawan Heron has done what he has said he would do. And now it is up to me to save myself." And he jumped into the sea and began kicking with his feet.

The truth is that mousedeer can swim. A little.

They often enter the water to escape their enemies. Like dogs, they move their legs as if walking. They can even hold their breath for four minutes. They have mastered the art of walking on the riverbed. But this was the sea, and the seabed was fathoms deep. The mousedeer's limbs being delicate and fragile, they tire easily. And so, after several minutes Sang Kancil felt himself going down.

At that very moment a young shark popped up. It had just left the shallow lagoons and mangroves that was its nursery, and like Sang Kancil, was out for adventure.

"Excellent! I shall have you as my meal, thank you," said the shark, his flat obsidian eyes glittering. He was very young.

"Me? With so little meat, that would be most unsporting," said Sang Kancil. "Why not instead, carry me ashore? Then I can teach you some magic that will save you from ever needing to hunt."

"You can? Excellent," said the shark. It was so young.

The gullible shark carried Sang Kancil on its back.

"Wait here," said the crafty mousedeer when he was safe on shore. "I shall go and get the simples (medicinal herbs)."

The shark waited impatiently. It was young. And eager to learn. Trusting.

Sang Kancil went some way inland before he could find some rattan. Securing a decent length, he returned to the shore. "Here are the simples I spoke of."

Then he proceeded to bind the shark's tail with the rattan.

Thinking this was part of the magic, the young shark stayed still but when it found its tail bound fast, he panicked. "Why have you tied rattan to my tail?"

Sang Kancil nodded his head sagely. "Just stay still for a while longer, and once I am done, I shall give you the rest of the simples that I promised."

But instead, when the shark's tail was bound fast, Sang Kancil proceeded to haul the shark up the beach.

Out of water, and unable to escape, the poor shark soon found itself butcher's meat.

Sang Kancil was about to feast on the shark when a young tiger came up.

"Here is a meal delivered without having to do a thing," said the tiger. It was also young.

"Oh, there is no meat to me, but look, here is the fresh carcass of a shark. We could share that if you like?" said the wily Sang Kancil.

Delighted that he would soon have a meal, without having had to do a thing for it, the tiger agreed.

"Happy to share what I have with you, but first can you wash the meat?"

"By all means." And the tiger went off to do as it was asked.

"Now we need water for the *priok* (pot)."

The tiger went off for the second time to fetch the water.

"Now we need to make a fire."

So far, every instruction from Sang Kancil had helped to contribute towards the meal, and so without any lingering suspicion, the young tiger congratulated itself that it would soon be feasting. It was so young.

The tiger set about making a fire. And when he was done, Sang Kancil settled the pot atop the flames and placed the meat inside.

Tiger lifted his head; half closed his eyes and inhaled the delightful aroma.

Stewed fish. Fresh.

"Almost done," said the crafty mousedeer. "Only now we need water to wash down the meal."

With a sigh, the obedient tiger went off.

As soon as the tiger was out of sight, however, Sang Kancil grabbed the shark meat and climbed to the top of a She-oak Tree. There he proceeded to feast until there was nothing left but bones. Then he took off.

And so, when the tiger returned it found the campsite empty.

"You have tricked me Sang Kancil," snorted the furious tiger, but there was nothing that it could do.

And from that day on, the tiger vowed enmity with Sang Kancil.

See Notes on Page 336

Sang Kancil and the Villagers

A TIGER WAS terrorising a village. The panicked villagers approached the mousedeer.

"Lie in a row with your heads facing the river," instructed Sang Kancil.

The villagers were baffled at his words, but they had alternative. Each night, one of them had gone missing. With their best warriors unable to capture the killer, and their homes no deterrent to the nocturnal predator, they decided to do exactly as the mousedeer commanded.

The villagers lay in a line with their heads facing the river. It wasn't comfortable as the ground sloped thus their heads were lower than their bodies, but they obeyed.

Sang Kancil placed himself opposite.

Then they all waited. But not for long.

In the night, the wind lifted the musky scent of fur.

Harimau(Tiger).

Moments later, at the edge of the jungle Tiger appeared, a beautiful and powerful figure in the moonlight.

Everyone held their breaths.

So did *Harimau* (Tiger). The beast had noticed the strange formation.

In all its years, Tiger had never come across humans forming a row on the ground. Curiously, their heads were all facing the river.

It was a mystery to the animal, going against everything that it understood.

When night came, most villagers were indoors or if they were out in the jungle, seated safely around a fire. But here there was no fire, no movement, no voices.

Just a strange silent row of villagers, obviously unafraid of being tiger food, simply lying in a row on the ground.

A tiger's strongest sense is its hearing.

Curiosity piqued; the tiger rotated its ears as it tried to make sense of the mystery.

But except for the soft breathing of the villagers, Harimau could detect nothing that could offer an explanation to this strange formation.

It padded up to the first house.

A tiger's second most powerful sense is its eyesight, about six times better than a human's but without detail, and which is particularly needed at night.

But the darkness held no answer either.

Tigers do, however, have a sixth sense.

Sang Kancil squinted one eye open and saw the great predator curl its upper lip.

Known as the *flehmen* (German for lip curl) response, this action allows scent to reach the roof of the tiger's mouth, where the tiger's Jacobsen (vomeronasal) organ is located, important for mating, and the marking of territory. In essence it allows the tiger to investigate different scents: to determine midway via smell and taste what is going on.

But in this instance, that vital organ was unable to provide an answer.

Harimau hesitated. So far, there seemed no sign of danger.

No one moved as the great cat came closer.

By now, the great beast was at the start of the line. It frowned, unable to determine the reason for this strange occurrence.

Thinking it might solve this nighttime riddle if it inhaled at a closer range, Harimau bent his great big head.

A cat senses the world through its whiskers, like fingertips.

But in this instance, the murderer's whiskers were of no help. For as soon as the tiger bent, its long whiskers entered the first villager's nostrils. Then the second villager's nostrils. And so forth…

The villagers could not help themselves. They sneezed. And sneezed. And sneezed.

"Gro-pft!" yelped the startled tiger.

One after the other, the villagers sat up and continued to sneeze; like a row of zombies coming alive.

Ah choo!

Ah Choo!

AH CHOO!

Terrifying.

The horrified tiger jumped.

Gave one panicked squeal.

Then it turned tail and fled, running straight into the river.

Of course, the crocodiles were waiting. They finished the tiger.

Quickly.

So, the villagers understood why their heads had to face the river.

Clever Sang Kancil.

Mousedeer and the Selfish Woodpecker

THERE WAS ONCE a woodpecker who was jealous of the mousedeer.

Now there are many species of woodpeckers in India and in Southeast Asia, the largest being the Great Slaty Woodpecker. Bald-headed and cloaked in grey, this bird measures up to 51 cm.

Woodpeckers are called woodpeckers because they peck. And they peck because they need to find food by uncovering insects. Pecking is also a form of excavating an area for nesting and marking territory.

But this woodpecker was especially noisy.

Ketok! Ketok! Ketok!

It is because the other animals do not like me, thought the Selfish Woodpecker. *So, I will make noise.*

But the other animals thought, it is because he makes noise that we do not like him.

Whatever the truth, the woodpecker decided to make a nuisance of itself.

Whenever Kera the monkey tried to sleep, Woodpecker would find him.

"*Alamat!* (Oh god!)" said Kera with a start as he was rudely awakened from his dreams. "*Terperanjat!* (What a shock!)"

Whenever *Tupai* (Squirrel) had a nice juicy grasshopper, along would come Woodpecker.

"*Adoi! Bising sekali*! (Oh dear! So very noisy!)" said Tupai, dropping the grasshopper in fright.

"*Telinga saya!* (My ears!)" Sang Gajah stamped his feet in annoyance as his ears filled with sound and pain.

The Selfish Woodpecker's pecking annoyed all the animals so much that they came to Mousedeer for help.

"*Keamanan Tuan Hutan, boleh tolong?* (Sir Peace of the Jungle, can you help?)"

Mousedeer decided that he would speak with the Selfish Woodpecker.

"Dear *Kawan Burung*, Friend Bird, the animals would like a favour," said Mousedeer most politely.

"What is it?" asked Woodpecker.

"Would you mind pecking a little more quietly?"

"What!" said Woodpecker, greatly annoyed. "Do I ask you to trick the crocodiles more quietly? Do I ask Sang Gajah to trample through the jungle more quietly? Or for Kera to laugh more quietly? Nonsense! It is my right to make as much noise as I want."

Mousedeer went away. He had a plan. He always does.

Kawan Burung needs to be taught a lesson.

Mousedeer decided that it would hold a picnic for the animals under a grandmother tree.

Now if you are wondering what a grandmother tree is, remember your own grandmother. Remember how much love and kindness your grandmother radiated. How she made you feel special. And how much you adored spending time with her. Kisses. Hugs. Love.

A grandmother tree is similar, only instead of a human being, it is a tree. So, a grandmother tree is a tree that feeds and nourishes and nurtures you and your spirit. These are generally more mature trees. They make you feel welcome just by being in their presence. They shade you from the world.

Mak Kera liked picnics. "But how can we possibly enjoy ourselves? That horrible woodpecker will turn up."

"Trust me," said Mousedeer. "And just do as I say."

Well, many of the animals came. They all liked picnics. And they liked the *buah-buahan manis* (sweet berries) on the grandmother tree. *Sedap!* (Delicious!)

They ate and ate of the sweet berries.

But like an uninvited guest, which he was, Woodpecker turned up, too.

Even though the animals begged the woodpecker to allow them to have their picnic in peace, he refused to leave. In fact, he made a nuisance of himself.

The animals didn't like the raucous pecking. They didn't like bits of bark falling into their food. And they certainly did not like their unwanted guest.

When they asked the woodpecker to go somewhere else and he didn't, the animals instead went somewhere else. To a second grandmother tree.

The woodpecker followed.

Again, he made a nuisance of himself.

Again, the animals asked him to remove himself and again he refused.

So again, the animals moved their picnic.

They found a third grandmother tree. As the other two, this one groaned with delicious, sweet berries.

How the berries gleamed, red and juicy and inviting!

The animals settled down once more, and once more the woodpecker followed.

Again, he made a nuisance of himself.

But this time, the animals did not taste of the sweet berries. And this time, the animals did not ask the woodpecker to remove himself.

"Well, I am not going," said Woodpecker.

"We are not asking you to go," said Mousedeer. "In fact, we like your noise."

"You're not? And you do?" said the woodpecker, shocked.

"Yes, we do."

"So, I can stay at this picnic?" The woodpecker cocked his head, suspicious.

"Yes."

"And peck away for as long and as loud as I want?"

Mousedeer nodded.

Too quickly. Woodpecker narrowed his eyes at Mousedeer.

"Peck all you want. Scatter bark. Stay at this picnic. All we ask is that you do not touch these berries hanging down."

"Why not?"

"Because I told you so."

"Well, I will do as I want." And with that, Woodpecker quickly dove straight for the bright red patch of berries. He pecked and he pecked, and he pecked.

Quickly, berries started dropping.

Bark and leaves went everywhere then-

From the pile of berries rose a horrible sound.

A sound so familiar to many of the animals. But before anyone could do a thing, from out the middle of the pile of berries shot a mass of bees.

They hovered in the air searching for the culprit.

"Stay still," Mousedeer warned the other animals.

And they sat and stared, unmoving.

The woodpecker continued to peck.

The bees dived. They had found the invader. Noise had led them to him. The bees stung the Selfish Woodpecker.

"Ow! They are attacking! Stinging me!" screamed the Selfish Woodpecker.

The bees stung him mercilessly for he had attacked their nest, well hidden under the pile of sweet berries.

That, of course, had been Kancil's plan.

But they did not attack the other animals.

And that of course had been Kancil's plan, too.

The Heart of the Earth

*S**UNGEI SEBIRIS* (THE RIVER SEBERIS) had dried up.

The earth was parched, and the animals were desperate for water.

The tortoise crawled along the banks of the riverbed, searching frantically for moisture, when it fell into a deep hole.

"*Tolong!* (Help!)" he screamed. And for a long time, no one heard.

But then a barking deer came by. "What are you doing down there?"

The tortoise thought quickly. If he said that he was trapped, he doubted that anyone would help him. So, instead he said, "Do you not know? I am eating the heart of the earth."

"The heart of the earth? Whatever for?"

"Why the heart provides moisture. Look!" And the tortoise buried his snout into the damp earth.

Memories of cold and wetness spiralled through his head at the first delicate touch of dampness.

"Eh, is that water I smell down there? Look out!" And before the tortoise could say stop, the barking deer jumped into the hole.

"Water! Water!" screamed the happy deer.

The other animals hearing the cries, all decided that they should share the water. And so, one after the other, the animals leapt into the hole.

Sang Rusa jumped in.

Sang Beruang jumped in.

Sang Kancil jumped in.

Sang Arnab jumped in.

Sang Harimau jumped in.

Even Sang Babi jumped in.

"But where is the heart of the earth?" shouted the animals.

"Ask the tortoise," said the barking deer. "He was the first to find it."

The tortoise thought quickly. "No wonder none of you can find the heart of the earth, why there is no room to look around. Don't you find it rather cramped down here?"

The animals agreed.

"This is what we must do. Sang Babi, you stand here. Sang Harimau you stand on top of Sang Babi." And so the tortoise got the other animals to form a pyramid.

"Let me see if this is tall enough," said the tortoise and he clambered over the other animals to reach the top.

"Hey what about us?"

"It is about to storm. You will be safer where you are," said the cheeky tortoise before crawling away.

And it was true. The sky grew darker and soon it began to rain.

It rained and rained.

The mighty Sungei Sebiris filled with water again and began to flow.

And what about the animals in the hole?

Well, I would like to think that they all were wise enough to swim away and so saved their lives, particularly a certain chevrotain.

See Notes on Page 336

Cruel King Cobra

CRUEL KING COBRA stole the kingfisher's eggs one day.

Poor *Mak Burung Rajawali* (Mother Kingfisher) sat on a branch and wept.

Along came the Mousedeer. "*Mengapa awak nangis*? (Why are you crying?)"

"*Raja Ular Tedung* (King Cobra) stole my eggs."

"Where did he take them?"

"There to that hollow log. I shall never see my eggs again!" And *Mak Burung Rajawali* wept, heartbroken.

Now cobras are common in Asia. In fact, the King Cobra, known as the largest venomous snake in the world, makes its home in Singapore. Extremely aggressive, they can stand as tall as six feet from the ground. They make a hissing sound when attacked and are of various colours. It loves to eat other snakes, rodents, lizards, and of course, eggs.

Cruel King Cobra was asleep when the Mousedeer crept up to the hollow log.

"There," whispered Mak Kingfisher.

"Wait here," said the Mousedeer. "I have an idea."

The Mousedeer trotted through the rainforest until he reached a *kampong* (village). In the village, the women were preparing the evening meal. Children were complaining they were hungry while the men sat around listening to a Penglipur Lara.

Good, thought the Mousedeer. He snuck up to one of the houses on the outskirts of the village and peered inside before entering.

In the shadows, he spotted what he was looking for. In a plaited reed basket, he found beads and a brooch. He selected the most sparkling adornment and taking it in his mouth he ran out, making sure to race across the open courtyard.

Of course, the woman of the house, the woman who owned the jewellery saw him.

"*Penchuri!* (Thief!)" she screamed.

At once, everyone turned to see what was happening.

"He has my brooch!" wept the distraught woman.

The chase began with the mousedeer leading the men further and further into the jungle.

Mousedeer was leading the men straight to Cruel King Cobra.

The snake was still asleep when something smacked him in the face.

"There!"

Cruel King Cobra opened his eyes to see something cut him in the eye. It was the sharp end of brooch pin. But he had no time to understand what was happening. For within seconds, he was surrounded by angry, shouting men.

"What? Why?" he stammered.

But there was no time to do anything but to run. Well, slither.

And in a swift movement, another chase was on. But this time, the aim of the men, after they reclaimed the stolen brooch, was to make an end of the dangerous snake. No one wanted a poisonous reptile so close to the village.

So, after the humans left, Mak Kingfisher retrieved her eggs and she and her children sang their praises of the clever Mousedeer forever and ever.

The Young, Black Elephant and the Tide

I T IS SAID that Kancil went down to the sea one day.

The tide was high when he arrived, and the black rocks half covered by the waves. He scrambled onto one outcrop plastered with dark green seaweed. Then he craned his neck forward and inhaled.

Wind dashed salt crystals into the air. Frothy waves lapped at the rocks, stretching, and then streaming away. Cool sea air pressed against him, pushing back his ears. Exhilarating!

Nearby, a young black elephant leaned lazily on a rock.

"*Apa Khabar?*" said Sang Kancil, only the young elephant barely gave him a glance.

"Have you had a bath?" said Kancil after waiting a while.

The young black elephant yawned rudely. "Yes. The sea is in the right place today. Sometimes it is far away, and then it is too much bother to walk all the way down."

Bother? Kancil smiled. Oh, if you had only bothered to speak with the crabs or Kua, the many-eyed pheasant, they would have gladly informed you that the reason why this is so, is because of a little thing called the tide.

Tide… hmmm. Maybe he could play a trick.

He turned to the rude elephant. "You do know why that is so, do you not?"

"Oh, there is a reason, is there? Tell me at once," said the young black elephant, deigning finally to cast an eye on the mousedeer.

"Raja Suleiman, of course!"

"Raja Suleiman?"

As the young black elephant shaded his tiny eyes with his truck as he peered around, Kancil recalled the story of how the elephant had small eyes. "Raja Suleiman drinks the sea away to let the crabs and turtles play."

"Is that so?" said the young, black elephant aghast. "But that would make him thirsty, would it not?"

"*Betul!* (Correct.) That is why he is offering a reward for any creature who can take on that task on his behalf."

Beady eyes blinked. "Reward? What kind of reward?"

"Why? It would depend on the creature who succeeded of course! If it was you, it might be a plantation full of *pisang* (bananas). Or *nangka* (jackfruit)."

"And if it was *you*, a single nangka! Haha!" The young black elephant laughed unkindly.

Kancil's cheeks heated. "Ah, would you like to know what my reward would be?"

"No, because it is I who will win the reward. When should I start?"

"Why not now? With the sea right where it is. That way you need not walk all the way down."

"What a good idea," said the young, black elephant, eager to win himself a whole plantation of bananas. He dipped the end of his trunk into the waves and began to drink. "Oh, oh! It tastes salty!"

"You can always drink river water later to wash away the taste."

The young black elephant frowned as he considered.

"Well, if you do not wish the rewar-"

"Nonsense! The reward is mine."

"Very well," said Sang Kancil, and trotted off to a cove nearby.

Celup-Celap. Celup-Celap.

Water splashed onto his legs and body. Deliciously fresh and cool!

For hours, Kancil watched the crabs and other marine creatures play, ducking in and out of the swishing water as the tide receded.

Finally, when the tide was gone, the young black elephant returned. The young black elephant was stunned to see that the cove was empty of water.

"Oh, oh, you have done as you have said," said the young black elephant, looking and feeling foolish.

"Yes," said Sang Kancil, "and now I am off to collect my reward."

The young, black elephant said nothing but stared and stared at the soft white sand and at the crabs frolicking.

Then he went off in search of the river, still none the wiser.

See Notes on Page 337

Sang Kancil and the King of the Jungle

*P**ADA ZAMAN DAHULU* (Once upon a time), there lived deep in the jungles of Malaysia, a mousedeer named *Sang Kancil* (Revered Mousedeer).

For many weeks, the chevrotain had been exploring an unfamiliar part of the jungle, and as much as he had enjoyed himself was delighted to be back home and to race again soon through his old grass tunnels.

Early morning mist blurred the air as trees and bushes emerged from the black of night.

Twigs cracked underfoot as his hooves clipped smartly on wet leaves while the surrounding light, blue and tingling, chilled his cheeks and chest.

How lovely to be alive! To glide through the rainforest!

Dawn was the time when the nocturnal predators returned to their lairs.

Excited to see his friends and to learn the latest news and gossip, Sang Kancil was trotting briskly when he heard crying.

Kancil wasted no time investigating. To his shock, he found his dear friend *Sang Kerbau* (Revered Water Buffalo) lying in a pool of his own blood.

This was not the welcome home Sang Kancil had been hoping for. "Sang Kerbau, I am coming! Hang on!"

Alone in a field of devastation, the buffalo blinked open bleary eyes. "Oh, Sang Kancil, if only you had been here!" he moaned, but before he could say another word, a shudder went through his massive frame, and his head rolled to the side.

The mighty beast was dead.

"What has happened? Who has done this to you?" wept Sang Kancil, bereft.

All around were the scenes of carnage. Bushes torn into pieces. Grass trampled. Raw clay mottled red with blood.

From the many wounds on its carcass, it was obvious that Sang Kerbau had been attacked.

Kancil's nostrils crinkled at the heavy scent of cat mixed with iron on the still air.

What did Sang Kerbau mean when he said, "If only I had been here"?

Grieving, Sang Kancil buried his friend in the orange clay where he lay. Then with a heavy heart, he continued his journey, unable to put the tragedy of what had occurred out of his mind.

Before long, Sang Kancil encountered two more friends: *Sang Arnab* (Revered Rabbit) and *Sang Rusa* (Revered Deer).

To Sang Kancil's surprise, he found Sang Rusa comforting Sang Arnab, the latter weeping bitter tears.

It took a while for the two animals to be able to relate the problem, so struck with grief were they.

But Sang Kancil persisted. Gently, he prodded and soothed until the two animals were ready to speak.

He was stunned by what they revealed.

Apparently, while Sang Kancil had been away exploring the limestone caves, *Sang Rimau* (Revered Tiger) had declared himself *Rajah* (King) of the Jungle.

Sang Rimau is greedy and selfish, thought Sang Kancil. This could only end in disaster, and he was right.

The false king's first command was to have a meeting, where he had ordered all the animals to provide him with a meal. The problem was that the meal was to consist of one of them. And that this was to occur at regular intervals.

"But this means that each of you, in turn, must sacrifice your lives to him," Sang Kancil choked out, his eyes wide with disbelief at the audacity of such a command.

Sang Arnab managed a tiny nod.

"The animals were not going to take this without fighting," said Sang Rusa.

"So, there was a battle," said Sang Kancil, shaking his head. He could see where this was all leading. "But the outcome was that Sang Rimau easily defeated you."

Sang Arnab wept anew.

"You understand," said the deer sniffling.

"He is Sang Kancil," said Sang Arnab.

"I found Sang Kerbau lying in a pool of his own blood."

The crying intensified.

"Sang Rimau told us that if we did not obey," sobbed Sang Arnab, his whole body shaking, "he would slay every one of us."

"We were shocked," said Sang Rusa, his own voice quivering. "What were we to do? You witnessed what he did to those who tried to oppose him!"

Remembering the bloody death of his friend Sang Kerbau, Sang Kancil nodded grimly.

"Each week, we met and cast a vote. And this week…" Sang Arnab's mouth opened but he was unable to go on. The terrified rabbit stared wordlessly at the mousedeer.

"It was Sang Arnab's turn," said Sang Rusa, finishing the sentence, his dark brown eyes swimming with tears.

The pair hugged each other and wept.

"Sang Kancil, you must help us," pleaded Sang Rusa. "You must save Sang Arnab."

If there was ever an animal the equal of Sang Kancil in wit, it was the tiger. The mousedeer bent his head, already deep in thought. Perspiration beaded his neck and forehead as he pondered and pondered.

"It is a hot day," said Sang Kancil, after a while. He smiled at Sang Rusa who towered over him. "Dear *kawan* (friend), can I trouble you for a drink of water?"

"No trouble at all."

The watering hole was a deep pit in the ground nearby, camouflaged by fallen leaves.

The animals pushed the leaves aside. Thankfully there was a bucket, but it was hidden down in the darkness at the bottom.

"Allow me to assist," said the deer generously, for the chevrotain was the size of a cat. He laid the bucket in front of Sang Kancil.

As the mousedeer bent his head to drink, for a fleeting moment he thought he saw in the glistening water the deep brown eyes of his friend Sang *Kerbau* peering back at him.

Startled, Sang Kancil jerked away. Then he shook his ears and leaned forward.

His loyal friend the buffalo seemed to be watching him, his placid expression full of trust.

Kancil's throat tightened. *If only I had been there. I would have helped.*

As Sang Kancil continued to stare at the watery reflection, an idea formed in his head.

I cannot defeat Sang Rimau in a battle of wits; it will have to be Sang Rimau who defeats himself.

"Quickly," Sang Kancil gasped, stunned at the simplicity of the solution. "Get the others. I have a plan."

"What is it?" Sang Arnab sat up.

"If you want to live," Sang Kancil panted, for he was thinking so hard, he could not spare much energy for breath. "Bring everyone. Bring them. At once."

"At once," said Sang Rusa with a grin. "I knew you could do it!"

"At once! He is Sang Kancil after all!" sang Sang Arnab.

Sang Rusa took off, darting through the bushes, scattering leaves in his haste.

Not to be outdone, Sang Arnab raced off. His tail flashed white and then he was gone.

In the time it took to cook a pot of rice (this is how, long ago, Malaysians used to tell time) the animals were back. They were not alone. So anxious were the other animals to realise a solution out of this nightmare that none lost any time in seeking out the mousedeer.

"Sang Kancil, what is your plan? Can you help us?" the creatures muttered as they stared at their friend.

Sang Kancil was silent as he gazed around at the terrified animals. He sensed their fear. Would his plan work? There was only one way to find out. "Sang Arnab, stop your crying," said Sang Kancil calmly.

Sang Arnab was overjoyed. "Thank you, thank you Sang Kancil. I knew you would help."

"But what is your plan?" asked the other animals, peeved.

"Sang Arnab will not die tomorrow because I will take his place," said Sang Kancil.

At the mousedeer's words, Sang Arnab fainted. When the animals patted him awake, he stared uncomprehending at Sang Kancil unable to speak.

"Sang Kancil you are speaking nonsense," said the others. "Do you want to die yourself?"

"Well, that is the question," said Sang Kancil as he gave a faint smile.

The animals melted away.

No one wanted to see what would happen to the mousedeer.

The next day, *Sang Harimau* (Revered Tiger), the fake *rajah* (king), was waiting.

He had heard of the mousedeer's determination to sacrifice itself in his friend's stead. In the end, it made no difference to him. An animal was an animal. Of course, something a bit larger would have suited him better, but a willing victim was always preferred to one that he had to hunt himself.

Time passed. The day grew hotter.

And Sang Harimau grew hungrier and still there was no sign of any mousedeer let alone any other animal. His stomach growled.

How dare he keep me waiting? When that stupid mousedeer comes, I will eat him at once. I am famished enough to devour two buffaloes.

The other creatures were wise enough to stay out of the way.

Sometime long after midday, the sounds of springing through the undergrowth reached the ears of the false king.

That must be Sang Kancil. I cannot believe he is really coming, but better late than not at all.

And so Sang Harimau continued to sit and wait for his latest victim to arrive, drooling. Mouth open, he inhaled, tasting the scent of his newest sacrificial victim on the wind.

Soon the bushes shook, and before his great yellow eyes, Sang Kancil appeared.

The tiger leaned forward, readying to pounce, when to Sang Harimau's surprise, his intended victim did something no other animal had ever done.

Without hesitation, it strode straight up to Sang Harimau/Rimau.

Impressed, the tiger paused his attack, curiosity overcoming him.

Sang Kancil bowed. "I apologise for my tardiness, Your Highness. I would have come sooner; had I not been detained by another tiger as large and as strong as you. He, too, wanted me for his meal but I had to persuade him that I was yours alone."

Sang Rimau could not believe his ears. "Who is this usurper?" he growled. "How dare he enter my domain! And as for demanding that my prey be his, his life is in mortal danger for his humiliation."

To Sang Rimau's delight, the mousedeer quivered at his words.

The tiger preened. "Show me this traitor! I will take matters into my own hands and do away with this fool. For fool he is to dare come against me!"

"You are indeed a true king!"

And when the mousedeer pressed its forehead into the ground in obeisance Sang Rimau almost died of happiness.

This was it! This was how the others should show their respect for me, instead of slinking away whenever I approach.

For a moment, Sang Rimau almost regretted the fact that he would soon devour the mousedeer - but only for a moment.

Sang Rimau lifted his head high and with what he assumed was a royal tone, hissed, "Show me where this usurper lives!"

Trembling, Sang Kancil rose. "Follow me, my lord."

With a disgusted sniff as if this was all beneath him, the false king followed.

Swiftly Sang Kancil led the way to the well. "Here is where the false king lives. This is his den."

"In this miserable hovel?" Sang Harimau sneered at the hole in the ground. He breathed in, and as he expected, inhaled the scent of numerous animals, which he assumed were the scents of the rival's victims.

However, these were only the scents of those who had drunk here. For many had used the watering hole.

Thus Sang Harimau was thoroughly convinced that this was indeed the home of another tiger. Perhaps, had Sang Harimau not been in such a hurry to impress the mousedeer, he might have asked himself the question: what hole goes straight down?

But Harimau is vain and impatient and right now, he was desperate to show himself as mightiest of the mighty.

"What wretch dares oppose me?"

"I do not know, my lord. I only know that I saw him further down."

With a snarl to prove his valour, Harimau peered into the depths of the well.

To the tiger's surprise, as he stared the vision of another tiger just as large as himself appeared down below. Sang Rimau did not know that it was his own reflection.

Instead, putting on a show of royal disgust, Sang Rimau did what every tiger does when they wish to instil fear. To paralyse their prey. To take over their mind. He roared.

Tigers roar to threaten potential enemies. They can produce low frequency sounds that can pass through objects, including bones.

Sound has physical and psychological effects. Long has it been known that sound and even music are effective forms of torture.

I will not give this fool a chance to escape. And so Sang Harimau roared as loudly as he could.

To his surprise, the guttural sounds of an enraged tiger reverberated up the walls of the well, almost deafening him as he stretched forward.

To Sang Rimau's shock, a chill passed through him. He did not know that it was the vibration of his own roar shaking and resonating the walls of the well, to echo back deep into his own being. His psyche.

I cannot be defeated, believed the proud king, and without another thought Sang Rimau lunged, opening his jaws to tear and to rip and to strike, only instead of flesh and fur and bone, to his surprise, he received a mouthful of cold water. Then-

Splash!

He entered the water.

Cold fear forked through him chilling his very being. He kicked, but there was no reassurance of solid ground to land on.

Undeterred, however, Sang Rimau dove, claws lashing out. Fatally brave and heroically valiant in his last dying moments, he attacked! Where was his enemy?

Where is the stupid fool of a tiger who has threatened me and everything that I have worked so hard to achieve?

But there was no physical being for Sang Rimau to strike.

Where was the tiger whose terrifying roar he had heard? Was this a trick? Black magic?

Even as his lungs filled with water, Sang Rimau suddenly realised what had happened.

There was no tiger.

There had never been another tiger. There had only been him. And his pride.

And in his deadly pride, Harimau had invented a foe as deadly and as terrifying as himself. There, in the reflection of the water when he had gazed down, his heart so consumed with pride and indignation that he had not the time to pull apart the truth from the lies.

That stupid chevrotain.

That foolish quivering meal.

That- that…

But Tiger had begun to sink, and whatever thoughts he had of revenge were soon overtaken by thoughts of survival. He paddled mightily with all four paws, yearning to feel the solidness of hard ground beneath his pads.

But a tiger, even a king, false or no, has only so much strength.

"Help me," he called out, only to have the cover of the well shut out all light.

In the darkness, Sang Rimau paddled. But one can only paddle for so long.

When the tiger finally drowned, the animals all wanted to elect Sang Kancil for their king.

"I think we have had enough of kings," said the chevrotain. And he went skipping about the jungle, free as ever.

See Notes on Pages 337

Sang Kancil and the Water Tortoise

A water tortoise is generally a terrapin, one of several small species of turtles, who live in either fresh or brackish water.

It is called Kikura.

KAWAN KANCIL (FRIEND MOUSEDEER) and *Kawan Kikura* (Friend Water Tortise) decided to set off together to find fruit.

They were in luck and soon found a tree laden with fruit beside a house. The tree was tall, but the friends were hungry.

As Kawan Tortise lumbered towards the tree, the mousedeer ran on ahead, skipping and leaping, hoping to be able to reach the branches where the fruit lay.

The thought of all that delicious fruit made Sang Kancil salivate, but to his disappointment, he was unable to reach the fruit. The branches were simply too high, even the lowest ones. By now Kawan Tortise had reached the foot of the tree.

"How goes the gathering, Kawan Kancil?" asked the Water Tortoise, yellow brown eyes blinking, as he craned his neck to look up at the tree.

Sang Kancil tossed his head. "As you can see, I have made little progress."

"Are we to starve then?"

The mousedeer winked. "Nonsense. I have another plan. As I cannot climb the tree, I have decided that I can push you up the tree instead."

"Very well, Kawan Kancil."

So Sang Kancil pushed the good-natured Tortoise onto the lower branches.

Once up, *Kikura* (Tortoise) threw down as much fruit as he could reach.

"Wonderful! You are doing well!" said Sang Kancil as he ate and ate.

"Leave some for me," grumbled the Water Tortoise. "I seem to be doing all the work."

"Nonsense," said Sang Kancil, continuing to gather fruit. "Who pushed you up there in the first place?"

"That is true. But now I am done," said the Water Tortoise.

Looking around at the bare branches, he saw just how high off the ground he was. His heart skipped a beat. "Oh, oh, I cannot get down."

"Have you tried?" said Sang Kancil, too busy to even look up, his mouth full of delicious fruit.

"Yes," said Tortoise, annoyed at being ignored. "I cannot get down by going forward and neither can I get down by going backward. What shall I do?"

"Throw yourself down," said the mousedeer without a second thought.

"What? Are you sure?" Tortoise blinked uncertainly.

"It isn't far to the ground. And you have your shell for protection," said Sang Kancil. "What could possibly happen?"

"True," said the gullible Tortoise. "Well, here goes!" And he threw himself off the lower branches.

Kikura made such a commotion as he tumbled that when he finally landed with a thud, the people living in the house nearby thought that a durian had landed. Durians are a great favourite.

All locals know this as fact: durians are never picked. The fruit falls to the ground when ripe. Most importantly, whoever gets to the fruit first has possession.

So, when the villagers heard something heavy landing on the ground, they all rushed excitedly out of the house.

Seeing what was happening, Sang Kancil at once escaped into the bushes. His belly was full and so he went on his merry way, while poor Water Tortoise was captured by the people and left to his own devices.

Tiger's Talking Bottom

Harimau has always tried to catch Sang Kancil.
Then one day, he did.
This then is the cherita (story) of Harimau's Talking Bottom.

HARIMAU CAUGHT SANG Kancil one day.

"Finally," said Harimau. "I have you!" The mighty predator opened his mouth wide and was about to devour the chevrotain when Kancil cried out.

"*Tolong!* (Please!) *Tuan* (Lord) Harimau!"

Harimau paused. It was not every day that the bane of his life referred to him as lord. The moment had to be savoured. "What do you want? Be quick about it though! I cannot wait much longer!"

To Harimau's infinite pleasure, Kancil prostrated himself on the ground. "If Your Lordship will permit your servant one last wish before Your Lordship does the inevitable, most kind, most powerful, mos-"

"Yes, yes, what is?"

"Consume me whole, please."

This was a change.

Harimau's ears twitched as he considered.

"Please understand that if you were to swallow me whole, then you would forever have the knowledge that you have eaten *all* of me. But should you decide instead to tear-" Kancil swallowed hard. "Umm tear me into bits, why then, there would always be a portion of me that is unconsumed. That portion will haunt you forever."

Haunt. Like most creatures of the Realm of the Deep Forest, Harimau was naturally superstitious. "Well, we certainly can't have that," said Harimau sounding magnanimous. "Wish granted. Now stop squirming while I-"

"*Tolong! Nanti*! (Please! Wait!) Just one more favour, Oh Most Noble One. Kind Benevolent Master-"

"*Chepat!* (Quick!) Out with it! I haven't got all day," said Harimau with a shake of his head. As Sang Kancil's first request had been a reasonable one, he was prepared to listen once more.

"*Terima Kasih!* (Thank-you!) You are most generous! All I ask is that you eat me headfirst. For if you were to eat me bottom first then you will surely perish."

Perish? Harimau frowned. He couldn't see how, but Kancil was silent and Harimau too embarrassed to ask. He did not wish his ignorance to become obvious. As there appeared to be no further requests, Harimau did exactly as Kancil had asked.

"No time to waste!" said Harimau matter-of-factly, and opening his jaws wide, he swallowed the chevrotain in one gulp, headfirst.

There! It was done!

Finally.

The deed done, Harimau wandered off, feeling pleased and warm. And full.

"Kancil was right! I am happy to know that I have eaten him, all of him. Haha ha!"

The jungle sighed and all was silent.

Meanwhile, what was happening to Sang Kancil?

The mousedeer found himself enclosed in a horrible heat that pressed against him on all sides. Pressure against his head pushed him forward, painfully stretching and elongating his whole body, slimy saliva easing the passage until with a pop, he burst into Harimau's belly.

I have been eaten.

But Kancil had a plan. He always has a plan. Now all he had to do was to put it into action.

The chevrotain squirmed forward. It had been easy to move from the mouth down through the gullet and into the tiger's stomach, thanks to peristalsis but from then on, if he was to survive, his task was harder.

If not impossible.

For what he was attempting had never been done before.

Kancil pushed with his head against the tough sphincter that was holding the contents of the stomach while digestion took place.

Digestion, that was happening to him. A heinous thought, but he knew that this was not to be his fate.

Acid burning him, close to blacking out, he persisted and pushed, hard, until he found the valve easing open. Which it does from time to time to allow small portions of the digested contents of the stomach, the yellow-brown chyme, to enter the next phase of digestion.

Now!

With a final massive effort, plop!

Kancil broke his way through at last into the start of the small intestine.

I can do this!

But his task was far from over. Kancil struggled for what seemed miles, shoving his way through the stinking rotting stew of whatever creature had met its demise before himself and knowing that if he failed then this would be his ultimate fate.

But somehow through sheer willpower, Kancil finally managed to push his way into the large intestines and up the colon, across and finally down towards the rectum where he remained, his quivering nostrils just hanging out of tiger's anus.

Finally, fresh air!

For he stunk of *taik* (shit).

Now all he had to do was wait.

Tiger, you are in for a surprise.

The unsuspecting tiger knew that something was happening within his belly but as he had just devoured a creature - hoofs and all, he assumed that it was simply his meal striking its usual way through his system.

After a quick rest, Harimau was again on the prowl. A mousedeer although delicious, was quite a small repast, and Harimau needed more. Much more!

To his delight, he soon came across *Babi* (Pig).

Babi was nosing out some roots, and completely oblivious to the fact that he was being stalked by Harimau.

Which was how Harimau liked it.

What an easy target! He salivated. The mighty tiger smiled and prepared to pounce. He launched himself into the air just as a voice sprang out from nowhere.

"*Lari! Run! Lari chepat-chepat! Harimau dekat*! (The tiger is near!)"

Startled, both Babi and Harimau jumped into the air.

Babi looked at Harimau.

Harimau looked at Babi.

Babi saw the Striped One and took off.

Tiger cursed as he saw his next meal shoot away through the underbrush. Baffled and angry, Tiger landed with a thump on the spot where Babi had been a mere second ago.

Tiger would have given chase only he was too stunned at the sudden appearance of that mysterious voice. And why did it sound so close?

Tiger turned round in circles, searching for the owner of that voice but he found no one. And all he knew was he had lost his next meal.

Harimau roared his anger to the trees, but it was too late. His prey had escaped!

Never mind. That was a pure accident. I will hunt again.

And Tiger did.

Next, he came upon *Rusa* (Deer).

Once again Tiger went through his moves. And once again, as Tiger launched himself into the air, a voice cried out again.

A small voice.

A very close voice.

But a voice that wasn't his.

Tiger landed, screaming with anger for once again his prey had escaped but this time Tiger did not waste any time searching for the owner of that mysterious voice. For Tiger recognised the voice.

"So now I know what trickery abounds!" said Harimau. "Come out! Come out!"

But of course, stuck in Harimau's bottom, Sang Kancil could not.

Never mind, thought Harimau after a while. Kancil is deep within me. A little while longer and he will no longer be around to plague me. And at the thought, Harimau smiled nastily.

Next, Harimau came across *Monyet* (monkey).

Harimau licked his lips.

Upwind, he stalked. Once again, he made to pounce, when once again Kancil's voice erupted from out of his bottom!

"*Lari!* (Run!) *Lari chepat-chepat! Harimau dekat!* (Run quickly! Tiger is near!)"

Of course, Monyet ran away.

"*Chelaka*! (Woe betide me!)" Wept Harimau as he saw his third meal escape. "This cannot be happening!" Frustration made him tear at his bottom, but Harimau's claws are sharp, and he stopped promptly as soon as he began to bleed.

Time, all I need is time. A little longer, and he will be done.

So Harimau waited a couple of days but when he tried again, the same horrible experience repeated itself.

A week passed and Harimau was ravenous.

Another week, and Harimau could take it no longer.

Every single prey he came across, was warned away by Sang Kancil.

If Harimau had thought that his troubles were over when he devoured the chevrotain, he was sorely mistaken. There was only one thing to be done.

"Out! Out! Out!" The famished and half-starved Tiger ripped and tore at his bottom. He pushed and grunted and roared and finally with a fart that sounded from one end of the jungle to another, Kancil flew out of his bottom.

Harimau did not waste any time looking at his nemesis. He took off and fled.

And as for Kancil, he too was starving, and he gobbled up whatever greenery was within reach.

And so here ends the interesting tale of Tiger's Talking Bottom, where Tiger finally got his wish and devoured Kancil only to learn that getting your wish may not always be the wisest thing.

Especially if it involves a certain chevrotain.

See Notes on Pages 337-338

Kantjil becomes a Raksha

GOSSIP STARTED THE whole incident.

Nonja Panther (Mrs Panther) had made her rounds and *Nonja Kantjil* (Mrs Kantjil) was livid from what she had learnt.

"That troublemaker started off by saying that you are smarter," said Nonja Kantjil, her heart pounding with fury. "But then she ended by saying that her husband does not believe it so."

"And how did you answer?" Kantjil's tone was placid. He could guess what was coming.

"Prove it." Nonja Kantjil nodded proudly, her ire easing as she considered her husband's handsome profile. "Prove it."

"Panther is powerful, but power does not equate to intelligence." Kantjil's eyes turned glassy.

"You are planning something," said his wife excitedly.

Kantjil refocused on his wife, grinning. "You know me too well. Perhaps it is time for the Kantjil to outsmart the Panther."

Nonja Kantjil hummed as she went and fetched some fresh coconut juice for her husband to drink.

Her husband did not disappoint. "Get me a pair of horns," said Kantjil, "and make a ruff of feathers. Then obtain clay, both white and red, and finally, a stick that I can wield as a sword."

His wife flew about gathering all the necessary equipment. "What are you planning to do?" she asked as she stitched feathers furiously.

"Become a Raksha."

Nonja Kantjil gasped, almost dropping her needle, for a Raksha was an evil spirit – part ogre, part beast, part human.

Totally terrifying.

But if a Raksha would not frighten a panther, then nothing would.

Nonja Kantjil's smile grew as she resumed her sewing. She made sure that their child, Anak, stayed indoors for the next few days.

Shortly after, a Raksha could be seen haunting their section of the jungle.

Attired in his costume and made up to look like a Raksha, Kantjil hid at the crossing of two grass tracks.

Soon elephant came along, absently swinging its long grey trunk as it ambled.

"Argh!" roared the Raksha, that was Kantjil. "Haha ha! Ha!"

"Ahhhh! Ah! Oh!" said Gajah as Kantjil revealed his identity. "It's you! Haha ha!"

And Gajah and Kantjil laughed together at the prank.

"But why are you disguising yourself as a Raksha?" asked elephant and roared even louder when Kantjil revealed the reason.

"Will you join me?"

"Certainly," said Gajah and the two lay in wait for the next victim.

Before long, Water Buffalo lumbered along.

"Argh!"

"Tru-u-m-phoot!" said the co-conspirator elephant.

So terrified was Kerbau that he almost urinated. "Wah! Adoi! Eh!"

"Ha ha ha ha!" laughed Kantjil.

"Ha ha ha ha!" trumpted Gajah, even louder.

"Oh, hah!" laughed Kerbau as he joined the pair. "What are the two of you playing at?"

They told him.

"I want to trick Panther, too!" said Kerbau, longingly.

Now there were three hiding by the crossroads.

When Panther approached, the trio were ready.

Kantjil crouched.

Gajah raised his trunk.

Kerbau swung his massive horns to one side and waited.

The trio held their breath. Everything rested on timing.

Panther had absolutely no inkling of what awaited him. He moved sinuously, enjoying how the cool of the morning pressed against his side, delighting in how the breeze tickled the thin straw ends of his whiskers. Sun warmed the top of his head and back, just enough to ward off the chill of night but not enough to cause him to sweat.

Me sweat? Nonsense! I am Panther the cool. Panther th- Ah!

"Argh!" Something black and hideous roared.

"Truuu-mm-phh!" Something large and grey bellowed.

"Mmmnooo – mo – nooo!" Something swarthy and muscley grunted.

Panther's thoughts vanished like tendrils into the air as these- these- things pounced onto the track right in front of him.

Devils! Monsters! A Raksha!

The gory red and white painted face of the Demon flashed before Panther.

"*Tolong!* (Help!) Save me!" And with a yelp of absolute terror, Panther fled back along the path he had just walked so confidently and disappeared into the jungle.

Whoosh!

Oh, how the three friends laughed and laughed. They had a tale worth sharing. How the braggart Panther had been scared half to death simply by a mousedeer dressed as a Raksha and an elephant and a slow-moving water buffalo.

Oh, ho ho! What an excellent prank to play on an unsuspecting victim.

The very next day, as was to be expected, Nonja Panther came calling to the home of Nonja Kantjil.

"Oh, let me tell you what happened to my brave husband!" said Nonja Panther, squealing with excitement.

"Oh tell, quickly!" said Nonja Kantjil, joining in the game. "It sounds like something big must have happened." She patted Nonja Panther soothingly on her shoulder. "Adoi! I can see from your face that it is something very important. *Besar*! (Big!)"

Nonja Panther pretended to swoon. Her tone turned dramatic, whispery, as if sharing a great secret that she could barely contain. "You will never believe it! Never!" And she lifted her proud jaw. "My husband was attacked by a Raksha! Yes, a Raksha I kid you not. He was going about hunting and- and…"

Only Nonja Kantjil was silent.

Nonja Panther frowned. She was midway through her recital and had been expecting her friend to join in with "ohs and ahs!", or perhaps some rapid fanning, to keep from fainting.

But all her performance had elicited from Nonja Kantjil was a wry look. Almost unbelieving. Nonja Panther stopped her spiel.

"I see," said Nonja Kantjil quietly.

"Yes!" said Nonja Panther, snapping shut her jaw and trying again, draping one paw over her forehead, and sighing heavily as if the weight of her story was pulling her down.

But the melodramatics did nothing either. "You do not believe," she said finally.

Nonja Kantjil coughed into her delicate paw. "You are correct. I do not believe it."

Nonja Panther shot up indignantly. Was she being called a liar? Rage burned through her. "But I have evidence!"

"Really?"

"Why, my husband was frightened of course. It was a Raksha, but being a panther, he was able to knock the Raksha down."

"I see."

"He had no fear of the Raksha's horn-"

"You mean these horns?" And nonchalantly, Nonja Kantjil placed the two horns that Kantjil had worn, in front of the dismayed Nonja Panther.

The liar blanched. "Oh, but these were great big horns. Then there was this magnificent ruff of feathers. And- and…" Nonja Panther trailed off as Nonja Kantjil produced the feather ruff that she had sewn.

"You mean these?"

Nonja Panther spluttered. "My husband knows a Raksha when he sees one. That Raksha's face was red and white…"

Nonja Kantjil produced the clay used to plaster Kantjil's face, then looked askance at Nonja Panther.

Well, of course, Nonja Panther went home at once and reported to her indignant husband exactly what had transpired in the home of the Kantjils.

Panther was furious.

The very next morning, Panther was up and about early. He loped up to every animal abroad at that hour and at once described his terrifying experience, only to be met with ridicule and laughter.

"Raksha? What Raksha?"

"Oh, you mean, *that* Raksha! That teeny tiny mousedeer-sized demon. Haha ha!"

And then the giggles began. And they didn't stop.

Gajah and Kerbau had done their job well. Too well, for before the end of the day, Panther was in a murderous mood.

"I will slay that Kantjil! He has made me a laughingstock," swore Panther.

Word was brought to Kantjil.

"Do you think you have gone too far this time?" Nonja Kantjil shook her worried head.

Kantjil nuzzled his wife's neck. "Do not worry, my dear. It just means that I will have to play another trick."

"What costume will you need?"

"The costume of a mousedeer. For this time, I intend to trick him as myself."

The next day, Kantjil was up bright and early, looking for vines with which to weave into rope. He made a net. Then he dug a hole and waited.

Gajah came along. "Oh, it is you, Kantjil. What are you up to this time?"

And Kantjil told Gajah.

"Let me help, please."

And Kantjil agreed to let elephant help.

The pair waited.

Soon Water Buffalo lumbered along.

"Oh, it is you, Kantjil. What are you up to this time?"

And Kantjil told Kerbau.

"Let me help, please."

And Kantjil agreed to let Water Buffalo help.

The trio waited.

Night fell.

And soon the panther came prowling along the jungle paths. As he was about to pass, Gajah swung into position. He was wrapped in bandages.

"Oh, oh, sakit (sick)," moaned Gajah.

"Oh, Kawan Gajah, what has happened to you?" said Panther, feigning concern.

"That Kantjil! *Alamat*! (Oh god!) All I was doing was trumpeting to scare some *anak musang* (baby civet cats). You'd think he has nothing better to do!" wept Gajah, "My bones, my poor bones."

Did Kantjil break Gajah's bones?

Panther swallowed.

"I shouldn't have bragged about my strength." Elephant sobbed. "Not in front of certain creatures anyway."

Panther had been about to share his story about the Raksha but thought better of it.

"*Selamat Petang, Gajah.* (Good evening, Elephant.) I must be on my way. Lots of mouths to feed," and bidding Gajah good night, Panther made his escape.

Minutes later, Kerbau swung into position. He, too, was wrapped in bandages.

"Oh, oh, *sakit* (sick)," moaned Kerbau.

"Oh, *Kawan Kerbau,* (Friend Buffalo), what has happened to you?" said Panther, feigning concern for the second time.

What is going on?

"That Kantjil! Alamat! All I was doing was stomping to scare some *anak mermerang* (Baby Otters). You'd think he has nothing better to do!" wept Kerbau, "My bones, my poor bones."

Did Kantjil break Kerbau's bones?

Panther swallowed. He suddenly felt very small.

"I shouldn't have bragged about my strength." Kerbau wailed. "Not in front of certain creatures anyway."

Panther had been about to share his story about the Raksha, but again thought better of it.

"*Selamat Petang, Kerbau.* (Good evening, Water Buffalo.) I must be on my way. Lots of mouths to feed." Bidding Kerbau goodnight, Panther again made his escape.

But he was thinking so hard about what he had heard that he was not paying attention to where he was walking. And so, minutes later, Panther fell into the net that Kantjil had lain over the pit.

The ground rushed past his head as he dropped like a stone. Right to the bottom where he landed heavily. "Argh!"

Blackness overcame him.

When Panther recovered, he gazed up to see large brown eyes looking down at him.

Did he see disgust in that face? Panther shivered, suddenly not feeling like the powerful predator that had left his home so confidently earlier in the night.

"Kantjil? Is that you?" said Panther, feeling and sounding small.

"Yes, it is," said Kantjil, his voice sounding like clear water.

"Can you please help me out? I find myself unable to climb out without help."

"Certainly, I will," said Kantjil. "Once you swear that you will stop all this boasting."

"But- but-"

Suddenly, what little moonlight there was blacked out. The night grew colder.

Panther gasped.

Then he realised that it was Gajah leaning over the sides of the pit. His enormous head had blocked out the moonlight.

Panther shivered.

"Boaster-cocks always have gossiping wives. And such gossips always cause trouble. Especially for their husbands," said Gajah ominously.

"But- but-"

Gajah leaned back and Kerbau took his place. His enormous, lethal pair of horns cast sharp shadows down the pit.

Panther winced. His throat was so dry that when he swallowed it felt like knives slicing.

"Boaster-cocks are cowards. Plain and simple," said Kerbau with a finality.

Kerbau leaned back as Kantjil took his place. His dulcet tones were the harshest rebuke. "*We*," said Kantjil, as Gajah and Kerbau moved to stand on either side of him, "we are sick and tired of boaster-cocks who brag about their so-called courage and strength."

Panther gasped at the show of strength and solidarity. "Please save me, and I will promise to do whatever you ask. Please I beg of you."

"Silence your wife," said Kantjil. "Silence yourself."

Panther hung his head.

The trio waited.

"But you will tell the others. You will say how you have made me promise, and then I will never be able to show my face in the forest. I will lose whatever pride I had." Emerald eyes glistened with tears. Hurt and the shame resonated in Panther's voice. The embarrassment of a once proud predator… Loss of face is very real to Asians.

While the three wished to stop the boasting, it had never been their aim to break Panther's spirit.

"Oh, you are mistaken," said Kantjil jauntily. "I am sure the three of you agree that I am the strongest animal here."

There was a murmur of agreement.

"If I were to say anything about how I dressed up as a Raksha and tricked you, then that would be gossiping."

Gajah and Kerbau nodded.

"And if I were to say anything about how I laid a trap and you fell into it, then I would be bragging."

Gajah and Kerbau nodded.

"Very well," Panther bowed his head. His cheeks were flaming. "By Gajah's tusks and Kerbau's horns, I swear that I will never boast again," said Panther.

"We are your witnesses, and so are these wise trees," said Kantjil.

For all knew that spirits dwelt in trees.

The three animals threw down a rope and helped Panther out.

And from that day forth, Panther never boasted or bragged about his strength.

But Nonja Panther still visited Nonja Kantjil and they are now quite good friends.

Crocodile's House of Tricks

CROCODILE WAS SICK and tired of Mousedeer playing tricks on him, so he decided that he could play a trick, too.

"I will catch Mousedeer. See if I can't," said Crocodile.

So he lay down by the riverbank and pretended to be a tree, which was easy, as crocodiles do look like logs when they float.

Kancil was thirsty; he trotted down to the river to drink. He spotted Crocodile. He decided to play his own trick. He called out, "If you are a tree, then turn over. But if you are a crocodile do nothing."

Of course, the silly crocodile turned over at once.

Kancil laughed. "*Bodoh!* (Stupid). Trees can't roll. You must be silly Sang Buaya!" Then he ran away.

Oh, how angry Sang Buaya was, but he was patient and bided his time.

The next day, he tried again.

This time he was a little smarter. He built a little house of leaves and branches. Just the right size for a mousedeer. Then he placed some peanut leaves, the sort that the mousedeer love to eat, at the entrance.

His job done, Crocodile went and hid.

Soon Kancil came trotting along.

Now mousedeer have good eyesight. Prey need to keep a sharp lookout if they wish to survive.

Kancil had noticed the change in the surroundings, and he was suspicious. Sniffing around he recognised the musty smell of Sang Buaya.

Aha! He is trying to trick me once more. But I am clever. Kancil trotted off to find Sang Harimau.

"Ho, Sang Harimau, dear Elder Brother," said Kancil.

"Hello, Sang Kancil, what can I do for you?" said Tiger.

"I just saw a fat little pig that I thought you might be interested in," said Sang Kancil.

"I am always interested in fat little pigs," said Tiger and he followed Mousedeer to where Crocodile's hut lay.

"Over there!" said Kancil before running away.

Harimau was hungry and he wasted no time pouncing onto the house. Imagine his surprise when the whole house collapsed, and instead of a fat juicy pig, he found himself between the jaws of Sang Buaya!

"You!" said each predator to the other.

Well, both were hungry and after a meal. And so, a fierce battle ensued.

Crocodile bit and slashed at Tiger, while Tiger clawed and ripped at Crocodile.

Trees and bushes were knocked flat as the animals rolled this way and that. The smaller animals all made sure to get out of the way as the two kings battled it out.

It was an even fight, however, and after a while, both animals were so exhausted that during a lull in the fighting they each crawled away to lick their wounds.

But crocodile was badly hurt and lying in water did not help him get better faster. In fact, his wounds got worse, and festered because of dirty water.

When next Kancil came down to the river to drink, he found crocodile. He was half dead.

Kancil felt guilty. The fight really was his fault. He found some medicine to put on crocodile's wounds.

Soon crocodile was better, and for a while, the mousedeer and crocodile were friends.

But somehow, I cannot see this lasting, can you?

Ancestor Buhum

This tale if any, shows the influence of the Malays in the Moken storytelling. Although many of the stories are recognisable to those of us who grew up hearing Sang Kancil folktales, these tales twist in unexpected ways.

PLEASE NOTE: In the original source, the author starts by stating that the snake predator is a python, but always finishes by calling the snake a serpent. I have continued that.

THE MOKEN ANCESTOR, Buhum, once took his son to the shore to chop down a tree. Mokens are sea dwellers, living in their boats for most of the year, and only forced onto the land during the monsoon period. This land is the Andaman Islands, in the Bay of Bengal.

That day, Buhum and his son were planning to make a boat. For this, they selected a Hopea odorata, a large tree that can grow to 45 m in height. Valued for its wood, it is native to Southeast Asia and grows near rivers.

The two were hollowing out the truck when a mousedeer showed up.

The chevrotain leapt onto the hull, and at once began to deride the skills of the pair, calling Buhum *grandfather* and telling him that he was ignorant and that he was continually making mistakes.

The pair had been sweating blood and tears over this project, so the insults were not welcome.

Father and son both tried to catch the pest, only the mousedeer eluded them by jumping from one end of the boat to the other. Eventually, the mousedeer vanished into the forest but that was not the end of the episode for the mousedeer returned for the next four days and continued his abuse.

So angry did the creature make Buhum that finally, he seized some of the wood shavings and hurled them at the pest. The wood struck the mousedeer on the rump.

"Let us see *you* suffer now!" said Buhum.

Since that day, the Moken say that the mousedeer bears the scar of that incident on its back. They also say that if caught and cooked, it is advisable that the back part of the animal be disposed because it contains a bad smell.

Do not worry however for although the mousedeer is considered big game by the Moken, and although they love going out hunting for mousedeer, they apparently seldom catch one.

But this is not the end of the story. Oh no!

For next the mousedeer encountered a tiger.

"I am going to eat you," said the tiger. "You are soon to die."

Everyone wants Mousedeer.

But again, do not worry. Mousedeer is agile. Quite. Did you not see what happened earlier?

And just as the human pair were unable to catch hold of it, so too, is the tiger unable to grasp the mousedeer.

The mighty predator lunges and pounces but all to no avail. Almost looking as if it were playing, the deft mousedeer leads the unsuspecting tiger to a part of the sea where there are especially enormous clams.

Celup-Celap. Celup-Celap go his thin legs in the water. Splashing, cool and refreshing.

Anyone who has gone diving knows that if you step onto one of these giant clams they will grip and never let go. And so, these shellfish do what they always do, they doggedly clamp onto the paws of the tiger who, unable to escape, screams in terror that the sea is rising. For it is.

Tiger is for good reason known as the King of the *Land*.

King or no king, no one can escape the rising tide.

Remember, Tiger had declared earlier that it would eat the mousedeer.

"Ah my friend," the mousedeer proclaims grimly, "It is you who is soon to die."

And as with each wave the tiger opens his mouth to shout for help, water enters, so that soon the greedy tiger perishes.

Once the mousedeer is sure that the tiger is dead, it returns to the jungle.

Hurray! Mousedeer has lost the tiger.

Only another tiger shows up.

Oh!

"You have tricked me and lied to me, and now I am going to eat you," says the second tiger.

Everyone wants Mousedeer.

Well, Mousedeer isn't about to sit down and let that happen. But it cannot lead the second tiger to the shore where the giant clams lie while the body of the first tiger floats on the rising tide.

"Ah my friend," the mousedeer proclaims, "I cannot let you eat me, either."

Only one thing to be done. Thankfully, mousedeer is a fast runner. It escapes into the forest.

Hurray! Mousedeer has lost the second tiger.

Only, a python shows up.

Oh.

Everyone wants Mousedeer.

But Mousedeer is not only quick on its feet; it is also quick in its thinking. Mousedeer seizes a reed from the nearby river and begins to play on the reed pipe.

At first, the python listens, lulled by the gentle melody, but soon its stomach growls, and it remembers its hunger.

"I demand that you hand me the pipe," says the serpent.

Again, the mousedeer is not having any of that. It knows what is coming. It also knows that pythons strangle their prey and swallow them whole. Hence, they are not fast.

"Ah my friend," the mousedeer proclaims, "I cannot let you have my pipe."

Darting about, the agile mousedeer seizes the serpent in its mouth, and just as quickly, tears out its eyes. These it tosses at the second tiger who has at that moment turned up.

Oh!

Tiger swallows. Then licks its lips. Looks around.

Quick as it can, Mousedeer escapes.

Hurray! Mousedeer has lost the second tiger for the second time.

Only an elephant shows up.

Oh!

Everyone wants Mousedeer.

"I have heard of the tricks that you have been playing on the other animals. I demand that you stop, or I will take matters into my own hands."

Tricks? All Mousedeer has done is try to survive.

"And what would you do?" asks Mousedeer politely.

"Why, kill you, of course!"

Now you understand why Mousedeer does what he does. He has little choice. Everyone wants to kill him.

So once again Mousedeer must rely on the skills he has been born with.

At the elephant's boast, the mousedeer laughs. "How? I can run faster than you."

That is true.

Even Elephant knows it. Elephant wants to chase after the cheeky mousedeer only the mousedeer persuades Elephant to have a contest instead.

Mousedeer states the rules.

Between the two of them, they will each select a tree. The first one who manages to hit the tree and make it fall will be the winner.

Elephant is large. So large that as it moves its huge bulk through the jungle, it always ends up pushing down trees, virtually redesigning pathways. Coincidentally, this makes it easier for the smaller animals to move around.

Elephant agrees. It cannot see any disadvantage.

Is Mousedeer then so foolish?

Mousedeer foolish? Never!

The competitors find a tree and take turns hitting it.

And here elephant discovers that although it is bigger and stronger than his opponent, he apparently has flat feet.

All elephants have flat feet.

> Elephants "hear" with their feet. Despite their enormous ears, elephants use their feet to pick up low-frequency rumbles that come from other animals. So sensitive are these pachyderms that they can detect underground vibrations from almost 20 kilometres away.
>
> They can do so because of a large pad of gristle under each heel that acts as a shock absorber. This is also why elephants walk so quietly.

Mousedeer patiently waits until Elephant has done the bulk of the work, and then, at the precise moment, it gently taps the mighty tree-

And the tree tumbles down.

It's all in the timing.

And Mousedeer is the Master of Timing.

Elephant screams in anger, unable to discover what has gone wrong.

Hurray! Mousedeer has lost the elephant.

Only two men show up.

Oh!

Everyone wants Mousedeer.

"We are hoping to exchange these fish for wood," say the two men.

"Wood," says the mousedeer, slowly looking around at the trees that surround them.

Can these humans really be so dumb...?

"Yes, wood," say the men in a louder voice, looking at the Mousedeer as if *it* is stupid.

Mousedeer shakes its head.

Stupid is as stupid does.

Mousedeer smiles at the two men. "I might be able to help you."

The two men grin. They sit and chat happily, their dogs gambolling, as the mousedeer drags branches of wood over.

"Here you go," says the mousedeer, handing over the branches.

The men hand over the fish.

Mousedeer is not stupid. It quickly eats the fish.

The men load the branches onto their shoulders. They start to head home only there is a problem. The branches have sharp thorns on them. And the thorns stab the men.

So the men rush off after the mousedeer.

"Ah my friend," the mousedeer proclaims, "I cannot let you catch me."

Elephant turns up. It joins the chase.

"Ah my friend," the mousedeer proclaims, "I cannot let you catch me."

Tiger turns up. It joins the chase.

"Ah my friend," the mousedeer proclaims, "I cannot let you catch me."

Everyone wants Mousedeer.

But Mousedeer is not about to let anyone catch him.

"Ah my friend," the mousedeer proclaims, "Help me! I must cross the river."

Baffled, the two men look at each other. The tiger and the elephant also look at each other.

Who is Mousedeer talking to?

But at that very moment, the centre of the river foams and froths as the King of the Water emerges. Crocodile.

Quick as a blink, Crocodile ferries Mousedeer to the other bank.

Done! Mousedeer is safe. Or is he?

The two men look at each other. The tiger and the elephant look at each other. Well, if Crocodile can ferry Mousedeer over, it can also ferry them over.

"Ah my friend," the men and the tiger and the elephant all proclaim, "Help us! We must cross the river, too."

So, the crocodile comes back and allows the two men, the tiger, and the elephant to clamber onto its back. And by the time the dogs get on, Crocodile is heavily loaded with passengers.

Crocodile starts to swim. It is slow going with so many to carry. But the good-natured Crocodile persists.

Halfway across, the men cheer. The tiger cheers. The elephant cheers. And the dogs bark.

Only in their excitement, the dogs also loosen their stools.

Oh! Oh!

Crocodile does what it must do at that insult.

It devours the lot of them.

And that is the end of the tale.

Two out of One

K ANTCHIL DECIDED ONE day, to steal mangoes…
The best mangoes grew from the trees of Matjan, the tiger. So, Kantjil grabbed a sack and headed towards the tiger's garden. It was April, and the aromatic fragrance of the delectable fruit filled the air.

Kantchil salivated as he imagined biting into the golden flesh of the mango. Sheer sticky sweetness soon to be his!

He trotted briskly, head up.

Mousedeer are not the only creature who loved mangoes. Monkeys, tortoises, mice, birds, and slugs all covet the fruit. Mangoes are best picked only when ripe. And on days when the wind sleeps, the fruit can be heard dropping onto the ground with a soft thud, the vibration sensed by animals who rapidly close in, using scent. Owners of mango trees are aware of this fact and can often be seen guarding their treasure during mango season.

So, when Kantchil turned up at Matjan's garden, the tiger was waiting.

Kantchil looked at Matjan.

Matjan looked at Kantchil. Then the tiger saw the sack and bristled. "So, *you* are the thief who has been stealing my mangoes?"

To be fair, Kantchil had yet to steal mangoes. Yet.

To Matjan's surprise, Kantchil's reaction was to sigh heavily. "Oh please. Just let me do my job, and that will be the end of it. I have been doing this all day for everyone. And now even the Raja has heard of what I can do. Let me just get this over and done with, and then I can present myself to him."

Matjan's ears pricked. *Raja?* "Do what?"

Kantchil's eyes widened in surprise. "You mean you have no idea? Why, it is the most wonderful thing in the world."

Tigers are big cats after all. "What? Do *what?* Please tell me at once before I die of curiosity."

Kantchil never blinked. "Make two creatures out of one."

Shocked, Matjan studied the mousedeer's face, but the mousedeer seemed perfectly serious.

"I have never heard of such a thing," he said finally.

"It is not my business as to what you have heard or have not heard," said Kantchil. "Everybody else has."

Tiger's face heated. "Well, maybe I have heard a little."

"Well, then," said Kantchil, with a tilt of his head. "The raja is waiting. That is all I care about."

"Please," said Matjan. "Please make two of me."

"What nonsense!" Kantchil's brown eyes rounded in horror. "I have to go."

"Please." Matjan's golden eyes turned limpid with emotion. "Please."

"Well…"

When Kantchil appeared to consider, the tiger gushed. "You can have as many mangoes as you want. For ever and ever."

That seemed a reasonable trade in Kantchil's books. *Something for nothing.* "Very well, then." He spread open the sack. "Get in."

"What?"

"Get in and hurry about it! The raja is waiting!" Kantchil stamped his hoof.

Matjan flinched at the strange request but squeezed obediently into the sack.

"There!" said Kantchil as he tied the sack up.

"Now what?" came the muffled voice of Matjan. "Oof! Hey! What was that?"

"Just making two out of one," said Kantchil, kicking the sack as he laboured to drag it to the nearby river.

"But, but-"

"I am kick- I mean making two out of one. Please do not disturb me," said Kantchil and kicked the sack again just to be sure.

Although discomfited, Matjan quietened. This magic does not appear to be a very comfortable process, he thought, but he stayed as still as he could and did not cry out, even when the bag started to get wet.

He panicked as he felt himself and the sack sinking. His heart pounded wildly. But before he could call out, Matjan felt something roughly seize the sack.

To his relief, he heard a ripping sound, and then the sack was opened.

Is it over? Is the process completed?

Eagerly, he pushed his head out, blinking gladly at the sudden light. Welcome warmth pressed on his cold, sodden head.

It appeared that the magic had worked, for he found himself staring back at two amber eyes.

"Oh!" Matjan blinked. "Oh! It's another tiger. But of course. Two out of one…"

This must be what Kantchil meant. I must be staring at a duplicate of myself.

Eagerly, he studied the duplicate's features.

Is this what I really look like?

Here was his familiar tigerish countenance.

His amber eyes… yes!

His strong neck… ummm…

No, not quite. Something was off.

As Matjan flicked his head this way and that, the other tiger cocked its head, as if it too was studying Matjan.

My duplicate is not as robust as myself. It's… it's smaller…

Matjan's whole body sank.

Much smaller.

"Oh," said Matjan, greatly disappointed. "Kantchil's magic mustn't have worked. My head's not as muscular."

To Matjan's surprise, his duplicate seemed to take offence.

"What are you talking about?" snorted the other tiger.

At the sound of the voice, Matjan gasped as sudden realisation hit. "Why! You're a girl. Kantchil's magic has really gone wrong!"

The other tiger growled. "Magic? What Kantchil? When I saw your sack struggling, I thought you were something to eat. That's why I pulled you out of the river."

"Wait, what!" Matjan shook his head. Then he realised a further truth. "That- that- trickster Kantchil! He promised that he would make two of me."

And Matjan explained what had happened.

To his surprise, when he finished the tigress said nothing but looked thoughtful.

"What is the matter?" said the furious tiger.

"How many tigers were there before you went into the bag," she said softly.

"One." Came the indignant answer.

"And how many tigers are there now?"

"Two." Matjan cocked his head. Realisation dawned… "Oh! Oh, I see."

The tigress nodded.

What beautiful amber eyes…

She turned her head to the side shyly. Sunlight poured down her silky hide, gleaming gold. Matjan's heart was pounding again.

"Well, well, well, that Kantchil spoke the truth after all. He did exactly as he had promised."

And so merrily, the two tigers padded through the jungle.

The Wisdom of Allah

IT WAS A day like any other. Kantjil was out exploring.

He had come across a road – a man-made road – all bitumen. Harsh scents of burning and scorching roughened his throat for the road was very new. *Black as night.*

Kantjil had seen such things before and normally he avoided them. But this morning seemed made for adventure and he was Kantjil!

What could go wrong?

But he turned and made his way back into the jungle.

Why does man do this? Is man the new architect of the jungle?

For it was Gajah who cleaved the emerald green of the trees, making welcome paths for prey and predator.

Allah no doubt has his reasons. Although I know not what they are.

Next, he came across a rubber plantation.

Here, man had stamped his ownership again, as Kantjil gazed upon miles of trees, all in neat straight rows. Where was the confusion of the forest? The safety of camouflage for the smaller animals?

He crunched through the fallen leaves, deep in thought.

Allah no doubt has his reasons. Although I know not what they are.

The next thing that Kantjil came across was a Raja Tualang tree.

The Raja Tualang tree (Koompassia excelsa) is one of the tallest trees in the world, reaching more than eighty metres in height. Its name comes from two words – tua, meaning old and helang, meaning eagle. They tend to be solitary trees and are valued for their timber as the wood is incredibly hard due to the silica content. The grey, whitish bark and handsome crown makes them stunningly beautiful. The Raja Tualang is also the home of spirits.

What a beautiful sight, thought Kantjil. How good it is that I have two eyes. A quick right eye that can look about and spot such beauties as well as danger and a keen left eye that turns inwards for meditation.

Kantjil came upon another road, only not as well made as the first one. He followed it some distance and soon reached a kampong. Like all kampongs, the houses were surrounded by vegetable gardens.

Kantjil could never say no to a meal and so he trotted up to the nearest patch. A familiar smell greeted him.

Pumpkins. His stomach rumbled. The warm bronze light had turned the orange of the pumpkins a deep gold. Delicious!

Kantjil nosed about the pumpkins for a while, feasting on the broken ones. As he moved about, he dislodged some of the pumpkins.

Chewing contentedly, he watched the golden globes roll about due to his movements. How strange that such a heavy fruit is attached to such thin withered green stems.

Allah no doubt has his reasons. Although I know not what they are.

The day was growing warm and as one could only eat so much of raw pumpkin, for it made one's mouth sticky, he trotted off in search of a drink.

He was sniffing about, following the scent of water, when he was startled by a sound.

There was something familiar about the noise. Looking about he found the source.

A man lay asleep in the shade of a date tree. An axe lay beside him, along with pieces of hewn timber. Old dates and fallen leaves littered the base of date tree.

The aroma of rotting dates reached Kantjil's nostrils.

No doubt this labourer had grown weary from his labour.

It was just at that moment that a ripe brown date dropped from the tree.

It hit the man- smack! On the head.

At once the man woke up. He did not notice Kantjil watching nearby, but he did spot the date, all fat and juicy, which he threw into his mouth and gobbled up.

Kantjils' head bobbed excitedly as he watched. Finally, he understood.

Allah has his reasons!

Had pumpkins grown from the top of trees this man would be dead.

Gratified to be brought one step closer to the wisdom of the Almighty, Kantjil trotted off greatly enlightened.

The Tiger and the Shadow

DEEP IN THE jungle was a place where the ground was saturated with the overflow from a hot mineral spring. Over time, evaporation had turned it into a salt lick. Many animals knew of this, which was why an old tiger had made it his hunting ground. And every day, he killed. For every day, an animal would come. It did not take long for word to spread through the jungle. But no one did anything. And so, the animals continued to be slain.

Finally, Pelanduk approached the old tiger. "Allow me to bring you a beast each day. This will save you having to hunt."

The old tiger agreed. Why work when you can do nothing?

The mousedeer knew that he had to make good on his word. So Pelanduk approached the other animals. "I have a plan."

But none would even listen.

"Can at least one of you come with me?"

After three days only kuwis dared to follow Pelanduk.

Kuwis are the smallest of the Malaysian flying squirrels and weigh less than a kilogram. They are arboreal, living within trees and feeding on fruits and seeds. Thanks to a small membrane that extends between their wrists and ankles, they can glide.

"Do not worry," said Pelanduk. "I have a plan."

Kuwis sat upon Pelanduk's back. They stopped in front of the old tiger.

"Salaam Raja Harimau, a thousand pardons for my delay but I was unable to return any earlier, as my way was blocked."

"How is that possible?" growled the old tiger. "By whom?"

"My way was blocked by a fat old tiger. There was a Kuwis balancing on his muzzle."

"Show me!"

The three animals set off at once.

Kuwis balanced on the old tiger's muzzle, with Pelanduk on his rump.

They reached a river.

"Here. Here is where I saw the fat old tiger with the Kuwis on his muzzle." Pelanduk pointed to a spot in the river.

The old tiger peered into the water.

"There! Can you see him?"

To the old tiger's surprise, there was indeed a fat, old tiger staring back at him. There was even a Kuwis balancing on the muzzle of the fat old tiger.

"It is true!" gasped the fat old tiger, finally believing. Not wishing to be deemed a coward, the old tiger leapt into the water.

At this point, Pelanduk jumped off, while Kuwis spread its limbs and took off.

And so, the waters carried off the fat old tiger, who drowned thanks to his greed and pride and stupidity.

See Notes on Page 338

Wit Wins the Day

PELANDUK DECIDED ONE day that he wished for the bulls to fight. So off he went to speak with the *Seladang Cherang* (Wild Bull of the Clearing). "The Bull of the Young Bush is angry with you and is swearing with the foulest of language."

He is, no doubt, trying to take over my territory, thought the Wild Bull of the Clearing. Then he stamped his hoof in anger.

> Bulls mark their territory using scent and urine. They utilise an action known as raking whereby they rub their horns against trees. This action scrapes off bark and sometimes even tears off branches. They also gather their cows in tight groups.

Pelanduk then visited the *Seladang B'lukar* (Bull of the Young Bush). "The Wild Bull of the Clearing is angry with you and is swearing with the foulest of language."

He is no doubt trying to take over my territory, thought the Bull of the Young Bush. And he also stamped his hoof in anger.

The next day, both bulls met at the boundary between the Clearing and the Young Bush.

"You are trying to take away my territory," each cried to the other.

After a single infuriated look, both bulls charged, locking horns, heads low to the ground as they pushed with all the strength they could muster.

Foreheads lock with mighty impact. The animals stand, horns intertwined, straining, and pushing as each creature strives to get a grip with the point of its horn. The horns are not sharp, but the bull has such tremendous weight behind it that the force of the pressure is enough to push the point through thickened hide and muscle.

Yet each animal is surprisingly clever enough to give the instant the tip of its opponent's horn touches its hide.

Pelanduk, seated upon a white ants' hill, rallied both combatants. "Hey, keep pushing. You have almost won!"

While Pelanduk urged the bulls, the annoyed termites extended their burrows around his back.

Head-to-head, back and forth the bulls fought, grunting and heaving. Each tried to stab the other.

Click! Click went the horns as the mighty blew and snorted, breathless with excitement.

The green grass all around is stamped into orange mud.

And then it happened.

A horn driven into yielding flesh.

The attacker pulled his hind legs under him and straightened his forelegs until the skin is drawn taut, and in this fashion, with his knots of muscle standing out like cord, he lifted his opponent. The wounded bull was lifted off his forefeet.

It hung for a moment on the point of the horn, legs kicking listlessly. Then stopped.

The Bull of the Young Bush had gone down.

The battle was over.

Pelanduk readied to stand on his feet, only to his shock he found that thanks to the white ants' work, he was trapped.

No matter.

He called out to the victor. "Wild Bull of the Clearing, come and disperse this ant hill, oh Mighty Victor!"

Thus, the Wild Bull of the Clearing did so, before making himself scarce for the termites sought revenge.

Alone, Pelanduk cut the throat of the Bull of the Young Bush and was skinning the carcass when Harimau turned up.

Blood always attracts predators.

Tiger saw the carcass and his large red tongue shot out. "I want some."

Pelanduk swallowed. Harimau was the larger animal. More powerful. More lethal.

There was only one thing that Pelanduk could say. "Certainly."

And so Harimau sat and waited while Pelanduk finished the job. But before Harimau could partake of the meal, the rain fell.

"Gather some prickly boughs for me to build a shelter," said Pelanduk.

Tiger did not argue. Cats do not like getting wet. "Certainly."

It was obvious that he was the larger animal. The more powerful.

Harimau found the 'Riseh' and the 'Tunggal Duri'. And the thorns scratched him.

But when Harimau returned, Pelanduk said, "We need to build a raft."

Tiger growled for he was hungry and wet. "What? Has the rain stopped then?"

"No, but man is on his way."

Harimau may be the King of the Jungle on the land, but there is one predator that he fears more than the King of the Water, and that is man.

"Where can we go, that we may be able to eat in peace?"

"Build a raft."

Tiger did not argue. "Certainly."

It was obvious that he was the larger animal.

Again, the thorns scratched him.

But when Harimau returned, Pelanduk said, "We need to carry the meat on board."

Tiger growled for he was hungry.

"Man is almost here."

Tiger did not argue. "Certainly." He was after all the larger of the two animals.

Again, the thorns scratched him.

But when Harimau had carried the meat on the raft, he was bleeding so badly that he had trouble clambering aboard himself.

I must be careful not to attract attention. Thankfully it is only me and Pelanduk. We just need to find somewhere we can eat undisturbed. Away from predators.

As Tiger stared at the bloody mess he was making on the raft, he noticed with a start the mousedeer. Kancil was looking at him, his big, wide brown eyes fixed and unblinking. To Tiger's shock, the chevrotain was shaking. Almost as if he could not control himself.

Almost as if the chevrotain tasted the blood in the air.

"Why are you shivering, Kawan Kancil?"

In answer, the mousedeer's long pink tongue shot out.

Harimau flinched.

Then Pelanduk's eyes gleamed, bigger, and darker. "Anticipation." Then he quivered even more.

Harimau gave a cry of anguish and leapt into the water.

And so Pelanduk was left with all the meat.

See Notes on Pages 338-339

Sang Kancil and the Gergasi

THERE ARE SO many versions of this tale that I found it easier to tell this story with some variants throughout. In fact, if you go to YouTube, you will even find a video. Basically, the story started with a giant appearing in the woods.

In one version, a *gergasi/girgasi/gergarsang* (giant) appeared in the rainforest. The animals (Elephant, Gaur, Monkey, Deer etc.), feared for their lives, and approached Sang Kancil to deal with the problem. Sang Kancil tricked the Gergasi into being bound. Sometimes, it was rattan that was used. Always, Gergasi allowed himself to be bound thinking that the rattan was a gift from King Solomon. Or that by being bound, it would relieve his pain.

But Sang Kancil bound Gergasi so tightly that it killed him.

One version said that the giant was a grandfather; in another it was a grandmother.

Sang Kancil is also known as Akal Pelanduk (Timeless Horn) throughout Southeast Asia. In my book THE GIRL SUDAN PAINTED LIKE A GOLD RING, I have written another version of Akal Pelanduk and the Gergasi.

In the version from the Borneo Literature Bureau – Iban Animal Tales – there is the added interest of new leadership.

Here, the story started with the animals picking Badak (rhinoceros) as their *penghulu* (head) of the village. Badak suggested tuba fishing. Now an event like tuba fishing was basically a chance for the Iban (formerly known as Sea Dyaks) to celebrate. And here they are no doubt celebrating the accession of Badak as the head. Badak thought he had made a good choice, but he was to soon learn that he was mistaken.

The animals met at the *pengkalan* (jetty) and travelled to the Sungai Kara. Now tuba fishing was when a section of a river or stream was blocked off and tuba roots thrown into the water.

The tuba roots emitted a toxin, so the fish, unable to breathe, rose to the surface. They are then collected. The poison is harmless to humans.

The animals happily smoked the fish that they caught. The next day, Rusa and Babi were to *jaga* (look after or guard) the fish while the others went off for another day of tuba fishing.

At noon, Rusa and Babi heard a voice and discovered that this was a *gergasi* (giant) which they called *Antu Raya* (Ghost Big). The Antu Raya ate the *ikan salai* (smoked fish). The returning animals were unhappy to have lost everything. Nyumboh and Kera were to *jaga* (look after) the fish the next day. But again, the Antu Raya came. The third day, because no one wanted to jaga the fish, Badak eventually volunteered.

He failed miserably. And was derided by the animals, in particular Pelandok, which is the name given to the mousedeer in Borneo. In the end, Terkura and Pelandok volunteer. They collected rotan and sharpened their *pasak* (wedge). When the Antu Raya comes, they welcomed him, politely calling him *aki* (grandfather). They even offered the Antu Raya rest and fed him. This had never happened before.

Antu Raya noticed them sharpening the pasak and asked them what they were doing, even using the term *uchu* (grandchild). This meant that so far, their actions had caused the Antu Raya to trust them. The two confided that the sky was about to fall. Then they let slip that because the Antu Raya was so tall, it was most likely to fall first on his head.

So here, the story followed the predictable pattern, Terkura and Pilandok laid Antu Raya down. They bound his head with rotan then placed the pasak against the soft part of his skull. They knocked. The Antu Raya screamed. He was dead.

When the other animals returned, they were at first terrified, for they thought the Antu Raya is alive. Finally, they were convinced that the giant was dead. They divided the fish but here there was a twist to the normal tale.

The animals did not divide equally! The larger animals got a larger share. Pilandok and Terkura were upset because it was, they who killed the giant, but they were ignominiously threatened with death.

When the mean animals slept, Pilandok and Terkura covered their eyes with fish scales then called out that the enemy was coming.

Awakened rudely, the animals could not see. They stumbled into the river, and some are drowned.

So, unlike all the previous tales, this tale did not have a happy ending. The story continued, as now, Badak, unhappy that he had been shown to be incapable as a leader, sought revenge.

See Notes on Pages 339-340

Sucking the Pond

B ADAK CRAVED REVENGE.
After the incident in the prahu when Pelandok and Terkura covered their eyes with fish scales so that they could not see, the other animals were unhappy.

"Pelandok and Terkura tried to kill us," the animals said. For some of them had drowned when they fell into the river.

"I never knew they would attempt such a thing like that," said Badak, still smarting from his previous failure to jaga the fish. "Ruthless."

The other animals exchanged knowing glances. "We must kill them."

Badak nodded, his ego satisfied.

But Pelandok and Tekura had heard the animals plotting and they fled.

Pelandok found a clump of bamboo and hid within, while Tekura sank into the depths of a pond.

All around the clump of bamboo, fallen leaves lay on their side in the mud, flashing like sharpened knives. The ground looked like a *tukak* (bamboo trap).

Pelandok dared the other animals. "Come then. Kill me if you dare."

No, we dare not, thought Badak. He knew that if he attacked Pelandok and failed, the other animals would replace him as their leader. He could not afford another disaster. "No, we will not attack you. We will look for Tekura."

At those words, a chill ran down Pelandok's spine. He cocked his head as he thought. Tekura was his friend. No doubt Badak would not stop until he achieved his aim. But Pelandok had a plan.

Badak had said that he would not attack. Therefore, Pelandok knew that it would be safe for him to leave the clump of bamboo.

"Very well. I will show you where he is hiding," said Pelandok, smiling as if they were the best of friends. He led them to the pond.

"Here he is," said Pelandok, laughing, and pointed to the dank water. "I shall leave you to your devices."

"None of us can dive," said Badak, looking with dismay at the water depth. "There is only one thing to be done. We must drain the pond."

"Suck the water out?" said the other animals, impressed.

Badak nodded, pleased that his suggestion had elicited such praise.

The animals all began to drink. They drank and drank and drank.

Then…

"Oh, oh, oh!" said the animals. "We can only hold so much. We need to let the water out."

"But if we do that," said Badak, "then the pond will fill again."

"What can we do?" said the other animals, all looking to Badak for a solution.

"I have an idea," said Badak, after a while. "We will put a cork up our anus. That way, we can drink and drink and be able to hold every drop in."

All thought it was a great idea.

As the pond was small, and as there were many of them, the pond began to empty rapidly. To their happiness, they could see Tekura. He was swimming around the bottom.

"Catch him!" commanded Badak.

But before the animals could do so, Pelandok leapt. He kicked the cork that was lodged in Badak's *burit* (bottom).

At once, all the water that Badak had drunk came gushing out.

"Oh, oh, what have you done!" said Badak stamping his hoofs on the ground and sending mud everywhere.

"I was only trying to help," said Pelandok, feigning sadness. "I saw Terkura and jumped down to catch him, only I bumped against you and- and-"

"Do not worry. We can suck the pond dry again," said Badak, magnanimously.

So again, the animals sucked and sucked and sucked. But when the pond was almost dry once more, Pelandok jumped again and again knocked the cork out of Badak's burit.

"Oh dear!" said Badak, still believing that Pelandok was on their side. "This isn't working. There must be another way."

The other animals waited. They were tired and full of water.

"We need someone who can dive," said Badak eventually.

Now while all this was happening, the animals that lived in the surrounding forest had been watching the proceedings intently. None had dared say anything in case the wrath of the tired and water-logged animals turned against them, but now the *Menarat* (monitor lizard) spoke. It could dive.

"I can help."

"Oh, oh, Menarat is coming," said the tired and full of water animals. "Please catch Tekura for us."

"Yes, I will," said Menarat, and so saying, he dived into the water. He had a parang *ilang* (meaning unknown) in his hand.

Menarat found Tekura lying at the bottom of the pond. But as he approached, he began to have doubts.

Tekura's shell is hard. It is useless for me to attack.

And while he thought about what he could do, Tekura spoke.

"Hello, *punggal* (friend)," said Tekura. "What are you doing here with your parang ilang?"

"I am here on the orders of Badak to kill you," said Menarat politely.

Tekura was shocked. "But why? We have never quarrelled. We are friends."

"The other animals want you dead," said Menarat, which wasn't quite true, for the other animals simply wanted Tekura – dead or alive.

Tekura tried to reason. "You know my shell is too hard."

"That is true."

"It is the other animals, not you, who want me dead?"

"That is true."

"We have no quarrel."

"That is true," said Menarat. "But Badak instructed me to kill you. Do not try to sweet talk me out of carrying out my task. I must return with your head."

"Let me tell you a *cherita* (story)," said Tekura smiling. "We are all of one family – the animal family. As such we are brother and sister to each other. What family kills a member of its own family? Tell me. What family acts in such a manner? Should we not protect each other as we are meant to do?"

Menarak listened and was silent a long while. "What you say is true. But Badak will not believe me. You know him."

"I know," said Tekura, "which is why I have a solution."

Menarak listened eagerly.

"Hold out your parang ilang."

Menarak did so.

Tekura smeared the juice of the betel nut over the blade, plastering it bright red. Like blood.

"There! Now return and show Badak your parang ilang. He will think that you have stabbed and slain me."

The animals cheered when Menarak returned.

"Menarak is our hero! He has killed Tekura! Brilliant warrior!"

And Menarak swelled in pride.

Now that the animals had accomplished what they had set out to do, and their honour was restored, they returned home, each congratulating the other.

Badak was particularly happy as he had not lost face but gained in stature.

So busy was everyone as they gloated that no one saw Tekura climb slowly out of the pond.

Tekura went in search of Pilandok. He found the mousedeer lying on the ground.

His mouth was open, and flies had landed and were crawling on him. He looked dead. Very dead.

But Tekura was Pelandok's friend. He knew Pelandok too well. So, he kicked Pelandok on his burit. It was the sort of thing friends do to each other. Good friends. No animosity meant. "Eh!"

At once, Pelandok jumped up. "Oh, it is you!"

"Of course, it's me."

"Sambi, (Friend), I thought you were dead."

"Sambi, (Friend), I thought you were dead, too." Tekura laughed. "He couldn't touch me."
And he told Pelandok what he had done.

Laughing together, the two good friends wandered off in search of food.

See Notes on Page 340

Measuring the Distance of the Sky

At Bukit Rabong, the new Penghulu/Tuai (Head or leader) Badak had an *aum* (meeting).

> Now the term Rabong is believed to mean the zenith or the highest point. Hence the mountain is supposed to be directly below the upperworld i.e., the home of the gods.

BADAK INFORMED THE animals of their task. The animals were to measure the sky.

There was a problem, though.

"I cannot fly," said Badak.

The animals all looked at each other. Then a voice spoke.

"I will," said Kenyalang (Rhinoceros hornbill), looking noble, as was his bent.

For Kenyalang is a revered bird among the Iban. It is the messenger of Singalong Burong, their god of war. The Kenyalang is supposed to be able to reach the *Pintu Langgit* (the door of heaven) in the sky.

The animals were glad, for who else but the best could succeed in such an impossible task.

"I will need a friend," said Kenyalang, looking around.

"Who will go with him?" said Badak.

"We have no wings," said the animals.

"Do not worry about wings," said Badak, full of confidence. "We can make some."

"Ah, then I would like to go," said *Kera* (Monkey, probably a Baboon), hopping.

"We will need to test your voice," said Badak. "First Kenyalang. Sing!"

"Boom! ENG-gang, ENG-gang," said Kenyalang, forceful and strong. It made a series of *toop*ing sounds. The voice was deafening.

Loudness was power.

In those days, Nusantara was an auditory world. A world where sound ruled. The more thunderous, the more powerful.

This is what predators have always known. It is why the lion roars. The elephant trumpets. And the ape screams and beats its chest.

After Kenyalang, it was monkey's turn.

"Sing," said Badak.

"KA-chik," said Kera, then as loud as he could, "KEra-a-ah! Whoop! Whoop!"

But it was no use, he was not as loud as Kenyalang.

"I would like to go," said Pelandok.

"We will need to test your voice," said Badak. "First Kenyalang. Sing!"

"Boom! ENG-gang, enggang," said Kenyalang, again loud and strong as again it made a series of tooping sounds.

Then it was the mousedeer's turn.

"Sing," said Badak.

Now mousedeer are not known for making loud noises. They tend to only make a shrill cry when frightened.

"Po-uut, po-uut!" said Pelandok, then as loud as he could he bleated and barked, "Su-ut! Su-ut!" But it was no use.

"No," said the animals. "*Nadai.* (No.)"

They looked about. Beruang was seated in the front, but he was deaf and had not heard anything.

"Beruang!" the animals called, but Beruang was hard of hearing and did not answer.

"We will need to test your voice," said Badak. "First Kenyalang. Sing!"

And once more Kenyalang sang.

Then it was the bear's turn.

"Sing," said Badak.

But again, Beruang did not answer.

"Beruang, why didn't you sing?" said the animals, disappointed.

"*Apa?* (What?)" said Beruang. "What do you want?"

It took a while to explain to the bear what needed to be done. But Beruang was not interested.

"I am hungry. Unless the sky has honey, I do not wish to go."

The animals were angry with him, but they could not punish him for not listening to their Tuai, for it was well-known that Beruang was unable to hear.

And the Iban are very kind to those who are not neurotypical.

"Let Tekura try," the animals said eventually.

"We will need to test your voice," said Badak. "First Kenyalang. Sing!"

"Boom! Eng-gang, enggang," said Kenyalang, again loud and strong. "Toop! Toop!"

Then it was Tekura's turn.

"Sing," said Badak.

Tekura may not have been keen to go. After all, the sky was very high. But when your chief gives an order, you have no choice but to obey.

Now turtles, tortoises and terrapins may be among the slowest animals in the jungle, and they may appear silent, but they can make noise. In fact, some never stop chatting.

They make a series of clicks, croaks, and grunts. One species even sounds midway between a croak and a bark.

"Croak! Chaengki-ingkoook-liok!" said Tekura, then as loud as he could, "CHA-ANG-KI-ingko-Oo-ok-li-Oo-OOKok!"

It was deafening. Everyone was surprised.

"Excellent!" said Badak.

"Excellent!" said the animals and clapped. "We have found a friend who can go with Kenyalang.

They made Tekura wings out of the upih from a betel-nut tree and affixed them to his shell. Then they handed him a young green coconut. "Use this to spray your wings when you get too close to the sun. It should stop your wings from shrinking from the heat."

Tekura grabbed the coconut. "I am ready."

Kenyalang took off, followed by Tekura who was surprised that he could fly.

Higher and higher the two friends flew.

But no matter how high they soared, the top of the sky seemed to elude them, the blueness thinning away as they flew towards it.

Soon, it grew hotter.

They were now very close to the sun.

Hotter it grew. Heat pressed against Tekura's face, his head, and then-

"My wings!" said Tekura for he could feel his wings shrinking. Quickly, he sprayed the wings with water from the young green coconut.

Hiss!

But there was only so much coconut water, and so much expanse of wing.

The pair flew even higher.

Still, the ceiling of the sky vanished before them.

After a while…

"My wings!" said Tekura for he could feel his wings shrinking again. Quickly, he reached for the young, green coconut, only there was no water left.

"Oh! Oh! With no water, I will fall!" said Tekura, and he knew that Kenyalang could not help him.

Kenyalang only looked at him sadly.

Tekura fell.

Down and down, he went.

Poor Tekura!

Down and down! As he fell, he did the only thing that he could do, he wrapped himself in his upih wings for protection.

Until with a horrendous sound, he crashed into a sibau tree. When he opened his eyes eventually, he found himself stuck between two branches.

"Oh! Oh!" said Tekura. But there was nothing that he could do.

Neither could Kenyalang aid him, for he was still up in the sky.

Tekura waited.

Now the tree that he had fallen into was ripe with juicy red sibau fruit. And many of the animals knew that, so they visited the tree throughout the day.

When Terkura saw them coming, he knew at once that they would gossip. So, he looked down sternly at them as they approached.

The animals were surprised to see Tekura up the tree. "Sambi, what are you doing here?"

"Guarding the tree for Kenyalang," said Tekura, with a lift of his head as if this was none of their business. Which it wasn't. "This is his tree."

Hearing that, none of the animals dared take any fruit.

Tekura was able to save face.

But poor Tekura was still up in the tree.

How was he to come down?

Ah, for that you will need to read on…

Eating the Liver of the Earth

TEKURA SPENT DAYS wedged in that sibau tree. And although the fruit was red and ripe, he did not eat any, for as he had told the animals - the fruit belonged to Kenyalang. So, he grew thin. And weak.

Kenyalang never came. But then he was never meant to.

Instead, someone unexpected came. Beruang.

Ah, Beruang the bear, you see, was always hungry.

"Hai Sambi!" said Beruang.

"Hai Beruang!" said Tekura, suspicious.

"*Nama berita*? (Literally: Name news. What is going on here?)" said Beruang.

"*Nadai berita.* (No news)," Tekura pointed to the fruit with his chin. "This sibau tree belongs to Kenyalang, and as you can see, I am jaga."

"Let me have some," said Beruang. "I am hungry."

"No, you cannot. If I do, Kenyalang will be angry with me."

But Beruang did not care. All he cared about was being fed. He clambered up the sibau tree and grabbed hold of Tekura. "Hoi!" Then he tossed Tekura unceremoniously out of the tree.

Finally, thought Tekura, *I am out of that horrid tree.*

And that would have been the end of the story, only instead of landing on the ground, poor Tekura landed in a pit. And not just any pit, but a very deep pit.

Oh dear, thought Tekura. He was hungry, and weak and desperate to get away. Thankfully, as he nosed around the inside of the pit, he found some of the old coconut that he had dropped when he fell from the sky. He fell upon the coconut at once for he was famished.

But soon the coconut was devoured.

Now what? thought Tekura. Thankfully, some animals came by, including Pelandok.

"Hoi Sambi," said the animals. "What are you doing in there?"

Although he was desperate, it was far more important that Tekura did not lose face. "Looking for *atau tanah* (liver of the earth)."

That sounded important. And it was.

In the world of the predators, it is the organs of their prey that are most valued, starting with the liver, for it is full of nutrition.

The animals drooled. "Is it delicious?"

Tekura smacked his lips. "Yes. Very delicious."

Of course, now the animals all wanted *atau tanah* and so they jumped into the pit.

"How do we find it?" They nosed about eagerly.

"You need to dig."

And so, the animals dug and dug. Unfortunately, the pit got deeper and deeper and still no atau tanah.

Soon the animals realised their predicament.

"We are in a lot of trouble," said Badak.

"Yes, we are stuck down here," said Babi. "How do we get out?"

"If we climb upon each other, the smaller animal on top of the larger animal, we could form a pyramid," said Badak.

"That is a good idea," said the animals, and they did as Badak instructed.

With the bigger animals at the base of the structure, Pelandok and Tekura found themselves at the very top. At once, they jumped out of the pit.

"Make a ladder!" said Badak to the pair. "Hurry!"

"Yes, Tuai!" said Pelandok and Tekura before they raced off. But rescue was the last thing on their mind.

When they felt that they were far enough way, the two friends stopped.

"Let us not make that ladder," said Pelandok. "Look at you. You are much too thin and weak. You must have been up that sibau tree for days."

Tekura's mouth was so dry he could only croak in answer. "Yes, agreed. I was up there far too long. I must eat or die."

And so, the two friends went off in search of food.

Meanwhile, back inside the pit the other animals were getting anxious. They waited and waited, but neither Pelandok nor Tekura returned.

Snorting from time to time, Badak searched the skies. If the two did not return, it would look as if he was a failure. For when a chief gave a command it needed to be obeyed. What kind of chief would he be if no one heeded his instructions?

So Badak continued to fume.

Finally, it was obvious that Pelandok and Tekura were not coming back.

"Scrabble at the sides of the pit," said Badak, issuing an order. "When we get out, we will kill those two."

To his relief, the animals obeyed.

The animals dug away at the sides of the pit, thoughts of revenge burning through their minds. Soon they were able to clamber out. As they exited the pit, all they could think of was retribution.

"Kill them," said Babi. "Kill them."

When Pelandok and Tekura found out that the animals were looking for them, they fled.

Each had a plan, however. And it was time to put their plans into action. Thankfully, Tekura had been able to eat. He was going to need every bit of his newfound energy to survive.

Tekura hung himself from a hanging *unak* (thorn) while Pelandok squeezed between two Belian logs.

> The Belian tree – Eusideroxylon zwageri – also known Bornean ironwood. A tall, slow-growing tree with buttresses that give the base an elephant foot appearance, it has pale yellow flowers. But what it is treasured for is its wood – impervious to termites and lasting 100 years after being cut. It is a giant among trees.

Now, the Belian tree is greatly prized for its wood which the Sea Dyaks use to make their longhouses from Belian timber because it is like iron. Tough and strong.

Which was how the two friends had to be.

Pelandok and Tekura played their roles.

"Aiyoh!" Tekura whimpered, sounding to all the world as if he was sorely wounded.

"Ah, ah!" wept Pelandok, sounding to all the world as if he was close to death.

Would their tricks work?

Kera found Tekura first. "There is one of them!"

Scaling the tree, Kera made to pull him down, only Badak stopped him. "Stop! Can't you see that he is in pain."

"Oh!" said Kera. He dropped his paw. Then looked around unsure.

"Help me, please," said Tekura. "I am in so much pain."

"Lift him up off that thorn," said Badak kindly.

The animals did as Badak instructed.

"Set him free." Badak looked down magnanimously. He wanted everyone to think he was a kind leader.

"Thank you, Tuai! It is my good fortune that you arrived so swiftly or that would have been the end of me," said Tekura. "I was trying to pull down some rotan when I got caught on that nasty thorn."

Rotan? Ah, so Tekura had been trying to help. "Not at all," said Badak beaming, feeling the power in his words. "Now we need to find Pelandok."

The animals found Pelandok lying on the ground stuck between Belian logs. His eyes were closed, and flies were crawling on him.

Rusa and Babi made to roll the Belian logs on him when Badak stopped them.

"Stop! Can't you see that he is in pain."

"Oh!" said Rusa and Babi. Rusa held up her hoof while Babi held back his. They exchanged a nervous glance.

"Help me, please," said Pelandok. "I am in so much pain."

"Lift the logs off him," said Badak kindly.

The animals did as Badak instructed. They took care as they lifted the logs off Pelandok.

"Thank you, Tuai! My good fortune for you to arrive in time or I would have been done for," said Pelandok. "I was cutting down some logs, when they rolled on top of me."

Ah, so Pelandok was trying to help. "Not at all," said Badak, overcome with his own generosity. "We are out of the pit, let us go home. For the day is almost over, and all is well."

Thanks to the ruses that the pair had played, the animals truly believed that Pelandok and Tekura had been trying to help. The animals believed that they understood the truth and went their separate ways, happy in the knowledge that they had not lost face.

Pelandok and Tekura, too.

They were happier than anyone else.

They had not lost face. Or anything else.

The End of Beruang

THE TROUBLE STARTED when Tekura and Beruang decided to build a two-door longhouse. Their aim was to live together. The longhouse was built in a few days, and when it was done, the two friends moved in.

Beruang was lying on the *ruai* (verandah) when he saw Tekura enter the jungle. "What are you doing, Sambi?

"Looking for food, of course. It is good that we have shelter, but there is no food," said Tekura, looking back over his shell.

"Why not plant some *pisang* (banana) plants around the house," said Beruang. "That way we will always have food nearby."

Tekura thought this was a good idea, so the two went off to collect banana suckers.

Now banana suckers are called pups, and the small ones are buttons. The pair made sure that the pups had plenty of roots and narrow leaves. They dug holes around their longhouse and planted the pups.

It was the tropics, so the banana pups flourished.

While Beruang watched the pisang plants grow taller, Tekura tended to his pups diligently.

Soon Beruang grew hungry. He decided to uproot and eat his. A short time later, he had devoured all that he had planted. But he was still hungry.

He watched Tekura's plants as they grew. The plants developed flowers. Banana blossoms are reddish-purple with tear-drop leaves. They emit an aromatic perfume.

Beruang swooned at the delicious smells that foretold of future feasting. Watered and tended, Tekura's pisang plants flourished. The tiny green fingers turned into dark green fruit. Then the dark green gave way to a light green and then a custardy yellow. Soon the pisang was almost ripe.

"Sambi," said Beruang, his voice husky. "Your pisang is almost ripe. Let me harvest them for us."

"No," said Tekura, sounding as stern as he could. "These are my pisang plants. I will harvest them when the time is right."

"I do not care who these plants belong to. When they are ripe, *I* will harvest them."

Beruang's words were ominous, but what could Tekura do? He continued his tending while Beruang sat underneath the pisang plants and waited.

Then one day, the pisang was ripe.

Beruang could wait no longer. The sweet smell was driving him insane. His stomach, empty so long, was making angry noises.

Although banana plants look like trees, they have no true trunk. They are plants, despite their height.

Beruang scaled the plants and plucked the pisang. He ate and ate and ate.

Tekura heard the racket. He came out of the longhouse. When he saw what Beruang was doing, he grew angry. "What do you think you are doing, eh, Sambi?"

"Why do you ask? Can you not see what I am doing? I can climb. I have climbed your pisang plants and I am eating the pisang. There!" And Beruang threw the skins onto poor Tekura.

Down below, covered in banana peels, poor Tekura wept. All his hard work for nothing.

Now banana peels are edible. Some cooks use them in banana cakes. But that was not what Tekura had put in all his hard work for.

Meanwhile, there was Beruang, caring nothing but to fill his stomach.

Tekura crept back into the longhouse. He needed to think. He said nothing when Beruang returned.

Beruang, thinking that he had gotten away with his theft, pretended that all was well.

And for a few days it was as if nothing had happened.

"Let us search for food," said Tekura after a while.

Beruang said nothing but he placidly followed Tekura out.

The pair were wandering around in the jungle when Tekura climbed up a tree. He hung himself on an unak thorn. The thorn was long and sharp.

Tekura began to swing. Back and forth. Back and forth. Then suddenly he called out. "Ah, ah! I can see *Apai* (Father) and *Indai* (Mother) in Hades."

Now the Sea Dyaks call the afterlife Hades. But it is not the Christian approximation of Hell with fire and brimstone. Instead, it is a land just like the world that the Sea Dyaks have left, and where the Sea Dyaks fully expect to go on doing the same things that they have done while living i.e., fishing and hunting and farming.

Beruang was startled at Tekura's discovery.

How was that possible? He had never heard of anyone being able to see into the next world.

"How is it that you can see into Hades?"

"I am seeing them now because I am swinging on this unak." Tekura continued. "Why, Indai is wearing a *tanggui seraung* (type of hat). And Apai is wearing a *Baju Burung...*"

Beruang's jaw dropped.

A *Baju Burong* was a bird jacket that allowed the wearer to fly. This was incredible!

Of course, he wanted to check if his parents had the same things as Tekura's parents.

"I want to see. I want to see my parents. Let me swing from your unak."

"No. This is mine, not yours. Besides if my apai and my indai see you, why, they will run away."

Beruang continued to plead.

"It is dangerous. You might fall."

"I am willing to take that risk."

Tekura pretended to consider. "Well, as you say, you can climb. Who am I then to stop you? But do not blame me if anything happens to you."

"I will not fall. I am a bear."

"Very well then, if that is your wish."

"It is."

Beruang climbed up to where Tekura swung.

"Hang on to this. Here is an unak. See how I have fixed it in your *burrit*." Tekura pushed and shoved the unak into Beruang's bottom.

The unak was long and sharp, but Beruang did not complain. If Tekura could do this, so could he. He was willing to bear a little pain if he could see his apai and his indai again. How he had missed them.

Sea Dyaks are a very close-knit family. And children are adored.

"Can you see your apai and your indai?"

"No, not yet."

"Let me help. Perhaps if I pushed this unak in further." And so, saying Tekura shoved the unak in deeper.

Beruang gritted his teeth, but he was desperate to see his apai and his indai.

"Can you see them?"

"No, not yet."

"Ah, I remember. You need to swing on the unak. Let me help you," said Tekura.

"Yes, please."

"Ready?"

"Yes, ready."

The thorn was long and sharp. The pain was excruciating as Tekura pushed the unak even deeper in, and then he swung Beruang.

Back and forth.

To and fro.

High and low.

"Can you see your apai and your indai now?"

But there was no answer.

Beruang was dead.

Oh dear!

Tekura was sad when he discovered that Beruang was dead.

But he stole my pisang. He was mean to me.

For a long time Tekura lived alone in the two-door longhouse.

Then one day, Pelandok came along.

"Can I stay with you?" said Pelandok.

"Certainly," said Tekura.

And so, the two friends lived together in the longhouse. They worked together, they planted together, and they harvested together.

And that is how it should be between friends.

And that was how the story ended.

See Notes on Page 341

The King's Chilli

TORTOISE AND MOUSEDEER are friends. They even live together in a longhouse and plant fruit and vegetables in their garden.

One day Monkey came for a visit.

"I am so hungry," said Monkey.

The two kind animals fed Monkey at once. This is what Southeast Asians do. They look after their friends.

Now Terkura and Kancil gave Monkey some of every fruit and vegetable in their garden except one: the chilli.

Chilli peppers are also known as chilli and are the berry fruit of the capsicum. They do a very important task and that is to give 'heat' to food. This is caused by capsaicinoids when ingested. Chilli was introduced to Southeast Asia by the Portuguese and Spanish who obtained them from Central and South America. In some cases, chillis are even used as medicine.

To the uninitiated, chillis are terribly hot and will cause a burning sensation when eaten that is not easily removed. Cold water doesn't work. I speak from experience.

At first Monkey said nothing. He was too busy gobbling. He was so hungry.

But when his hunger pangs eased and he began to look around, he spotted some pretty plants with bright red shiny fruit.

"*Apa tu?* (What are those?)"

"Chilli," said Terkura kindly.

"I want some."

"No, you don't," said Kancil quickly. "They are the king's fruit."

Well, that was the wrong thing to say.

As soon as the words were spoken, Monyet plucked half a dozen fruit and popped them into his mouth.

Terkura gasped, but he was too slow to stop him.

Monkey bit down hard and chewed.

Fire exploded into his mouth!

"Oh! Oh!" gasped Monkey, and he spat the fruit out at once. Sadly, that didn't work.

The burning did not ease.

Instead, it intensified. The chilli had brushed against the soft passages of the mouth, inflaming them. It was as if the flames within were being stoked. Nothing could put out the burning sensation.

"I have eaten fire," wept poor Monkey. "Ah! My mouth!"

The animals tried to help but nothing worked.

The chillis had done what they were programmed to do: release heat.

The tender palate of Monyet experienced extreme stinging. It made no difference whether he jumped around or vomited or rubbed grass over his very sore and very tender tongue. Nothing could ease the pain.

Nothing except time.

And so, weeping and sobbing and rolling around on the grass, poor Monyet learnt his lesson.

The two friends also learnt their lesson.

They learnt that they could no longer trust Monyet. This meant that he was no longer their friend.

It is sad when a friendship breaks up.

But sometimes there is no choice.

Chilli Cakes

TIGER IS ALWAYS out to get Mousedeer.

But this morning Tiger finds Mousedeer.

At once Mousedeer flees.

Oh, Kancil! Run!

He tries to elude Tiger, but Tiger seems to know what Kancil is thinking. Each time Kancil swerves left or right, Tiger is there.

Oh no!

In the end, Kancil realises that he is being herded towards the river.

Buaya lives in the river. What is Kancil to do?

As he thinks, Kancil suddenly remembers he has cakes in his possession.

Naturally, the cakes had slipped his mind because he was being chased. When you are being chased there is little room for anything else except where to run.

"You must be very hungry, Sang Harimau, to lead me on such a chase today," says Sang Kancil politely.

It is hard to speak politely when you are being chased.

"I am always hungry," says Tiger puffing hard.

It is also hard to speak politely when you are in pursuit.

"I have some cakes that you may have."

In other words, eat them and leave me alone.

But Tiger knows what Kancil is planning. "I want the cakes *and* you!" said Tiger.

How rude! What is Kancil to do?

As he thinks hard, something unexpected happens.

A wave of water slams over the two animals.

Mousedeer looks up and blinks in shock.

Tiger gasps as his feet slide about. He too, looks up in astonishment.

Buaya has joined the fray. He has also overheard the conversation. "I will have Kancil and the cakes!" he says very politely.

It is easy to speak politely when you are only watching.

How is it possible that in a split-second things have changed so quickly? For the worse! But that is life in the jungle.

Sigh.

Harimau and Kancil change direction.

Kancil has a plan.

"Here are the cakes!" Kancil tosses the cakes as he doubles back.

Tiger is stunned but he manages to turn and open his mouth at the same time. To his delight, the cakes topple into his mouth. He can smell the wild honey and the eggs!

Yum! Yum!

Tiger's eyes half close in ecstasy!

But there is another aroma! Something familiar only… what?

Chasing is hard work. This backtracking and high-speed chase has taken all of Tiger's brain power and there is little left to ponder. Automatically, his powerful jaws close on this sweet treat.

Tiger swallows. But a moment later, a fire explodes along his tongue down into his gullet.

Roar!

It is a volcano!

Earth-shattering fire!

Red, hot fiery chilli that leaves its lingering unmistakable touch wherever it goes.

Tiger's eyes flood with tears.

Tiger wants to explode. He is in so much pain. One or two chillis he can handle, but Kancil has loaded these cakes with handfuls of the explosive red fruit.

Shiny red daggers.

Tiny, shiny red daggers.

Chilli padi.

The smaller, the hotter.

Cutting and slicing Tiger's insides with fire!

I wonder why Kancil did that.

Was he really expecting to eat those cakes himself.

Or did he know that he would be chased.

With Kancil, you never know.

In agony, Tiger races after the trickster.

Kancil is not giving up.

He swerves back and forth until he nears the river.

Tiger is in too much agony to pay attention to where they are headed.

Kancil jumps just as Tiger leaps after him. Tiger lunges forward, jaws snapping just as Kancil twists in midair and lands safely.

Back on the land.

Meanwhile, Tiger still in agony is not quite as fast.

He tries to twist but lands heavily in the water.

Where Crocodile is waiting.

Crocodile is king of the water.

"What are you doing?" Tiger spits out as jaws enclose him. "I am the king of the land!"

"And I am the king of the water!"

"Stop!"

What is Buaya to do?

Then a voice calls from the shore.

The two kings spot the mousedeer.

"Buaya! Eat him! He is far bigger a meal than me!" says Kancil.

And that is true.

So that is the end of Tiger.

Or is it?

Full of Beans

Mousedeer always thinks he is right.
He is full of beans.
As much as I love Mousedeer, we all know what happens to those who think this way…

ONE DAY MOUSEDEER was so full of himself that he decided to have a competition.

"I will give a bag of beans to any animal who can catch me," said Mousedeer.

He knew that he was the fastest animal in King Solomon's jungle and so he was assured that no animal could catch him.

Cheeky mousedeer! Boaster-cock!

Pig decided to try.

Pig was always hungry, and Pig liked food. Pig was also intelligent, and so he knew that he would have to trick mousedeer in order to catch him. This was what Pig did.

Pig placed some ripe bananas outside Mousedeer's house.

Not just any old bananas but *pisang raja*! the king of bananas.

Pisang raja is the most delectable banana with unparalleled sweetness and oh so custardy creamy! They are used for *goreng pisang* (banana fritters.)

The bananas were a golden yellow with little brown spots. This meant that they were just ripe. Ripe bananas emit a lovely, sweet aroma and so of course Mousedeer soon smelt them.

He looked outside to see where the fragrance was coming from and at once spotted the bananas. Pisang raja! But that was not all that Mousedeer noticed. He also saw the tracks that Pig had left behind.

"Oh Babi! I see the pisang, thank you very much. But I also see your tracks. You are clever, but not clever enough to catch me. Sorry, but no bag of beans for you."

Pig was sad, but he ate the pisang raja and so cheered up a little.

Next, Monkey tried.

Like Pig, Monkey was always hungry, and Monkey liked food. And just like Pig, Monkey was also intelligent.

He had a plan.

He wasn't going to use food. Or at least not the way you and I would think.

Monkey tied his dog and his goat in front of mousedeer's house. But then he placed rice and grass in front of the two animals. Only instead of putting the rice in front of the dog and the grass in front of the goat, he put the wrong food before each animal. Then he climbed a tree and went to sleep.

As well as Pig and Monkey being hungry, so were the dog and the goat.

Newly plucked grass emits a strong fragrance, while newly cooked rice emits a sweet, succulent aroma that makes you salivate. Just like I am now. And I hope you are, too.

Southeast Asians all love rice. It is our staple food.

Soon, the dog started barking. It was hungry.

That set the goat off, and he started bleating. It was hungry, too.

Of course, in the middle of all this racket, Mousedeer stuck his head out.

"Hello, 'Nyet! What are you doing with your Anjing and your Kambing? Can't you hear them making such a noise?"

Monkey opened his eyes. "Morning, 'Cil, how are you today? My animals are only a little hungry, but please do not worry. I have placed food before them."

"Oh Nyet, can't you see? You have grass before the dog and rice before the goat. No wonder your animals are crying out! You need to swap them immediately."

"Oh, thank you for your kind concern, 'Cil, but there is no mistake. I have rice for my goat and grass for my dog. All is as it should be." So, saying, Monkey closed his eyes and went back to sleep.

In the meantime, the dog and the goat were getting hungrier. Dog barked louder. Goat bleated louder.

And Mousedeer could get no peace. He stuck his head out once more.

"Hey Nyet! *Bising sekali*! I think it might be an idea if you swapped the food. Or swapped the animals. Either way, I think that might be the solution to your problem."

"To what problem?" Monkey huffed and then went back to sleep again.

Mousedeer was getting a headache.

He had not wanted to say straight out that Monkey had made a mistake. That would cause Monkey to lose face.

But there had to be something that could be done. And then Mousedeer knew.

All I must do is swap the food. Monkey is asleep, so he will never know. With the right food in front of each animal, the food will be eaten, and so the evidence devoured. Monkey will never know what I have done.

Quick as he could, Mousedeer snuck out of his house. Quick as he could, Mousedeer swapped the food. Then quick as he could, oh, but not so quick, because Mousedeer being Mousedeer always must stop to admire his handiwork.

It was a mistake.

Because quick as he could, Monkey caught Mousedeer!

"Oh 'Nyet! What are you doing?"

"Waiting for my bag of beans."

And then of course, Mousedeer laughed. And so did Monkey. Mousedeer gave Monkey the bag of beans as promised, and all was well.

That is until the next time another trick was played.

But for now, the dog and the goat were happy.

And Monkey.

And so was Mousedeer. He admired a good trick.

But then he is the king of tricksters!

The New Creature

A NEW CREATURE entered the jungle one day.

Mousedeer heard him first. *What a strange noise.* Mousedeer went closer to investigate.

It walks on two legs like Kera and Burung. But has no wings. Though it sings like a bird. It has some… fur.

Mousedeer took off, racing as fast as its pencil thin legs could carry it. He had to find the other animals.

The others were interested but they were cautious.

"On which side are its eyes?" said Tiger frowning.

That was a very important question as you will see.

"In the front," said Mousedeer and swallowed.

The animals all nodded grimly.

This was a predator, for front facing eyes gave predators the ability to focus on prey. This was not good news.

"Can it fly?" asked Tiger.

Mousedeer shook its head. "No wings."

The animals all sighed in relief. At least the new predator could not spot them from above. No aerial advantage. That was something.

"You will need to investigate further," said Tiger.

"What? Why can't you go?" said Mousedeer. "I have done my part by bringing news of this new predator."

"Because I say so and because I am the King of the Jungle."

Mousedeer went back to investigate. The creature had a bag on its back.

As Mousedeer crept closer, he smelt a familiar smell.

Kerbau (Water Buffalo).

The bag was made from Kerbau's hide.

A frisson of fear went down Mousedeer back. He went back and reported what he had found.

The animals all looked at each other worriedly. If this predator could carry Kerbau's hide on his back, what other animals could it attack? Skin?

"There is no alternative, but you must return once more," said Harimau. And when Mousedeer opened his mouth to protest, he added quickly, "do it as a citizen of the jungle. For all of us."

Mousedeer shut his mouth and took off.

This time, from a secluded spot he watched as the new creature removed a box that contained little sticks from his pack. The creature struck one of the little sticks, and fire suddenly sprang from the tip of the tiny stick.

The aroma of smoke wafted over. Burning. It was unmistakable. Fire.

Mousedeer took off at once.

"It has fire at the end of the stick," he reported.

The animals all shivered. Their fear was palpable. Fire was capable of great destruction. And now there was an animal that could make it!

"Mousedeer, you will not like what I am going to ask, but you must go back and find out more about the new predator."

Mousedeer stamped his hoof. "I have seen the new predator three times already, while none of you have even seen it once. I have done my fair share."

"But that is only because of your size," said Babi condescendingly.

"Yes, that is true. If we were to go, why that new predator would spot us at once," said Beruang, a smug smile on its hairy face.

Mousedeer shivered but it was not from fear. In agitation, he whipped his tail in a circle.

"Listen, this is what I will do," said Harimau. "I will roar my loudest if there is trouble. How about that?"

Mousedeer shook his head and again stamped his feet, and that looked to be the end of the matter until Terkura spoke up. "I will go with Mousedeer. He is my friend."

The other animals all looked gratefully at Terkura. Especially Mousedeer.

"You see, if such a small animal can go, what are you afraid of?"

Mousedeer said nothing, but he and Terkura set off towards the new predator.

Trot-trot.

Crawl-crawl.

Neither were in a hurry. If the predator was gone by the time they reached the area, they did not plan to search for it.

But the new predator was still there.

He had had a nap and was now puffing stinking clouds from his mouth.

The unfamiliar stench of nicotine reached the animals' noses. They wrinkled up their noses in disgust. *What a horrid smell.*

The stench made the animals' throats raw.

The man, for it was the first human that Mousedeer and Tortoise had ever seen, reached into his leather bag, and pulled out a towel to dab away his sweat.

His perspiration smelt sour, with the tang of onions.

So, this is the creature's scent.

The pair exchanged a knowing glance.

They noted how the towel was striped: purple, and red and blue and green.

How strange that the animal could change its skin.

Next, the animal pulled a water bottle from his pack and drank.

The scent of stale water reached the pair.

Mousedeer smacked his lips.

Nervous, Terkura eyed Mousedeer. How long should they watch? He was itching to get away.

Kancil was about to reply when the man pulled a long stick from the ground.

The pair watched, mesmerised. They felt that something momentous was about to happen. And they were right.

The man lifted the long, black stick to his shoulder-

Bang!

The gun thundered.

It was as if their hearts had exploded from within.

The acrid scent of smoke and sulphur and metal polluted the air as both animals darted off as fast as they could back to the others.

Mousedeer reached the other animals first.

"He carries the clouds in his mouth," said Mousedeer, describing the smoke from the cigarettes.

The animals stared at the ominous words.

"And the rainbow, too," said Terkura, describing the towel.

The animals shook their heads, unable to believe the horror that was unfolding.

"He has taken our water."

The animals began to moan. "We are doomed," they cried.

"But worst of all, he carries thunder in a stick."

Thunder!

This was the way the ancient Malays believed their gods spoke.

Was this creature a god?

"It cannot be true," said Harimau.

"But it is true," said Terkura crawling into the centre. Tears stained his cheeks brown.

Numb, the animals all parted to allow the weary tortoise into their midst.

"Feed them. Water them," said Harimau softly. "They have done all this for us."

And so, because of the kindness that the other animals showed. Terkura and Mousedeer agreed to go back. One last time.

By now, the sun had set.

In the blackness of night, under the dense jungle canopy, the pair returned.

"At least we won't be seen," said Terkura, trying to sound hopeful.

Kancil nodded, tight-lipped.

Imagine then their shock when, as they neared, they saw a ray of yellow light slanting about the trees.

Whatever the ray of light touched, it lit up.

It was the man using his torch. But the animals did not know that.

"The sun," gasped Mousedeer, stunned.

"He has the sun!" wept Terkura.

How powerful was this new beast? What chance did they stand against it?

It had to be a god.

But why had it come? What wrong had they committed?

Without a word — for what was there to say? - the pair raced back.

The animals heard them coming from a long distance away and knew from the sounds of their flight that the news was not good. Still, they were aghast at the latest discovery.

"Can it be true?" said Harimau.

"It is true," said Terkura panting. "We saw it with our own eyes."

The animals all huddled together as the night grew darker.

"The creature has taken the sun from our sky."

"With no sun nothing will grow."

"We will perish."

"The creature has taken the water from our rivers."

"With no river nothing will grow."

"We will perish."

"The creature has taken the clouds from our sky."

"With no clouds nothing will grow."

"We will perish."

"The creature has taken the rain from our sky."

"With no rain nothing will grow."

"We will perish."

Teeth chattered.

Heads drooped.

Shoulders hunched.

The animals lay down together, comforting one another.

The night grew darker.

So dark that no one could see a thing. The night was silent.

The black grew colder.

Everyone shivered.

No sun.

No rain.

No clouds.

No water.

All was quiet.

The darkness shivered a bit.

Eyes blinked.

Were they mistaken?

But no for even as they watched… Black turned into grey.

"I- I think I can see my whiskers," whispered Tiger, awed.

Eyes were rubbed.

In the haziness of early dawn mist, the animals gazed through tired eyes. For none had slept.

But the darkness was dissipating.

The animals turned their heads from side to side. They could see each other's pale faces! Oh!

Then they leapt to their feet. All except Terkura, but he leapt in his heart.

"The clouds are back!" the animals cheered. For a heavy mist covered the ground, blurring everything white.

And as they watched, a faint line of gold gleamed in the horizon.

"The sun is back!"

And as they watched, a rain cloud drizzled faint drops of water on them painting their faces wet.

Their hearts beat.

"It has all come back!" said Tiger with an astonished growl.

"The creature has given these things back to us," said Mousedeer stunned.

"Why?" said Tiger, his voice heavy with foreboding.

"I do not know." Mousedeer shook his head. His voice was a whisper. "Perhaps in exchange for something else."

"What does he want?" echoed the animals.

Wordlessly, they stared at each other, their hearts heavy.

Section 2-Menteri belukar = vizier of the underwood or brush

In this section, you will find stories of Sang Kancil in the service of King Solomon or else as his judge – Salaam di Rimba (Peacekeeper of the Jungle.) Also, as Chief War Dancer.

I have also included tales of King Solomon's treasures – his flute, gong, belt etc.

Here you will also find other animals who have been given titles by King Solomon.

And war.

Warfare, according to Godinho de Eredia's DESCRIPTION OF MALACCA in 1613, was in the form of an ambush along a narrow path or thicket. This is probably why Kancil often uses this method of attack.

Poison is also used, especially in blowpipes. The Sea Dyaks were well-known to have constructed palisades. Many mousedeer stories talk of traps with pointed sticks at the bottom. These traps were covered with branches.

Writing these stories, I had no idea that the mousedeer's defences were taken from real life.

Who killed the Otter's babies?

*M*EMERANG (OTTER) SAID to Sang Kancil one day, "*Kawan* (Friend) Kancil, could you *jaga* (watch) my children? I am going to fish, and when I come back, I shall share my catch with you."

Sang Kancil agreed and so Memerang went off to the river for a day of fishing.

But Mousedeer was the Chief Dancer of the War Dance and whenever the War Gong was beaten it was his duty to dance.

War Gongs were only beaten in times of great need to summon help during war.

So, when the *Kutok* (Woodpecker) sounded the War Gong, Sang Kancil had no choice but to dance.

Kelentang. Kelentang. Kelentang.

At once, Kancil broke out into a twelve-step Silat move.

And while he danced, his hooves stomping here and there, he trod upon the Otter babies and squashed them flat.

Hours later when Otter returned, bringing with him a string of fish, he found to his horror that his babies were dead.

"Sang Kancil, what have you done?" wept the distraught father.

"It is not my fault but Kawan Kutok's," said Sang Kancil by way of explanation. "As you know, Kutok is one of the Omen Birds, and when they call out, we have no choice but to listen and obey. So, when Kutok beat the gong, I had no option but to dance. And when I danced, I forgot all but the dance itself, and in my forgetfulness, I trampled upon your children."

Memerang knew that what Sang Kancil said was true, but he was a father and he wanted vengeance, so Memerang sought an audience with King Solomon.

Prostrating himself before the king, Memerang addressed the mighty monarch. "Pardon your Majesty's most humble slave for appearing before you in this fashion, but Kawan Kancil has murdered your slave's children, and your slave craves to know if Friend Kancil is guilty, according to the *adat* (Law of the Land)."

"If Kawan Kancil has done the thing that you have said he has done, and done so wittingly, then he is indeed worthy of death."

And so, King Solomon summoned Sang Kancil before his throne.

When Sang Kancil entered the palace, he made obeisance before the great king. "Oh, Mighty King Solomon, to hear is to obey. You have commanded your slave to appear before you, and so here I am as you commanded."

"Kawan Memerang has brought a complaint against you." Then turning to the Otter, King Solomon directed. "Relate your charge."

"Your slave accuses Sang Kancil of the murder of my children and your slave wishes Sang Kancil to be brought to justice according to the adat (Law of the Land.)"

"Is this true? Was it through your doing that the Memerang's children were killed?"

"I crave pardon, but it is true, Mighty King Solomon. Your slave did trample upon the Otter's children."

"How did this come about?"

"When Kutok sounded the War Gong, your slave had no alternative but to dance."

"That is true. There is no fault to be found," said King Solomon. "And you are my Chief Dancer." So, King Solomon summoned Kutok.

When Kutok entered the palace, he made obeisance before the great king. "Oh, Mighty King Solomon, to hear is to obey. You have commanded your slave to appear before you, and so here I am as you commanded."

"Did you sound the War Gong?"

"Yes, I did. Your slave sounded the War Gong when he saw the Great Lizard wearing his sword," said Kutok.

So, King Solomon summoned the Great Lizard.

When the Great Lizard entered the palace, he made obeisance before the great king. "Oh, Mighty King Solomon, to hear is to obey. You have commanded your slave to appear before you, and so here I am as you commanded."

"Did you wear your sword?"

"Yes, I did. Your slave wore his sword when he saw Tortoise don his coat of mail," said the Great Lizard.

So, King Solomon summoned Tortoise.

When Tortoise entered the palace, he made obeisance before the great king. "Oh, Mighty King Solomon, to hear is to obey. You have commanded your slave to appear before you, and so here I am as you commanded."

"Did you don your coat of mail?"

"Yes, I did. Your slave donned his coat of mail when he saw the King Crab trailing his three-edged pike," said Tortoise.

So, King Solomon summoned the King Crab.

When King Crab entered the palace, he made obeisance before the great king. "Oh, Mighty King Solomon, to hear is to obey. You have commanded your slave to appear before you, and so here I am as you commanded."

"Did you trail your three-edged pike?"

"Yes, I did. Your slave trailed his three-edged pike when he saw Crayfish shoulder his lance," said King Crab.

So, King Solomon summoned Crayfish.

When Crayfish entered the palace, he made obeisance before the great king. "Oh, Mighty King Solomon, to hear is to obey. You have commanded your slave to appear before you, and so here I am as you commanded."

"Did you shoulder your lance?"

"Yes, I did. Your slave shouldered his lance when he saw Memerang coming down to devour your slave's own children," said Crayfish.

"If that is the case, then you, Memerang, are the guilty party," said King Solomon. "Your complaint does not hold up against the adat. Sang Kancil is innocent."

And so, saying, King Solomon dismissed the case.

See Notes on Page 342

The Magic Flute

S ANG HARIMAU (REVERED TIGER) was chasing Sang Kancil (Revered Mousedeer) through the jungle. As the mousedeer ran for his life, his deep brown eyes searched desperately for an escape route. But there was none.

"Oh, oh," thought Sang Kancil. "Sang Harimau has almost caught up to me and I am tiring."

"I am going to eat you, stupid fool!" roared Sang Harimau.

And it did look as if this would be the end of the Kancil. He could literally feel the tiger's hot breath on his tail.

Just at that moment, however, the wind blew, lifting the most lilting music to Sang Kancil's ears. His eyes rounded as an idea came to mind.

"Hear that wondrous music, Sang Harimau?" said Sang Kancil as he continued to spring for his life.

Sang Harimau slowed to hear better. He cocked his ears. "Where is that coming from?" he asked, curiosity getting the better of him. Besides, he could see that even his prey had slowed.

To the tiger's complete surprise, Sang Kancil had indeed halted.

The chevrotain was standing in a grove of bamboo from whence the most delightful strains originated. He almost appeared to be waiting for the tiger to catch up, his head bobbing along to the melody.

But surely that could not be the case?

"Did you not know Sang Harimau, that this is a magic flute?" said Kancil, his brown eyes limpid with desire as he stared at the tall yellow and green stalks.

"A flute? What is that?" asked the inquisitive tiger, pushing forward his snout, his whiskers twitching to sense the ethereal vibrations in the air.

"Why a flute is a musical instrument. Only the very cleverest and the very best learn how to make music on such a device."

And that must be true for the mousedeer's whole body quivered with delight as he listened.

Even Tiger was charmed.

"Cleverest? Best?"

"Even better," said Sang Kancil. "Listen." The mousedeer pushed forward his head and stuck his pink tongue between two long poles of bamboo just as the wind lifted.

At that moment, the most refreshing melody played.

To Sang Harimau's disbelieving eyes, it appeared as if the creature was performing a tune.

Music contains the ability to lift spirits, and even Sang Harimau found himself thrumming as he listened to those delicate notes.

When Sang Kancil finished, he turned to the tiger and whispered as if sharing a great secret, "Whoever masters this flute will be healthy forever."

Healthy forever? Was this why he had always been unable to catch that foolish chevrotain?

Sang Harimau snarled. "Teach me at once, fool."

"Certainly," said Sang Kancil in the most obedient of tones. "It is so simple. You only need to put your tongue between these two poles just as I did earlier." Again, he demonstrated with his tiny pink tongue.

Once more, the most delicious melody emanated from the bamboo grove.

Again, envy ate at the enormous predator.

"Move aside," said Sang Harimau gruffly. "I do not wish for you to get all the benefits."

"Of course, I understand," said Sang Kancil, hastily moving to the side.

In great anticipation, Sang Harimau stood in the place of the mousedeer. He leaned his great big head forward, opened his great big mouth and then he poked out his great big tongue.

His rough, raspy, red tongue.

Sang Kancil pricked his ears up. "Ready?"

A frisson of excitement rose in Sang Harimau's chest. He swallowed.

"Ready, ready," whispered Sang Kancil, his body quivering with anticipation.

"Yes!" hissed Tiger.

And at that very moment, the wind rose again.

"Blow!" shouted the mousedeer.

The air between the poles of bamboo moved, repeatedly the poles clicked together as the tiger blew, only this time-

"Argh!" screamed the foolish tiger for the moving poles had pinched the great big rough tongue of Sang Harimau.

The rough, raspy tender tongue.

No music rose, or if it did it was drowned in the screams of pain emitted from the tricked beast.

Laughing merrily at the tongue-trapped tiger, Sang Kancil escaped. Again.

See Notes on Page 342

The King of the Tigers is sick

DULU-DULU (ONCE UPON A TIME), the Great King of All the Tigers fell prey to a mysterious ailment. Although all the *bomohs* (witch doctors) were summoned, none knew of any remedy to cure him. The king grew sicker and sicker.

The Tiger *Raja Mudah* (Crown Prince) entered the king's presence and made obeisance. "If my Lord would taste the flesh of every beast of the jungle perhaps the cure lies therein."

And so, the Great King commanded the Raja Mudah to summon every kind of beast into his presence. Only Sang Kancil, the mousedeer, refused to obey. And when he learnt of the fate of his friends, he knew he had been correct to do so.

But soon the Great King learnt of the disobedience of the mousedeer, and his wrath was kindled. Before long, Sang Kancil found himself summoned once more to appear before the throne.

When the Wise One turned up at the palace, he found the Great King pacing, his long orange and black tail lashing in anger. The Great Tiger's ears were twisted back, his eyes wide, his whiskers quivering as if already tasting flesh.

Sang Kancil approached and bowed, then looked up.

The Tiger King's pupils were black dots in swirling yellow balls.

"Why did you not attend when commanded? All my subjects appeared except you," roared the Great King.

"Because of a dream," came the faint answer.

"A dream?" The Great King cocked his head, his wrath partially subsided, for dreams were mysterious messages from the Land of the Dead, and all knew that disobedience caused madness. "Tell me of your dream."

Sang Kancil swallowed hard. "I dreamt of a medicine that would make your Majesty well."

By now every eye was on the chevrotain.

"And?"

Not one subject breathed as they all waited for the words that the mousedeer would speak. Would this cure the Great Tiger King? Would the carnage end?

The mousedeer lifted his voice. "Your slave dreamt that the cure of your Majesty's ailment was near at hand."

The Great King smiled at the news. "Even better," he purred.

The Tiger Rajah Mudah who was seated beside the Great King smiled, too. After all, this had been his idea. He leaned closer to his father.

Sang Kancil's gaze went from father to son. "The cure is to seize and devour that *which is nearest your Majesty-*"

With a growl, the Great King's eyes widened. He darted a glance at the startled Raja Mudah, who gave a piteous mew. Then before anyone could protest, the Great Tiger King seized the Raja Mudah and devoured him.

Immediately, he was cured.

And from that day on, the Great Tiger King was never sick again.

And as for the previous Rajah Mudah?

No one missed him.

For the Great Tiger King declared that Sang Kancil would become the Tiger Raja Mudah.

See Notes on Page 343

Sang Kancil and the King of
the Tiger's Whisker

It is rumoured that a tiger's whiskers may be used as a mechanical poison. Whiskers form a small part of the tiger's body, measuring on average fifteen centimetres, with the Sumatran species the most generously endowed. Resembling sticks, it is possible to stab yourself with one although a porcupine's quill is sharper. Whiskers function to allow the tiger to navigate in the dark, to sense prey, determine where to inflict a bite, jump, crouch, or slide.

In this story, however, whiskers are also a sign of virility.

THE KING OF the tigers summoned his emissaries one day. "I have decided to send you to Borneo."

The dedicated emissaries bowed. "Certainly, Your Majesty. May we enquire as to the purpose?"

The tiger king gave a growl. "Let us see what tribute, food and slaves the king of Borneo has to offer."

The dedicated emissaries bowed again.

"Before you depart however," said the tiger king, "take this." And in front of the shocked eyes of the emissaries, the king plucked a single whisker from his jaw. "Here."

The emissaries gave the king a highly impressed bow. "With this as evidence, everyone will see what a big and *virile* tiger you are."

The king of the tigers smiled smugly, as that had been his intention.

The enormous whisker was respectfully retrieved, and the dedicated emissaries departed at once.

The journey was swift.

When the emissaries landed on the island of Borneo, the first creature encountered was the mousedeer.

The emissaries scoffed.

What a puny creature!

But at least judging from its size, they believed it should show no great resistance.

"Hey you! The tiger king demands tribute, food, and slaves. Take this to your king at once as proof of our serious intent."

The mousedeer, who just happened to be Sang Kancil, gingerly received the whisker. "Your slave obeys. I will go at once to inform the king."

Only what king? thought the baffled chevrotain. We have no king. We don't need a king. We don't want a king.

But wisely he did not stay to argue that point with the emissaries.

Hurrying out of sight, Sang Kancil raced off to locate his friend the porcupine.

"If you value your life and ours," said Sang Kancil when he came upon the porcupine, "give me your biggest, fattest, sharpest quill."

This the porcupine did at once.

Sang Kancil returned to the emissaries. He bowed low, which being so close to the ground anyway was no ordeal. "My king welcomes your king to Borneo, and he looks forward to meeting your king in battle. It has been too peaceful for his liking, and he grows bored. In return for your generous gift, here is one of his own whiskers." And with the sincerest expression he could muster, he handed over the porcupine quill.

The eyes of the emissaries rounded as they caught sight of the generously endowed quill.

"Hmmm," said the emissaries, stunned as they massaged their jaws. "Hmmmm, we will certainly relay your message to our king. In fact, we will do so immediately."

The emissaries returned.

Bowing to their tiger king, they relayed the message.

"Hmmm," said the tiger king, as he stared at the quill. "Hmmm, judging from your tale, the creatures of Borneo are so puny, it would prove no great advantage to make them our slaves. I do not think it worth ever visiting again. Let us see what tribute, food, and slaves the elephant kings of Sumatra have to offer."

See Notes on Page 343

The Mock Funeral of the Great Commander Harimau

ELANDUK WAS HUNGRY. Searching for food since early morning, he had been vastly unsuccessful and so rejoiced when he encountered Dame Rusa.

"*Selamat Pagi,* (Good morning) Dame Rusa, *awak dari mana*? (Where did you come from?) *Awak pergi mana?* (Where are you going?)" said Pelanduk.

"I have come from home. *Saya chari makanan.* (I am looking for food.)"

"Why not let us seek food together then?" said the mousedeer, and the two animals trotted along, both in search of sustenance.

Pelanduk, however, was ravenous and the idea of a moveable feast alongside him only whetted his appetite. A plan soon emerged, but he needed Harimau to carry it out.

At the first opportunity, he bid Dame Rusa goodbye and sought out Harimau's presence.

"*Selamat Pagi,* (Good Morning), Great Commander of the Deep Forest! *Awak dari mana?* (Where did you come from?) Awak pergi mana? (Where are you going?)" said Pelanduk.

"From home. *Chari makanan.* (Looking for food.)"

"Then let us not waste any time. Listen to what I have to say. I know the whereabouts of Dame Rusa. *Dia sangat gemok.* (She is very fat.) *Tolong saya.* (Help me.) Help me trap her and we can both feast together. *Sama Sultan!* (Like a king!)"

Harimau was intrigued. "How do we do this?"

"Easy. All you need to do, Tiger, is to play dead. *Buka mulut.* (Open your mouth). *Semua lalat boleh masok.* (Let all the flies enter.) I in the meantime will summon the others to come. We shall mourn your passing, but while all this is going on do not move or flinch or twitch. Do nothing at all until I give the signal. Then do your deed and we will feast."

Tiger promised and at once played dead.

In the meantime, Pelanduk ran off in search of his unsuspecting victim. He also summoned the animals.

First came Kijang, then Badak and Babi, followed by Grandfather Gajah. Last, and most importantly, Dame Rusa joined the throng.

Now, there was a reason why each animal had been selected.

The animals of the Deep Forest were as superstitious as the next human. And digging graves was considered bad luck. So, then, who better to dig the grave for Harimau than Babi, who was well-known for digging up graves?

Kijang had been invited to put Dame Rusa at ease, for Kijang, the Barking Deer, was of the Deer family.

Badak had been invited, because like Harimau both were predators.

Finally, old Grandfather Gajah was invited, not only because his age gave a respectable veneer to the proceedings but also because he possessed a trunk – the only means of carrying water. For Harimau's corpse, like a human corpse, needed to be washed before the burial.

And then of course, a group of mourners was essential at every funeral.

Standing before the prostrate form of the tiger, the mousedeer began. "Raja Suleiman has summoned us to attend the funeral of the late Great Commander of the Deep Forest."

Grandpa Gajah presented the water to Pelanduk who sprinkled it over Harimau's body.

Next was the job of carrying the body to the grave.

An argument broke out. While many offered to carry the tail, none wished to carry Harimau's head.

"*Bodoh!* (Stupid!)" Pelanduk cast a disgusted eye over the embarrassed throng. "The Great Commander is no more. Why then do you quarrel over who gets to carry the head?" The mousedeer stamped his foot.

Mousedeer are known to stamp the ground with their four-toed hooves whenever angered.

Ashamed, the animals stared at the ground.

Pelanduk shook his head sadly.

"But who can blame us?" said Kijang.

"Is it not said that the spirit of the dead hangs around?" said Badak.

"Waiting to return," said Grandpa Gajah.

Pelanduk smiled at the elephant. "Grandpa Gajah, you have carried the water."

And Grandpa Gajah nodded, pleased to be excused.

"Babi, you have dug the grave."

And Babi nodded, pleased to be excused.

"Badak, you and our Great Commander were great friends, it should be you no doubt who should carry his head, however…" And here Pelanduk frowned at Badak's horn, "we do not wish to damage the body. We therefore need an animal who is gentle."

The mousedeer cast his eye appreciatively at the two remaining animals but then he smiled at Dame Rusa. "Two deer, elegant, gentle, and therefore most perfect. However, it is obvious that one is so much more capable than the other." Pelanduk nodded at significantly larger Dame Rusa. "Would you mind, Gentle Lady?"

Dame Rusa preened at the compliment.

And after Pelanduk had put his request in such a logical manner, who was Dame Rusa to disagree? Much against her instinct, she took up her place at the head of the corpse while the other animals gathered up Harimau's belongings, for they would be needed after the burial to decorate the grave.

With all eyes upon him, Pelanduk then gave the signal. "*Sekarang!* (Now!)"

A death curdling roar split the jungle as the prostrate tiger suddenly came back to life.

The animals fled at once. All except poor Dame Rusa, who, to her great surprise, found herself between the jaws of the tiger.

One heart-rending scream and it was over.

Blood sprayed in all directions.

Dame Rusa would never more frolic in the Realm of the Deep Rainforest.

All that remained was to share the spoils.

Harimau was extremely pleased. Pelanduk divided the carcass of the deer equally.

Nearby was a field set alight by a farmer wishing to clear the land for paddy, so the two culprits took turns keeping the flames burning while they cooked the first half of the deer. Poor Dame Rusa.

"Great Commander of the Deep Jungle, may I offer a suggestion? As to be expected, this meal will take a while so let us share the work. While one of us cooks, let the other sleep. This way we will both wake refreshed to a magnificent repast."

"Let it be as you say," said Harimau, and prepared to take the first watch for he did not trust the mousedeer.

"Take note though, Elder Brother," said Pelanduk. "It may not be well-known, but my tusks are poisonous with a venom that will strike at your being. Whatever you do, do not touch them."

"Never fear, Little Brother," said Harimau. "I wish nothing of the sort."

"One last peculiarity we mousedeer have is that we think with both eyes closed. Only when one eye is open, are we deemed to be asleep."

"I understand," said Harimau.

And so Pelanduk closed both eyes.

Harimau waited, hoping that it would not take long for the chevrotain to fall asleep. And soon Pelanduk opened one eye and rhythmic breathing filled the glade.

"Only two pots of rice," said Harimau for that was how they counted time, both the animals and the humans of that era. Which meant that an hour had passed.

Harimau was consumed with curiosity, because after all what is tiger but a large cat?

So, as soon as he was able to, he reached out to stroke the two tusks of Pelanduk.

Harimau sniffed at the ivory then snorted in disgust. "What utter nonsense! These two toothpicks are not the least bit poisonous! I wonder why Pelanduk told such an outrageous lie!"

Soon the time came for the change-over, and Harimau woke the mousedeer. "My turn."

Pelanduk yawned and said nothing, but as soon as he was sure that Harimau was sound asleep, he fell upon the first half of the venison, and so great was his hunger that he devoured the entire slab without hesitation.

Replete, Pelanduk dashed into the jungle and returned with a chunk of reddish bark from a tree. Then he cooked the second half of the venison.

When morning broke, Pelanduk woke the sleeping tiger. "*Bangun*! (Wake up)! Come let us carry our meal to where man cannot find us, and we can eat in peace."

Harimau set off to find creepers to tie up the meat while Pelanduk came back with a thorny pole. But unseen, Pelanduk cut the thorns off his half and left the remaining thorns on the other half. Then the two animals fastened the meat to the pole and set off to find a spot where they could eat in peace.

Pelanduk had his piece of real venison behind him while Harimau had the reddish chunk of bark.

Tiger was ravenous.

"*Nanti, nanti!* (Wait, wait!)" said the mousedeer but Tiger began picking bits of meat off and devouring them.

Imagine then, Harimau's great surprise to discover that the delicious meal he had dreamed of was as bitter as herbs.

"Disgusting! Yuck!" he complained. "How can this be? Did we overcook the venison?"

Pelanduk shook his head. "I should have seen this coming."

"What do you mean?"

"It is as obvious as the whiskers on your face that you touched my tusks. Confess," said Pelanduk as Tiger blushed. "Be thankful that the poison only entered the meat and not your person. Just think that we almost lost our Great Commander of the Deep Realm!"

And Harimau went white.

"Have some of mine, Great Leader," and so saying, Pelanduk generously tore off some of his meat and offered it to Harimau.

"*Sedap sekali! (*So delicious!)" said Harimau.

"You see, you see!"

With hunger partially appeased, soon Harimau was overtaken by a dreadful burning sensation in his shoulders. "Adoi! Adoi! What is this horrible pain!"

"Whatever it is you must learn to bear it with patience for we cannot stop here. If King Solomon's guards were to find us, he will exact punishment. Remember we did not ask permission to hunt Dame Rusa."

And so Harimau bit his lips and proceeded on as the thorns continued to pierce his flesh.

Harimau was in dreadful agony. To keep Tiger moving, Pelanduk fed him from time to time from his half of the meat, but Pelanduk made sure to consume his half by the time the pair reached the river.

The river flowed straight and swift, and as the two looked on, a raft fashioned from coconut trunks floated past.

"*Lekas!* (Quick!) Before the farmer comes," said Pelanduk and leapt onto the raft.

Harimau followed suit.

The current was swift, but they needed to reach the other bank, so Harimau rowed with his mighty paws.

"Help me, brother!"

But Pelanduk held up his fragile legs, pencil-thin, and Harimau continued to row on alone. However, he was weak with hunger and so it took a great amount of effort to make any headway.

Eventually, the raft reached the other side. Not wasting a moment, Pelanduk jumped off leaving Harimau open-mouthed as the raft, bereft of one rider began to spin back unbalanced into the middle of the river.

"*Kesian!* (Sad!) What an unlucky day for you, dear brother. Row quick, before Sang Buaya catches you."

And so, saying, Pelanduk laughed and skipped away, full, and happy.

Harimau roared as he finally understood the trick that the mousedeer had played on him.

"I will get you, Pelanduk! If that is the last thing I do!" And Harimau promised with all his heart that he would revenge himself on the crafty chevrotain.

The river, however, was full of crocodiles...

See Notes on Pages 343-344

The Pact between Harimau and Buaya

BUAYA MADE A pact with Harimau one day.

It was no ordinary pact because Buaya was King of the Water, and Harimau was King of the Land.

Together, the two monarchs vowed eternal hatred on a certain common enemy. Sang Kancil who had fooled Sang Harimau with not only a hornet's nest but also with a snake.

Sang Buaya related how Sang Kancil had wanted to eat the chadong fruit on the other side of the river and how he had smacked the crocodiles across the head while crying out, "*Satu, Dua, Tiga,* (One, Two, Three)! Crick! *Kepala kechil, kepala besar!* (Small head, big head)! Crack!"

"Very well, then. Carry me across the water so I can hunt for him on the other side. If he enters the water, he is yours. And while he is on the land, he is mine."

"The domain of the water is mine," swore Buaya.

"And the domain of the land is mine," pledged Harimau.

And so, saying, the two promised to honour the pact.

Kancil, of course, had heard everything - he had the knack of being in the right place at the right time. He called out, "Hey *Bodoh* (Stupid)! *Malas*! (Lazy)! You can't catch me!"

And even before he had finished calling out, he leaped and skipped over the muddy bank, just under the noses of Buaya and Harimau.

Well, of course they could not take that lying down.

"Hey, did he call you stupid?"

"No, he called you stupid!"

"I thought he called me lazy!"

"No, he called me lazy!"

"Why *that* Kancil!"

Both predators launched into action.

Harimau pounced. Buaya snapped his powerful jaws. But of course, neither was able to catch the crafty chevrotain. And so, a chase began, one that started on land and soon ended up in the water as Kancil skipped from stone to stone in the shallows and soon was leaping from back to scaly back of the mighty crocodiles who snapping and smashing the water, tried to catch the crafty mousedeer.

Not to be outdone, Harimau joined in. "I have you now Sang Di Rimba!"

"Ho, ho! You think you are so smart! Catch me if you can then!"

Sang Harimau could not resist. He leapt at once but of course Sang Di Rimba ran off. He was perilously close to the edge of the bank where the crocodiles all waited. Closer and closer he came.

Closer and closer came Sang Harimau as well.

Tiger sprung.

And Kancil jumped high and twisted mid-air.

Oh!

And he sprang back inland, while Sang Harimau landed with a great splash in the water! Oh! Oh! Oh!

But Harimau was out in a second. He gathered himself for another leap but again he missed.

Kancil bounded and whipped round and then they were back at the water's edge. There was Sang Kancil almost within reach, but he was shooting high up, almost ten feet into the air to the disbelieving Harimau's eyes.

Harimau sprung once more. Twelve feet. Only straight into the water! Into the jaws of the buaya!

The crocodiles ripped into him. They thought he was Kancil!

"*Kawan!* (Friends!)"

"*Makanan!* (Food!)"

"But what of our pledge? Did our promise mean nothing?"

"The domain of the water is mine," swore Buaya.

"And the domain of the land is mine." Harimau screamed.

He was outnumbered.

"Take him *Si Rangkak* (Mister Crawler). He is a larger meal than I any day," said Kancil.

"And so, the crocodiles did.

Beware the fealty of the crocodile.

See Notes on Page 344

Sang Kancil the Judge

LONG HASSAN AND Ngah Ali were friends. They worked side by side planting *padi* (rice) and *jagong* (corn).

For many years they had good crops but then a drought came.

Long Hassan ran out of food, so he approached his good friend Ngah Ali.

"Can I borrow some padi and corn, please? I will repay you in two moons."

Ngah Ali lent him the padi and corn at once.

The following month, it rained heavily. Both farms did well.

In the second month, Ngah Ali approached Long Hassan. "Please pay me back what you owe me."

Only Long Hassan refused. "I promised to repay what I owed when there were two moons. Look in the sky. How many moons do you see?"

Ngah Ali was furious. But what could he do?

Then he knew. He would approach the Judge of the Jungle.

Sang Kancil will know what to do.

And so, he approached the mousedeer.

Of course, Kancil knew what to do. This was why he was Salaam di Rimba.

"Tell your friend to meet us at the foot of the hill tonight."

That night, when the moon came out, both friends met at the foot of the hills.

Sang Kancil was already waiting.

"Is it true that you will honour your debt when there are two moons?"

Long Hassan swallowed. "Yes, it is true."

"Look into the well beyond the trees."

Both men found the well.

When they peered into the darkness, they saw the clear reflection of the moon in the water.

Two moons…

Long Hassan gasped.

"Pay your friend what you owe him. Friendship is more important than money."
Long Hassan repaid his debt.
But although Ngah Ali had been paid in full, he never trusted his friend fully ever again.
And I don't blame him.

Two Men and an Axe

King Solomon is renowned for his wisdom. But here are two cases where even his legendary wisdom appears to have failed.

Of course, it is a certain mousedeer (Selang Dirimba) who comes to the rescue!

IT WAS SAID that two men appeared to *mengadap raja behawa beliung yang di pinjam oleh salah seorang daripada mereka telah dimakan ulat* (confront the king (the great Raja Suleiman) with a pickaxe that one of them had borrowed and had been eaten by caterpillars).

The first complained that his neighbour had borrowed his axe some time ago, and when he asked for the *beliung* (pickaxe) to be returned, had instead received a story of how the axe had been devoured by *ulat* (caterpillars).

"The caterpillars ate the axe head," swore the borrower.

"Give me back my axe!" swore the owner.

Only how could metal be devoured? King Solomon was puzzled. "Summon Selang Dirimba, do you know where he lives?"

Sang Serigala (Wolf) searched for half a day until he found Selang Dirimba. "Hai Selang Dirimba, you are summoned by King Solomon."

At once, the mousedeer obeyed.

At the court of the Great Raja Suleiman, he made obeisance.

"Selang Dirimba!"

"Raja Suleiman!"

"I have sent for you because of this dispute."

And Selang Dirimba listened well. When he had heard all that there was to be heard, he bowed before King Solomon. "Will you allow your slave to go and bathe?"

Raja Suleiman frowned for it was customary for any of his subjects to bathe before they presented themselves to him. Not after.

But he gave a curt nod.

Selang Dirimba set off. He bathed in the river, and when he had finished, he went over to a burnt patch of lallang and *gulang* (rolled) in it. He rolled like a popiah until his little body was black with ash. Then he *naik ke darat* (went ashore), looking worse than before.

King Solomon was stunned. "Toh Selang Dirimba! What sort of bath has caused you to return even blacker and more dishevelled than before?"

"A thousand pardons, Your Majesty, who is the wisest of the wise. It is true that your slave went away to bathe but just as your slave exited the palace, your slave found to his horror that Your Majesty's Garden was on fire. Your slave lost no time is rolling over the flames to put the fire out." Selang Dirimba bowed low. "And this is why your slave's body is so black, for it has been singed."

King Solomon stroked his beard. "Hai, hai, hai. What nonsense is this, for the river to be on fire?"

Both the borrower and the owner shook their heads at the imbecilic tale.

"Pardon your slave, Your Majesty, a thousand pardons, but why is that so unbelievable? According to the knowledge of your slave it is just as improbable to him for an axe head to be devoured by caterpillars."

When King Solomon heard the words spoken by Selang Dirimba, he at once made judgement.

The borrower was to either return the axe or replace it with an equivalent.

And so, the king held his Selang Dirumba in higher esteem than ever before.

See Notes on Pages 344-345

The Rich Man and the Poor Man

ONCE THERE WAS a very *kaya saudagar* (rich merchant) in a village who loved to eat and drink from morn to night. Nearby lived a *miskin* (poor) man and his wife. One day, the poor man's wife was speaking with a *teman saudagar* (friend of the rich man.)

She inhaled languorously. "I eat when the rich merchant cooks, whether he does *rendang* (cook by slowly stirring until dry), *tumis* (stir fry), prepares a *gulai* (curry), or whatever. This is how I am so fat."

The saudagar kaya (rich man) was angry when he learnt of this. He complained to the king, who ordered the poor man and his wife to attend the court.

The rich man explained about his *aiap* (food – special term used by a subject to refer to his food before royalty) and how the *bau* (smells) when he cooked it made the poor man and his wife fat while he, the rich man, and his own wife remained thin.

Maka berfikir raja itu (Then thought the king) that he could not judge, so he instructed the gong to be beaten about the country.

But no one would answer the summon of the gong.

The pelanduk queried the beater of the gong, the king's herald.

"*Apa susah raja didalam ini?* (What is the king's difficulty in this?) Where are his enemies breaking in? Which warrior or captain has committed murder? Where is the wall of the royal fort that needs repairing?"

The herald told the pelanduk of the case before the king.

"Inform the king that I will be the judge."

"*Salam di Rimba*, (Judge of the Jungle,) come then."

"Have you found any who can settle this case?" said the king.

"*Harap diampun*. (Please forgive me.) A thousand pardons Your Majesty," said the herald. "Salam di Rimba has come forward to give judgement."

"*Akulah yang chakap menyeliseikan pengaduan saudagar.* (I am the one who resolves merchant complaints)."

"If you are not able to do so then I will slay you," said the king.

"Then if your *hamba* (slave) is slain, you will be one slave poorer."

"Give your judgement!"

So Pelanduk sat on the judgement seat while the rich man and the poor man sat before him.

Salaam di Rimba turned to the rich man. "How much of your cooking smells has been consumed by the poor man?

"One thousand duit."

Salaam di Rimba turned to the poor man. "Is it true that you eat in the middle of the time of cooking, of rendang and tumis and gulai of the rich man?"

"It is true that I eat whenever I smell the cooking of the rich man, of the rendang, the tumis, and the gulai drifts over," said the poor man.

"Have you ever entered the house of the rich man?"

"*Tiada.* (No.)"

"Have you ever entered the village of the merchant?"

"*Tiada.*"

Salam di Rimba turned to the rich man. "Is it true that the poor man has never entered your village?"

"*Betul.* (True.)"

Pelanduk borrowed a thousand duit from the king. He ordered a state curtain to be placed in the middle of the hall, between the poor man and the rich man.

Pelanduk then ordered the poor man to count out a thousand duit while the rich man was to listen intently.

"*Satu,* (one), *dua,* (two), *tiga…* (three…)"

When he finished, Pelanduk turned to the rich man. "Here, sir, is the full and complete settlement of your account."

The rich man rubbed his hands. "Bring the money to me."

"Why, sir, do you want the actual dollars?" Pelanduk looked askance. "You have received your account, and it is all settled. The poor man took away by smelling and you have received compensation by hearing."

See Notes on Pages 345-346

Kancil and Raja Suleiman

Some say that Raja Suleiman wanders about the great jungle as quiet as a mouse. Some say that he may or not be visible. That he is supposedly tall, as tall as a tree sparkling with raindrops or that he may be found amid a gathering of peacocks, or that his face may be seen shimmering in the white light that shafts down through the great canopy.

KANCIL WAS HURRYING along the jungle when he came upon a herd of mousedeer. Was this part of his mousedeer family?

An ancient mousedeer was making a speech. "Not safe," he said. "Not safe."

"We should move," said a mother.

"But where?" said another.

"Why is it not safe?" asked Kancil, prancing, excited to finally be part of a group.

"Men."

Ah! Kancil understood. He opened his mouth to tell the stories of how he had tricked men time and again, but-

"*Diam!* (Quiet!)" said the rest of the mousedeer.

It is one thing to be told off by someone whose opinion you do not care about, quite another thing to be told off by someone whose opinion you value.

Kancil's heart twisted. So off he went, to find a place where he could be appreciated. He had been alone for so long that his aloneness had worn a hole in his heart.

Trip-trap. Trip-trap.

There was consolation in movement. On and on he went, his mind a blank, unthinking, until with a shock, he found that he had reached the Perak River. To his surprise, the river was dry.

Oh, what has happened?

"No rain," gasped the fish.

And everywhere that he looked, he found whole families of fish, flapping desperately about in what little remained of the water.

"Help us Kancil!" they cried.

Kancil's heart twisted even more, but this time it was not for himself. Already flocks of birds were descending. Soon the fish would be gone.

And so, he forgot about the little hole in his heart. He forgot about tricking.

"Great Raja Suleiman," he called out. "*Tolong.* (Help.) Please help the fish, for they desperately need water."

Almost before he finished speaking, a chill swept through the valley. Kancil shivered.

But it wasn't a breeze. It was the voice of Raja Suleiman. He was speaking to the Spirit of the Mountain.

You see, the Spirit of the Mountain had, in his moving about while everyone was asleep, accidentally pushed a small dam onto the river, the result of which meant that the fish families found themselves on one side, while the water was on the other.

The mist made a bed of moisture for the fish while Raja Suleiman speared a respectable fat cloud. It rained at once, and soon the river was full of water and bursting with happy fish families once more. Everyone was happy except for the birds who flew away grumbling. But they had had a good feed, and all had fat bellies so really, they had little to complain about.

The place where this all happened is called Fish Trap Mountain.

It was a part of the jungle that Kancil had never been visited before and so, he was startled when almost immediately the sky darkened.

At first, he thought it was a thunderstorm. He searched around for shelter when a muster of peacocks – all in brilliant iridescent blue - paraded into the clearing.

It was then that he realised that the darkness was caused by Raja Suleiman, his height blotting out the sun.

At once, Kancil bowed low.

He waited for Raja Suleiman to pass but to his shock, the Lord of the Jungle lowered his hand and scooped up the trembling Mousedeer.

Heat radiated from the large palm.

Then Raja Suleiman breathed upon Kancil, and the fear that had been in Kancil's heart evaporated.

The mousedeer's shoulders sagged with relief.

"Ah, my little one. You have been selfish and proud but also rather clever and kind. You thought of others when you called for help for the fish."

Kancil lowered his big brown eyes. He could not quite bear looking into the deep gaze of Raja Suleiman.

"I want you to help your family the mousedeer, for they do not think before they act. They always run into difficulty. Help them think first."

Kanchil nodded. Garnering up his courage, he cocked his head at Raja Suleiman.

The great king smiled. And it was as if the sun shone in the clearing and everything was lit bright as day.

"It is wise to be afraid of men. But even men are beginning to tell tales of your cleverness. But do not be proud. Stay humble. Stay yourself."

And so, saying, Raja Suleiman lowered his hand, and Kancil trotted off, shaking his head as if waking up.

Only the voice of Raja Suleiman remained. "Do not be like the deer and damage the trees with horns, or like the elephant and plough through the corn, or like the tigers and crocodiles. Instead, stay sweet and serene."

Eyes closed, Kancil promised. He inhaled deeply, swaying a little.

Trip-trap. Trip-trap. Trip-tr-

Trot. Trot. Trot.

Who was that?

Kancil opened his eyes to see a delightful lady mousedeer enter the clearing. Her legs were pencil thin. She dropped her gaze shyly when she spotted him, but not before Kancil noticed her big brown eyes, darkly lashed.

Kancil swallowed hard, suddenly unable to speak.

Smiling serenely, she lifted her head, then trotted up to Kancil and gave him a kiss.

Kancil's heart fluttered.

Kancil wedded the Lady Mousedeer, and they lived happily ever after.

And he helped not only the other mousedeer but all the rest of the animals in the jungle. And all loved him.

Mousedeer are well known as being extremely solitary animals and only socialise when breeding and raising their young known by the term asses. The lesser Malay mousedeer is monogamous.

While some mousedeer are nocturnal or crepuscular, the lesser Malay mousedeer may be diurnal.

The Midday Dream

A DEER ONCE foolishly fell asleep in the middle of the jungle. When she awoke, she found a lion looking down at her.

Fear raced through her being at the huge furry face above her head, but somehow, she managed to stammer out these words. "*Apa khabar, Sang Singa*? (Hello, Mr Lion). Sorry, but I would like to go home, please."

Her last word ended in a bleat.

The lion smiled. Even though he was old, he was significantly bigger and more powerful than the little deer.

"No, you may not. I have had a dream, and, in my dream, I dreamt that I ate you." The lion laughed.

Of course, the poor deer began to cry. That is what I would have done, too, had I been in her situation.

Thankfully, a mousedeer just happened to be walking by.

"*Selamat Tenggah Hari, kawan-kawan*, (Hello, or Good Afternoon, friends!) What is the matter?" said the mousedeer.

The lion explained his dream.

Now in those days, it was believed that dreams come true. It was also believed that by not obeying a dream one would go mad. Everything appeared to be in the lion's favour.

The mousedeer frowned hard. "I think it would be a good idea to seek out the king."

Well, the lion couldn't see anything wrong with that suggestion, so, he agreed.

And as for the little deer, if seeing the king meant delaying the inevitable, well, she certainly had no problem with that.

So, the three set off to see the king. Now the king was of course the great and magnificent King Solomon. It was always King Solomon in these stories.

As to be expected, there was a crowd. You see, it was the job in those days for the king to judge his people. He did so to keep the peace. And as there were constant disputes among the animals, the king was kept busy.

While the three waited their turn, the mousedeer had a nap.

The lion and the little deer waited and waited.

I said that there was a queue, didn't I?

But finally, it was their turn.

They woke the sleeping mousedeer and made their obeisance before the mighty King Solomon and his queen.

King Solomon had seven hundred wives, so which one was sitting beside him on this day? I have no idea.

"What do you want?" said King Solomon.

"I only want what is due to me," said the old lion. "I had a midday dream. And in that dream, I dreamt that I would eat this little deer."

The deer cringed.

"Ah, midday dreams. Everyone knows that midday dreams come true. So why then have you come to bother me?" said the king.

"Oh please, please do not let him eat me," said the little deer, crying most piteously.

"Midday dreams come true," said King Solomon. "There is nothing I can do about it."

"Oh please, a thousand pardons, for interrupting these proceedings, but I have had a dream, too," said the mousedeer yawning as if he had just woken up.

"As I said, midday dreams come true. Why are you bothering me?" said King Solomon.

"Oh good, because in my midday dream, I dreamt that the queen was my wife!" And so, saying the mousedeer trotted up to the queen, looking extremely pleased.

At once, the queen screamed.

Gegak-gempita! (Uproar!) There was an upheaval at court.

Guards blocked the mousedeer from coming any closer.

"What! What nonsense!" King Solomon thundered. He rose to his feet and stood protectively before his wife.

Everyone froze.

Silence.

Then King Solomon laughed. He chuckled loud and long as everyone stared baffled at each other.

"Haha! Well done!" said King Solomon, gazing down at the mousedeer.

"Midday dreams come…" said the Mousedeer as his lips spread in a smile.

"True." King Solomon slashed the air. "No longer."

The crowd gasped.

"As of right now, midday dreams no longer come true," said King Solomon, and he sent for his vizier and had the law changed that very day.

So, the old lion lost his meal, the little deer gained her life and never went to sleep again in the middle of the jungle.

And that is the end of the story.

Moral: Never go to sleep in the middle of the day in the middle of the jungle. Or you might end up in someone's middle.

See Notes on Page 346

Section 3-Sheikh Rimba

In this section, Kancil becomes king.

These are the stories of how he accomplishes this.

But first, you might ask, why does a mousedeer wish to become a king?

A good reason would be he doesn't want to be eaten. This is the reason given in a story from Borneo. There are other reasons of course.

But first…

King of the Jungle

MOUSEDEER HAD NO desire to be eaten. But he was small, and except for his wits, defenceless.

So, one day Mousedeer came up with an idea.

He covered a hole in a tree with leaves, so that the hole would be hidden. Then he invited the other animals to a kicking competition.

"Let us see who is the strongest," said the mousedeer.

Of course, Tiger wanted to go first.

Needless to say, Tiger made barely a dent.

Lion went next, with much the same result.

All the other animals tried but none were able to do any damage.

Finally, Mousedeer spoke up. "It is my turn."

The other animals all laughed. But they let Mousedeer have a go.

Imagine then their surprise to see a hole, right where the mousedeer had kicked.

"I am stronger than all of you."

"Ah, that is true," said the other animals. "We are sorry that we laughed at you."

And so, from that day on, Mousedeer became king in Borneo.

The animals all did what they could to honour Mousedeer, and he lived a long and happy life.

Harimau berdamai dengan kambing

The Tiger makes peace with the Goat (Original Title)

THE JUNGLE SMELLS different after rain. The air is cleansed, cooled, and soaked with the aromas of wet earth and washed plants.

Pelanduk Jenaka (Trickster Mousedeer) skipped along, stopping to watch pale pink earthworms wriggle out of the ground, skirting long black leeches when he came across a paddy field, splashed yellow gold in the morning sun. Stepping out from under the jungle canopy, he felt warmth upon his head and throat.

Peace.

Today was a good day, and if he had his way, it was the start of many more good days. For the night before, he had had a dream. And in that dream, an old man had announced that Pelanduk was to be king!

King!

Pelanduk king!

When he woke, he had spoken of his dream at once to his wife, breakfasted and then set off, full of anticipation.

On his jaunt, he came across a pack of elephants.

"*Selamat pagi, kawan-kawan*, (good morning, friends)!" He greeted them, only to be met with disdainful glances.

"Of course, it is a good morning," they had answered. "For animals such as us! Ha ha ha! We have nothing to fear, and if any animal were to go against us, why, we trample them down!"

"Do you think that is wise?" said Pelanduk. "Should not every animal be seen as a friend?"

"Who are you to lord over us?" The elephants trumpeted in shock at being spoken to in such a manner. Then they laughed before stomping off.

Who am I to lord over them?

Pelanduk was struck by the elephants' words.

Was this indeed another sign that something big was about to happen?

Well, the dream certainly had been the first indication, only, how was he to accomplish such a phenomenal task?

Allah no doubt has his reasons. Although I know not what they are.

While he was busily pondering, *Babi* (Pig) showed up.

"*Selamat pagi, kawan,* (good morning, friend!)" Pelanduk greeted the pig only to be met with a snort.

"What are you up to at this hour, Pelanduk? Out to play your perpetual tricks? I don't want any trouble."

"Trouble? Why that is the last thing on my mind," said Pelanduk speaking the truth.

"Well, you would know."

Pelanduk's cheeks heated but he replied politely. "What I do know is that if one animal is in trouble, then should not the other animals assist? Are we not all denizens of the jungle?"

Babi grunted. "And yet, we prey upon each other. If only there was a king who could establish peace."

Peace.

Was this yet another sign?

Only how am I to accomplish peace?

Pelanduk shut his eyes as he pondered deeply. He could almost see the old man from his dream again.

"Reign over the animals…"

Pelanduk Jenaka blinked opened his eyes, inhaling the sweet air, as he made his way home. Sanctuary was a *pusu* (an anthill) atop a hillock. This was Pelanduk Jenaka's Hermitage, where he had a clear view of his surroundings. Directly ahead in the distance rose a plateau, beyond lay jungle.

Pelanduk Jenaka had barely arrived back at the hillock when he noticed at the foot of the plateau, a herd of goats grazing peacefully.

Goats are intelligent albeit curious creatures. The long horizontal pupils of a goat allow the animal to see panoramically, a distinct advantage when you are prey. Seeing clearly in a forward direction also aids flight across rough terrain especially when predators can come from any direction.

Although a goat's instinct is to flee from danger, when cornered they will charge at any predator in defence. A charging goat, horns lowered, is a formidable sight.

Pelanduk Jenaka then turned his head toward the second slope to the right. He noticed a group of tigers. His heart pounded.

Tigers generally are solitary animals and hunt every eight to nine days. A single tiger is a phenomenal threat. But here there were hundreds. Which was why he had spotted them, for they were not even bothering to seek camouflage.

An ambush of tigers.

This was a massacre waiting to happen.

Only one thing to be done.

Hatta Maka (Even then) as he made his way towards the goats, he knew that there was a chance he would not be believed. He had to do something.

Pelanduk Jenaka went up to a giant banyan fig tree. He scraped at the bark until sticky sap seeped out, then he smeared the rubbery white stuff onto his brow and moustache and beard.

Next, he went over to a field of sharp lallang grass and rolled.

Finally, he approached the herd of goats.

"Eh, *kambing semua*! (Hey, all you goats!) Tiger scouts have come over to your hill many times. But I have a magic spell gained while I did *bertapa* (religious penance) which warded off any danger."

"Penance?" said the *tuah* (elder or head) of the goats, his lavender blue eyes rounding.

"I did penance for three years, three months, and three days in my cloister. Then I pronounced the spell which God had given me. It is a potent spell. And when I do so, all the animals will obey me. For then I will become king."

The Tuah Kambing observed that Pelanduk Jenaka must have indeed lived an ascetic life for his brow and moustache and beard were white.

Allah has brought Pelanduk to us, and Allah no doubt has his reasons, although I know not what they are.

"Yes, for when I spoke the spell, the tigers were not able to smell you. Even their eyes were clouded, and they could not see you, either. How then do you explain that your herd and theirs were able to co-exist for so long while practically side-by-side? But" — Pelanduk Jenaka gave a dramatic pause — "if you do not believe me, then I will tell you when next the tigers will come round."

Sakti. (Supernatural powers.) The old Tuah stood silently for a moment as he digested the news, then he arched his head. Sunlight glinted across the curve of his horns.

"Let it be so then, according to the power of the incantation," said the Tuah Kambing, believing. "If it is true, then we will become your subjects and you, our king." Then he turned to his flock. "Do not panic. We have Pelanduk on our side. He will tell us what to do."

"Pelanduk, Pelanduk," cried the herd, "what must we do? Please tell us, and we will do it."

Pelanduk's heart skipped a beat when he saw how determined the goats were. But the task was hard. "Tigers will always want to eat you. And you will desire revenge. Thus, there will be eternal hatred between you unless the cycle can be broken."

"Tell us," bleated the herd. "Tell us then what we must do."

"But first," said the Tuah Kambing, "we will send a young kid to Harimau to check and report on this state of affairs. If she comes back alive, then we know that what Pelanduk said is true. For we believe that you possess a powerful and magical formula."

But as the goats looked up, they found that Pelanduk had already left.

As Pelanduk approached the ambush of tigers, his steps slowed, and he bowed his head as if traumatised. When he drew near, he sobbed out loud. "*Adoi! Adoi*! (Oh dear! Oh dear!) *Tuan-tuan Harimau* (Tiger lords!) The end of the world is upon us. Everything that we have known has come to pass. And everything is turning upside down."

"By the Coiled Whiskers of the Elder," said the Tuah Harimau, "what nonsense are you babbling?"

"*Pak Matjan*, (Father Matjan) are you not aware of the prophecy of the Great Catastrophe?

When events reverse? When prey and predator swap? This is why I weep! For you and for your mighty clan. Hear the prophecy and heed it well, for this is the last time that I will speak it. For rain will fall back up into the clouds. The Jinns' hair will grow outside in. Nagas will be devoured by worms and you, my lords will be slain by goats."

By now the group of tigers had gathered around the chevrotain. They had all seen the white of his brow and his moustache and his beard. That this was the result of ascetic living they were in no doubt. What he was saying – how could it be true?

"I will send two scouts tomorrow to check that what you have reported is true," said the Tuah Harimau, but when he turned back to Pelanduk, the mousedeer was gone.

Pelanduk wasted no time in returning to the first hill where he once again, addressed the goats.

"Follow my instructions to the letter if you want to live in peace."

"Tell us. Tell us what we must do."

"See those red flowers? Early tomorrow morning, all of you must eat those flowers. But not only must you eat them, you must let the sap from those flowers run down to coat your mouths and beards." Then Pelanduk told them what they must say.

"We hear and obey."

Night soon passed and the dawn came.

Few had slept, so worried were they.

At the first touch of morning's golden light, the herd of goats carried out Pelanduk's commandment. They gorged themselves on the crimson flowers until the bright sap spattered their fur and ruff and bled down their throats as red and fresh as blood.

The goats then turned and raced up towards the second hill. There in the bright morning sun they saw the figures of the two tiger scouts looking down upon them.

"Two! Two! You have only brought two! What miserly pickings, for we are ravenous!" screamed the herd of goats as they rushed at the two terrified tiger scouts.

"Eeek!" The two scouts squealed. They turned tail and fled.

Loud was the lamenting when they reached the herd of tigers and related their news.

"Father, dear father! What Pelanduk told us is true, indeed! The end of the world is upon us. The prey has become the predator and the predator, the prey.'

"Pelanduk, you must help us," said Pak Matjan, when Pelanduk appeared a few minutes later. "Tell us what we must do, or we shall surely perish!"

"Very well. The only way out is to establish an everlasting peace between both your tribes. Go up now to the top of this hill, while I approach the tribe of goats. Do not worry about me, for I have done penance for three years, three months, and three days in my cloister. Then I pronounced the spell which God had given me. It is a potent spell. And all the animals will obey me. For then I will become king. And only when I become king will I be able then to keep this everlasting peace between your two tribes."

"Let it be so then according to the power of the incantation," said the Tuah Harimau, believing. "If it is true, then we will become your subjects. And you, our king."

The old Tuah stood silently for a moment as he digested the news. Turning his head to one side, sunlight fell upon half his face, lining each whisker white, etching his fine hair in glorious pale gold. "Do not panic. We have Pelanduk on our side. He will tell us what to do."

But as the tigers looked up, they found that Pelanduk had already left.

Pelanduk returned to the goats.

"Remain on that side of the hillock until I call you," he said.

Then he went and drew a line in the middle of the plateau, dividing it into two equal halves.

Having done so, Pelanduk called the tribe of tigers. At the same time, he called the tribe of goats, indicating to both groups that they were to remain on each side of the line.

"The two leaders please approach," said Pelanduk and the two leaders approached.

"Noble kambing and noble harimau, I have gathered both your tribes to this mountain to make an eternal peace among you. Swear to me both of you never to attack the other and on my honour and the strength of the magic spell, you must keep your word. The day that you break your word will be the day that your tribe drowns in *sungei darah* (rivers of blood)."

"I swear," said the Tuah Harimau and the Tuah Kambing. "By the magic and the power of your spell, we swear to live in peace side-by-side. And we also swear allegiance to you as our king, Sheikh Rimba."

"Two days ago, I would have never dreamt of such a thing happening," said the Tuah Harimau.

"Two days ago, I would have never dreamt of such a thing happening," said the Tuah Kambing.

Dreams.

All this happened because of my dream after all.

And so, because Pelanduk had made peace between the goats and the tigers, he made them both his ministers. And the strength of his kingship lay in the strength of their promise never to attack.

And thus began the journey to Pelanduk to becoming king.

See Notes on Page 346

Pelandok, his adopted son, Harimau the Man Eater and what happened in the end which may not be believed...

Here follows a series of stories of Pelandok and his dealings with the strange race called Man.

IT WAS THE drum beat that first caught Pelandok's attention.

Deram-deram! Tat-tat-tat!

Sharp and loud and merry. Sounds of excitement.

The drum beater was announcing his daughter's upcoming marriage.

Everyone in the kampong was celebrating because a wedding is always a special event.

The beat seemed to enter Pelandok's entire being. He could not keep still. In fact, the music so consumed him that he skipped straight up to the kampong and trotted undaunted right into the middle of the celebrations.

Oh, what joy! For the next thing to catch his attention were the heavenly smells!

Fragrant saffron! Rice! Pelandok's stomach rumbled as he inhaled the enticing sambals and spiced meats. Oh, and there was *udang* (prawns), and *kambing* (goat), and *ayam* (chicken)!

Pelandok salivated. His eyes teared from the sizzling of frying chilli in the air.

He bounded from one end of the house to the other, scattering the *bunga rampai*, the finely cut pandan leaf that sprayed with perfume had been laid out in trays for the guests to toss over the newly married couple.

The sweet aroma of rose water drifted in the air.

"Oh! Oh! Stop him! Stop that horrid Pelandok!" cried the guests, aghast at all the effort gone to waste.

And they chased Pelandok from one end of the verandah to the other. But Pelandok was too quick for them.

The heavenly, heady smells of all that cooked rice was making him too excited to keep still. Nasi lemak! Nasi bryani! Nasi minyak! And more, more, more!

Oh! Oh! Oh!

Scattering rice! Flour! Fluffy white! Saffron yellow! Turmeric orange!

The ground was soon plastered with rice flour; the guests covered with rice. White! Yellow! Orange!

Oh! Oh! Oh! Rice is precious!

Especially saffron rice!

Then Pelandok ran over the top of the gifts. All of them! Even the *Bunga Telur* (the symbol of fertility) which is offered to the guests in return for their gifts.

Oh! Oh! Oh!

But Pelandok knew his luck would soon run out.

He grabbed a pillow and headed down the stairs.

The wedding guests followed, but they were not quick enough.

When they reached the ground, they saw the end of the pillow deep under the house.

Oh! Oh! Oh!

"Catch him!" And they ducked under the floorboards, swearing and cursing, while dressed in their finest. They were sure to catch the rascal now! For the house overhung a river and they had surrounded the house, on all three sides.

But Pelandok wasn't under the house.

As soon as he had tossed the pillow into the depths of the *bawah rumah* (under the house), he had snuck back into the house, found a cauldron, and tipping the contents out, managed to find a slab of clotted rice at the bottom conveniently shaped like a cauldron. He pushed the clotted rice cauldron into the river below and jumped in!

There! Escape!

And so Pelandok sailed away, far, far away. Away from the feast. Away from the kampung. And away from the land of the Gaping Mouth.

He travelled for a while before he spied a youth on the banks of the river.

"*Buat apa*? (What are you doing?)" said Pelandok.

"*Tak apa*, (Nothing,)" said the youth.

"*Mari!* (Come!) Join me," said Pelandok.

And so, the youth leapt into the clotted rice cauldron and joined Pelandok.

The two sailed on. Past rocky headlands, past tall trees, oh could they be durians? On they sailed and soon Pelandok and the youth saw Pak Si Bajok, Father Ape.

"*Buat apa*? (What are you doing?)" said Pelandok.

"*Tak apa*, Nothing," said Pak Si Bajok.

"*Mari!* (Come!) Join me," said Pelandok.

And so, the ape leapt into the clotted rice cauldron and joined Pelandok and the youth. The three sailed on.

Past more rocky headlands, past more tall trees until they came to a land where the fields lay untilled, and the fruit hung rotten on the trees.

They had arrived in a land abandoned to a tiger. The threesome sailed on until they perceived a man walking wearily on the banks of the river.

"*Buat apa*? (What are you doing?)" said Pelandok. "Why is this land so silent?"

"*Tak apa*, (Nothing)," said the man. "There is nothing to do. Nothing because this land has been laid waste by Harimau. This is why it is silent."

"What! Go tell your king that it is not difficult to kill Harimau," said Pelandok, Salaam Di Rimba.

At once the man went and let the king know.

And the king summoned Salaam di Rimba to his court.

Immediately, Salaam di Rimba presented himself before the king.

"Is it true what my slave says? That you Salaam di Rimba can kill the tiger that has been plaguing my kingdom?"

"It is true. Your slave can kill the tiger. But please grant your slave a vessel of liquid rubber and two bags of cotton."

And it was done as he commanded! Salaam di Rimba was presented with the rubber and cotton.

"*Ampun Tuanku.* (Pardon my lord king). *Sa ratus ribu ampun saya*, (a hundred thousand pardons from me), but when I slay Harimau, what will be my reward?"

"If you keep your *perjanjian* (promise), you will *nikahkannya* (marry) my daughter."

"*Baiklah.* (Good)," said Pelandok and began his preparations. "From what direction, and at what time does the tiger arrive?"

"Evening." The men took Salaam di Rimba to the place where the tiger hunted, for tigers are known to return to their kill. They carried the rubber and the cotton with them.

Salaam di Rimba sat down. "You may return to your homes." Then he waited, but he did not have to wait long, for a short time later the tiger arrived.

"*Ka Sang Harimau ini hendak kemana?* (Mister Tiger, where are you going?"

"*Melanggar* (Violate) this country."

"How long have you been doing this work?"

"About three months." Came the smug reply.

"What? You have been running amok through this land for three months and have yet to subdue it? Perhaps you have no magic. For if you had the proper magic, you would have subdued this country."

Tiger frowned. This was not the response he expected. Still, this was salvageable. "Teach me this magic."

"Ah, but what if I teach you and you do not believe?" The tone was coy.

"Teach me and I will believe," said the tiger furiously, and as he looked around saw the fresh rubber and the cotton. "Oh, what is this?"

"This is it. *Hikmat yang sangat besar.* (Great wisdom.)" Pelandok nodded at the rubber and cotton. "If you were to wipe this over your body, you would be stronger, and your courage would increase."

Tiger roared. "*Kenakanlah pada badan aku.* (Rub it over my body.)"

And so, Salaam di Rimba did as he was ordered. He smeared the fresh white liquid rubber over the impatient tiger's body.

As well as Tiger's face. And eyes. Effectively blinding the tiger.

"One more thing," said Pelandok, before Harimau realised what was happening.

And the greedy tiger waited, eyes glued shut, eagerly contemplating the ensuing rampage.

Salaam di Rimba covered the foolish tiger with cotton. And then it was done. There in the field of lallang waited the foolish, greedy tiger for the magic to take effect.

"Now it is done!"

But of course, with his mouth covered, the tiger could not respond. And of course, his ears were stuffed with cotton. So, he did not hear Pelandok move away or call out.

"Come!" said Salaam di Rimba to the men. "Set fire to the lallang."

And so, the field was set alight.

White and yellow edged along the tiger's vision, becoming in minutes, blindingly white. Then there was the heat. The radiant heat. And the acrid scent of smoke.

At first, the tiger turned its head left and right, unable to see, unable to believe that he smelt fire. Perhaps it was the magic about to work, but soon he knew that he had been tricked.

That cursed Pelandok! If only he could get his paws on him. But tiger could not see.

The tiger ran. *Hulu. Hilir.* (Upstream. Downstream.)

But Salaam di Rimba's plan had been too well thought out. The field had been set alight at its boundaries. Tiger was surrounded by raging flames.

Orange glowing, red flaming, and brilliant white.

And soon the fire ate the tiger and he perished.

Ah!

The people told the news to the king and the king was greatly pleased with their story.

Shortly after, Salaam di Rimba presented himself at court. "Pardon my lord, but now that the tiger is dead, will you grant your slave your promise?"

"*Telah aku sempernakan perjanjian aku itu.* (I will fulfill my agreement)," said the king and he ordered preparations for the royal wedding.

But Salaam di Rimba stopped him. "Do not bother with me because I am an animal. But marry your daughter to my adopted son."

The king was delighted to marry his daughter to a human rather than to an animal.

The royal wedding feast lasted seven days and seven nights.

Seven is a special number.

And so, the adopted son of Pelandok lived in the palace with his new bride, and for a while, all was well.

But one day, the young man approached Pelandok. "I would like to return to my home to see my mother whom I miss very much."

Pelandok was happy to hear this and the two set off back to the young man's home. When they reached the house of the young man, the young man's mother was so happy to see her son that she wept, for she had thought him dead.

The pair stayed together in the young man's house for many days. Then one day Pelandok approached his adopted son. "Why is your mother living alone?"

"If I ask, she may be angry with me."

"*Jangan kamu berchakap itu waktu ia tengah lapar, dan jangan waktu ia tengah berkerja.* (Don't ask when she's hungry, and don't ask when she's in the middle of work.)"

And so eventually at the right time, the young man approached his mother.

"I have no wish for a husband," said the mother.

Five or six days later, Salaam di Rimba approached the boy. "Speak with your mother once more. What has she done that she prefers to be alone the rest of her life?"

The young man began to see that Pelandok was right, and at the right time, he approached his mother.

By now, Pelandok had lived with them for a long time. And the mother agreed to marry Pelandok.

The three lived together happily until one day, Salaam di Rimba felt a desire to return to his own home. The young man liked the idea. The three set off together.

Masok hutan. Keluar hutan.

(Into jungles. And out of jungles.)

Masok gunung. Keluar gunung.

(Up mountains. Down mountains.)

Masok Padang. Keluar Padang.

(Onto plains. Across plains.)

Maka tiba-tiba berjumpa dengan sabuah negeri terlalu rameinya. Maka tiba ini Salaam di Rimba mejadi manusia, dia-lah raja didalam negeri itu.

(Then suddenly they came across a country that was filled with people. Then Salaam di Rimba became a human, for he was the king in the land.)

Maka dudoklah ia bersuka-suka dengan anak isterinya.

(He lived there happily with his wife and child.

His adopted son returned to his wife, the princess, and lived happily, too.)

See Notes on Pages 346-348

Grandmaster and the Gergasi

Pelandok jenaka menipu gergasi –
The Joker deceives the Giant (Original Title)

One of the first tasks that Pelandok undertook once he was King of the Rainforest was to slay the giant – Gergasi / Girgasi / Gergarsang etc.

In this version, he is only king over the tigers and the goats.

A T THE COURT of Seladang, the Gaur, were gathered Badak (the Rhinoceros), Landak (the Porcupine), Rusa (the Sambar Deer), Kijang (the Barker), and other ambassadors.

"Our children are being devoured, even as we assemble," said the denizens of the rain forest. "What can we do about the monstrosity?"

Thus, they referred to Gergasi, the giant sometimes also known as Antu Raya and other names.

Seladang had no answer though he pondered long and hard.

Eventually, Serigala, the red dog also known as the wolf, spoke. "A thousand pardons my lord but may I have leave to speak?"

"Speak," said Seladang the Gaur King.

"It is said that Pelandok the Trickster possesses miracles directly from heaven by way of meditation."

"Explain."

"He meditates and is thus given a talisman. It is rumoured that this is how he has been deemed Grand Master of the Jungle and now holds court under the cassia tree."

"*Bohong*! (Lies!)" Rusa leapt to her feet.

"I have heard that the tigers and goats have made peace. And that it is all his doing," said Seladang, eyes half closed as he thought deeply.

The animals debated.

Was this *sakti* (supernatural powers)?

The argument went back and forth until at last, Landak, known as the Wise One, suggested, "Let us send Serigala to Pelandok. We have nothing to lose. And if it is true, much to gain."

And so, it was agreed to despatch Serigala, who shot through the jungle in search of the one that had been known as Pelandok the Trickster who may indeed be Pelandok the King.

Only how was it possible?

Over *sungei* (rivers), *bukit* (hills) and *gunung* (mountains), through *hutan* (jungle), and *paya* (swamps), Serigala journeyed tirelessly until at last he reached Pelandok's court.

Even before he reached his destination, a floral scent permeated the air, hinting of glorious wonders to come.

Thus, in great anticipation, Serigala entered the grove. He looked up, heart beating rapidly. He was not disappointed.

The monarch mousedeer was seated on a white rock under the shade of a golden shower tree (cassia tree), its canopy of hanging yellow flowers resembling a huge parasol.

Serigala blinked, inhaling deeply of what seemed indisputable evidence of nobility.

For the Cassia fistula is the national tree and flower of Thailand, and its flowers symbolize Thai royalty. They also give off a strong floral note reminiscent of mimosa.

And if that was not enough, reclined around Pelandok were the people of Kambing and Harimau, eternal enemies, discoursing peacefully.

Serigala's throat grew dry. And he would have retired except that Pelandok had already noticed him. In fact, from the ongoing conversation, it seemed that he had been seen from afar.

"Here is Serigala," said Pelandok, turning his head as if to deign to cast his glance on Serigala.

Serigala trembled. But what cemented Serigala's belief that Pelandok was indeed the new ruler of the jungle were the words the mousedeer spoke next.

"I know why you are here."

Serigala almost swooned, so heady were the feelings that throbbed through his body. He barked his request in the greatest of faith that he would be granted a miracle, and when Pelandok turned and said, nay, promised, "It is an easy task."

The mousedeer's words sealed the red dog's loyalty forever.

And from that day onwards, Serigala became Pelandok's most faithful follower.

"Approach."

Trembling with fear, Serigala came forward. Close to the new leader, he could see that Pelandok had a white moustache and brows and that he was seated on a white rock. All signs of ascetism.

Indeed, I am standing on Holy Ground!

But what Serigala did not know was that just moments earlier, Musang the Fox had informed Pelandok of the appearance of the Gergasi, and Pelandok, seeing Serigala approaching, (he does have exceptional eyesight) in such haste, had put two and two together.

Pelandok now turned to the goats and the tigers, and it was indeed unnerving to see how all the beasts fawned before him.

"It is known," said Pelandok, "that giants are not allowed into the jungle. Their domain is the mountain known as the Mountain of the Giants and there they must stay according to the gods."

The beasts gasped at his wisdom.

"But your Majesty," said Harimau, unable to stop shaking with fear. "How is Your Majesty to keep Gergasi in his place?"

"Giants are big, and their weakness lies in their size. They think slowly and are gullible. All we need do is get him into a position where he must think or be lost and then we have won."

All the beasts nodded appreciatively. Including Serigala, although he had no inkling how the impossible was to be accomplished.

But wasn't this the domain of a monarch – to protect his people against incredible threats? And thus, his love for Pelandok only grew.

"Get me fresh glue," said Pelandok and at once the animals went forth to do his bidding.

"Dig a pit," said Pelandok.

The animals did his bidding.

Pelandok turned to Serigala who bowed until his forehead touched the ground. "Now go! Tell the beasts of the plains and of the Jungle, that by tomorrow, Gergasi will be no more. It is a shame that they took so long before they came to me, but what is done is done. By tomorrow the jungle will be rid of this monstrosity."

"Yes, your Lordship," said Serigala, almost falling over his feet as he sped away to carry the incredible news back to the Court of Seladang the Gaur.

Back at the Court, when the animals heard the glad tidings, they scattered to spread the news even further.

"The Gergasi will be no more. Pelandok, the new Lord of the Jungle has seen to it. By tomorrow the giant will be gone. Celebrate! Rejoice!"

Back at the Court of Pelandok, the mousedeer headed off to find the giant.

He trotted until he reached the middle of the jungle, where a hole had been dug by the wild pig and the panther. This had been done on his command.

Pelandok approached and began to scrabble away at the sides, calling out at the same time, "*Bini, anak! Datang! Chepat-chepat!* (Wife, son! Come! Hurry, hurry)!"

His frantic calls soon attracted the giant.

"Quick! The end of the world will soon be here! Hurry!" Pelandok continued to call to his absent family.

"*Apa khabar, Pelandok*! (Hello, Mousedeer!)" said Gergasi as he approached.

The Mousedeer looked up but did not stop the frantic digging. "Have you not heard?" said Pelandok, panting with exhaustion. "There is a great shaking coming and soon everything will fall."

"What? I never heard of that?"

"I dreamt it."

"Ah," said Gergasi. "If you dreamt it, then it must be so." And his belief increased when the ground around him shook.

But it was only Gajah, stamping as instructed earlier by Pelandok.

"Hurry, my wife and child, hurry," said Pelandok and scrabbled some more at the sides of the hole.

Gergasi peered down the hole, curious. "What are you doing?"

"Digging a hole for my family and I to hide in."

"Why, that looks like a good idea. I am very tall," said Gergasi, but failing miserably to look modest. "Perhaps I could hide in there as well."

"How I wish you could, but as you can see, the hole is not big enough."

"Let me help you." And Gergasi jumped into the hole.

The giant and the mousedeer dug and dug. But it was hard work.

"Why not have a rest?" said Pelandok.

"Don't mind if I do," said Gergasi. He clambered out and within seconds was snoring loudly.

Pelandok waited a few moments to make sure that the giant was really asleep. Then he called out, "Quick, bring the glue."

The animals brought the rubber. On Pelandok's instructions they carefully poured the fresh glue into the pit and then covered the bottom and the glue with leaves.

Then Gajah danced once more.

Startled, Gergasi woke to find his surroundings moving! The giant screamed, thinking that the end of the world was already here.

"Quick, into the hole at once!" shouted Pelandok, "You first and then me and my family."

Gergasi did not hesitate but leapt into the hole, only-

"Oh, oh! What is the matter, I cannot move!"

"Oh, you are silly, Gergasi! You couldn't even dig a hole well. Why you have left your head sticking out."

"So, I have! What can I do?" blubbered the giant.

"Nothing!" said Pelandok. "You are well and truly stuck. In fact, so stuck that if I were to dance upon your head there is nothing that you can do!"

And to prove his point, Pelandok danced a *joget* (dance)on Gergasi's head.

At first Gergasi screamed and shouted but when he found himself well and truly stuck, he began to weep and plead. "Please Pelandok, mighty Pelandok, generous Pelandok, please let me go."

By now, the animals had gathered round the pit. They were amazed to see the monstrous giant trapped exactly as Pelandok had promised. Soon the other beasts from the court of Seladang began to gather round, including the Gaur King himself.

All were amazed and glad to see that Gergasi was unable to move or escape.

All except Pelandok who was thinking hard.

"Please, please Pelandok. Let me go and I promise never to come back again," said Gergasi.

Pelandok looked around at the cheering animals. "Very well, Gergasi. You have made a promise and the trees, these all-knowing trees, will hold you to your word."

For it was accepted that certain trees were the homes of the spirits.

Gergasi nodded, understanding what Pelandok was alluding to. "I promise!" thundered the giant.

And so Pelandok ordered the birds to pick berries, and he and the animals squeezed the juice over Gergasi for these berries' juice dissolved glue.

Now Pelandok had been planning a speech but as soon as Gergasi was free he fled back towards his mountain and was never seen again.

"God may end the world, but a mousedeer can end a giant."

And at those words, Musang the fox fell upon his knees and paid obeisance to Pelandok. "From this day forth, we are your subjects."

Pelandok beamed. Looking over the astonished crowd of animals, he spoke. "Animals of the plain and jungle, Landak and Serigala are to be my heralds from this day forth!"

Then Beruang burst forward. "Tuan, here are the offerings from my people." And the bears laid tray upon tray of tamarind fruit before Pelandok.

Not to be outdone, the Gaur king came forward and bowed.

"Tuan, you have done as you promised," said Seladang, his voice quavering. "Ride upon me so that the animals can see your triumph!"

And Pelandok did so, riding in state upon the noble Seladang as all the animals cheered.

And that was how the domain of Pelandok the Trickster grew even more. But there was one group that refused to acknowledge Pelanduk.

See Notes on Page 348

Monkey Business

Sang Singa terta'alok kapada pelandok jenaka –
The Lion is Attracted to the Joker (original title)

*I*T WAS THE *monkeys.*
It was always the monkeys.
Kera, the monkey king, was eating rambutans and hurling abuse at the absent Pelandok when Serigala passed by.

"Pelandok a king? Why, did he not flee to Buaya for protection not so long ago! And even the golden collar that he cursed us with, was that not given by man! False king! Fake monarch!"

Serigala bristled, barely able to restrain himself from ripping into Kera. "If it were not for the commandment of Tuan Pelandok to maintain peace in the jungle, I would come over and tear you to bits!"

In response, Kera waggled his head and rolled his eyes. "Adoi! *Saya takut!* (I am scared!) Are you planning to trick us like your fake lord tricked everyone? There is no true kingship in a trickster. Let him meet us in battle as a real king would do!"

And so Serigala returned to the court of King Pelandok and reported *verbatim* the treasonous words.

"I will go at once-" said Pelandok, but King Beruang held up one paw.

"*Nanti!* (Wait!) Do not demean yourself by the antics of this nobody. You are our great and mighty king. Do not lower yourself to meet this troublemaker on equal terms. Let myself and Serigala do so on your behalf," said King Beruang.

"Do as you have spoken, Prince of the Bears," said Pelandok, granting permission.

And so, the very next day, a strange conglomeration formed of animals readying for battle against the monkeys.

They were out for revenge. Out to guard the honour of King Pelandok, but when they reached the monkey kingdom, it seemed that the monkeys were out.

Kera, who had spies everywhere, had heard the rumours of the invasion and fled to the kingdom of the lions.

Kera threw himself on the mercy of the king of the lions, Singa. "Oh, great and mighty *Singa* (Lion), is it not said that the lion is the king of the jungle?"

Singa pushed out his chest but said nothing. He didn't need to. Being king afforded him many luxuries. And one of them was the ability to look mysterious. This was what he did when he was still deliberating his response.

Kera, perfectly knowing the rules of etiquette and diplomacy continued fawning. "And as you are the-" he paused for effect, fluttering his eyelashes— "the *true* king of the jungle, we come to you for protection." And Kera then proceeded to tell the stories of how Pelandok had tricked the monkeys time and again. Wringing his long tail in his hands, Kera told the piteous tale of how he had lost his wife and children…

Singa's heart bled. He had heard the stories, too.

And so, the Lion King, Singa, granted Kera and his people protection. But then he really didn't have a choice.

He was king and while being king came with many privileges it also came with many rules. One of them was affording sanctuary to another ruler.

When King Beruang and Serigala reached the domain of the lions, they set up camp on the border and waited. But days passed, and still Singa refused to meet them in battle.

"We want peace," said Singa. "Why wage war over an usurper?"

When news of this stalemate reached Pelandok's ears, he sent forth his heralds: Landak and Serigala.

But they, too, were refused an audience by Singa.

"Imposters! Hypocrites!" taunted Kera, seated on the sidelines.

And the pair were sent off smarting, a string of abuse in their ears.

"This cannot go on," said Pelandok. "If *might* cannot win." And he nodded at the great army that Serigala and Beruang had assembled. "And *diplomacy* has failed," and he pointed his snout at Landak and Serigala.

The animals waited with bated breath.

Pelandok sighed. "Then there really is only one option left."

The animals cringed with fear.

But then their king smiled, deep brown eyes turning liquid with love.

The animals swooned, so passionately in love were they with their new king.

"But, but Your Highness, what do you mean?" said Serigala, fearing the worst.

"Simple. Tell Singa that if it is a battle that Kera wishes, then it is a battle that we will wage. Only it is to be single combat between myself and Singa. King to king."

Hearing the news, half the court fainted.

A mousedeer versus a lion.

There was only one way such a battle could end.

And how Singa the Lion King laughed when the news was related to him.

"Let it be said that Singa the Lion King is magnanimous," roared Singa with glee. "Very well. To prevent the bloodshed of all our subjects, it will be single combat."

Serigala quaked, panic evident in his dark eyes. "And the method of combat, Your High-ness?"

Singa gave a derisive nod. Sunlight shone upon his skin, reflecting its golden sheen. And his entire court gasped at his splendiferous beauty, cementing even further his aristocracy. He opened wide saintly amber eyes. "Let my opponent decide."

Ironically, the proud lion king sealed his fate with that humble decision.

Pelandok on hearing the news, smiled. "Blowpipe."

Deadly.

The entire court shivered. Even so, how could Pelandok win?

On the selected day, the two kings and their people gathered on the plains to watch the outcome.

The rules were simple:
1. The two combatants were to face one another;
2. Each combatant would have his mouth open;
3. The blowpipes were to be loaded with *sa-biji Mata Kuching* (one Cat's Eye seed) the translucent flesh peeled away;
4. The winner was the one who placed his Cat's Eye seed in his opponent's mouth;
5. The winner would accept the undisputed total surrender of the loser and his people.

It seemed straightforward.

And, Singa had had enough of the monkeys. His unwanted guests had ploughed through all his food stores, rumour-mongered from morning to night, and annoyed his entire harem to the eyeballs with their constant tricks and dramatics. If he won, they would have to go home.

What could Singa do but agree?

As Pelandok had chosen the form of battle and created the rules, Singa had first go.

The entire jungle had gathered to observe the momentous occasion. Everyone waited.

All knew of the Lion King's skill. His prowess. His accuracy.

Singa stepped up to the mark. He knew the whole jungle was watching. Expertly, he held up the blowpipe. There was power in the way he loaded his weapon. Brought the end to his mouth. Took a deep breath. Centred his aim at the distant mouth of Pelandok.

The world stopped spinning.

Everyone stilled.

Sound stopped.

And then-

Pfftt!

The shiny black Mata Kuching seed shot into the soft earth with a thunk.

Right by Pelandok's delicate feet.

Feet? Not mouth?

Wait! What? Did that mean that… *The mighty Singa had missed?*

Missed.

Everyone gasped.

Groans and whispers of disbelief erupted from the audience. His face heated with shame. Before the whole world.

Enraged. Furious. Disappointed with his wretched attempt - *in front of the whole rain forest* - he opened his mouth even wider to roar his anger to the entire jungle.

Arrrrrgggghhhhhhhh-

It was at this point that Pelandok's berry hit its target.

The red open mouth of an angry lion is always an easier target than the tiny pink mouth of a mousedeer.

Singa's eyes widened at the shock of something small hitting his soft palate.

So stunned that he inadvertently swallowed.

Grave error.

You see, had the pellet been a Cat's Eye seed as had earlier been agreed upon, all would be well.

Yes, Singa would have lost. And that would have been it.

Pelandok is Pelandok, however, and when no one was looking, he had substituted the shiny black seed with an ant. Several ants. More than several as these are so tiny.

Maybe a hundred ants?

But they weren't the black ants that love sugar and are found throughout Malaysia and Singapore. The harmless kind. No, they were the red ants. The ones that sting and bite and make your life a misery. The painful kind.

These were what Pelandok had shoved down the nozzle of his blowpipe.

They didn't want to be in anyone's mouth.

And so, they stung.

Gnawed.

Sliced with their pincers.

Oh, how Singa screamed and wept and gagged.

But it was too late.

Everyone in the jungle had heard his scream of agony. Seen how he had gone down. Capitulated. And so, in the end, the mighty Singa, King of the Jungle was forced on bended knee to pay homage to Pelandok.

Oh, Pelandok! Once again you have won.

And that you would think would have been the end of the story and of the dispute between Pelandok and Kera.

But if you do, then you don't know much about monkeys.

Because even before Singa landed on the ground, Kera fled.

He fled to one who was wise and respected.

There was only one such animal left.

Oh dear!

See Notes on Page 348

Kicking: Shaikh 'Alam berbenteh dengan Raja Gajah

Shaikh 'Alam quarrels with the Elephant King (Original Title)

KERA ESCAPED.

Monkeys are smart. And the King of the Monkeys was known to be particularly smart. "Hurry!" he called to his subjects.

And thus, the kingdom of the elephants soon found itself overrun by the kingdom of monkeys.

Nobody likes an invasion of monkeys.

And Raja Gajah was about to be inundated.

Elephants like their freedom. And thanks to their size, they can move about the rainforest unimpeded. And so, the events of the deep jungle unfolded while the elephants went about loftily unaware. Even when a rumour reached them, so powerful and mighty the entire herd deemed themselves, that they chose often to ignore the little creatures' talk, considering the missives beneath their regard.

Kelelawar of the bats flew in one day.

"Greetings, Rajah Gajah," said Kelelawar.

"What news?" asked Rajah Gajah, half asleep.

"I hail from the domain of King Kancil. We are indeed fortunate to come under his protection."

"King? A kancil is king? What nonsense!"

"I assure you that it is not nonsense. Why I have literally left the lion lying with the goat. Even the tigers bow before him." And so, saying Kelelawar nodded again before flying off.

Gajah sat up, now wide awake.

"You are a raja, and a raja is far more important than a king any day!" said Gajah's cousin.

"Hail the great and mighty Raja Gajah!" shouted another cousin.

It is as if they already believe. For no one is even denying the fact that Kancil is king.

Thus, when Kera turned up a few days later, Gajah was not completely surprised.

"King Gajah, the wise! King Gajah the kind! King Gajah the generous!" called out Kera as he and his people approached.

King Gajah sighed, knowing that an enormous favour was in the offing. But the rules of etiquette and diplomacy had been drilled into him. There was only one way to respond. "King Kera, it is good to see you. Welcome!"

Kera threw himself at Gajah's feet. "We beg sanctuary."

Gajah had heard of the devastation that Kera had brought to the kingdom of the lions. He did not wish that repeated in his own domain. But how to wiggle out of this imposition without appearing powerless? Ungenerous? Ignoble?

"You are our *last* hope," said Kera and waited expectantly.

Well, what else could Gajah do, except smile and grant the monkeys leave to remain in his domain? And when Kera began to praise and compliment old, fat Gajah, he burst out, "Why I am Gajah. I shape the jungle and I will shape this boaster cock!"

And he believed he could.

Empty praise inflates ability.

Now Pelandok had sent out Beruang and Serigala again, but not before he had bestowed titles upon them. This is how rulers win the loyalty of their followers.

Serigala and Beruang were now Maharajahs – great princes.

And so, the two great princes camped on the boundary of King Gajah's land. With great pomp, they went forth to speak with King Gajah.

"You troublemakers, what do you want?" said King Gajah. Now another advantage of an elephant is height. Elephants tower over every other creature in the rainforest. So, Gajah loomed impressively over the two envoys. It had always worked in the past.

But not now. Instead, the vassals of Pelandok stood tall, having the backing of their king for reassurance. This defiance disconcerted Gajah, although he knew better than to let it show.

"We are here for Kera."

Gajah raised his trunk. "Kera is under my protection and in my domain he will stay. Go tell that to the Trickster."

And so Pelandok was duly informed. "Very well, if that is how it is. Gather our forces. In three days, we march."

And that was exactly how in three days' time that the two kings, Kera, and Gajah, found themselves nervously staring at the strangest procession they had ever seen.

Earlier that morning a heavy cold had pressed upon the jungle canopy. Mist veiled the tops of the trees like a white scarf. The absence of the dawn chorus that morning was unnerving.

A sign everyone waited for something to happen.

Gajah squinted. In the distance, he noted several black dots wheeling and soaring. His heart constricted with foreboding.

"What are they?" gasped Kera, for monkeys dwelt beneath the jungle canopy. "They are too far to make out."

"Vultures," said Gajah.

Even the gods are on the side of Pelandok.

"How can you tell?"

"Height." And Gajah sighed. "I smell war on the wind."

For vultures soar high to seek their prey.

"They desire blood."

Ours. Gajah shivered.

When Kera looked askance, he said simply. "It is the cold."

Deram-deram!

Distant rumbling sounded from afar.

Only a faint glimmer of sound, but so silent had been the land that the tiny echo was enough to frighten Kera, whose nerves were already on edge.

Thunder? Or drums?

For creatures of long ago, the loudest sound was thunder. Especially to those on the Malayan peninsula where there were no volcanos. They believed thunder was the voice of the gods.

The sun rose, a brilliant line of gold edging the horizon. The early morning light lit Kera's pale face.

Petir!

"What was that sharp clap?"

"The drums of war."

Further evidence that the gods were indeed on Pelandok's side.

Kera squealed.

"Trees being pushed down," said Gajah, astonished and discomfited, for it was elephant who was the architect of the jungle because being of massive size that when elephant moved about, he dislocated trees and destroyed shrubs.

Elephant was being replaced. And elephant did not like that.

Gajah shaded his eyes with his trunk. He began to make out faces. Figures.

Badak, the Rhinoceros King, leading his troops. His armoured retinue had their massive heads lowered. It was they who had pushed down the trees to clear a path.

Crash! Smash! Boom!

Just how big is this invasion?

Out of the dust of destruction came a parade of lions, padding noiselessly on soft paws, sunlit golden eyes sparkling like jewels.

Kera and Gajah exchanged a look of horror. But there were more to come.

Goats. Hundreds of them. White-bearded, soft ears twitching, wielding mercilessly ridged horns.

Next came Kijang and his people of the Barking Deer, followed closely by Sambhur. All looking mild and deceptively gentle until you caught a glimpse of the fight in their clear brown eyes.

No, no mercy to be had there either. King Kijang turned his head to one side and a stream of stars sprinkled silver down his side.

Kera began to quake.

And even Gajah had turned white.

But the procession was far from finished.

Next came Beruang and his people.

Shaggy, thick-muscled, white-snouted, some bore the emblem of the dazzling sun on their chests. All looked eager to strangle and clasp and murder.

Kera swallowed hard.

Gajah stamped nervously.

King Kerbau now led his troops.

Black glossy hides, black eyes, and horns that stretched widely end to end. Wicked.

Kera slumped, barely able to stand, his arms and tail limp.

Gajah bobbed his head continuously, swaying anxiously from side to side. A full-blown headache was coming on. Blood vessels strained to bursting.

Then came Harimau, the Tiger King leading his troop. Each tiger held its head proudly as they moved sinuously along the ground, golden eyes peeled for anything out of the ordinary. Striped gods of the deep jungle. Terrifying. Majestic.

And then finally, at the very end of the parade, came King Seladang.

Kera blinked.

Gajah strained to look.

Here indeed was Pelandok, mounted atop Seladang, and both kings further flanked by king after king.

It was then that Gajah's last hope died.

But Gajah was a true king. "Come," said King Gajah, lifting his trunk magnificently. "It is time to meet."

Kera hung his head and followed listlessly as the pair prepared to meet Pelandok the Trickster.

There is a saying: When elephants battle, mousedeer get crushed underfoot. But riding upon the back of King Seladang the Gaur, Pelandok went straight up to Gajah without blinking or dismounting.

"Greetings, King Gajah," said Pelandok, "I salute you as an equal."

Gajah baulked. "Equal? Since when! You have tricked everyone, but you shall not trick me."

"I wasn't planning to," said Pelandok, calmly. "In fact, I have come to challenge you to a contest."

"A contest?" said Gajah, recovering slightly at the sound of that.

"Yes. A kicking contest. Shinbone against shinbone."

Shin kicking is a martial sport that began in 1612 and is still played today. Also known as shin diggings or purring, it involves two contestants. The event requires both agility and the ability to endure terrific pain at close quarters.

Gajah began to hope. He narrowed his eyes craftily as he began to plan his escape.

Look at those pencil thin legs. Why, there is no way I could lose, thought Gajah as he studied Pelandok's physique.

Pelandok waited. He could almost read Gajah's mind.

"Very well," said the Elephant King. "What are the rules?"

The rules were simple:

1.   Gajah's troops remained on one side while Pelandok's troops remained on the other
2.   Each opponent got three kicks
3.   Everyone else was to be a witness
4.   The first opponent to cry out in pain or weep is the loser
5.   The winner is the undisputed king.

Gajah agreed. He really could not see how he could lose. But then neither could he see the pointed piece of belian (ironwood) hidden deep in the lallang.

This was Pelandok's secret weapon.

The contest began.

"King Gajah may begin!" said Pelandok and straightened his foreleg, offering it to Gajah.

Everyone gasped at what seemed sheer stupidity.

Pelandok smiled.

Distraction as usual was his weapon. While everyone was shaking their heads and discussing this foolishness, no one had noticed that he had adjusted his leg *behind* the ironwood.

The entire crowd watched. Jaws opened in anticipation. Eyes were wide.

"Let it be the defamer or the defamed who shits himself. I will get to the point. Your subjects and mine are the witnesses. Watch my eyes. Check to see if tears roll down my cheeks. Check to see if screams of pain hurl from my mouth. Then when you are done, check to see if my leg is broken or bruised."

The crowd roared. So excited were they with Pelandok's urging.

They would look! They would check! They would verify!

And thus, they fell once more into Pelandok's trap: distraction.

Pelandok raised his hoof and the cheering stopped. His face was deadly serious. "I say, to the witnesses, watch, watch, watch. You must watch or be struck down by God. May you be cursed to the second and third generations. Crushed under a mountain. Crushed under a tree."

Eyes widened. Jaws dropped. Hearts tightened.

Then elephant gave a shout and raised his trunk. Gajah eager to put an end to this fiasco, took his place.

Steadying himself, he prepared to kick.

Ready, one, two, three! Kick!

The thick stump that was Gajah's leg shot out, swinging perilously close to Pelandok's leg but of course it stopped short. Thanks to the jagged piece of belian.

And as Gajah's foot contacted the belian-

Pain exploded throughout Gajah's entire being.

To stop from screaming, Elephant bit his lip. The taste of iron flooded his mouth. Extreme agony shot up his foot, spreading through from his toes up to his gut. But just in time he remembered the rules of the game. And stopped himself from showing any emotion.

Perspiration beaded his entire being. He swallowed his blood then darted a look at the mousedeer's face in hopes that perhaps he had done what was necessary and had won the contest.

But a single glance at that noble face only showed him the impossible.

Pelandok was unmoved. In fact, he appeared completely untouched.

This cannot be, thought Gajah, in complete disbelief.

How can he be untouched when I am in extreme agony?

And as he watched, Pelandok leaned and nuzzled his slender leg.

Impossible! Gajah blanched.

Pelandok flicked one ear lazily and smiled up at elephant. "All good. You may begin again when you are ready. I promised three strikes."

Gajah shook his head, unable to believe what his eyes were telling him: that Pelandok has escaped unhurt while he was aching beyond belief.

But elephant is a noble beast. He gritted his teeth, refusing to show any weakness, even though his wound was starting to bleed. Even though his injury was smarting beyond belief. Even though he could barely move. Gajah was determined to get this over with.

Gajah struck once and then twice!

Kick! Kick!

And once again Gajah contacted what seemed a rod of iron.

This time, sheer misery numbed Gajah's entire being. He felt as if he were paralysed and indeed his entire body was wracked with excruciating pain.

How Gajah wanted to scream! To take off for the nearest river and to soak his agony in cold water. He felt as if he had broken his toes, cracked a bone, torn muscles, and ripped ligaments. A wetness spread between his toes. He smelt blood – his blood - soaking into the ground. But Elephant could not move even if he wanted to.

Enough, he wanted to plead.

But the context was only half over.

For it was now Pelandok's turn.

Three kicks to come.

Could Elephant endure them?

Gajah squeezed his eyes shut, blinked rapidly to dry his tears.

"Are you all, right?" came Pelandok solicitous query.

Unable to speak without screaming, Gajah simply nodded.

Just bear a moment longer. This will be over soon.

In complete disbelief, he watched as Pelandok tilted his head slightly as if testing the wind. The mousedeer's eyes, big and brown, glinted.

"Ready?"

Gajah nodded furiously. Praying that he could bear just a little more pain.

"Can you move a little?"

Gajah gritted his teeth. He was unable to lift his leg. Squeezing down his pain with everything that he had, his small eyes widened as he searched furiously for an answer that would not shame him.

Pelandok's big brown eyes shot left then right as if studying the situation. As if understanding. "Very well. You do not have to move. Just hold still."

Hurry, hurry. Sweat poured down Gajah's forehead. He was so cold. But he refused to shiver. No!

Pelandok gave a tiny tap.
His delicate hoof swung.
Right between Gajah's bloodied toes.
"Arghhhhhh!" Screams tore from Gajah's throat.
The entire jungle looked on in disbelief.
Then they cheered.
How could they have ever doubted their king?
Pelandok had won.
But Pelandok wasn't the only one to use distraction.
While Gajah screamed and sobbed and pooed himself, the monkeys had taken off.
Again.
To the last king left.

Sang Rangkak kena hukum
The Crawler is Punished (Original Title)

It has been said that when Kera fled from King Kancil that he sought sanctuary from three kings:

First, the mighty lion King Singa.
Second, the noble elephant King Gajah.
Third, the despicable King Buaya.

This then is the alkesah (story).

SO FAR, THE battles that King Kancil had waged had all been in the domain of the land.
But there remained the domain of water.
And here King Buaya ruled supreme. He had grown strong.

> The Damansara river runs from Sungai Buloh to Shah Alam in the state of Selangor. A century ago, steamboats used to ply the river. 'Sara' means precious or important in Sanskrit while 'damar' means resin, used to make varnish. Today, the river is polluted with animal and human waste and is a part of the Damansara Sewage Treatment Plant. But once it was mighty and clear… and its estuary spread for miles in the sunlight glittering silver.

King Buaya's dominion was the water realm and here he ruled as absolute monarch. The numbers of his kin grew and as they multiplied, they fed upon the animals who came down to the water's edge to drink and none were safe from the voracious jaws of the bloodthirsty.
Then the animals of the land cried out.
"King Kera has sought the court of King Buaya. And Raja Buaya is killing us all."
Delegation upon delegation brought news of the menace of the Damansara. Others

gathered at King Kancil's court to hear the outcome. For miles around, the delegations came, with their tribute and retinue.

The gendak drums beat. Each delegation took their turn performing obeisance and offering gifts. And all the requests were the same: Curb the appetite of the damnable crocodiles.

"We are thirsty. Decimated. War-ravaged. A thousand, thousand pardons, oh merciful one! But we seek justice! Aid! A demonstration of your magnificent might!"

King Kancil listened.

And when his people had finished, an enormous silence grew as they awaited the reply of the monarch.

Kancil's deep brown eyes watered as he surveyed the waiting multitude who had gathered before him. Row upon row of unblinking eyes.

There was fear in those eyes and yet, there was more.

Anticipation.

Hope.

Slowly, he rose to his feet.

Heads that were bowed lifted. Eyes that were heavy with tears brightened. Jaws quavered in hope.

And when Kancil lifted his noble head and spoke, his words fell like welcome drops of rain on parched soil.

"Three years, three months, and three days have I done penance. I will pronounce the spell. It is a potent spell. And then I will be king. And king of all the jungle, land and water!"

The animals were enthralled. "Master! It is as if the deed is already so."

"So will it be. In three days, we march on King Buaya! And all will bow to me!"

Like the skies' opening, an endless drought breaking, the cheers of his people reached to the heavens! So excited and pleased and eager were they to see the end of that despicable rogue. And so, the love that they bore their monarch grew and swelled.

At Kancil's bidding the animals gathered tuba roots. And then the forces prepared themselves. This was the time.

Revenge. Reprisal! Retaliation!

The troops marched on the dawn of the third day, a host of angels marching down the hillside, in glorious raiment, arrayed victorious row upon row until the eye grew weary, for infinite appeared the forces of King Kancil.

Meanwhile, the spies of King Buaya brought news.

> Biawak, the Malayan Water Monitor is of the genus Varan, and the largest of the three common monitor lizards found in Singapore, growing up to 3 m in length. Carrion eaters, they secrete venom and are found in the jungle, swamps and sometimes canals. They perform a useful function - keeping the environment clean as scavengers, while also being a food source for crocodiles.

Biawak swam up to Buaya and bowed. His blue forked tongue darted. "The entire jungle is headed this way, Master. We are doome-"

But the warning came too late.

From the skies overhead pounded the sounds of imminent onslaught.

An uproar boomed throughout the jungle! Pulsing!

"Beat the drums!"

The drums of war!

Drumming reverberated through the jungle announcing the start of the advance.

Gegak-gempita!

A hubbub, an upheaval swiftly began.

King Buaya and Biawak watched, hearts in mouth as the cacophony intensified then-

Tanda kebesaran!

Big thunder!

As air exploded!

A deafening combination of concentrated sound fanned out relentlessly from that single point throughout the entire jungle.

Trees bowed in the mighty wake. Shrubs and bushes flattened.

To Biawak and Buaya this was the indisputable signal of greatness.

The beat changed.

This was followed immediately by the terrifying sound of trees uprooted.

The elephants were on the move.

"Gather the troops!" said King Buaya.

"We have been greedy!" screamed Biawak.

"We have committed terrible crimes, alas!" wept Buaya, shedding tears. But no one believed him.

Crocodile tears! Pah!

They launched themselves into the middle of the river hoping that the deep would provide sanctuary.

It did not.

For the first time ever, the depths failed.

For the forces of King Kancil overran the reptiles.

The elephants had been sent into the river first and as they ploughed in, thanks to their bulk and numbers, the river flooded and overflowed onto the banks.

How the crocodiles snapped and bit, but the tough hide of the elephants were no match and anyway, soon the rhinoceroses followed.

The river was emptying rapidly of water.

The crocodiles were being trampled.

The tempo changed once more.

Now came the creatures of the land. All eager for a rout.

Water buffalos next entered the fray. They threw their massive bodies down, wrestling the scaley vermin.

There was no place to hide.

Suddenly a heavy weight pushed up against Biawak in the water.

He gasped, spluttering to see who had hold of him. It was Singa the Lion King who had placed a heavy paw on Biawak's neck.

"Hold, miserable creature! You are the servant of the Devourer Buaya! Today we do away with all your kind!"

Biawak prostrated himself. "Alas, mercy! Mercy! We plead for mercy, my lord!"

But there was no mercy to be had in those golden eyes.

To Biawak's relief, a disturbance caused Singa to look away.

Tagar! (A thunderous peal!)

Had Biawak looked he would have seen King Kancil entering the battle while seated atop a white rhinoceros, but Biawak's only thoughts were of escape.

So, while Singa and the others cheered, Biawak escaped. But not for long.

Biawak was pounced up on by Harimau.

"Ah! I have you! Say your prayers! For I can hold back no longer!" said Harimau loftily.

"Please, mercy! I beg for mercy!" Biawak found himself trampled upon for the water was teeming with all the inhabitants of the jungle.

Mud splattered and blood spattered.

Biawak gulped. Then screamed an unearthly scream for Harimau was lacerating his back.

But Harimau was unable to hold on and so slipping and sliding, Biawak twisting this way he ended up before King Rusa.

"What? You!" said King Rusa with a lordly toss of his head. Polished bone antlers glinted in the morning light.

"Mercy! Mercy! Before I am done for, I beg that you take me to your lord and master, King Kancil! I wish to beg for mercy!"

King Rusa looked down upon the miscreant. "Then do so."

But Biawak only cringed and turned baffled eyes this way and that.

Perhaps it was something in Biawak's unblinking eyes which made Rusa feel pity. Rusa snorted. "Very well, I will take you to him."

"Thank you, thank you! I will never forget your kindness."

The rhythm in the air changed becoming lighter, triumphant, glorious!

Kancil had reached the water's edge.

"Crush the tuba roots and toss them into the water!" commanded the king of all kings.

There was another cheer and the sky darkened with the weight of hundreds of tuba roots being flung into the river.

The crocodiles stood no chance.

No sooner had the tuba touched the water than the poison seeped out.

Buaya and his family puked and gagged but it was useless to try to escape. Their way was blocked in every direction.

"Mercy! Mercy!" wept King Buaya as he found himself before King Kancil. Fear flooded through him.

"King Buaya, what have you to say?" said King Kancil, lifting his noble head. Glistening big brown eyes considered the crocodile.

In response, the crocodile cringed. "I am nothing before you. This day is yours. I am yours and my people are yours," wept King Buaya as he prostrated himself before King Kancil. "I throw my crown before you."

Looking down from the back of the white rhinoceros King Kancil surveyed the scene of desecration. His heart bled.

So much unnecessary suffering.

"Enough."

That single word softly spoken filtered down from the largest elephant to the smallest tortoise.

The chaos ended. The calamity ceased.

Calm. In an instant.

Heads turned expectantly in the king's direction.

Silence pressed upon the land.

The only sound to be heard was the gasping of the crocodiles as they struggled to breathe, overcome by the poison of the tuba roots.

The animals gazed enthusiastically at Kancil.

Had they all heard right?

Their king nodded at Buaya. "Now that I have your word, I will order King Gajah to fetch water."

All looked on eagerly as the elephants did as King Kancil commanded. They collected water from an uncontaminated stream.

"Drink this magic water and you will be well once more. But if you ever break your word, your punishment will be twice as severe."

"Never! We swear from now and forever to be your subjects and your slaves."

All heard the declaration.

And so, the crocodiles drank of the magic water, and they were cured, and the jungle became once again a safe place. All thanks to King Kancil.

And all in the jungle were pleased.

All?

All except for the monkeys.

Again, they fled.

Oh dear!

Guardian of the King's Soul

Shaik 'Alam berlawan dengan raksaksa - Shaik 'Alam
fights with monsters (Original Title)

THE MONKEYS ESCAPED.

Only now there was no king to save them.

They were on their own.

Yet despite everything that had happened, the monkeys continued to deride Kantjil. In the entire jungle, they were the sole objectors to the rule of King Kantjil.

Everyone else agreed that Kantjil had become king in a fair manner and as he was doing an excellent job, everyone was very happy.

Everyone except the monkeys.

Each day Kantjil trotted about his kingdom greeting his subjects.

"*Apa khabar, Buaya?* (What news or Hello, Crocodile.)"

"Khabar baik, King Kantjil (Good news, or I am good, King Kantjil)," said the crocodile.

"Apa khabar, Memerang?"

"Khabar baik, King Kantjil," said the otter.

"Apa khabar, Terkura?"

"Khabar baik, King Kantjil," said the tortoise.

"Apa khabar, Monyet?"

"*Eh, siapa tu? Semut atau kanchil?* (Eh, who is that? Ant or mousedeer.) Haha! Ha!" the monkeys laughed and pointed derisively at Kantjil.

But that was not all.

Whenever an animal approached King Kantjil for help, the monkeys with the blessing of the Monkey King, Kera, tossed abuse.

"Go find your useless king to help you!"

But when Kera tried to get other animals to join the monkeys, Musang decided that it was time. He approached King Kantjil.

"A thousand pardons, Your Majesty! But I believe that you need to do something about the monkeys," said Musang the Fox.

"The monkeys are up to mischief. No doubt about it. But that is what makes them monkeys," said King Kantjil, peaceably.

"A kingdom may be lost over a drop of honey." Musang bowed low to show no disrespect.

Kantjil's eyes narrowed as he considered Musang. Then he sighed. The last thing he wanted was war. "Very well, then, it is time *I* finally put the monkeys in their place."

His king's swift answer confirmed in the fox the belief that the king must have been thinking about this for a while. He looked up eagerly. Kantjil did not disappoint.

"Follow me." Kantjil led the fox to a path of grass that had recently been set fire to by man. He rolled in the blackened dirt, over and over until finally he resembled a patch of movable dirt, so dust-coloured and ash-painted was he.

"You- you look like a Raks-" Musang gasped, "I meant no disrespect Your Highness!"

"I *look* like a Raksha," said Kantjil, finishing Musang's sentence, and looking anything but upset. "Perfect."

Musang squinted, unsure what his king was planning.

"Follow me." This time Kantjil led Musang to a beehive. "Notice its silver colouring."

"It looks like an urn. The sort in which the Kings of Men place their souls," gasped Musang.

"Everyone knows that an enemy cannot kill a man whose soul is kept safe in one of these urns." Kantjil winked. "Perfect."

"It is important then, to ensure that each urn has the right caretaker," said Musang catching on.

Kantjil winked. "Now dear Musang, if you could please dig a hole at the base of this ancient tree. See its many knots. It is-"

"Perfect!"

Kantjil smiled.

While Musang dug the hole, Kantjil approached the bees. They had recognised their king but were still a little wary. This was their home after all.

"I have need of your hive," said King Kantjil, "but please do not be alarmed. Soon you will have my thanks!"

The thanks of a king! What would any beast sacrifice to be granted such an honour?

So, the bees buzzed around, comforted that they were playing a part in the governance of the jungle, although they had no idea yet what was happening. All they knew was to sting and to make honey. And sting some more.

In the meantime, Kantjil removed their hive and tenderly placed it half in the hole that Musang had dug.

The freshly disturbed earth around the hive gave the impression that someone had been trying to hide the 'urn' when they had been disturbed.

"Follow me." This time Kantjil led Musang to the domain of the monkeys.

While Musang hid and watched, his king strode up the path towards the chattering monkeys.

Bending his head to the ground as if distraught, Kantjil stamped as he paced. "Stupid Kantjil! Who does he think he is? Ordering me about as if he were king!"

Stamp! Stamp!

The monkeys stopped their gossiping and peered down at the intruder.

What was a demon doing in their domain?

"Who cares if anyone finds the urn of King Kantjil!! How dare he make me—*me*—a guardian of the Underworld his slave!"

Stomp! Stomp!

The scent of scorching was strong, thanks to the fact that Kanctjil had rolled in ash.

Reassured, the monkeys looked at each other and scrambled to the lower branches to get closer to the Raksha.

"The rope which fastened the urn to the sacred waringen tree has broken," muttered the Raksha.

Seethe. Seethe.

Now the waringen tree is the fig tree and it is a holy tree. Many years ago there lived a mighty king in Java whose second wife longed for her own son rather than for the son of the king's first wife, to be king. The mighty king who was growing old acquiesced and banished his first son. But that devious deed alone was not enough for the second wife who then poisoned the true heir. When the heir lay dying in the jungle his devoted wife pleaded with the gods. While the gods could not undo the work of the poison, they chose instead to turn the heir into a fig tree and his wife into a spring.

But that is not the end of the story for the younger brother (the child of the second wife) missed his older brother. The gods turned the child into a bird that searches futilely for his brother.

So, it made sense to have the urn of a king attached to such a sacred tree. And a rope stolen foreshadows the death or decline of the monarch…

Even better!

More reassured than ever, the monkeys rubbed their hands.

Kera dropped to the ground in front of the Raksha.

"Pardon me for overhearing, but did you say that you are the guardian of the urn of King Kantjil? It would be the greatest of honour to be able to look upon the sacred artifact."

"Guardian I was, but no longer. Come with me and I will show you the urn. But do not expect me to do more than that. I have had enough of the monarch and plan to return to my domain at once," said the Raksha.

Kera followed the curious black figure to where the urn lay, half buried in the dirt.

To Kera's greedy eyes, the urn did indeed resemble a vessel in which the ancient kings used to store their souls.

As the demented Kera stared, a shaft of light fell upon the urn so that it gleamed silver.

Any remaining doubt vanished.

He glanced about, the demon who had so providentially taken him to this prize was nowhere to be seen.

No doubt he has flown back to the Underworld, thought Kera. But no matter. I have Kantjil's soul, and the time has come to wreak utter and complete destruction on that fake monarch!

With a howl of triumph, Kera and the monkeys tore into the sacred urn, ripping it apart as they screamed and laughed and cried and danced!

As they fought to each get a piece of the urn, a curious grey smoke poured out of the vessel at the first tear.

Now the soul is believed to take the form of vapour, so the insubstantial mist only confirmed that this was indeed the mousedeer's soul.

The half-crazed monkeys squealed even louder.

"Here finally is the soul of King Kanjil!"

"Lost! Lost!" they howled with happiness.

Half-possessed, the monkeys gambolled and cheered and leaped while the smoke only grew blacker.

But what the monkeys assumed was the soul of King Kantjil emerging from the urn was really a swarm of bees.

The enraged bees gathered in a mighty cloud. Thousands of bees. Hanging over the hundreds of unsuspecting monkeys.

It was only a matter of time…

Attack!

Sting!

Bite!

The howls of delight from the monkeys soon turned into howls of pain.

"Oh! Oh! Ouch!"

"Stop, please stop stinging!"

"Help! Please go away!"

Terrified and confused by how their simple plan had gone awry, the desperate monkeys fled, down the path and straight into the river.

Their screams and cries for mercy echoed for a long time through the jungle.

As soon as the scene was clear, Kantjil and Musang popped back up.

"Datok Beruang will appreciate the honey," said King Kantchil. And Musang delivered the honey to the old bear.

That night the whole jungle listened to the weeping of the monkeys.

And in the morning, no one was surprised to see the monkeys turn up to the court of King Kantjil.

"A thousand mercies, Your Majesty," said Kera, bowing low. The rest of the monkeys followed suit, all prostrating themselves on the ground in line upon line.

The rest of King Kantjil's court looked on appreciatively.

"We wish to pay tribute to King Kantjil and to be King Kantjil's loyal subjects forever more."

Without hesitation, Kantjil rose and nobly accepted the monkeys. "You are welcome to be my subjects!"

And the whole court of King Kantjil cheered and leapt to their feet and the love that they bore for their king only grew and grew!

The first Miracle: Pelandok jenaka berlawan minum ayer dengan raayat-nya

The joker fights drinking water with his people

P ELANDOK LED HIS closest subjects down to the river one day.
It was the end of the dry season and the many rivers that fingered through the jungle had been reduced to streams.

When they reached the riverbed, only a small trickle could be seen. The ground lay cracked and dry like crusts of rice, disintegrating into dust as the animals trod upon its cracked surface.

"I wish to make a bet," said Pelandok.

"Willingly, we will bet, but a thousand pardons, Your Highness. Just what are we betting on?" said his devoted subjects.

"Drinking the river dry."

The companions exchanged startled looks among themselves. "But Your Highness, that is impossible! Even if the entire jungle were to get together, this is a feat that is beyond any of our powers."

"I can," said Pelandok quietly, and proceeded to trot over to a section of the river near the river mouth. There in the rocky gully, surrounded by sheer cliffs sparkling silver in the morning sunlight, Pelandok bent his head and began to drink.

Now the timing was such that the tide was going out, and so after a long time, the riverbed was dry. But Pelandok's subjects did not know that.

Instead, Pelandok's loyal subjects were wracked with wonder at the seeming miracle.

Once again, their beloved king had proven beyond a shadow of a doubt that his abilities were beyond their ken. Truly, he deserved to be their monarch.

They prostrated themselves before him with many utterings of love and devotion. "Forgive your doubting slaves, My Lordship!"

"You are truly the Great and Mighty Kancil!"

"Oh, my King, rule over us forever. Forgive our ignorance!"

Pelandok closed one eye as he considered the group. Then he winked. "Your turn."

All looked at their monarch in horror. Had they heard correctly?

But already Pelandok was moving aside and beckoning for them to take his place.

As if even the river was waiting, a sheen of wetness shimmered on the sands as the river began to refill.

It was simply the tide coming back in.

But the subjects were not to know.

Eagerly, as they had seen their king do so earlier, they all bent their heads to the task.

If their monarch could do it, surely… they could?

They drank. And drank. And drank.

Water lapped at their feet initially. The level rose. And continued to rise. Past their ankles…

For hours the animals drank until their stomachs groaned. They drank until their necks ached from the strain of bending down for such a long time. They drank for fear of losing face. For the shame of not wanting to be the first to admit defeat. They drank.

For surely if their king could do it, why shouldn't they be able to as well.

They drank and drank…

If only the wretched water wasn't up to their haunches! Still!

An idea grew in their heads.

Unwilling to admit that they had failed, the subjects asked a boon. "May we call our kin?"

Pelandok gave a nod, and so the grateful subjects summoned their kin.

But whatever relief they must initially felt soon evaporated.

For the river kept flooding in, higher and higher and higher. It had no eyes and no ears, and it could not hear their cries of despair. Or see their swollen bellies.

At long last, the weary and sodden subjects threw themselves onto the riverbank. Some urinated. Some vomited. Some simply passed out.

"We admit defeat, Your Highness!" came the weary reply.

Pelandok smiled a little smile as he studied his prostrate and moaning subjects. "Very well, if that is the best that you can do."

His ploy accomplished; he trotted back to his throne.

Badak and the Raksasa

A day of tuba fishing is always seen as a holiday.

This must be why kings love to celebrate such an occasion with their subjects. Everyone has fun. Everyone has lots of fish. And everyone has lots to eat. And bring home. Hence, the day is always a success. Moreover, at the end, everyone thinks even more highly of their king.

It is a win-win situation.

Unless a raksasa shows up…

IT ALL STARTED when Sir Jipan the Tapir reported finding a crystal-clear river full of fish.

"Where is this wondrous place?" asked the animals back at the court of King Kancil.

"I have heard of it," said Kijang the barking deer. "I remember my ancestors telling of the river Tinam that flowed into a lake. By the shores of that lake rose a mighty city ruled by a mighty king. But the city is no longer."

"What became of it?"

"It sank into the waters," said Kijang.

The animals grew silent.

Then Badak the rhinoceros and Kerbau rallied the others. "Let us have a fishing expedition."

Perhaps it was the idea of an easy meal. Or, perhaps, just perhaps, it was the fact that no one wanted to lose face. After all, hadn't they all enthused only a short while ago about going fishing? No one wanted to be considered a coward. And besides, there is always strength in numbers. And there certainly were a great many who were going.

Babirusa was going. So was Ungka the Gibbon, his cousin Siamang, Binturong the Perfume Maker and his cousin Dame Musang the Civet cat, Beruang the Bear, Kerbau, Badak as well as Jipan who started all this in the first place and even Singa the Lion. If so many strong and mighty warriors were going, surely it must be right? Safe.

They found the river easily enough but when a suggestion was made to set up camp on its shores, the more wary spoke up.

"Where a city sleeps, there be dragons."

And so, they journeyed upstream and further into the land of the misty mornings until finally they found a place on white sands that satisfied all and they commenced fishing.

As Jipan had said, the fishing was good, so good that it was not long before they were able to spread their catch under the leaves of a breadfruit tree.

> The breadfruit tree grows up to 18 metres and has glossy large leaves. Cultivated in the Malay Archipelago, it spread throughout the South Pacific, carried on ships by explorers such as Captain Bligh. The round green fruit fully ripe tastes like a nutty potato.

Kijang's warm brown eyes ringed yellow, darted left and right anxiously. "Who will guard our catch while the rest of us continue to fish?"

"I will," said Beruang the Bear.

"Very good," said Kijang, "but I must warn you that I have only now remembered that I have also heard it said that this place is the dwelling place of a Raksasa."

Oh! Could not Kijang have mentioned this earlier?

Everyone looked at Beruang to see if he would retract his statement, for a Raksasa is a terrible foe.

But if anyone does not like to lose face it is Beruang. He launched into a demonstration of his skills. "Watch what I can do to this monster!" And he gave a mighty swipe with his powerful paws.

The others all cheered.

And as no one had lost any face, the rest returned to the fishing, leaving Beruang with their precious catch.

Now the land of the Misty Mornings is highland, and highland is where Raksasa are known to dwell. And a Raksasa soon turned up.

Unknowingly, Beruang was seated with his back to the demon and his front to the fire. He soon realised the presence of the Raksasa when the earth shook. Turning around, Beruang screamed at the sight of the monster.

The Raksasa was truly terrible.

The demon towered over the tops of the trees, crimson eyes aglow with the fires of damnation. Covered in detritus and debris, his coat stank of blood and raw bone.

"Arrrrr!" The Raksasa raked and scored the bear.

Beruang fled, his furry back bloody and bleeding. He ran and ran until he collapsed. Hours later, when he awoke and finally found the courage to return, the campsite was empty.

Beruang's deep brown eyes filled with tears of shame. He knew what would happen.

When the others returned, happily carrying their latest catch, Beruang was teased mercilessly.

"I was almost devoured. See the lacerations."

"The demon was able to rip your back because that is all you showed him."

Beruang hung his head and kept his peace.

But who was to guard the fish?

Seladang gored the earth. The black Gaur raised his head high, his pale green, black-tipped horns glinted dangerously.

And so, it was agreed that Seladang would take the next watch.

But the defeat of Beruang was repeated.

Again and again, no animal seemed able to defend their fish.

Finally, Badak spoke.

No doubt there were many less armoured animals who, licking their wounds, wondered why he had not spoken earlier.

Of all the animals, it was Badak who hated most to lose face.

Surprisingly, a rhino's eyes are small compared to its body size. Males have red eyes while females have white.

And their vision is notoriously poor.

They are near-sighted; their eyes located on opposite sides of their head, hence their binocular vision is abysmal. They also lack colour vision. Some hunters have reported that rhinoceroses were unable to tell the difference between a man and a tree at 20 metres.

They make up for this with their sense of smell and hearing.

So maybe it was a brave thing, after all, for Badak to volunteer.

The Raksasa turned up again.

"Stand your ground," said Badak as he lowered his horns.

The demon only laughed.

Badak prepared to charge. He was quailing inside, but with his head down, all he could see was the ground. Which probably explained what happened next.

The rhinoceros launched himself at the Raksasa, trampling the earth and whatever was in his way. He ripped up bushes, tossed them high in the air and continued to swing his mighty head this way and that.

After a while, he looked up, and then behind. There lay a scene of chaos and destruction. But where was the Raksasa and the fish and more importantly – *where was the camp?*

Badak frowned, baffled, but he was not about to give up. So far, he had yet to feel the wrath of the Raksasa on his body. That had to be a good thing, surely.

He bent his head once again and charged.

Trees were gored. Shrubs unearthed. The earth ripped up.

Vines and lantana wrapped themselves around his horns. Time and time again, Badak had to stop and disentangle himself, but he did not give up.

I am victorious!

By now, Badak's back was bleeding, and his horns were ripped and broken. Destruction lay in every direction. Breathing heavily, the rhinoceros stopped to survey the wreckage.

"What is happening, Badak?"

Badak blinked and squinted.

Daylight twinkled through the shadowy canopy overhead, and as he peered, he made out Kera the monkey.

"Oh Kera! It's you." Badak laughed nervously.

"Why, who were you expecting?"

Badak feigned nonchalance. "I am battling a Raksasa, that's all."

Kera's eyes widened and he scanned the area. All that could be seen was a swathe, the width of the rhinoceros's girth, of trees trampled and bushes pushed down to the ground.

Shafts of light slanted into the clearing in Badak's wake. The scent of twisted vegetation and bark was strong.

What madness was this? But this was not a sentiment Kera was prepared to share with any animal with horns. Perhaps there really was a Raksasa about?

If so, then better that Badak continue.

Kera thanked the bleeding rhinoceros and hurried out of the area leaving the defender of fish to tear apart vast portions of jungle.

Back at camp however, the others had returned. They were not astonished to find that their haul of fish had disappeared. They had expected that.

What they were astonished to find, however, was that their defender of fish had also disappeared. They had *not* expected that.

Had the Raksasa devoured Badak?

Harimau volunteered to search for Badak. The animals agreed and so he set off. Soon, he came upon Tiung the mynah bird.

"Have you seen Badak?"

"He charged through a short while ago, goring flies and trampling ants."

"I see." Harimua thanked Tiung and continued his search eventually finding Badak collapsed on the ground.

"So here you are at last. Did you enjoy the fish?"

"Do not joke, Sir Harimau," said Badak, panting heavily. "I was lucky to escape with my life."

"Indeed," said Harimau. "It might be best if we returned."

"Why, I attacked and lunged, and the Raksasa pounced-"

"Sir Tiung told me how he saw you plunging through the jungle after you taught the Raksasa a lesson."

Badak blushed. He kept his jaws shut until the two returned to the camp.

"Ah, Badak, it is good to see you. We worried that the Raksasa might have devoured you," said Seladang.

"Me? Me! Why it was all that the Raksasa could do to hold his own! I hit him with everything I had."

"Which is why there is no fish."

Badak hung his head and clamped his mouth shut as the animals laughed. It was the truth.

"You injured yourself when you fled, that is all."

Badak's face heated.

The next morning, the animals left, but they agreed that this was an excellent fishing spot.

How then, were they to protect this location from the Raksasa?

There was only one solution and that was to appeal to King Kanchil.

This they did.

King Kancil listened to their complaints when they returned and at once announced that he would deal with the Raksasa.

The animals cheered.

If anyone could solve the impossible, it would be their king.

On the seventh day, the animals went back to the fishing spot, but they were not alone, for King Kancil was with them.

"Go fish. Do everything exactly as you have done before. Lay the catch under the breadfruit tree then leave," said Kancil. "And bring me long ropes of rattan."

The animals did as they were instructed and then left.

Kancil rolled and unrolled the rattan.

Then he lit a fire.

The fire roared into life: the next second, staring back on the other side of the flames, was the Raksasa.

So unnerving was the sudden appearance of the creature that a frisson of fear shot up Kancil's side. He caught his breath.

Grit your teeth and do not jump.

The Raksasa was truly a monster. Huge and demonic, matted fur that stank of rotting flesh and swirling red eyes that sucked in your soul.

Kancil made sure he did not gaze into the Raksasa's eyes.

"*Sua makan?* (Have you eaten?)" asked Kancil, smiling sideways at the creature.

Now everyone knows that when you are asked such a question that the polite answer is to respond in the affirmative.

Everyone except the Raksasa.

"No. I am hungry."

"I have fish."

"I know," said the monster and it proceeded to devour the fish.

The slurping sounds were horrible to hear.

But Kancil remained, rolling, and unrolling the rattan, so consumed by his task that he appeared undisturbed by the ghastly sight of the demon relishing its meal.

The crunching of the fish, bones, tail, fins, and all; the noisy sucking of air as the demon gagged and choked, so much in a hurry was it to devour what was before it that only towards the end of the meal did it notice that the mousedeer was still around.

"What are you doing?"

Kancil beamed conspiratorially. "Getting ready to bandage my body. It is a remedy that I have learnt from an old master that allows me to deal with the aches that I have. Aches from collecting so many fish from the river."

The Raksasa felt its back. "I have aches, too."

"Indeed, it is hard to avoid such a thing. Might I ask you why it took so long to share a meal?"

The Raksasa cursed and flung down a heavy hand. "Aches of course! All throughout my body. Give me your remedy at once!"

"Certainly! If you will understand though, that I have barely enough for myself-"

"I want it! Give it to me now! Or-"

Kancil jumped up. "Adoi! I had no idea that you were in such pain. Of course! I will give you whatever I have."

And he mollified the Raksasa by immediately wrapping up its tortured body with the rattan. "See, see, do you not start to feel relief?"

The Raksasa closed its horrible eyes. It breathed out and its breath stank of half regurgitated fish. A bone fell from its half-closed mouth.

But Kancil stuck to the job at hand, even though he was close to vomiting. "Now that I have bundled you up securely, you must try to see if you can wriggle. If you can, then it means I have not done my job properly, and I must fasten the bandages even more tightly."

The Raksasa moved and stretched and jiggled. "A little more here. And here. I can just twist my neck a little."

"Certainly, certainly." And Kancil continued to wrap and tighten and pull.

"Umm, that does feel better, only there is still pain."

"You know what, I forgot one last part."

"What?"

"Your mouth," said Kancil making an apologetic face.

"Hurry!"

Kancil did not need to be asked a second time. In a great hurry, he wrapped rattan around the mouth of the Raksasa so firmly that the monster could not swallow. Around its head. All around the Raksasa until it was covered with rattan.

Perfect.

"Can you move?"

"Mmmm."

"Try harder."

"Mmmmftt."

"Harder."

"Mm."

Kancil lowered his arms. It was done. The Raksasa was so bound with rattan that it could not move. Or breathe.

The Raksasa must also have suddenly realised its dilemma for little rapid movements made its chest rise and fall.

"Oh, let me see." And Kancil pulled and tugged and tightened the rattan until the chest of the Raksasa stiffened and froze.

All done.

The Raksasa was dead.

Then Kancil called his followers.

All jubilant were the animals. Hooray! Hooray! Hooray!

Once again, their king had triumphed over insurmountable odds.

The river was theirs! The fish was theirs!

And the monster was no more!

The celebration was intense, for this was a *Raksasa* that had been destroyed.

Kancil nodded benevolently. "Gajah and Kerbau, you may carry my share back to my palace."

And so once again, Kancil rode upon the back of a rhinoceros in triumph to his throne and the stories and songs of his victory were sung throughout the land.

Gongs were beaten and the Penglipur Laras were busy for many days, writing of the epic victory of King Kancil and the Raksasa.

As for Badak, he lowered his horns once again and chased away enemies, imaginary or otherwise.

And the jungle breathed a sigh of relief, for everyone and everything was well under the kingship of Kancil.

As it should be.

A Crossing of Crocodiles

The skin of crocodiles is sensitive to touch, heat, cold and the chemicals in the environment thanks to tough epidermal scales made of keratin and bony plates that contain dome pressure sensors.

ONE DAY, KANCIL smelt some delicious fruit from the other side of the river. Naturally, he wanted to cross.

Only how?

He observed the river. There were crocodiles lazing in the water.

It had not been so long ago when they had sworn obeisance to him. Would their fealty still hold true? There was only one way to find out.

"Oho Sang Buaya! How are you today?" said Sang Kancil. "I wish to conduct a survey! You are to line up from one end of the river to the next in the form of a bridge."

Without a word, the water began to froth.

Magically, the crocodiles began to assemble themselves. It took a while, of course, for lining up is no easy task especially if you are swimming and there is a strong current, but eventually the deed was done, the command obeyed, and there in the afternoon light glistened a bridge formed of crocodiles.

Kancil beamed. *Oho! Here goes!*

Seizing a half-shell coconut, Sang Kancil leaped lightly from the back of one crocodile to the other. He gave each *kepala* (head) a knock with his nut, calling out as he did so, "*Ketok sini! Ketok sana!* (Knock here! Knock there!)"

To his delight, the crocodiles held firmly still, or as still as was possible in a rapidly moving river.

Kancil grew more daring.

"*Ketok Enche! Ketok Nonya!* (Knock Mister! Knock Miss!)"

"*Ketok kechil! Ketok Besar*! (Knock Small! Knock Big!)"

The bridge of scales held firm through the knocking.

By the time Kancil reached the other side, he had no doubt that the crocodiles had learnt their lesson.

He was their king!

And so assured and elated was he that he leapt onto the bank and proceeded to reward himself with a feast of rambai fruit.

Yum!

King Gajah and King Semut: Gajah berperang dengan semut

Elephants fight with ants (Original Title)

This is a political story… although the original two kings have been lost in the annals of time.

There will always be disputes among family. The family of the jungle was no exception. And as was the usual case, it was always the big bullying the small. My family had a saying used among us, "Bully kechik (small)."

KING SEMUT, THE ant, was getting married.

The wedding of a king of any size is always a big affair.

That morning, King Semut had set out bright and early. It was customary for the groom to be accompanied by friends as he goes to the house of the bride, and in King Semut's case, he was escorted by thousands of his followers. So excited and enthused were they, that they spread out over *gunung* (mountain) and *bukit* (hill), blanketing the landscape.

Black and red dots. Moving, squirming sea.

It was a moving scene in more ways than one. And impossible to wade into the teeming masses without committing murder.

By sheer coincidence, the largest of the inhabitants of the jungle happened to be heading in that direction.

"Adoi! What is going on?" King Gajah swore as a flood of ants suddenly appeared and, in an instant, blocked his path.

A sentry halted, antennae waving as he replied, "We are preparing to celebrate the wedding of our king."

The horde of ants marched on, covering everything in red and black. The very ground appeared to move.

To a smaller beast. It was unsettling. Terrifying. Threatening.

But this was Gajah. The largest of them all.

Gajah squinted. Elephants have little eyes and there is a reason for this. "King? What king? I see no king."

"What? Why, there he is. Right over there."

Gajah towered above the ant. "I say again, what king?"

The sentry bristled. "Your answer shows a lack of breeding. *Tak ajar adat.* (Not taught the law.)"

It was sadly not the first time Gajah would be accused of such a failing. Fury burned through the King of the Elephants.

"Law? Breeding! How dare you comment on me, you miserable creature. Why a single stamp, and hundreds of you perish! You are so insignificant that I shall proceed to do so!" Gajah danced on the ants, killing thousands.

The massacre was hideous.

The acrid scent of the mangled ants fouled the air.

Heads separated from thoraxes. Thoraxes from abdomens.

Yet… Feelers continued to wriggle. Limbs continued to wave. Eyes continued to blink. Thanks to a decentralised nervous system, each insect part is capable of independent movement.

Even after decapitation.

Seething, King Semut watched heartbroken as his followers retrieved the mangled carcasses of the slain.

Only one thing to be done.

Turning to Gajah, he lifted his head. "Pray stop your pounding. What have my subjects ever done to you that you murder them in such a manner? If you wish a battle, then please, one on one with me."

Gajah stopped. Elephant laughed. "What? One on one. One on nothing is more like. *Satu Kosong!* (One Zero!)"

"I have challenged you to single combat," said King Semut proudly.

"Sing- ahaha! Single? Are you serious?"

King Semut tightened his jaw. "I ask for seven days."

"Why seven days? Why not seven weeks or months?"

"Seven days is all I require."

Perhaps something of his tone did manage to reach the floppy ears of Gajah. The elephant's mood sobered. "Very well then. Seven days from today." Then he turned and tramped off, leaving King Semut to deal with his dead.

Thus, a day of celebration turned to a day of mourning.

King Semut put off his wedding to prepare for battle.

"Turn your head to the side so that your tears do not blunt your weapons," he ordered. "We need spend every moment preparing our revenge. We will look for help from the four corners of the world."

Semut's people stopped and listened.

"Collect everyone who has survived. Then come together and dig. We will dig the deepest pit we have ever dug. One deep enough so that an elephant can fall in and never climb out."

And so, the ants dug and dug and dug.

The ants with the strongest mandibles took charge.

> Today scientists are discovering that ants use physics. They tend to dig straight tunnels that descend at the angle of repose. Somehow more through luck than knowledge, ants select just the right grains of sand so that the ground around them does not collapse. This is how ants create tunnels many feet below the ground that last years.

When the pit was deep enough that three elephants could stand one on top of the other, King Semut gave another command.

"Well done, good and faithful servants. But the task is only half complete. Collect branches and disguise the pit. This area is to look as if it has not been touched."

> Mandibles - an ant's most powerful tool — are used in place of hands to hold and to carry things. Despite being small, ants carry up to 50 times their body weight as their muscles have a greater cross-sectional area relative to their body size. This means they can experience forces of more than 3,000 times their own body weight. Without breaking.

King Semut's people worked without rest. Soon the area was camouflaged.

Now as you can imagine, the other inhabitants soon realised something was happening. King Kera swung by.

"*Apa khabar?* (Hello)," said King Kera, and was duly informed as to the declaration of war.

No one likes watching family members feuding. Kera set off to see if he could make sense of what was happening and if there was a chance that Gajah would call this off.

"Dear King Gajah, surely it cannot be true what I have just heard?"

Gajah lifted his head loftily. "Dear King Kera, that would depend on what it is that you have just heard."

"That you have decided to wage war against your brother, Semut, king of the ants."

Gajah snorted. "Brother?"

"Please Gajah, did you not as I, swear fealty to King Kancil? Did you not agree to come to him to settle any dispute?"

Gajah turned his head away.

This angered Kera. "I cannot understand your behaviour. You need to report at once."

Moodily, Gajah closed his eyes.

"Or you will regret your action."

Suddenly, Gajah blinked open eager eyes. His face broke into a smile.

Encouraged, Kera sat up. "That's it! That's the right spirit."

"I shall go at once."

Kera rubbed his hands, pleased his diplomacy had worked. "Excellent!"

"King Kancil must be informed."

The Monkey King nodded approvingly. "That's right."

"We need a witness for the battle."

"Witness?" Kera could not believe his ears. Before he could respond, Gajah had stomped away leaving only large leaves swaying and slapping in his wake.

Unbelievable. Kera shook his head. He had a bad feeling about all of this.

Unstoppable, Gajah marched up to King Kancil.

Kancil was sitting on his white rock surrounded by his retinue. He was white. To the elephant, he looked ancient and wise.

"A thousand, thousand pardons, Your Majesty. But I bring word of a matter of dire consequence."

Kancil's ears pricked. "Dire consequence?"

Gajah to his credit, blushed a little. "Well, yes, of course, dire, dire consequence."

Kancil lifted one brow. "To whom?"

"Why to King Semut of course! Why did you think?" stammered King Gajah. "Why I am so large…"

King Kancil looked over his own small frame.

King Gajah turned red. "Not that size has any bearing on what I am about to report."

"And that is?"

"That King Semut has decided to declare war on me. One on one."

"Oh, I see." Kanchil looked thoughtful. "Well, then as I am Peace Maker in the jungle, it makes sense that I should bear witness."

King Gajah bowed respectfully. "You honour me greatly."

Kancil smiled to himself.

The next day, Gajah set off to meet King Semut.

Kancil, followed by his troops, and seated on a white rhinoceros, followed.

When they reached the clearing which had been set aside for the battle, Kancil sent King Kambing as messenger to King Semut.

King Kambing was met by King Semut's Minister of War – Kerengga the red ant. Although smaller than the black ants, red ants are deadlier.

"Hail, King Kambing, my king greets you," said Kerengga. He was also Prime Minister.

"Hail, semut merah (red ant), I wish to inform your king that my king is waiting to greet him," said King Kambing.

Kerengga bowed and at once set off to get his king.

When King Semut discovered that it was none other than King Kancil who was to be witness, he panicked.

Had Gajah really assembled all these animals as witnesses or were these troops out to eliminate the entire ant kingdom? Only one thing to be done.

"Find out why they are here."

Kerengga set off again. He approached Singa who was at the head of the line and asked the question.

"It would be best to speak directly to our master."

"How do we recognise your king," said Kerengga, hesitating.

Singa almost choked. "There on the white rhinoceros. That is King Kancil."

Kerengga turned and spotted the mousedeer atop the white rhinoceros. He had no idea that Kancil had rolled in sap from the fig tree and then in grass seeds. He was white. To the ant, he looked ancient and decrepit.

Kerengga went forward and bowed. "Hail, King Kancil, my King Semut greets you this day. I am Kerengga, Prime Minister of the Ants."

"Hail, Kerengga, Prime Minister of the Ants. I greet your Excellency and am here as witness. Though why your king wishes to waste his time on this I do not know."

Kerengga's cheeks heated. It seemed that King Kancil did not know the true story. But he went back and reported to King Semut.

"Were there any people near Gajah?"

"No, Your Highness."

"At least that is that then."

King Semut bowed his head as he thought long and hard.

Only one thing to be done.

"Go ask Gajah for two more days. Two more days and we will be ready. He agreed before. He should agree again."

Gajah agreed but stipulated that in two days they would attack. There would be no more delay because the whole world of the jungle was looking on.

He was eager for this to be over as the delay made him look foolish. Yet he had to agree to the delay because the whole world was watching. He needed to appear benevolent. He stamped the ground anxiously and waited.

"Seven plus two makes nine," said Kancil to himself when he learnt of the delay. Of course, he knew based on the numbers what King Semut was planning. Plus, Weaver Ants, did not dig.

With the whole world of the jungle present, King Semut rallied his ants.

"Kerengga, call your people," said King Semut and told them what they had to do.

The Asian weaver ant is known as Semut Kerengga and is a species of ant that dwells in trees. They weave nests of leaves using silk thread produced by their larvae. These structures are called leaf houses and last years.

So, for two long days the weaver ants wove and spun and stitched while the other animals entertained themselves as they waited.

And at the end of the two days, the two kings assembled themselves opposite each other. They were ready.

The animals were also ready. This was what the entire jungle had been waiting for. Would the bigger, heavier animal win?

Kancil lifted his hoof. "We are here as witnesses. Let the outcome be final."

Both kings charged.

Both saw red.

Both craved vengeances.

Across the ground.

Across the branches.

Across the hidden pit-

Argh!

Gajah fell. In a flurry or leaves and branches and dirt! The whole world seemed to spin. As Gajah dropped like a *batu*. (Stone.)

Being big.

Heavy.

Weighty.

Crash!

Through the first set of leaves!

Kercrash!

Through the second set of leaves!

Kercrash! Kethruash!

Through the third set of leaves!

Down to the ground.

Boom!

Splat!

The mighty Gajah was dead.

Semut was still charging. He of course, had a longer area to cover relative to size.

Only there was no longer any need.

His enemy was dead. At the bottom of the pit that Semut and his people had dug for seven days and seven nights. Some were still slowly making their way out, for ants are tiny.

Stunned silence fell upon the animals watching.

"No!"

And before the astonished eyes of the animals, Gajah's brother plunged after him. He died instantly.

Eyes glanced unseeing this way and that. So sudden and so swift had been the conclusion of this dispute; the demise of two massive beasts.

Wailing began.

King Kancil rose. He lifted his hoof.

The wailing ceased.

"My people. Observe what comes out of pride. Of feuding. Of anger and hatred. We should instead see to the welfare of our brothers in the jungle. For we are all brothers regardless of our size."

"We will," swore the inhabitants.

And so, to honour the dead, the animals fetched kindling and burnt the bodies of the two elephants.

As the flames died, Kancil lifted his voice. "King Semut and his kin were prepared for Gajah to perish in a cruel manner. What of his kin?"

"Roasted in the same fire."

"Entirely?"

"Those that remained in the pit perished. But some had already returned above ground."

"Then everything is as it should be. Let us return."
And so, it was the way of the jungle. Everyone returned silent and contemplative.
Until the next event.

See Notes on Pages 348-350

Kantjil to the Rescue

I T IS NICE to lie asleep as the world around you slowly awakens. Even nicer when someone is preparing your breakfast while you stretch and stir and decide whether to open both eyes… Or just one.

"Life can be sweet," said Kantjil.

"What makes you say that?" asked Bibek Kantjil. She laid a fresh green coconut in front of her husband and went back to her chores.

"Well, sweet for some," said Kantjil opening his eyes. He made a face.

"Is the coconut sour already?" said his doe, returning to check.

"No, no I have yet to taste it. I was just thinking aloud. Here I am in my home, all safe and snug, and yet for others, remaining in their homes may not be the safest."

"You speak in riddles. Is not the rainforest a safe place now that you are king?"

"It should be, but there is man to content with."

His doe twitched her ears. "Man." She gave a little shiver.

"Yesterday I came across Nonya Ground-owl. She had her nest hidden in among the paddy fields."

"And yet…"

Kantjil shook his head. "As you said. Man. In a few days, they will come with weapons and reap the paddy for the grain is already golden."

"A mother and her children…" Bibek Kantjil mused. "You have your work cut out for you. She will not shift her eggs. No, she will not."

She trotted over to where Anak lay sound asleep. Kantjil joined her and he nuzzled her throat as they gazed upon their sleeping baby.

The pair were silent, enjoying a quiet moment of parenthood. Then Kantjil sighed. "I must be off."

His doe said nothing for she understood that he was father to the animals in the jungle since becoming king. And she did not wish to have to comfort a weeping Bibek Ground-owl. If anyone had wisdom it would be her husband and although she begrudged the jungle for stealing her husband away, she knew that the jungle could not be in better hands.

Kantjil started on his rounds at once. It always pleased him to see how the jungle changed each day and to greet its inhabitants.

All in all, life was good.

At the edge of the jungle where the cultivated fields lay, he took a deep breath and trotted over. Even before he could reach the nest, he heard weeping.

He hurried over and found Bibek Ground-owl sobbing.

"What is the matter?"

"Men! Over there! They have scythes." Bibek Ground-owl bobbed up and down in great agitation.

"Then flee," said Kantjil gently, steeling himself for the reply which he knew would come.

"Flee! Never! What parent would abandon their children?"

"You have but moments."

"Moments? In moments the first of my babes will hatch. Can you not hear the pecking on the shell?"

But you do not have moments.

Kantjil leaped boldly in the direction of the reapers.

"Eh, *tengok*! Kancil! (Eh, look! Mousedeer!)" The reapers cheered and began to surround Kantjil.

At once Kantjil took off.

He ran and leaped.

The chase was on!

The reapers dropped their scythes. Across the golden landscape of swaying padi they raced.

Kantjil continued to elude them. And when the chase slowed, he danced on his two hind legs.

The reapers called out excitedly. "*Tengok*! (Look!) What a shame to turn him into a curry." The first reaper pointed with a crooked brown finger, the result of years of reaping.

"Curry! You curry food that is about to go off. No, when I catch him, I will give him to my children."

The second reaper wiped his arms across his forehead. "When? You mean 'if', don't you? I don't think any of us has a chance. See how fast he scampers off."

"What? Have you given up already?"

"Give up? Never! You *gila*! (Mad)!"

"Hahah!"

And the reapers then proceeded to try to round up the mousedeer.

But Kanchil knew where the tunnels were.

And while the men were busy scouring one section, he lay panting in a tunnel, ready to scoot off as the men came nearer. In this fashion, he kept the men from the precious nest. But he was stiff with exertion. For the men were relentless in their pursuit.

At *Sinjakala* (twilight), he came exhausted and weary up to Bibek Ground-owl. To his relief, he heard cheeping.

"Congratulations!" he said admiringly.

The newborn hatchlings were dark with wet fluff.

Bibek Ground-owl looked on proudly.

"You will be able to find a new home now."

"My babies cannot fly. How then am I to move them?" came the annoyed answer.

Kancil's shoulders dropped. Biting back his retort, he watched as Bibek Ground-owl fed and nursed her brood. "I shall be back tomorrow."

Then he went home and grumbled to his wife.

"If something were ever to happen to you, and I was alone, I would pray that there was someone who could help me protect Anak."

Kancil said nothing. To that there was no answer.

Quietly, he ate his dinner then went straight to bed.

He slept well that night, exhausted by the day's activities.

For the next six days, he led the reapers on an exhausting chase. The chase was also taking its toll on him. Exhaustion was his constant friend. Limbs that refused to bend. Skin damp with constant perspiration from his labour. He lost weight. His muscles ached constantly. There were times when he grew dizzy and even a moment or two when he had almost fallen into the hands of the reapers. He was moody and put that down to the fact that he had a constant headache.

He could not go on for much longer. What would happen when his limbs refused to obey him?

When he woke that seventh morning, he rushed off to check on the nest. To his surprise, it was empty.

Aghast, he looked around.

Warm golden stalks of padi heads bowed and danced in every direction. The reapers had not finished their work. What then?

The answer settled before him.

Wings darkened the sky as Bibek Ground-Owl landed on the ground.

Anxiously, he searched her face. But to his surprise, the most serene expression greeted him.

"You are an inspiration! For days my little ones have been watching you outrun and elude the reapers. You have convinced them that you so care for them that they wanted to help, too."

Kancil could only stare.

"And so, this morning, they took off. They…" Bibek Groun-Owl's eyes grew luminous with heavy emotion.

"You mean?"

"Yes." The new mother nodded emphatically. "They flew."

And as relief flooded Kancil, the sky overhead darkened and he was surrounded by Bibek Ground-owl's newly flying brood.

"Kantjil! Kantjil! We love you so!" cheeped the little ones in excitement as they landed on the ground.

"You can fly!"

"Yes, yes, we can! Join us!"

"King Kantjil!" wept their very proud mother.

"Ah, flying is the skill of birds," said Kantjil with a sigh. They were so young and had so much to learn.

"Ah, but how then will you be safe?"

"Do not be rude! This is your king! He knows better than us, how to stay safe!"

And so, the admiring brood flapped their wings and cheeped their thanks and Kantjil was just as proud of them as their mother was.

When he returned to his home that night, he stared long and hard at his sleeping son.

His doe came to join him.

"Do not worry," said Kantjil.

"I do not," replied his doe as she leant into his strong neck.

"I love you Kantjil."

"I love you, too.

And that is where we will leave the happy family.

The Celebration

THERE WAS TO be a celebration. *Satu hari raya*! (A big day!)

King Kancil had decided.

"A celebration in time of peace," his doe had remarked dubiously when he first voiced his intention. "But that is not the way. We celebrate *after* winning a war."

Kancil's dark eyes glowed with passion. "Maybe it is time to make new traditions."

And as her husband was the king of tricksters, who was she to argue? And besides there was no harm in a celebration. Only good.

So, for *tiga minggu* (three weeks) the entire jungle prepared.

Everyone was so excited.

Buzz! Buzz! Buzz!

The bees went about making honey to feed the animals. The monkeys collected fruit. While the pigs dug for peanuts.

Not one animal wanted to miss out.

This was their way to show Sang Kancil how much they admired him. Every beast wanted the day to be a success for the king whom they loved so much!

The night before the celebration, the animals retired early.

King's orders: get a good night's rest, so they could be at their best the next day.

They were happy to do so. Especially Kanchil who was the most tired of the lot. He was really looking forward to a good long rest. And the shiny, wonderful celebrations tomorrow.

If this was the way the animals wanted to show their love, then this was also the way he wanted to show his love.

But before he could sleep, he took it upon himself to check that everything was in order.

Three times.

Because each time he checked, there was something that needed to be done. Or re-done.

Finally, he crept into bed.

Exhausted. Drained. Depleted.

Ah! Sleep! How much his body craved it. Needed it.

In fact, so tired was he that he overslept the next day.

When the sun peeked out that glorious morning, gossamer white tendrils of mist still lay on the ground. Dew sparkled like diamonds on dark green leaves, turning the entire celebration grounds into a fairyland.

His doe and their son crept out softly, not wanting to awaken their very tired husband and father. And so, for a while, Kancil slept on blissfully. What woke him was the thumping of heavy feet.

Kerthump! Kerthump!

What was that?

Kancil blinked open sleepy eyes to find Gajah's face smiling down on him. Large, wrinkled, grey.

"*Selamat pagi, raja yang baik sekali*! (Good morning, best king of all)," said Gajah, his deep grey eyes blinking excitedly.

"Selamat pagi, Raja Gajah," said Kancil in reply as he jumped to his feet.

The day was already bright with the yellow sun halfway up the blue sky.

He had overslept. What a dilemma!

"I noticed that you were not at the celebrations and so, thinking that you might have overworked yourself the day before, I decided to come and give you a ride on my back," said Raja Gajah, his tail swishing excitedly from side to side.

Even as he spoke, he lifted King Kancil onto his head. And so, moving along quickly, the pair reached the celebration grounds where they were greeted enthusiastically.

On three sides, the ground was hedged by trees forming a bright green grass rectangle, while the river bordered the fourth. Water was the domain of the crocodiles and so pleased were they to have been invited to a real celebration that they had proclaimed themselves *mata-mata* (police). And they took their role most seriously.

Like a curtain rising, the ants lifted a wave of dark green leaves, glistening and shiny as if they had been polished and indeed, they had been!

Kambing cleared his throat. He had cleaned and shined his horn for the special occasion as he wanted to look his best. His golden eyes scanned the ground, black slit pupils rotating horizontally, before he began his introductory speech. "Glory be to God, who hath magnified himself in His works, ordained Kings and Kingdoms; exalted alone in power and majesty! "King Kancil is our blessing and may his peace be over us all! You have been proclaimed as our king and we your servants are not slow to show our love! And… and-" Tears of gratitude ran down Kambing's face as he concluded, so overcome was he with the peace that had befallen his precious herd ever since Kancil had become king.

"And let the celebrations begin!" concluded King Kancil kindly, his big brown eyes radiating love for his subjects.

The animals cheered! How they worshipped their king! But now it was time to begin.

One by one, the animals took turns performing the acts that they had practised for the last three weeks.

First the bears danced.

> In nature, scientists have discovered that bears communicate by twisting their feet into the ground. This 'sumo strutting' or 'cowboy walking or bear dance' is to leave the scent on the ground. There are apparently 26 different volatile compounds with six unique to males that allow them to leave messages. Sadly, scientist have yet to determine just what those messages say.

Next came the turn of the crocodiles. They demonstrated sliding down the muddy slopes into the water. They were fast. Scarily fast.

With their hearts pounding, gasps rose from the watching crowd.

More than one animal was glad crocodiles were now friend, not foe.

To top it off, most of the crocodiles gathered at one end of the river and with their tails swishing in rhythm, sent wave after wave downstream so that they could demonstrate surfing.

The eyes of the watching animals rounded. But not just from the dramatic performance. The surfing was spectacular, but an unexpected consequence of all that moisture sponging the air was droplets reflecting shimmering rainbow after rainbow in glorious iridescent prisms.

Ah! How beautiful! One could almost expect to see peri-peri (fairies) descending from heaven.

It was a radiant, glorious moment.

Harimau was next. The tigers performed a series of growls, roars chuffs and moans.

Of course, the unexpectedly memorable performance of the crocodiles had won the show, but still everyone clapped most politely at the conclusion.

Kerbau then launched into his own rendition with a series of grunts, snorts, coughs, and growls.

Everyone cheered enthusiastically when the birds took over.

> Birds have a specialised organ called the syrinx that is the equivalent to our larynx. This allows them to sing. An astonishing 40% of the birds are Passeri i.e., songbirds. They sing to defend their territory and to woo their mates. Their songs can be heard a long distance away.

Clear and sweet their notes rose and fell in delightful harmony so that with their low tones and long notes the listeners calmed immediately.

Seated atop Gajah, sun warming his own head and with a cooling breeze ruffling his fur, so engrossed was Kancil in enjoying the melody that it took a while for him to notice that someone was trying their hardest to catch his attention. But then he was high above everyone else on Gajah's head.

"Adoi!" Raja Gajah suddenly jumped.

Kerthump!

"Oh!" Kancil sprawled, but he managed to regain his bearing almost immediately for mousedeer are light on their feet.

The concert stopped at once as the animals looked around to see what had caused the largest of them to interrupt in such a manner.

And because the perpetrator was so small, it took a while to spot him.

It was Siput the Snail.

He had taken upon himself to climb the elephant's grey trunk.

Helpfully, Gajah lifted his trunk, bringing the grey tip up to Kancil, still on Gajah's head.

The snail bowed.

"*Ma'afkan saya*! (Forgive me!)" said Siput, blushing. "But I have been trying for a long time to catch your attention, Your Highness!"

"Indeed," said King Kancil leaning forward. "And what can I help you with?"

"A race!" said the snail, both tentacles waving vigorously, "I wish to race King Kancil!"

"You wish to race me?" Kancil's big brown eyes widened in surprise.

A few titters started which stopped as soon as Kancil turned his head to glare.

Everyone continued to stare; how would this request play out?

"But why would you wish such a thing?"

"Why not?"

Kancil smiled. He liked Siput. "But what if you lose?"

"Then I have the honour and fame of saying that I was beaten by King Kancil," said Siput. "But I will not lose."

The watching animals gasped at such a bold statement. But their king only smiled. And so, their love for him only increased.

"Very well," said Kancil, his admiration of Siput growing, too. "We will have a race."

Kancil smiled and it was as if stars danced in his eyes.

Surely this was the best king that the rainforest had ever had!

How the watching animals cheered. They loved their king, and they liked races! Especially ones when they knew that it was impossible odds for one competitor. What was Siput planning?

He had to be planning something.

Ah!

The excitement grew.

The rules were:

1.   Race along the riverbank;
2.   Start at the otters' site;
3.   Finish at the nagka tree.

The nagka or Nagkassar tree is the Mesua Ferrea also known as the Ceylon ironwood, or cobra saffron. It is a slow-growing tree valued for its hard timber. It has greyish-green foliage with large, fragrant white flowers. Its oil is an excellent hair tonic favoured by English sea captains. Back at home as these men reclined on their chairs, the oil made grease spots on the backs of the chairs, so their wives crocheted tidies that were easily laundered and called them antimacassars.

"This race will last a mile," confirmed Kancil.

And so, it was decided.

"Satu, dua, tiga!" Kambing kira. "One, two, three," counted the goat.

The race was on!

Kancil ran.

Tripitty-trap. Trippity-trippity trap!

Many of the animals raced beside him. They wanted to see who would win.

Halfway up the river he was tiring. "Where are you, Siput?"

He thought he heard a voice call.

Musang the fox cocked his head, whiskers twitching as he scanned the area. "The voice seems ahead of you."

Well, Kancil was not having any of that, so he set off once again.

Trippity-trippity-trap! Trip-trap-trip-trap!

Finally, he reached the nagka tree.

"Siput! Oho! Sang Siput, here I am!" said Kancil, looking around.

For a moment, there was silence.

Kancil shook his head. Perspiration beaded his body. He stamped his weary feet and was about to speak when a voice called out.

"King Kancil! Here I am!"

It was Siput.

The snail was resting on a twig close to Kancil's feet.

Wah! Good thing I did not stamp hard.

For a moment Kancil's heart sank. Then he grinned. So that is how the snail had triumphed. No doubt he had clambered onto that twig and allowed the river to do the work – sweeping him downstream.

"Well done!" And King Kancil gave a little bow.

Siput beamed.

"I should have made a bet." Kancil winked. "Does anyone else know how the snail defeated me?"

"Does it matter?"

"But you hailed him at the half-way point."

"Well, I had to pretend that we were racing, did I not?" Kancil lifted one brow as if to say, 'did I fool you?'

Musang frowned.

Kancil's dark eyes were pools of limpid innocence.

Was Kancil aware of Siput's plan all along?

Or was he even to the end, bluffing his way out of a dilemma?

For Kancil is the king of tricksters.

And that is why I love him so.

He will ever be my favourite trickster.

Musang and the animals mulled this over as Kancil made his way back to his waiting family. Then the entire family of the Deep Rainforest sat down together to enjoy a repast.

Golden honey dripping from the comb. Crunchy *kachang.* (Nuts.) Deep yellow bananas perfectly ripe. Luscious mangos. And lots of smoked fish. And plenty more food. Like durian!

Yum!

For that is the way of Southeast Asians. To eat together and to become one in fellowship and love.

Tamat!

The End!

Section 4-Sang Kancil the not so nice

There are apparently quite a few stories where Kancil does things that are not so nice.

In the interests of completeness, I have included a couple. But as I love Kancil so much I have not gone out of my way to find more.

Sang Kancil and his wife the tiger

KANCIL WAS ONCE married to a tiger.

His wife being pregnant, and about to give birth, she requested that Kancil bring her some medicine.

Kancil did as instructed, only the leaves were the wrong type and maggoty. However, Kancil handed them to his wife.

The tiger wife placed the leaves on her vulva.

But they were the wrong type, and the maggots entered her womb.

Kancil then informed his wife that she had broken the birth pantang, for they were the wrong leaves.

Sadly, the tiger wife died.

See Notes on Page 350

Harimau's child

SANG KANCIL AND the tiger's cub went into the jungle one day. Both hungry, they decided to look for food. After a while, they came across many fruit trees.

Sang Kancil placed some fruit on his knee and ate it.

The tiger cub cried out noisily to be fed.

"Feed me! Feed me!"

Sang Kancil granted the tiger cub its request. He gathered some fruit and then in the same manner as he had feasted himself, he placed the fruit on the tiger cub's kneecap.

"There, you have plenty to eat now," said Sang Kancil, and went back to its own feasting.

Greedily the tiger cub tucked in. "Oh, oh, I am so hungry!"

Unable to control itself, it ate and ate and ate.

"More, more!" the tiger cub cried ravenously.

What a nuisance, thought Sang Kancil.

In its eagerness to sate its hunger, it bit off its own kneecap.

Amid screams of pain the tiger cub bled to death.

See Notes on Page 350

Beginning of the end of the stories

And so, concludes the stories for now.

In the latter section of this book, I have included a few. For various reasons, it made better sense to place them there rather than in the previous sections.

The following sections contain additional notes, examples of the order of some stories as well as other bibs and bobs.

If you wish for more mousedeer stories you may wish to get hold of my books on folktales:

THE GIRL WHO BECAME A GODDESS
THE GIRL SUDAN PAINTED LIKE A GOLD RING

In the first book, I have created a brand-new tale on Kancil.
I hope that you have enjoyed coming on this journey with me.

Theresa Fuller
Sydney
4th of January 2024

King Solomon's Treasures

THERE ARE MANY versions of these tales. There are no right or wrong versions, and one version is never superior to another. Remember these are folktales.

Version A
- Monkey's Poo
- Magic Belt
- Royal Drum

In most versions, it is the tiger – Harimau – who is after Sang Kancil.

This version starts with Tiger getting fooled into thinking that a pile of monkey poo is King Solomon's cake and that Sang Kancil has been guarding it. Tiger, being a cat, albeit a large cat, is curious and asks for a taste. The mousedeer pretends that he must go down to the river for a drink and so, Tiger tries the cake and realises, too late, that he has been fooled.

Next comes the magic belt. Kancil tells Tiger that whoever wears it can wish for whatever they want. The belt is of course a snake and Kancil allows Tiger to put on the belt, saying that he needs to get far away from the belt before Tiger does so, so as not to get into trouble.

Tiger survives and finally catches up to Sang Kancil who has stopped beside a wasps' nest. Once again Sang Kancil fools Tiger into thinking that the nest is a drum. Tiger refuses to believe Kancil and so Kancil says that he will allow him to beat the drum just to convince himself that it is indeed a drum. Once again Kancil gives a reason to be allowed to leave. He says that the noise will deafen him.

Tiger beats the drum, gets stung by hornets and must escape by jumping into a river. But he is alive.

Version B
- King's Sweetmeat
- Enchanted Violin

- Magic Gong
- Lilit the Sash, the Great Indian Python

In this version, the tiger is Sang Pahlawan – the Imperial Warrior.

Sang Kancil, who has been up to his usual tricks, is fleeing Tiger when he comes across a pile of cow dung. Sang Pahlawan shows up a moment later and is told that Kancil is guarding the sweetmeat of Raja Solomon and that he is not allowed to fail on pain of death.

In this instance, Sang Pahlawan is threatened with death should he even come close to the treat, which only makes Tiger long even more for the treat. Like the previous version, Sang Kancil uses an excuse to distance himself. He knows only too well what the result will be. He begs to be allowed to ask permission for Tiger to taste a morsel. We know only too well what will happen next.

After Tiger recovers, he goes after the chevrotain and finds him next to a grove of bamboo on the edge of a promontory. Kancil speaks quickly of the enchanted violin of King Solomon. He tells how that after one has listened to the enchanted music, food will appear magically daily. He then offers himself to Tiger in place of the food.

But Harimau is intrigued. He puts off devouring Kancil in the hopes of hearing the magical melody. Tiger believes that he has convinced Kancil to fetch the violin when the chevrotain trots off, calling words of advice: to leap and to poke his tongue into the grove of bamboo. The wind lifts, Kancil heads off and Tiger jumps, sticks out his tongue only to find it pinched mercilessly between the sticks of bamboo.

Kancil is beneath a hornets' nest when Sang Pahlawan arrives.

He tells the tale of King Solomon preparing to hunt, how when he beats his drum, all the animals not being hunted that day will fall asleep. Kancil then begs Tiger not to sound the drum. In fact, he even offers Tiger anything, including himself if he were not to beat the drum.

The greedy tiger, hoping for an even bigger feast decides he will beat the drum. Kancil goes off to get permission and as he leaves, he hears the hornets' nest being beaten, then the screams of pain from Tiger as he is mercilessly stung.

Tiger is upset that he has been fooled three times by a lowly commoner – Kancil – while Tiger is *Sang Pahlawan*, the Imperial Warrior. He comes across the mousedeer who is standing on the top of what looks like an anthill but is in reality Ular Sawa – the Great Indian python.

Kancil derides Sang Pahlawan for not recognising the colours of his master and that the sash is to be worn on the anniversary of King Solomon's coronation. When he announces that this is the most precious of all King Solomon's treasures, Tiger is ensnared. He must have it.

Sang Kancil offers his life. The mousedeer would rather that Sang Pahlawan eat him than let him touch the precious object. This only convinces Tiger more.

He weeps. Begs.

Kancil says that this will be the very last time. When Tiger hears his instruction, he is to don the sash immediately.

Lilit the Sash so rudely awakened tightens his coils. Tiger struggles but is losing. It is only at the end when he is almost unconscious and unmoving that Lilit stops and uncoils. And so, Tiger once more escapes with his life.

In another version contained in the Journal of the Straits Branch of the Royal Asiatic Society, 45, 1906, the drum is instead a gong, and the belt is a turban.

These are stories told throughout Malaysia and belong to everyone.

Version C

Indonesian legends & folk tales by De Leeuw, Adèle, published by Nelson, New York, 1961.

- Guarding the king's food
- Guarding the king's girdle
- Guarding the king's trumpet
- Guarding the king's drum

Kantjil is resting in the shade when Tiger approaches. Kantjil knows that Tiger only has one aim and that is to eat him. He starts to fan rotting leaves with a large palm leaf. When Kantjil declares that he is guarding royal food, Tiger at once wants it.

Next, Kantjil finds a snake. This he tells Tiger is the king's girdle and whoever wears it will have magic powers. Tiger kills the snake and escapes.

Lastly, Kantjil awaits Tiger beside a clump of bamboo. This is the king's trumpet. Tiger fancies himself a fine musician and once again Kantjils is a great distance away before he declares that Tiger can put his tongue between the reeds and wait for the wind to blow. Tiger gets his tongue pinched. Tiger roars in anger and pain and finally finds Kantjil beside a wasps' nest.

This nest is supposedly the king's drum. Tiger, believe it or not, still insists that he has a go. Tiger is stung, he jumps into a pond of water and is never seen again,while Kantjil congratulates himself.

In other versions, it is a rock that Kancil guards, pretending that it is a dessert of the king. Or eggs which are in reality the sour fruit of a Rhu Tree.

A Pelandok Tale (I)
as narrated by G.M Laidlaw

I *HAVE CREATED composites of stories from various sources, this is the general order that the stories come in:*

- The Mock Funeral of the Great Commander Harimau
- Harimau and King Solomon's Gong
- Harimau and King Soloman's Belt
- Sang Kancil crosses the river
- Sang Buaya catches hold of bamboo thinking it is Kancil
- Harimau and Buaya make a pact
- Two Men and an Axe
- Tiger has a Dream.

A Pelandok Tale (2)

This tale is believed to have originated from the late
Penghulu Mohamed Noordin bin Jaffar.

(Note: Generally, the word for mousedeer is pelanduk with a 'u'. However, here it is spelt with an 'o'.)

This tale has been summarised as many aspects are repeated in the stand-alone stories in this book. Again, this is simply one point of view.

Many storytellers have their own versions. Who is to say which is right? Or which is the original?

THIS STORY STARTS off with a king of a certain country who goes out hunting. As the king and his courtiers make quite a racket, they end up chasing away all the animals, including a certain mousedeer. The mousedeer in his escape, falls into a *kolam* (pool) and is unable to climb out.

An elephant comes along and sees the mousedeer in the *telaga* (well). There is also, coincidentally, at the same time a storm. The mousedeer tells the elephant that the sky is falling as evidenced by the lightning.

"Hei, Ka Sang Gajah, langit hendak runtoh."

"Hey, you Revered/Mister Elephant, the sky is about to fall."

The mousedeer is, of course Sang Kancil, only he is referred to as *Salam di Rimba* or the Judge of the Jungle. This title no doubt lends him authority.

Kancil shares his two reasons for being in the well:
1. The sky is going to fall
2. There is *endah* (beautiful) game rarely seen by *datoh nenek moyang* (ancestors) in the well. (The story started off with a pool, which now has turned into well. Is this simply a mistake of the storyteller, or the fact that each animal sees things differently? Mayhap what appears to be a pool to one animal is a well to another? Remember this is an Asian well, not a European well. Asian wells are basically holes in the ground.)

The elephant believes that Kancil is seeking refuge in the well to escape the sky falling. He, too, wants refuge and to see the game. He is also afraid that he may die.

More animals come.

Kemudian lalu pula harimau demikian juga.
Then the tiger as well.
Kemudian lalu pula badak demikian juga.
Then the rhinoceros as well.
Kemudian lalu pula rusa demikian juga.
Then the deer as well.
Kemudian lalu pula babi demikian juga.
Then the pig as well.

All jump into the well. Then the pelandok says, "*Hei, kechek aku sahaja.* (Hey, I'm just kidding.)"

The tiger declares that if he ever gets out of the well that he will kill the mousedeer.

So, the mousedeer grabs a piece of wood and annoys the elephant until the elephant kicks the mousedeer out of the well. He then takes off and tells some men about the animals in the bottom of the well.

After a few days, the mousedeer comes across a large hornets' nest. He is seated beside the nest, fanning it with a leaf when the tiger finds him.

The mousedeer tells him that he is watching the gong of Raja Suleiman and that it makes *merdu* (melodious) and *lazzat* (delicious) music.

Of course, what happens is that the tiger beats the gong and is bitten by the hornets. Once again, he swears to eat Sang Kancil.

After another 2-3 days when the mousedeer is still on the search for food, he comes across an *elok rupa belang* (good looking striped) snake in a *sawah* (paddy field.) When the tiger turns up, the mousedeer describes the cloth as King Solomon's *ikat bengkong* (twisted tie). However, the tiger puts the article of clothing around his *pingangnya* (waist). (So perhaps it is a loincloth? Only why would a king wear a loincloth? In Baba Malay *tali pinggang* (rope waist) is a belt so perhaps it is more correctly a belt?

This tali pinggang was also mentioned by some Kuala Kangsar boatmen on the Perak River to R. V. Winsedtt in 1905.)

Once again, the tiger is tricked.

Five or six days later, the tiger finds the mousedeer. This time the mousedeer seems to accept its fate and asks to be telan (swallowed) and not di-kunyah (chewed.)

He gives the excuse that he will die if swallowed. And live if chewed.

Also, he is to be swallowed headfirst. Not tail first. Again, the same reasoning.

Eaten whole, the mousedeer *tersembor* (bursts) out of the tiger's *burit* (arse.)

Tiger thinks all is well, and unwittingly is on the lookout for more prey when he comes across a pig. He is about to pounce when something unexpected happens.

The mousedeer who is still alive calls out.

Ho, babi, pergi-lah angkau lari!
Ho, pig, go and run!
And the pig escapes.

This warning happens each time the tiger is about to pounce on prey. After a while, the tiger becomes famished. He scratches at his back until it bleeds.

Desperate, he finds a man clearing his farm but again the mousedeer warns the man. Finally, unable to obtains any sustenance, the tiger dies. The mousedeer then escapes.

At a river, the mousedeer manages to assuage his thirst, but he is still ravenous. He spies fruit on the other side of the river and wonders how to get across it as he is still very weak.

He is then inspired to *titah* (command) the *Kakak* (Elder Sisters) of Sang Garagi (If anyone knows the meaning of Garagi, please let me know. Or is it a misspelling for gergasi?) to *bersusun* (arrange) themselves for him to count them as this he says is a command of King Solomon. So, the crocodiles *ditimbul* (arise) from the depths and arrange their heads together at the edge of the river for the mousedeer to count them. The choice of words is interesting as he *panggil* (calls) them, *bilang* (speaks) to them, and eventually *titah* (orders) them.

Once across, being Sang Kancil, of course he reveals that he has tricked them. The crocodiles vow to catch him when he goes down to the river to drink.

And when he does go down to the river to drink, he is caught by a crocodile. The mousedeer thinks quickly and says to the luckless crocodile that it is a twig and not his leg (the term used is *tangan* (hand) for leg, not *kaki*, which makes me wonder if it is his front paw) that the crocodile has in its jaws.

The crocodile, not tasting any meat, agrees. It releases the mousedeer. Again, the mousedeer cannot help but reveal that it was his leg after all that the crocodile had.

The mousedeer arrives at the sea where he overhears men complaining that their catch of fish has disappeared and that this recurs daily. Curious, the mousedeer hides to discover the thief. He learns that a *nenek girgasi* (grandmother giantess) has been devouring the fish.

So, the mousedeer decides to give the giantess some medicine. In the meantime, he collects some rotan to make a noose.

When the giantess returns to eat the fish, she not only recognises him as Judge of the Forest (Salam di Rimba) but asks him what he is doing there.

He replies that he is *beramalkan almu* (doing good deeds). One of which is *ubat lengoh segala sendi tulang-tulang* (medicine for all joints of the bones).

Once again, he does a similar trick with his eyes – when I am awake and when I am not awake. He pretends to sleep and when they swap places, he places *bara api* (embers) on the hand of the sleeping giantess. She wakes complaining of pain.

Then she admits to having teased the mousedeer while he slept. The mousedeer explains that this is the cause of her pain. The giantess is curious as to why the mousedeer had fashioned rings with the rope and is told that if one has many aches and pains, then being tied up with these rope rings helps alleviate the pain. Of course, the giantess asks to be tied up.

Once tied and unable to move, the people return and beat and stab the giantess until she is dead.

Still on the lookout for food, the mousedeer travels *hulu* (upstream) and *hilir* (downstream) until he meets a man working on a sampan.

"Ini olah-olah jong, olah-olah ngin."

(Supposed to mean "perhaps or perhaps not". Meaning is unclear.)

The man observing and understanding what the mousedeer says, is enraged. He *lotarkan* (hurls) *sa-keping tatal* (a scroll of wood) at the mousedeer that injures its back.

The mousedeer returns to *perempuannya* (his girl) and says *barangkali kita bercherai* (maybe we will breakup).

Not understanding, she asks the reason for his saying this and he tells her that he has been hit in the *punggong* (back) with scrolls of wood.

Ten days later, the mousedeer is dead, leaving his pregnant girl behind.

And so, the tale ends by explaining that this is why every mousedeer has a scroll on its back.

Tamat.

Over.

See Notes on Pages 350-351

From the Philippines - Natalo rin si pilandok (Pabula)

A fable of How the Mousedeer Lost

Here is another sample of how stories were arranged, this time from the Phillipines:

A BABOY-RAMO (wild pig in Tagalog) spots Pilandok.

"My dinner!

But Pilandok tells the pig that he is too scrawny to be able to satisfy the pig's hunger. Instead Pilandok suggests that the pig tries eating a human.

A human is the most powerful animal in the world, he tells the pig. Eating a human will satisfy the pig's hunger.

The pig is famished as he has not eaten all day. But he agrees that the mousedeer will not satisfy him.

The pig wonders if he can overpower man but Pilandok assures the pig that with his sharp teeth and claws and his amazing speed, it would be no problem to catch a man.

The two come across a child.

The pig asks if that is a man.

Pilandok says that the child is a man not yet grown to full stature.

The pig won't let Pilandok out of his sight as Pilandok is his backup meal in case he cannot find a man.

The two next come across an old man.

The pig asks if that is a man.

Pilandok says that the old man is a man who has already grown to full stature. Now he is too bony and scrawny.

The pig agrees.

The two next come across a hunter.

The pig asks if that is a man.

Pilandok finally says, yes, that is a man in perfect condition.

The pig is overjoyed. He charges and is about to gore the hunter when there is a loud sound. Bang!

The hunter has spotted the pig and shoots him dead.

So that is the end of the story for the pig, but this is not the end of the story for our hero – Pilandok.

After all this excitement, he is thirsty. He goes down to the river to drink, only a buwaya (crocodile) spots him and clamps on to his foot.

Pilandok tells the crocodile that he doesn't know the difference between a stick and his foot.

At first the crocodile does not believe him but eventually he does and releases the foot. This he does after he is shown Pilandok's other foot. Then Pilandok runs away laughing.

Next Pilandok comes across a snail.

Pilandok boasts that he can beat the snail in a race.

The snail uses his many relatives to pretend to be him each time Pilandok calls out, during the length of the race.

In the end, Pilandok collapses.

He admits that he is not as wise as he thinks he is and promises to avoid playing tricks on the other animals.

The White Mousedeer

This is probably one of the first stories that I have ever heard in school about Sang Kancil and I be-
lieve that this is Sang Kancil and not some other mousedeer. The source is the Hikayat Hang Tuah.

My first sight of Sang Kancil was unfortunately as a taxidermized animal in my Primary Two
classroom in Methodist Girls' School.

Original English translation.

"The Raja of Bentan went one day with the Ratu of Melayu to Pulau Ledang to hunt. A white
mouse-deer turned on their dogs and the prince decided to found a settlement, calling it Malacca
after a tree on the spot where Hang Tuah and his friends afterwards built his palace."

My rewrite:

PURE WHITE ANIMALS are generally prized by hunters. And so, when the King of
Bentan and the Queen of the Malays saw the white mousedeer, naturally they gave
chase.

The preferred prey in Southeast Asia tends to be monkeys, deer, and large squirrels with only
a few hunters choosing to hunt the more dangerous gaur, sun bear or tapir. Hunting larger
animals such as the elephant and the tiger is generally unheard of. This makes sense when you
realise that the traditional hunting methods hundreds of years ago were mainly blowpipes,
spears, snares and at times fire traps. The latter used to smoke animals out of burrows.

But on this occasion, the hunt was with dogs.

White mousedeer are very rare.

And somehow this one had survived into adulthood.

Formerly, hunting with dogs, meant running.

A lot of running.

The dogs might have been the Telomian, which today is deemed the rarest breed in the world.

The Telomians or Anjing Kampong (Village dogs) are generally a medium size short-haired dog with a distinctive blue-black tongue. They were domesticated by the Orang Asli (the original inhabitants of Malaysia much like the aboriginals are the original inhabitants of Australia.) They are trained to catch small vermin and snakes.

> These dogs are also great guard dogs: they are seen by some to be unlucky and treacherous, and to even desire the deaths of their owners. Feral dogs were considered especially dangerous as they were believed to harbour evil spirits.

How I remember my grandparents calling me to stay close to them whenever we encountered such an animal. Now it all makes sense.

As expected, the dogs cornered their prey.

Across the white mousedeer's path rushed a wide green river, behind rushed the slavering pack.

The white mousedeer turned. Baring its teeth, tusks glinting in sunlight, it faced its attackers.

Snapping and barking, the hunting dogs closed in.

To the watching king and queen, the mousedeer's dark brown eyes gleamed with a sudden intensity.

Then to their shock and surprise, the white mousedeer attacked!

A single slight mousedeer against several medium sized and well-trained hunting dogs - yet the fight was over in seconds.

All the observers could recall was loud growling.

A white tail held vertical then-

Biting! Ripping at ears, necks, and shoulders.

White canines flashing!

Howling and whining, dog after dog turned tail and fled, leaving the tiny mousedeer triumphant.

Standing tall, the mousedeer considered the royal pair for a moment, dark brown eyes luminous.

Wind ruffled its snow-white fur.

Then it stamped its front hoof on the ground.

A single stamp, as if to say, "This is my victory! Mine!"

Then the white mousedeer dashed off into the depths of the jungle, never to be seen again.

The pair turned to each other, astounded.

Did we really see what we just saw?

But what the king next noticed was the Melaka tree.

"If such a place can breed such fierce animals, then this is the place to set up a kingdom," said the King of Bentan excitedly.

And so, the Kingdom of Malacca was born that very day. And as history attests, the port of Malacca gained fame as one of the best ports in the ancient world, bringing renown and riches to its Sultan.

But why the city was not named Kancil I do not know. After all, it was the mousedeer that fought the dogs, not the tree.

The Mousedeer

Mousedeer are generally seen as prey in the wild. With no antlers or horns, they lead lonely, secluded lives with some species seldom seen.

They often come together only to mate. And some species are nocturnal. They communicate with a series of smells and noises.

"Mouse deer can breed at any time of the year. The gestation period is usually 4 1/2 months. Breeding females produce one fawn" (Jinaka, 1995). "The young are precocial when born and can stand within 30 minutes of birth" (Grzimck, 1994). "Mouse deer are shy, and their fawns tend to be "hiders". The fawn is weaned for 10-13 weeks. It reaches sexual maturity at about 5-6 months. Lesser Malay mouse deer can live for 12 years." (Jinaka, 1995)

Name
Most known as Sang Kancil in Malaysia and Singapore.
Sang Kancil = Bahasa Melayu
Kanchel = Baba Malay
Pelanduk/Pelandok = Borneo, Malaysia, and Indonesia.
Pilandok = Philippines
Mīminnī – Ceylonese or Sri Lankan

Europeans have spelt his name as Pelandok or Kantchil or Kantjil or Kunchil or Plandok etc.

Sang – 'Revered' although sometimes translated also as 'The'.
Kancil – Mousedeer

Akal Pelanduk
Akal – Timeless or sometimes intellect
Pelanduk – Mousedeer or horn or moth

Nickname = Sometimes referred to as Close Only One Eye
In Indonesia, Kancil or Pelanduk tricks the tiger, crocodile, elephant, buffalo and even the hyena. He is part of living folklore.

Kanchil's wife – like all wives, she writes To Do Lists, only these are upon banana leaves.

And everyone knows how broad these leaves are. Sometimes referred to as Bibek Kancil or Nonya Kancil.

In the collection of tales published by G.C.T. van Dorp in Semarang in 1871, Serat Kancil, apparently tells the story of the mousedeer from its birth to its death in Egypt. The mousedeer is believed to be born of the Goddess Sungkawa, who dies in childbirth. The mousedeer eventually marries an Egyptian princess, is later taken prisoner and ultimately murdered.

Sadly, I only found this mention towards the end of my two-year search. By then, my manuscript was bulging with stories that I was keen to share. And my grasp of Javanese is negligible. If someone can translate and share the stories with me, I would be very grateful.

Here is a link to the Serat Kancil.
http://anyflip.com/dukss/rjsk

Titles
Menteri Belukar = Skeats also describes the mousedeer as Ment'ri B'lukar or 'Vizier of the Underwood' or 'Brush' as no difficulties are too great for it to overcome.

A vizier is a high-ranking official in the king's court, so this authority aids Pilanduk, as the animals believe and trust him.

Salam di Rimba = Chief Councillor or King Solomon. According to A Pelandok Tale by G. M. Laidlaw who was told the tale by the penghulu of Pulau Tiga, Lower Perak, Haji Mahomed Ali bin Haji Mahomed Perak, the Mousedeer is the Chief Councillor of King Solomon.

Tuan Syeikh Alam in Rimba = Lord Judge of the Forest

Selang Dirimba = Judge of the Forest

Sekh/syekh Rimba = Lord of the Forest Realm

Species
In Malaysia, Singapore, and Indonesia, Sang Kancil is the Tragulus javanicus: Or the Tragulus Kancil.

Tragulus Kancil is one of the smallest-hoofed mammals in the word, measuring 45 cms.

"Tragulus Javanicus are found in overgrown primary and secondary forests in Southeast Asia. They often reside around rocks, hollow trees, and dense vegetation near water." (Nowak and Paradiso, 1983).

In the Phillipines, Pilandok is Tragunus Nigricans which lives in the southwest regions of the Palawan Islands. He is the trickster and the best friend or protégé of the cobra with whom he can apparently be dangerous.

And in India, it is the Moschiola Indica. There are many species of mousedeer throughout the world and the list here is not exhaustive.

Skeat describes Kancil as a favourite character in Malaysian folktales, "… a beautiful animal, with big dark pleading eyes and all the grace and elegance of a gazelle."

While others have described the mousedeer as a mash-up of a deer, a mouse, and a pig. I prefer Skeat's description.

Although the mousedeer has a sub-order with deer (Ruminantia), they are not considered "true deer" and have their own family, Tragulidae.

Mousedeer have fangs not horns and these are especially elongated in males. Females lack these canines. Both sexes are even-toed and have a three-chambered stomach.

"The pelage of mouse deer is brown with an orange tint. The underside is white. There is also a series of white vertical markings on the neck." (Grzimck, 1994).

"Lesser Malay mouse deer tend to form monogamous family groups. Some are solitary. Mouse deer are very shy and try to remain unseen. They are usually silent; the only noise mouse deer make is a shrill cry when frightened" (Jinaka, 1995).

"Mouse deer are hunted for their skins. The pelage of mouse deer is smooth, and the skin is used to make handbags and coats" (Jinaka, 1995).

Mousedeer tend to either be solitary, or else live in pairs. Their territories are small, and neighbours tend to ignore each other rather than compete. They possess chin glands for marking each other as mates or antagonists while the water chevrotain had anal and preputial glands for marking territory.

Adult weight: 3.85 kg (8.47 lbs)
Maximum longevity: 14 years
Female maturity: 167 days
Male maturity: 167 days
Gestation: 144 days
Weaning: 84 days
Litter size: Generally, one offspring.
Weight at birth: 0.37 kg (0.814 lbs)
Body mass: 1.616 kg (3.5552 lbs)

Mother Mousedeer clean their offspring by licking. They are more active than males and sit on their hind legs or crouch.

A young/baby of a lesser mousedeer is called a "fawn or ass". The females are called "doe, hind or cow" and males "buck, stag or bull". A lesser mousedeer group is called a "herd".

Thankfully, the lesser mousedeer is listed as Least Concern (LR/lc), lowest risk.

Which probably explains why mousedeer are seen as tricksters because they survive despite great odds.

Trickster

Tricksters are multifaceted. They live in a grey area. They can be seen as the champion, the defender and even the saviour for mankind in the role of the magician.

The Trickster is the representative of the oppressed individual. He becomes their hero by taking on unjust and corrupt powers without direct confrontation.

He is subversive.

Sang Kancil is able to do this by employing strategies such as changing life skills, influencing thinking and behaviour to strengthen the position of the King and be certified as a leader in the jungle.

Strategy One: Shifting his self-image.

Mousedeer are small-bodied animals with fur that is brownish black and shiny.

Interestingly, the word 'pelanduk' can also be taken to mean moth.

To influence the other animals Kancil uses materials such as rubber wood to colour his head and beard to influence others into believing that he will be the next king based on his teacher's sacred instinct. And white of the ascetic.

"…maka lalu dicakar-cakar batang kayu itu dengan kukunya."

"…then clawed the trunk with its nails. Proving that he has undergone the ascetism process for a long time…"

This he can do because he realises that the animals value objects based on what they see.

Strategy Two – Influencing thought and behaviour.

In the story of the goat and the tiger, both creatures have cohabited in the same neck of the woods yet have never met the other. Sang Kanil takes advantage of this for his own benefit.

He tells them that the peace they have so far experienced is due to his prayers.

He prods them into believing that this is the case, when he asks the goat if he can number the times when he has encountered the tigers.

Of course, the goat must answer in the negative.

He pretends to be an aulia – a saintly Muslim Believer. He also pretends to be a mustajab/ mustajib (one whose wish comes true) when he says he will recite his prayers for the animals' safety.

Animal Names

The animals of Nusantara are sometimes referred to as a 'Beast from the Soil', or a 'Beast of the Trees' or a 'Beast from the Waters'.

Animals sometimes have the prefix 'Sang' in front of their names. 'Sang' means 'Revered' so 'Sang Kancil' means 'Revered Mousedeer'. Sometimes Sang can be taken to mean simply 'The' as in 'The' Mousedeer. or "Sir" or "Mister". Always look at the context.

The prefix "Si" is used when the animals are friends. So instead of saying Sang Kancil, they refer to him as Si Kancil. 'Si' infers a familiarity.

Sometimes animals are addressed by their physical characteristics: Hence the buffalo is 'The Horned One' or 'The Horny One' because of its horns.

Male characters, especially those that are fathers are sometimes referred to as 'Pak' or 'Father'.

Female characters often have the prefix 'Ma' or 'Mak' or 'Mother' or 'Nonya' or 'Bibek'.

Older female animals can be referred to as 'Dame' as in 'Dame Katak', the frog. Or Dame Rusa, the Sambar Deer.

Sometimes 'Mister' can be used i.e., 'Enche' or 'Inche' shortened to 'Che'. So Harimau is 'Mister Stripes'.

Or 'Tuan' which is 'Lord' and is used for someone on a higher social status i.e., having more rank. Not to be confused with 'Tuhan' which means 'god'.

Sometimes more familiar terms can be employed such as 'Elder Brother' or 'Little Brother' even though the animals are completely different species.

Adjectives can also be used to aid the description as in the case of Dame Rusa – the Daintily-Hoofed Lady.

Then there are the terms employed under the sovereignty of King Solomon or Raja Suleiman. The Great Commander of the Deep Forest – Harimau - initially owned this title.

Pak si Bajok is a Berok Tunggal, a solitary ape.

The Animals of the Great Rain Forest

The animals can basically be divided into three types:

Beasts of the Trees
Beasts of the Soil
Beasts of the Waters

However, for ease of use I have organised the animals in alphabetical order.

Ant = Semut. Symbol of industry.

Anteater = Tenggiling. *Manis Javanica*. Scaly anteater. Currently endangered.

Ape = See Monkey. Apes are tail-ess, whereas monkeys have tails, but I do not know if this was understood by the storytellers. I have read stories where both apes and monkeys were treated as the same.

Bat = Kelelawar

Bird = Burung
Ayam or chicken. Symbol of intelligence but also of cowardice.
Gagak symbol of weakness and ugliness. Crow. Black is associated with evil. Linked with humans with bad attitude.
Hornbill represents powerful people. Grandeur.
Eagle is a symbol of strength. Powerful people.
Owl or Burung Hantu is a symbol of weakness.
The Tiptibau is believed to be the *lyncornis temminckii.*
Tiung the magpie represents goodness. *Graculus Religiosa.*
Pretty birds tend to represent a person of high rank and status while less attractive birds represent people who are poor or lower class.
The peacock represents beauty and arrogance.
Sparrow represents commoner.
Swan = Commoner who likes to travel but still remembers their roots.
Woodpecker = Burung Belatuk. Pecking at wood that is old and unsafe just to find a meal.

Layang-layang or the House Swift *Apus Affinis.*
Burong Tukang Kayu or the Carpenter bird or *Burong Malas* the lazy bird.
Mak Burung Rajawali (Mother Kingfisher).

Bear = Beruang. Unclear if this is *Helarctos Malayanus.* Sometimes also referred to as Grandfather Bear.

Bear-cat = Binturong. Arctictis Binturong. A viverrid.

Bison = Gaur also sometimes called Seladang or Wild Bull (See Water Buffalo)

Buffalo/Cow = Mister Horn. See Water Buffalo. A symbol of stupidity. Probably because it does the work for humans such as farming and even as a form of transport.

Butterfly = Their king is sometimes called Raja Brook.

Crocodile = Buaya is 'The Crawling One' or 'Mister Crawler' or
Sang Bedal or Kakak Sang Geragi (A Pelandok's Tale) or Buaja or Si Rangkak. *Crocodylus Porosus* or *Crocodylus Siamensis.*

Dog = Anjing who is also Sang Koyok. See Wolf.

Deer = Kijang the Barking Deer also called the Barker. Muntjac. Manjangan. Rusa.
Kijang is *Muntiacus Javanicus.*
Rusa is the Rusa Sambar Deer in Malaysia.

Dragon = Naga. Another symbol of strength.

Elephant = Gajah, Gadja. *Elephas Maximus* is the Asian Elephant. Generally, a symbol of power due to its size. As it moves about the rainforest, it re-designs the forest while pushing down trees, etc.

Fox = Musang or Civet Cat. Interestingly a symbol of evil. Malays see it as a symbol of the male predator. Possibly because it steals chickens.

Flying Dragon Lizards = Gecko-Draco.

Frog = Katak or Kadok. The smaller the frog the noisier it is in the tropics. Garuda = A very large bird that may be capable of destruction on an epic scale. Another symbol of strength and power. See eagle.

Giant = Gergasi, Gergasang (many spellings), or sometimes referred to as Antu Raya or a

Raksasa. Referred to as Grandpa in A Pelandok's Tale.

Goat = Pak Kambing. The goats of Southeast Asia are diverse and impossible to classify into breeds.
There is another type of goat – the Kambing Gurun – Capricornis Sumatraensis, which is black and shaggy and known as the Goat Antelope.

Iguana = Great Lizard. See Monitor Lizard.

King Crab = Limulus.

Lion = Singa, Singa the Mighty. Another symbol of strength. Unclear whether it is the African or the Indian lion that is referred to. Interestingly quite a few cities in Southeast Asia are named after the lion. Not just Singapore.
Sometimes also referred to as Emperor Singa.

Monkey = Kera. Monyet. Pak si Bajok/Ap' Si Bago which is a Berok Tunggal.
Some sources say that Kera is an ape while others say it is a monkey. Unclear. Kera is most likely the macaque.
Lotong (the long-tailed Spectacle Monkey).
Siamang is Hylobates syndactylus – a gibbon. *Hylobates.*
Bero = Berok monkey or coconut monkey. Likely a baboon.

Monitor Lizard = Menarat or Biawak. Possibly *Varanus*.
Kabaragoya, the Asian water monitor or Varanus salvator.

Orangutan = Man-ape.

Otter = Memerang.

Pheasant = Kua (Many eyed pheasant).

Pig = Sang Babi. Possibly *Sus scrofa*. Surprisingly, a symbol of humiliation. In Sea Dyak culture, pigs are known to dig up graves. In Singapore, pigs used to be fed on swill.
Babirusa is *Babyroussa Babyrusa*.

Porcupine = Landak also known as the Wise One and a friend of Kancil.

Snail = Siput or Siput Kiyong (King of Sea Snails from Some Mousedeer's Tale).
Squirrel = Tupai.

Tiger = Harimau, Arimo, Rimau, Madjan, Matjan or Pak Matjan. *Panthera Tigris.*

Harimau or Rimau or Arimo is 'The Striped One' or Si Rangkak (the Crawler or Crawling One) according to A Pelandok Tale by G. M. Laidlaw who was told by the penghulu of Pulau Tiga, Lower Perak, Haji Mahomed Ali bin Haji Mahomed Perak and he is also the Hulubalang or Chief Warrior of King Solomon.
Also known as Matjan. Tiger-in-Chief. Another symbol of strength.

Rhinoceros – Possibly *Dicerorhinus Sumatrenis*. Smallest species in the world.
Mrs Rhinoceros is the supposed mount of the mousedeer. She is white and lives in a thorny valley. Once she had a jumping competition with the mousedeer and got stuck between bamboo. But she is not the only mount.
The male is known as Batang in Malaysia and Singapore but Badak in Indonesia.
Badak, the male rhinoceros, is also a Tuai i.e., chief, depending on where the story takes place.

Tortoise = Terkura. Might be the long-necked turtle judging by a picture from IBAN ANIMAL STORIES.
Terrapins are Kikura.
Labi-labi = huge turtle with hard scales.

Snake = Ular. Raja Ular Tedung = King Cobra.

Squirrel = Tupai or Kuwis (Malaysian Flying Squirrel).

Stork = Upeh.

Tapir = Jipan. *Tapirus Indicus*.

Water Buffalo = Known as Seladang or Kerbau. *Bos bubalis? Bos Gaurus?*
Seladang Cherang – Wild Bull of the Clearing.
Seladang Belukar = Wild Bull of the Bush.

Wolf = Serigala sometimes also referred to as a Dog or the Red Dog. Wolf or Lupus in Sanskrit. Also, possibly *Cyon Rutilans* or the Red Jungle Dog.

Woodpecker = Kutok.

The Victory of the Buffalo

This story does not contain a mousedeer, but I have chosen to end with this to demonstrate how much the people of Southeast Asia love and imitate the mousedeer. This is the final story.

> The name Minangkarbau/Minangkerbau means the Victory of the Buffalo, and this is how the name came about.
>
> Indigenous to the highlands of central Sumatra, their culture is matrilineal with property owned by women and passed down from mother to daughter. Their distinctive homes – rumah gadang – are basically long houses with multiple gables forming a buffalo horn-like end.

HUNDREDS OF YEARS ago a Javanese king attempted to conquer the people of Minangkarbau. The people knew that if they fought, they would be defeated.

Finally, after days of debating, it was decided to follow in the footsteps of Kantchil and to fight with their wits.

They negotiated with the Javanese king – Raja Sanagara – that they would fight with the karbau.

The raja produced a very powerful karbau.

The Minangkarbauans were discouraged. How could they win against such a strong opponent?

But again, they were reminded to fight like Kantchil.

So, they went into the fields and took a bull calf who was still being nursed by its mother. They attached sharpened iron points to his budding horns. Then they kept him in a pen. They did not feed him for three days.

Now calves should not be allowed to go without food for more than 24 hours. Ravenous, the calf screamed with hunger. As the days passed, it took on a cold, hunched up look. Its head drooped and the folds of its skin were obvious as it had lost much of its fat. It had started to lose muscle. How long could it last?

It struggled to stay on its feet.

Finally on the day of the fight, the people of Minangkarbau took their calf to meet the Raja's champion.

When anyone saw the calf, they roared with laughter!

But the people of Minangkarbau kept silent. They had a plan.

When the two buffalo were turned lose in the pen, the bull calf was so hungry that he gave a roar of hunger and tore across the ground towards where the other bull waited.

The powerful bull was stunned. It heard the calf's anguished cry and saw its desperate lunge for food. It knew the calf was not attempting to attack.

And it wasn't.

That was the trouble.

Instead of trying to gore and attack, the starving calf shot under the bull's body and began to try to feed. But the bull had no udders.

Enraged, the ravenous calf began to meow piteously while all the while it dug its horns into the soft underbelly of the baffled bull.

The horns pierced the underside of the champion bull. Within seconds the bull began to bleed.

The adult bull screamed. But it was too late. It could not get away.

Bloodied and desperate the calf continued its actions until finally the adult bull dropped dead.

By this, Raja Sanagara knew then that these people would never allow themselves to be ruled by him, and so he removed his army.

The people of Minangkarbau celebrated.

See Notes on Page 351

Sounds

Sounds were an important component of the Malay culture. It was aural world.

Here are some examples where sounds played an important part:

Celup-Celap. Celup-Celap. = Splashing of water.
Kelentang = Gong clanging.
Gegak-gempita = Uproar.

Thunder – As the east coast of Sumatra, the Malay peninsula and the West Coast of Borneo do not have active volcanos, the loudest natural sound was thunder. In this animistic culture, the belief was that thunder was the voice of God and that the thunder god was capable of *baliw* (punitive storms). In tropical Asia the atmospheric conditions cause thunderstorms to occur with frequency and intensity. Writers (William Marsden 1754) have described thunder occurring without rain. Of forked lightning, of a sky on fire and of the ground quaking. This is probably the reason why the Mousedeer told of the earth ending and the sky falling, taking from nature what he had experienced.

There is even description and words to depict objects thrown down supposedly by the gods – gigi guntar (thunder teeth) or batu lintar (thunder stones.)

Tagar = Thunderous peal.
Deram-deram = Distant rumbling.
Petir = Sharp clap of thunder.

It was assumed that loudness was synonymous with power. Therefore, the louder the sound, the more powerful it was presumed the maker of the sound.

This is probably why Tiger literally salivated when he discovered King Solomon's gendang drum. A slit allowed amplification of the sound. And the drums were even anthromophised, with a male and female pair.

Kerab kerab kertub kertub = The sounds of gobbling.
Gegak-gempita = Hubbub or uproar.

It appeared that a cacophony seemed the way to greatness with booming, beating, banging, blowing, and clanging reaching a thunderous climax that resulted in being considered as having reached the pinnacle of success. The tanda kebesaran = sign of greatness.

This necessary increasing of sound appears to even be the case with music. According to Skeat, the multiplication of notes was in accordance with the traditions of the king's musical instruments in Malay romances.

The example, Skeat (Malay Magic), gave is that of Raja Donan's magic flute.

"The first time (that he sounded it), the flute gave forth the sounds of twelve instruments, the second time it played as if twenty-four instruments were being sounded, and the third time it played like thirty-six different instruments."

Magic and Beliefs

Beliefs from long ago.

According to Skeat (Malay Magic), it was believed that landslips were caused by dragons. After heavy rains and floods, the Malays used to believe that a *naga* (dragon) who had been performing *bertapa* (religious penance) had broken forth in the mountains and was making its way to the sea.

Demons were also thought to play a part in the landscape with waterfalls and rocks of unusual shape being attributed to the agency of demons.

Spirits descended via the *Pelangi* (rainbow) to drink, or via a spirit snake.

The most dangerous time of the day was Sinjakala or twilight as this is when the evil spirits have the most power. As a child, I remember my grandmother calling me indoors at that time. The yellow glow of the dying sun is termed 'mambang kuning' or the yellow deity.

The king - like kings around the world - was 'Divine Man' and so able to 'slay at pleasure.' It is understandable then Pilandok's dread when he is awoken by Prince Sumusong sa Alongan. So why is he asleep during the day? Possibly because mousedeer are nocturnal.

The king was sacred. There was more of the god about him than the man. The following from MALAY MAGIC is a description of just his waistband:

His waistband (*kain ikat pinggang*) was of "flowered cloth, twenty-five cubits in length, or thirty if the fringe be included; thrice a day did it change its colours — in the morning transparent as dew, at mid-day of the colour of lembayong, and in the evening of the hue of oil."

The king had Daulat (Divine Power) which extended to his regalia.

Generally, the regalia consisted of the *silasila* (book of genealogical descent), a code of laws, a baju (vest) and weapons such as a kris, kleywang and spear.

Regalia also had supernatural powers.

No wonder Harimau yearned to touch the regalia.

Anyone who touched his regalia or broke a religious taboo was subject to *kĕna Daulat* (struck dead) by a quasi-electric discharge which resided in the king's person.

Yellow was the colour or Malay royalty with Sultan Muhammed Shah the first to prohibit the wearing of yellow clothes in public other than for royalty.

White may be a more exalted and sacred colour used by Medicine men as it is believed to conciliate the spirits and demons.

Royalty also used umbrellas but, in this case, the white umbrella was superior to the yellow mainly because it stood out better from a distance. The yellow umbrella was reserved for the raja's family.

The *semangat* (soul or sevenfold soul) interestingly took the form of a 'thumbling' or what we would today term a 'mini me' that could leave the body when the person was asleep, in a trance, ill or dead. Generally invisible and about the size of a thumb, it resembled its human but was a vapour and could fly.

I remember having discussions about this. I was told that when a person had a shock that it was customary for the soul to leave the body and that we must call the soul back into the body. The words used were, "Kus Semangat."

When I asked why, I was told that this was how you would call a bird. But when I asked why a bird, no one could provide an answer.

On researching this topic, I discovered that it was believed long ago that the soul could fly and hence was treated as if it were a bird. The words finally made sense.

The original entreaty was probably something like this but has been very much shortened (I doubt whether the word 'hither' would have been used but this was written by Skeat, an Englishman):

"Hither, Soul, come hither!
Hither, Little One, come hither!
Hither, Bird, come hither!
Hither, Filmy One, come hither!"

I wonder whether *mari* (come) would have been more appropriate?
Sometimes rice is also used to tempt the soul to return.
The thumbling held the person's life and resembled the person. Hence the story of storing of the mousedeer's soul in an urn makes more sense.

At the time, this was an animistic society. There was belief that you could call a *riang sĕmangat* (carefree soul) back or even abduct the soul of a person whom you may wish to get into your power (*mĕngambil sĕmangat orang*). To do so you would have to induce it to take up its residence in a vessel. Again, the story of GUARDIAN OF THE KING'S SOUL makes more sense. I wonder if this was like the genie in the story of Aladdin with his domicile of the lamp.

The number seven is important in Malay magic. This could be why the snail asks for seven days to prepare, and so does the ant. Kancil starts a war on Kera in seven days.

And nine is a well-known lucky number.

Animals, minerals, and vegetables also had souls, with animal souls, like the human souls, resembling the animal itself but in a mini me form. Tree souls or ore souls however resemble either animals or birds with the Eaglewood tree resembling a bird, the souls of tin ore - a buffalo - and the soul of gold - a deer.

Fasting or religious penance was performed in a solitary spot, often at the top of a hill or a mountain to reach a state of spiritual exaltation or to acquire *sakti* (supernatural powers). This is probably the reason Pak Kambeng believed Kancil.

A lower hill or even a plain that possessed an unusual rock or tree was also used. This was possibly because landscapes with waterfalls and rocks of unusual shape were attributed to demons.

Fasts weren't complete fasts as ketupats (handful of rice wrapped in plaited coconut leaves) were allowed and hence fasts could go on for an indefinite period.

"Jins" or "Genii" were the link between gods and ghosts. The most powerful was the Black Genie who is described as having black organs i.e., liver, heart, lungs, spleen, tusk-like teeth; a scarlet breast; inverted body-hairs, and finally a single bone.

He lives in the heart of the earth. The animals wanting to eat the heart and the liver of the earth makes more sense.

The Nabi are the prophets, and they are:

Muhammad, Solomon (king of the Genii), David (beauty of his voice), Joseph (beauty of his countenance) and even Noah (lord of trees.)

According to Skeat (Malay Magic), there are sheikhs *di-kandang* (penned) in the Four Corners of the Earth respectively.

Thus, the phrase "Ask pardon of the Four Corners of the World," i.e., of these Sheikhs makes sense.

Giants appeared to be plentiful in those days:

Bota or Bhuta from Sanskrit, Raksasa from Sanskrit, and Gargasi (See Glossary for the many different spellings), or Hantu Tinggi (Tall Demons/Ghost).

There are also fairies or good people - Bidadari or Bĕdiadari (my grandfather was buried at Bidadari cemetery before it was turned into a housing estate) or Pĕri (fairies and elves).

How I remember being told that when I slept, I was not to be awakened. My grandmother would point to a sleeping child and say see how her eyes move – she is dreaming of fairies.

According to Skeat the Malays loved to watch buffalo fighting to the point of addiction. Thus, the story of WIT WINS THE DAY makes more sense.

These animals have been prepared and trained for months. Their coats glisten blackly and their necks gleam from having chilli water poured over them to increase excitement. They stamp the ground, blowing clouds of smoke from nostrils full of blood.

Omens and dreams are a part of this landscape.

According to Skeat (Malay Magic), omens are drawn from the acts of men or the events of nature.

Sneezing is a sign of driving away the demons of disease.

Yawning is a bad sign.

Stumbling is a bad omen for obvious reasons.

The Iban believe that dreams were the way the gods or spirits spoke to them and that they had no choice but to carry out the dream or else they would go mad.

Charms were also popular.

They were to control the weather, birds, building ceremonies etc.

Notes

2 – Sang Kancil and the Elephant

"T. javanicus are most active during the night. Lesser Malay mouse deer travel through tunnel-like trails of thick brush to reach their feeding and resting sites, which are often in the cracks of rocks, hollow trees, and dense vegetation." (Grzimck, 1994).

"The male mouse deer are territorial. Mouse deer regularly mark their territories, and their mates, using secretions from an intermandibular gland under the chin, an action that is usually accompanied by urinating or defecating." (Nowak and Paradiso, 1983).

Their territories are around 13-24 hectares and often mousedeer ignore their neighbours rather than attack.
"Male mouse deer protect themselves, and their mates, against rivals by chasing or slashing them with their sharp canines. When threatened, lesser Malay mouse deer rapidly beat their hooves on the ground at speeds of up to 7 times per second, creating a 'drum roll'." (Grzimck, 1994).

3- Pilandok and Sumusong sa Alongan

This story from the (Maranao, Philippines) comes in many forms as you will find when reading through the book. Although in Malaysia it is a tiger – Harimau – who ends up beating the gong and getting stung.

While we accept that Kancil allows the tiger to be tricked to escape being eaten, here we find that it is a human being, and one who appears to have no evil design on the Mousedeer's life.

So why then does the Mousedeer trick the prince?

According to Dehino and San Jose (THE STORY OF PILANDOK: A POST-COLONIAL READING OF TRICKSTER TALES by Peachy Cleo Dehino and Ariel San Jose, Arete, vol 2, no 1, 2014.) Prince Sumusong-sa-Alongan may be interpreted as the symbol of the Colonial Powers. Notice how he comes riding along on his horse with the trophies of his conquest in full display for all to see.

By urging Pilandok to acquiesce, he is usurping authority where he does not belong. His very name itself, 'Sumusong', appears to translate as 'one who invades', or 'one who creeps into'. Hence an outsider who does not belong.

Pilandok is the trickster, albeit already a rebel at such a young age.

4 - Sang Kancil counts the crocodiles

Believed to have originated from Hikayat Sang Kancil (Tale of the Mousedeer.)

In another version contained in the Journal of the Straits Branch of the Royal Asiatic Society, 45, 1906, the mousedeer decides to cross a river simply to get away from his enemies.
He tells the crocodiles that he is a messenger of Nabi Sleyman (Prophet Solomon). And that it is the will of Nabi Sleyman that he counts all his slaves. So, the crocodiles float on the river while the mousedeer counts them one by one. After the mousedeer gets across, he simply states that he has reckoned correctly and that the crocodiles may now sink back down.

The mousedeer counting the crocodiles is told throughout Malaysia. Often, it is the jambu air tree that is the mousedeer's aim. In some versions a crocodile grabs the mousedeer's leg as he goes down to the river for a drink but is convinced that it is only a twig and so releases the leg. Sang Kancil then goes on to mention that it is King Solomon who has ordered the headcount.

This is one such verse. There are many.:

One, two, three, knock!
Male, female, I knock,
Four, five, six, seven,
Eight, nine, ten, eleven,
Twelve, thirteen, fourteen!
Keep your tails straight!
Fifteen, sixteen, and seventeen.
King Solomon must be obeyed.

Not in every case does Sang Kancil admit that he has tricked them, and in one instance he thanks the crocodiles for obeying. Not once, however, does he reward them.

Indonesian legends & folk tales by De Leeuw, Adèle, published by Nelson, New York, 1961.

The same tale which ends with Kantjil teasing the foolish crocodiles in the end.

This is followed by Kantjil drinking at the river's edge. The oldest crocodile was waiting and seizes Kantjil's leg. Kantjil pretends that it is a stick of wood. The crocodile lets go and Kantjil escapes.

The story ends with Kantjil and the log floating upstream.
Mousedeer stands on the edge of the bank and spots the old crocodile.
Mousedeer says that if it is a log he sees then it will float upstream but if it is a crocodile then it will float downstream. At once the silly crocodile floats upstream.

The Filipinas also have their own version – Pilandok and the Crocodiles.

The story starts off with Pilandok wanting to cross the river while not wanting to be the crocodiles' next meal. Again, the excuse is that the Sultan wishes to know how many crocodiles there are in the river. He promises a gift to each. Pilandok crosses and then in true mousedeer fashion admits his prank. The crocodiles are upset but Pilandok does not care and trots off.

6 - Mousedeer and the Crocodile have a tug of war

Again, a composite of tales.

From: Borneo Literature Bureau – Mousedeer and the Crocodile.

7 - Tiger gets his deserts

Pp 20-21

So many sources, one of them being Fables & Folk-Tales from an Eastern Forest, Collected and Translated by Walter Skeat, M.A., Cambridge: At the University Press, 1901.
Also, in the Hikayat Gul Bakhtiyar.

In another version, the chief of the crocodiles is lying in wait by a water pool when the teak tree that he is lying under breaks, thanks to a freak storm. The crocodile is then trapped. Kantjil who happens to be there when this happens asks for help to free the crocodile. Kantjil believes the crocodile's promise to stop his predations in return for help.
The first creature to come onto the scene is a silver gibbon, but the gibbon refuses to help, saying instead that the jungle would be better off without such a predator. The silver gibbon calls for help and other animals answer – lemurs, monkeys, orangutan, a fox, and finally a bull.

While the bull rolls the log off, the others shout encouragement.

Crocodile then asks for assistance to get back into the water. Bull rolls the crocodile into the water, and as thanks, crocodile tries to eat the Bull.

Crocodile says that it makes sense to eat Bull as he is hungry.
But Bull says that there is such a thing as gratitude.
The pair consult the other animals. This is a very Asian tradition of asking a group to decide

on the outcome of a matter.

A pot floats by and its opinion is gathered. The pot speaks of the ungratefulness of humans. Crocodile is about to devour the Bull when Kantjil speaks.
He derides the Bull for his stupidity. He reminds the Bull of how weak the crocodile is after his ordeal and that the Bull should take advantage of this and toss the crocodile into the river. Bull obeys.

Crocodile is gored and then tossed into the river where his body is swept away by the swift-flowing current and never seen again.

And that waterhole is now a safe place for drinking.

8 - The Kinot

As much as possible, I study all the sources, determine the heart of the story, and then I write the story.

Here are some sources:

In Harold Courtlander's Kantchil's Lime Pit: and other stories from Indonesia, published 1950 by Harcourt Brace, New York, in The Crocodile's Share, a similar tale is told.
Only it is a Javanese farmer and his small son. They are in the jungle far from home. They decide to stop for the night and lie on the ground. The son wishes to sleep on the inside because it is cold on the outside. The father acquiesces although he says it is a silly thing to want with only two of them. They go to sleep with the son's head on the father's stomach. The man covers them both with a blanket.

A tiger comes along and smells man but is puzzled by the strange shape. And when he investigates, he discovers four arms and four legs, but only one head.

He goes off and finds a crocodile who wisely says that there must be two, not one man, and that the tiger should toss one of the men into the river as his rightful share.
The tiger returns to investigate. He bends over the sleeping man and his whiskers tickle the man who sneezes. The sudden sound terrifies the tiger who is in a panic. He races to the river and is devoured by the crocodile.

Reference: Pp 20-21

Fables & Folk-Tales from an Eastern Forest, Collected and Translated by Walter Skeat, M.A., Cambridge: At the University Press, 1901. However, this version does not have a mousedeer in it.

9 - The Leopard and the Mousedeer

This story (31) has been rewritten from VILLAGE FOLK-TALES OF CEYLON Vol. I, Collected and Translated by H. PARKER, Late of the Irrigation Department, Ceylon LONDON, LUZAC & CO, Publishers to the India Office, 1910

North-western Province.
The notes below are verbatim from the journal above. It makes you wonder where the story originated.

"This story is given in The Orientalist, vol. iv, p. 79 (D. A. Jayawardana), but the animals that went to the cave are wrongly termed tiger and fox, which are not found in Ceylon.
It is also related in vol. iv, p. 121 (S. J. Goonetilleke), the animals being a hind and a tiger.

In vol. i, p. 261, there is a Santal story (J. L. Phillips), in which a goat with a long beard, which had taken refuge in a tiger's cave frightened it when asked, "Who are you with long beard and crooked horns in my house?" by saying, "I am your father." A monkey returned with it, their tails being tied together. When they came to the cave, the monkey asked the same question, and received the same answer, which frightened both animals so much that they fled, the monkey's tail being pulled off. When the tiger stopped, and began to lick himself, he found the monkey's tail so sweet that he went back and ate the monkey.

In the Panchatantra (Dubois), a bearded goat frightened a lion that he found in a cave in which he took refuge, by saying, "I am the Lord He-goat. I am a devotee of Śiva, and I have promised to devour in his honour 101 tigers, 25 elephants, and 10 lions." He had eaten the rest and was now in search of the lions. A jackal persuaded the lion to return, but the goat frightened them again.

In Old Deccan Days (Frere), p. 303, a pandit (Hindu scholar) frightened a demon in this manner, by scolding a wrestler who brought for dinner an apparent goat which the pandit recognised as a demon.

In Wide-Awake Stories (Steel and Temple), p. 132 ff - Tales of the Punjab, p. 123 ff — a farmer's wife frightened a tiger that was going to eat a cow. A jackal persuaded it to return, their tails being tied together. On the tiger's running off again, the jackal was jolted to death.

In The Indian Antiquary, vol. iv, p. 257, there is a Santal story by Rev. E. T. Cole, of a tiger which was frightened by two brothers. The three sat round a fire and asked riddles. The tiger's was, "One I will eat for breakfast, and another like it for supper." The men expressed their inability to guess the answer, and their riddle was, "One will twist the tail, the other will wring the ear." When the tiger was escaping, they held the tail, till it came off.
In Tota Kahānī (Small), p. 98, a lynx took possession of a tiger's cave, and behaved like

the mousedeer when the tiger arrived. When the tiger returned with a monkey, the lynx frightened it like the mousedeer, by telling its young ones that a monkey friend had sworn to bring a tiger that day. On hearing this, the tiger killed the monkey, and fled.

10 - How Beruang lost his tail or Pickled Tiger's Eyeballs

This story is supposed to have originated from Selangor.
In other versions, the mousedeer is supposed to be in a cave.
In one version it is the sun bear and in yet another version, it is a black bear.

Many sources, one of them Penghulu Haji Mohamed Nasir, who cannot recollect where he heard it.

"Kerab kerab kertub kertub. Kerab kerab kertub kertub. Kertab kertub kertab, kertub."

These are the actual sounds in the original version.

11 – Sang Kancil and Sang Beruang

Again, another national story in Malaysia.

12 – The Golden Collar

In another version contained in the Journal of the Straits Branch of the Royal Asiatic Society, 45, 1906, the mousedeer is thirsty. It sees a river and believing that there are no crocodiles around it, drinks.

A crocodile however bites the mousedeer's leg. The mousedeer pretends that his leg is simply a dead branch and even suggests that the crocodile taste it carefully but not by biting because then the crocodile would miss the flavour. Surprisingly, the crocodile agrees and releases the leg.

The mousedeer then admits that it was his leg after all.

14 - Sang Kancil and the Deep Pit

Believed to have originated from Hikayat Sang Kancil (Tale of the Mousedeer.)

In Harold Courtlander's Kantchil's Lime Pit: and other stories from Indonesia, published 1950 by Harcourt Brace, New York, Kantchil is passing a farmer's house when he sees a fresh banana cake wrapped in banana leaves.

He steals the cake and is so engrossed in eating it, that he falls into the farmer's lime pit.
Now lime pits are where limestone is quarried or burnt to make quick lime. They can be quite deep.
Kantchil called out to tuhan (god) while holding the banana leaves.
Babi the boar looks down and sees him.

Kantchil pretends to be reading. He announces that god has determined that today is doomsday, and that all who wish to live should take refuge in a cave.
When Babi the boar questions the mousedeer, he confirms that he has been reading from the holy book. Then he adds that only those who stand in the sacred lime pit will be saved.

When Babi says he wishes to join Kantchil, he is turned away as he is apparently unclean because he is constantly sneezing.

Babi promises that he will not sneeze and so joins the mousedeer at the bottom of the pit.

Matjan the tiger is next. He, too, promises not to sneeze.
Gadja the elephant follows.

The four sit at the bottom of the pit looking at each other. Then Kantchil tells Gadja to get out as he looks as if he is about to sneeze.

Gadja is upset. He promises to stand on his truck so that he will not sneeze.

Kantchil pretends to read. Then he accuses Matjan of being about to sneeze.

Matjan denies it.

Then Katchil sneezes.

The other three accuse Kantchil of defiling this holy place and flouting the words of the law. They then throw him out of the limepit…

Indonesian legends & folk tales by De Leeuw, Adèle, published by Nelson, New York, 1961.

Same tale. Kantjil is running through the forest when he falls into a pit. Elephant comes along and is told the story of the sky falling. Elephant jumps in, and Kantjil jumps onto his back and leaps out of the pit.

In yet another version, Kanchil falls into a pit. He calls for help but when that doesn't work, he calls out that there is a market down in the pit. The other animals join him in the pit. When enough animals are in the pit, Kanchil jumps onto their backs. The remaining animals are upset but Gajah helps them all out and, in the end, Kanchil leads them off to the real market in the jungle.

15 – Rimau – Part I

Believed to have originated from Hikayat Sang Kancil (Tale of the Mousedeer).

In the Moken version, the tiger and the mousedeer meet on a shore in front of a hollow tree. This makes sense as the Mokens were sea nomads and lived for most of the year on their boats.

Tiger, of course, wishes to eat the mousedeer to which the mousedeer replies that he may if he beats the bees' nest.
The mousedeer removes himself a little distance while the tiger beats the nest and of course what happens next is that the bees swarm out and attack the foolish tiger who only manages to escape by hastily running away.

The second day the two meet again, this time beside a sleeping python. Again, the mousedeer says the same thing, that he will allow himself to be eaten but only if the tiger wears the python as a necklace.

"Place the python round…"

The silly tiger agrees. The serpent strangles the tiger enough for it to develop a limp.

The third day, tiger encounters the mousedeer. This time the mousedeer is busy collecting chilli pods.

When the tiger says that this time there is no escape, the mousedeer agrees. In fact, the mousedeer then says that he has even prepared an appetiser for Tiger.

Well, Tiger eats the chilli pods and experiences the horrible burning sensation – as if his throat was on fire. It managed however to pounce. The mousedeer runs off and during the chase both prey and predator end up in a deep waterhole.
Angered to find itself in this mess, Tiger takes a swipe at the mousedeer and so powerful is its swipe that it sends the mousedeer out of the pond. The mousedeer ends up escaping while Tiger perishes miserably.

16 – Sang Kancil and Siput the Water Snail

Believed to have originated from Hikayat Sang Kancil (Tale of the Mousedeer).

In another version contained in the Journal of the Straits Branch of the Royal Asiatic Society, 45,

1906, the race is by the sea, and it is the king of snails – Siput Kiyong whom the mousedeer races. In Harold Courtlander's Kantchil's Lime Pit: and other stories from Indonesia, published 1950 by Harcourt Brace, New York, in the back of the book (page 135), a similar tale is told, only instead of the water snail it is the crab. Each time he calls out, another crab answers and of course, one crab appears very much like another.
In some versions, according to Courtlander, Kantchil or Pelanduk gets revenge by asking the elephant to trample on the crabs.

Courtlander states that the role of the trickster is sometimes taken by the ape or the tortoise. When Pelanduk tricks there is a 'cunning sharpness' and a 'humourous pomposity' present.

In Fables & Folk-Tales from an Eastern Forest, Collected and Translated by Walter Skeat, M.A., Cambridge: At the University Press, 1901 it is a King Crow in place of the mousedeer.

In another version, it is the Gecko and not Siput who tricks the mousedeer.

In another version, Kanchil challenges all the animals to a race. It is Pelan (Slow) the snail who beats all the animals. Such tales are common also in other parts of Asia and Europe. The difference is the type of animals involved: tortoise and Garuda, tortoise and hare or rabbit.

17 – The Tragic Tale of Tiptibau the Nighthawk

Believed to have originated from Hikayat Sang Kancil (Tale of the Mousedeer). But stories of men chopping down the houses of their mothers'-in-law are not uncommon.

19 – Mak Rimau – Part II

Believed to have originated from Hikayat Sang Kancil (Tale of the Mousedeer).

22 - Sang Kancil and the Buffalo

Believed to have its origins from the Hikayat Sang Kancil (Tale of the Mousedeer).

In another version contained in the Journal of the Straits Branch of the Royal Asiatic Society, 45, 1906, there are three and not one buffalo: the mousedeer comes up and berates the buffalo for asking stupid questions. Then he shows the buffalo the folly of his ways by first asking a sleeping mat that was drifting downstream, about its treatment by men.

The account is not a pleasant one.

The mousedeer next asks a dish cover, and again it is to discover it, too, was ill-treated by men. The mousedeer then suggests that the crocodile lets go of the buffalo because it is tough and there is a young buffalo nearby. The tale ends with the mousedeer saying that it needs to see the crocodile under the tree before it will believe.

This story is told throughout Malaysia.
Crocodile is referred to as Sang Bedal (Badass). And when Sang Bedal is once again trapped, both the buffalo and Sang Kancil run away.

In Harold Courtlander's Kantchil's Lime Pit: and other stories from Indonesia, published 1950 by Harcourt Brace, New York - War between the Crocodiles and Kantchil, a similar tale is told.

Crocodile is Buwaya. Kerbau is Karbau. When Karbau finished lifting the tree, he is asked to push Buwaya into the water. This is when Karbau's leg is bitten.

Here Kantchil declares that this is a matter for legal judgement and assumes the role of the judge. The crocodile is left pinned under the tree and so declares enmity against the mousedeer.

Next, Kantchil goes to drink, and a crocodile shouts, "War against Kantchil!" The crocodile attacks but manages only to grab a tough root. Kantchil, though, pretends that he has been seized and screams that he will be drowned.

The crocodile believing that he has indeed caught Kantchil pulls harder while Kantchil escapes.

Kantchil goes down to the river once more to drink and spies another black crocodile. He pretends to be talking to himself and asks whether it is a log or a crocodile. He finishes by saying that if what he sees is a log, then it will float upstream.

The crocodile floats upstream at once and is chided by Kantchil because everyone knows logs cannot float upstream.

Kantchil continues and this time smells sweet fruit from the opposite side of the river.

He sees more crocodiles and so he commands them all to arise from the water and be counted by order of Allah.
Thus, he counts them in the name of Allah and once on the other side, simply thanks them and goes off to eat his sweet fruit.

23 - The Elephant has a bet with the Tiger

In Harold Courtlander's Kantchil's Lime Pit: and other stories from Indonesia, published 1950 by Harcourt Brace, New York - The Bet Between Madjan and Gadja, a similar tale is told.

It was a time when animals were friends. Madjan and Gadja were walking beside the Mandau River. Madjan was eating small bugs while Gadja was eating bamboo stalks.
Again, Lotong appears and makes a pest of himself, chattering, making faces and eavesdropping. Unlike the story earlier, it is Madjan who makes the bet while Gadja, who is a vegetarian, goes along with it, thinking that it is idle conversation.
Pp 41-48

Like many of the stories in this book, the above story is a composite from many sources. Here is another source: In Fables & Folk-Tales from an Eastern Forest, Collected and Translated by Walter Skeat, M.A., Cambridge: At the University Press, 1901 it is a King Crow in place of the mousedeer.

It is also popular in Indonesia.

24 - Monkey and the Kueh

This story has its origins in Perak although, it is supposedly two monkeys arguing about sharing a piece of cake. They turn to a cat for judgment and the cat does exactly what Sang Kancil does.

The sad pair are left with the words that in life it is better to share than to be greedy.

25 - Sang Kancil and the Farmer

Believed to have originated from Hikayat Sang Kancil (Tale of the Mousedeer).

In another version contained in the Journal of the Straits Branch of the Royal Asiatic Society, 45, 906, the mousedeer comes across a cucumber garden.

The gardener paints dry coconut husks and makes a scarecrow using the gutta of the jackfruit. The mousedeer gets stuck to the scarecrow but is saved by the Ketupok bird.
The mousedeer feigns death and is tossed onto the rubbish heap, but immediately jumps up and runs away. The mousedeer eats more cucumbers and is caught in a trap. He escapes by telling the farmer's dog that he is the bridegroom. The dog, angry at this, opens the cage and orders the mousedeer to exchange places.

This story is told throughout Malaysia. Although sometimes it is yams and tapioca that the mousedeer is feasting on, and it is a noose trap and not a scarecrow that is the downfall of the mousedeer.

In another version, a deer (unclear if it is a mousedeer) is trapped by a farmer. While the farmer's wife is getting ready for dinner by preparing the spices the dog Sang Koyok comes along, and it is the dog who is tricked. The deer says that he is going to marry the Pumpkin Princess. Or the Farmer's daughter, Siti.

In another version, it is the animals who want to feast on the farmer's vegetable garden, and it is the Mousedeer who goes over to ask permission and becomes ensnared by the gummy scarecrow.

26 - The Stork and the Mousedeer

A story known throughout Malaysia.
It bears a strong resemblance to The Mousedeer's shipwreck (at least in the beginning.)

28 - Pilandok in the Kingdom of the Maranaw Sea or Si Pilandok sa Kaharian ng Dagat Maranaw

In one version, Pilandok is not a mousedeer but a young man. In another version, the greedy merchant dies, and the princess is the Datu's daughter.
Manaraw also spelt as Maranao.

The Maranao race live on the southern Philippines island of Mindanao. The name Maranao means "people of the lake" and the Manaraw Sea most likely refers to Lake Lanao in Lanao del Sur.

29 - The Mousedeer's Shipwreck

PP 5-8

Fables & Folk-Tales from an Eastern Forest, Collected and Translated by Walter Skeat, M.A., Cambridge: At the University Press, 1901.

The water chevrotain is known to retreat to the water on the approach of a predator. It can dive and can walk on the bottom of rivers and streams, and avoid being swept away. They grab onto plants and reeds to stay tethered and can hold their breath for around four minutes.

As some species show such affinity to water, this discovery has lent support to the idea that whales may have evolved from animals that looked like small deer.

32 - The Heart of the Earth

A story from Sarawak.

34 - The Young, Black Elephant and the Tide

In another version, it is a buffalo instead of an elephant.

35 - Sang Kancil and the King of the Jungle

In another version of the story above, an old tiger tells the other animals that he wishes to live in peace with them. Elephant, the leader of the animals, does not believe the old tiger until he is told a story about two hunters who have come to this neck of the jungle.

The deer is sent off with the old tiger to investigate the story. Only there are no hunters, and the poor deer is instead slain by the old tiger. After the deer is killed, the elephant seeks revenge.

When elephant is defeated in a battle with the old tiger, he is forced to daily sacrifice an animal to it. Unhappy, the animals seek the aid of Sang Kancil who takes the old tiger to a jungle pool whereby the light of the moon, the old tiger is tricked into believing that there is another tiger deep within.

The old tiger leaps into the pool and is drowned.

In another version, the mousedeer is eating grass when he is surprised by the tiger. Tiger at once announces that he is going to eat the mousedeer and is surprised to hear the mousedeer say that while he may do so, that if Tiger eats him, then his fate is to be eaten by an even bigger tiger.

Tiger is curious.

Sang Kancil leads him to a pond. There in the water, Tiger sees his own reflection.

Sang Kancil goads Tiger to fight the reflection.

Tiger jumps in and is drowned.

37 - Tiger's Talking Bottom

In another version contained in the Journal of the Straits Branch of the Royal Asiatic Society, 45, 1906, the tiger spots a pointed stick and ends up with the stick piercing him and thus dying.

In the Moken version, it is a tigress and not a tiger. But the events are the same although shortened.

The mousedeer is going along the shore when he was caught by the tigress.

The mousedeer persuades the tigress not to bite him but to swallow him whole if she wanted him dead, which she does.

The tigress devours the mousedeer whole but when it next goes to hunt and spots a wild boar, a voice cries out," Beware of the tiger!" frightening both the tigress and the wild boar.

This happened repeatedly, and finally, the mousedeer made itself thin enough to slide out when the tigress was at stool. It then pretended to be dead and part of the tigress's faeces.

But being a mousedeer, it could not resist the urge to jump up and taunt the tigress. Thus, the reason why all predators rip their kill apart.

43 - The Tiger and the Shadow

Pp 28-29

There are so many versions of the Mousedeer tricking the tiger, but this particular tale comes from Fables & Folk-Tales from an Eastern Forest, Collected and Translated by Walter Skeat, M.A., Cambridge: At the University Press, 1901.

44 - Wit Wins the Day

This is a story about territorial dispute although it is not clear in the beginning. Here are the hints:

Hint #1 – While most animals are introduced either by their names or description, the two bulls are introduced by where they are from i.e., their territory.
The first bull is named - Wild Bull of the Clearing while the second is Bull of the Young Bush.
Hint #2 – Where the fight took place which was the boundary between the two lands.

Hint #3 - Pilanduk sits on an anthill which would have been built a long time before the fight. The anthill is the territory of the white ants. While Pelanduk watches the battle, the white ants seek to make Pelanduk part of their territory by extending their burrow into his back.

Hint #4 – Harimau enters the scene. It does not matter whether Pilanduk is on Pilanduk's own territory, Harimau goes wherever he can find food. He acquires what he needs through might.

Hint #5 – Pilanduk shifts territory to that of the water. Remember, Harimau is only King of the Land, not the water.

I wrote the above story months ago but in January 2024 I found this below in Malay Magic by Skeat, who states that Kipling spoke of the Law of the Jungle which really is only the code of man but adapted to beasts. But those familiar with buffalo are aware that they are highly territorial.

Do not trespass.

I remember visiting the grounds of Kandang Kerbau Hospital in Singapore as a young child and seeing water buffalo wallow in the mud. My mother warned me not to go near them.

I remember feeling very vindicated that I had read the hints/clues in the story correctly.

Pp 30-32

This folktale is from Fables & Folk-Tales from an Eastern Forest, Collected and Translated by Walter Skeat, M.A., Cambridge: At the University Press, 1901 as well as many other sources.

'Riseh' and the 'Tunggal Duri' – names given in Skeat's writing.

45 - Sang Kancil and the Gergasi

In the version from Borneo, it was the mousedeer, the tortoise, an ape, and an elephant. They caught fish, and it was the elephant who first stood guard. They all failed, and of course the mousedeer was the last to guard the fish. The mousedeer set four stout poles into the ground, attached four rings. When the giant came, he told him that this was a cure for backpain. The giant insisted on being treated and was trapped and killed.

In the version from Indonesian legends & folk tales by De Leeuw, Adèle, published by Nelson, New York, 1961:
Here, (still in Borneo) the animals are the mousedeer, tortoise, ape, and elephant. They all decided to go fishing on the banks of the river and were visited by a giant. When the animals all failed to prevent their smoked fish from being eaten, it was the mousedeer who volunteered to guard their catch. The others laughed but the mousedeer insisted. When the others left, the mousedeer planted four posts into the ground. He then wove rattan into four strong rings. When the giant turned up, he kept on hard at work.

Curious, the giant asked him what he was doing. Mousedeer explained that he was fashioning a cure for his friends, who have back pain.

The giant asked for the remedy, and Kantjil agreed to help him. He told the giant to pull his elbows and knees close to his chest. He explained that he intended to massage him but instead slipped the rings over the giant's arms and legs, and pulling them tight, hitched the rings to the posts. The giant began to get suspicious, but Kantjil simply told him to wait and see.

Too late, the giant found that he could not move. When the others returned, they killed the giant.

Charles Bryce, Mousedeer, published by Darling Newspaper Press 2009.

In this version, mousedeer rode a white rhinoceros. He was out to impress the animals who tried to fight off the giant but failed.

The giant stole their food and water, and although the animals fought him, none succeeded in defeating the giant.
The white rhinoceros took the mousedeer to the giant then ran away. The mousedeer gathered honeycomb and placed them in an old well. He told the giant that he was guarding the honeycomb, which was a gift for the Giant.
The giant knew that he had misbehaved, so he was puzzled as to why the animals wanted to present him with such a wonderful gift.
This was where the Mousedeer came into his own. He could have simply given the giant the honeycomb, but instead he said that the honeycomb was the second-best gift, in fact a distraction from what the animals valued most.

The Mousedeer admitted that the real treasure was down the well. And so, the giant jumped into the well. Unable to get out, the animals buried him in the well.

46 - Sucking the Pond

This story was a delight to write. A few years ago, I had written a book on the Sea Dyaks, and writing these stories brought back so many memories.

I loved the little details like the mention of the head collecting, for the Sea Dyaks who are now called Iban were head-hunters. Collecting heads was how a warrior increased his status. This whole story was about status.

I loved how, even though it appeared that Pelandok had betrayed Tekura, they were friends to the end. For nothing is stronger than family to the Sea Dyaks.

Menarak had volunteered to win honour in the eyes of his chief, another typical Sea Dyak behaviour.

But the best part was the cork.

How many times had my late father told me stories about humans and animals stuffing a cork up their bottoms. This was a very common ploy in the stories that he told. I have since learnt that this is a common device in stories from Southeast Asia. This familiar device brought back so many memories of the days when he told me story after story.
In this story, Badak continues to try to live up to his new role as leader. He picks little challenges that he knows he can win. But in the next story, he attempts the impossible.

49 - The End of Beruang

These last five stories had their source in the Iban Animals Stories published by the Borneo Literature Bureau, illustrated by Benjamin Hasbie.

Again, the theme is the very Asian dilemma of what to do about possible 'loss of face.'

It is interesting that while some animals worry about this – Badak and Tekura, there are others who do not seem to care – Pelandok and Kera.

So why did Badak do what he did?
He made a mistake when suggesting tuba fishing but then saved face with his next task. Why did Badak next suggest the impossible – measuring the distance of the sky?

The answer is because he wanted to keep his people busy.
This is what rulers do.

Keep their people busy, so busy that they don't think of overthrowing their ruler.
There is another version of this story: the monkey and the mousedeer decide to plant bananas.
Monkey doesn't care for his plants and so his plants die.

Monkey picks the bananas and throws the peel down onto the ground. Mousedeer is unhappy and when the time comes to harvest his bananas, he refuses to give even one banana to monkey.

But mousedeer cannot climb trees. So, he knows that he is forced to obtain monkey's aid unless he can come up with a solution.
Mousedeer begins to call monkey names.

Monkey is furious and grabs bananas and hurls them down, trying to hit mousedeer with them. Of course, mousedeer ends up with the bananas.

This is like the story of the man with the hats who fell asleep one day and woke up to find the monkeys had stolen his hat.
He tries everything to get his hats back, but nothing works. In the end, in complete frustration he throws his hat on the ground.

The monkeys imitate him and throw the hats on the ground, and this is how the man gets his hats back.

How I laughed when I was told these stories as a child.

54 - Who killed the Otter's babies?

PP 9-12

This folktale is a composite from Fables & Folk-Tales from an Eastern Forest, Collected and Translated by Walter Skeat, M.A., Cambridge: At the University Press, 1901 as well as many other sources.

Writing these folktales has brought back many memories and this is probably one of my most vivid memories from childhood.

I remember crying when I was told this story. How could Sang Kancil be so horrid? Those were children that he trampled.

I remember how I hated this story.

But now when I recall this story, what I remember most is my grandfather and his great love for me.

And so now this story only holds sweet memories for me – of my grandfather. Of course, it was still awful for the children to have perished.

It is true that mousedeer drum their hooves to warn other animals.

Clock stories are common in Southeast Asia. Another name for them is cause-and-effect stories. In essence, it is a riddle that has been lengthened into a narrative.

The war dance that the mousedeer is stunned into performing is the twelve-step Silat.

55 - The Magic Flute

Believed to have originated from Hikayat Sang Kancil (Tale of the Mousedeer).

In another version contained in the Journal of the Straits Branch of the Royal Asiatic Society, 45, 1906, the flute is a viol. This is also the reason why the tiger, to this day, has a short tongue.

In another version, faeces are supposed to be a cure for a sore tongue, which was why the tiger did eat it in one story, even though it was bitter.

All these stories are well-known in Java.

56 - The King of the Tigers is sick

PP 3-4

Fables & Folk-Tales from an Eastern Forest, Collected and Translated by Walter Skeat, M.A., Cambridge: At the University Press, 1901.

57 - Sang Kancil and the King of the Tiger's Whisker

In Harold Courtlander's Kantchil's Lime Pit: and other stories from Indonesia, published 1950 by Harcourt Brace, New York - The Tigers' War against Borneo, a similar tale is told.

As well as in Indonesian legends & folk tales by De Leeuw, Adèle, published by Nelson, New York, 1961 – Why there are no tigers in Borneo.

This is a popular and well-known story.

58 - The Mock Funeral of the Great Commander Harimau

Believed to have originated from Hikayat Sang Kancil (Tale of the Mousedeer).

In one version, Pelanduk saw some red-shooted shrub (lamah-lamah) and upon eating the shoots, stained his mouth red.

A Sambur Deer came upon him. When asked why he was slavering red from his jaws, the mousedeer replied that he had been given some red betel to eat by the villagers. When the Deer learned that the villagers were generous to strangers, and because betel was apparently something that Deer were particular to, the Deer headed for the village where it was instead ensnared and slain. The villagers thought that she was the culprit who had destroyed all their betel.

The mousedeer next came upon the Deer's fawn, who enquired as to his mother's whereabouts. When the mousedeer feigned that he was unaware of the Sambur Deer's whereabouts he was rushed at by the fawn.
The fawn accused the mousedeer of lying and stated that his mother was dead.

The mousedeer leaped into a pit.

He then called out to the other animals, saying that the sky was falling. The story then followed the predictable tale of the animals jumping in to save themselves and the eventual escape of the mousedeer who jumped onto the backs of the animals.

"In the wild, lesser Malayan mouse deer are commonly herbivores and folivores, eating leaves, buds, shrubs, and fruits that have fallen from trees. In zoos, mouse deer tend to eat insects as well as leaves and fruits." (Nowak and Paradiso, 1983).

I was horrified to learn as I researched that some mousedeer have also been observed eating arthropods and small animals.

59 - The Pact between Harimau and Buaya

Believed to have originated from Hikayat Sang Kancil (Tale of the Mousedeer).

From A Pelandok Tale by G. M. Laidlaw who was told by the penghulu of Pulau Tiga, Lower Perak, Haji Mahomed Ali bin Haji Mahomed Perak.

Charles Bryce, Mousedeer, published by Darling Newspaper Press 2009. A similar tale.

61 - Two Men and an Axe

In A Pelandok Tale by G. M. Laidlaw which was told by the penghulu of Pulau Tiga, Lower Perak, Haji Mahomed Ali bin Haji Mahomed Perak, it is not caterpillars but weevils, while in others it is worms which have eaten the axe.

In other versions, it is not an axe but an adze.

In another version, the mousedeer rolls in dust.

Raja Suleiman is King Solomon.

It is the river which caught on fire. And to save the palace from catching alight, Kancil rolls to put out the fire.
In the interests of preservation, here is one source in the original Malay:

Dua orang lelaki datang mengadap Raka Sulaiman bahawa beliung yang dipinjam oleh salah seorang daripada mereka telah dimakan ulat. Kancil dipanggil untuk menjadi hakim. Laul dia ke Sungai mandi berliamu. Bila naik ke darat, Kancil bergulung di dalam debu. Lalu dikatakan pada Raja Sulaiman, air Sungai tersebut sedang terbakar. Kerana takutkan istana turut terbakar, dia berguling untuk memadamkan api. Mereka tidak percaya dengan cerita Kancil itu. Lalu, Kancil pun mengkiaskan bahawa beliung dimakan ulat juga tidak boleh dipercayai kerana ia adalah mustahil.

English Translation:

Two men came to confront Raka Sulaiman that the pickaxe borrowed by one of them had been eaten by a caterpillar. Kancil is called to be a judge. Then he went to the river to bathe. When he went to land, Kancil rolled in the dust. Then it was said to King Sulaiman, the water of the river was burning. Fearing that the palace would also catch fire, he rolled over to put out the fire. They didn't believe Kancil's story. Then Kancil alluded that a pickaxe eaten by a caterpillar is also unreliable because it is impossible.

NOTE: Berliamu meaning unclear.

I have kept as close to the original plot as possible but also provided my interpretation of events to help clarify the situation. As can be seen, the above appears more of a summary than a story. At least to me. And I go by the basis of the stories told to me as I grew up, by my grandfather.
Perhaps paper was too expensive at the time that this tale was recorded. Perhaps the storyteller was too shy to expand upon his tale. Or terrified of Europeans. Whatever the reason, thankfully there are quite a few variations of this story and so I have taken the gist of the story and built it up according to what was needed to be enjoyed.

This was also one of the stories from memory.

Sadly, this is not the case with every story.

The Burmese have a similar story where a traveller stops to eat his meal beside a woman who is selling food. The woman accuses the traveller of stealing her food and demands payment. Here it is the Princess Learned-in-the-Law who comes to the rescue by determining that if the price of a plate of fried fish is a silver coin, that the price of the smell of fish frying is the shadow of a silver coin.
Isn't it wonderful how similar stories are shared around the region.

62 - The Rich Man and the Poor Man

Believed to have originated from Hikayat Sang Kancil (Tale of the Mousedeer).

"Reason is a better paragon of virtue than a thousand stupid and foolish friends."
Author of the Hikayat Sang Kancil.
The more popular version is that of two orphans instead of the poor man and his wife.

Here is the original story of one of them in Malay:

Malay
Saudagar menuntut dua anak yatim yang berjiran membayar sjumlah 1,000 wang emas. Sedangkan dua anak yatim ini tidak pernag memakan apa-apa dari rumah saudagar. Hakim

Sang Kancil hanya membayarnya dengan dentingan wang emas yang dijatuhkan ke latai sebanyak 1,000 kali.

English
The merchant demanded that two neighbouring orphans pay a sum of 1,000 gold money. Whereas these two orphans didn't eat anything from the merchant's house. Judge Sang Kancil only paid him with a sliver of gold money that was dropped to the floor 1,000 times.

Another one of the stories told to me as a child.

64 - The Midday Dream

In another version, it is Kantjil who goes to sleep beside a well. He awakes to find Tiger staring down at him. He tricks Tiger into thinking that he has been appointed guardian of the well by King Singa, and when the tiger bends over to drink, Kantjil pushes the tiger into the well, and he drowns.

66 - Pelanduk Jenaka becomes King:

Originally from Hikayat Pelanduk Jenaka.

Jenaka could also mean a sacred or Pure Place. In the Hikayat Pelanduk Jenaka (published in 1885 and 1893) the story is told of how the mousedeer becomes king.

He obtains his strength by (1885) rubbing his body with the sap from a ficus tree and in (1893) rolling in lallang. (I hated lallang as I have been cut by this ubiquitous grass so many times as a child.)

67 - Pelandok, his adopted son, Harimau the Man Eater and what happened in the end which may not be believed...

There are two secondary sources for this story. The first is Tales from the Deep Forest, The Very Curious Adventure of Kancil the Mouse Deer by Georges Voisset, and The Journal of the Straits Branch of the Royal Asiatic Society.

The story was told by Penghulu Noordin of Kota Stia who learnt it from a woman - Lekah binti Jaman. I find this interesting as this is the first instance of a female storyteller. Yay!
In the second source, the story starts off with a man digging a well. Pelandok passes by and makes fun of the man, then runs off. When the well is done, Pelandok comes back to investigate and unfortunately falls in. The well itself being deep, Pelandok is unable to escape. The story follows the predictable pattern of other animals coming by: Ka Sang Babi the Pig, a rhinoceros, a barking deer, a Sambhur deer and a bull elephant.

The difference is the excuse that Pelandok (referred to as Salaam di Rimba) gave: he is playing and amusing himself. And that the animals are only to join him for a short period. But by this stage, Pelandok is using the familiar excuse of the sky falling in.
Conveniently there is a thunderstorm overhead.

The elephant joins the crowd at the bottom of the well. Pelandok then picks up a piece of wood and starts to hit the elephant. He annoys the elephant to the point of that the elephant tosses him out of the well.

Mission accomplished. And of course, Pelandok can't help himself but boasts of how he tricked the others.

The story then continues onto the wedding feast. Here Pelandok relates to the wedding guests that there are animals trapped in the well.

The wedding guests find and kill the animals.

Pelandok creates mayhem at the wedding feast and so the wedding guests now want to kill him. Pelandok grabs a pillow and climbs onto the ridge pole of the house. As the villagers chase him up and down the house, he lets the pillow fall.

The guests stab the pillow thinking that it is the mousedeer, but while they are engaged with the pillow, Pelandok escapes down the river on a slab of clotted rice.
The story was originally called Pak si Bajok (Old Bago of a Thousand Faces), the character being a solitary ape. But all I can find is a mention of Pelandok coming across the ape and inviting it on board the clotted rice cauldron. There is no further mention of this character which is strange as this is the name of the story.

As much as possible I have gone back to the original Malay source which is in The Journal of the Straits Branch of the Royal Asiatic Society.

So how is it possible for our Mousedeer to become human?
This question was put tothe late Mat Nordin, a storyteller, and his answer was:

"Those who possess the tales possess only the words. They know neither the truth of the Fireflies nor the truth of little Mouse Deers. Not even the truth of Men."
The truth lies in many other tales. Here is one:

It was believed that once upon a time humans could become animals and that animals could become human.

In the tale of the white crocodile, Nakhoda Ragam sailed from Jering with his beautiful wife,

Cik Siti. Now, his wife was sewing but despite her multiple warnings, Nakhoda could not resist the urge to cuddle her. She pricked him with the needle, and he died. His spirit entered an old crocodile.

Whenever the crocodile was seen, the people would ask person to pass, "Nakhoda Ragam, your descendants would like permission to pass."

The crocodile would then disappear from the waters.

Other races such as the Moken also have stories when people routinely turn into animals. It is believed that they inherited these stories from the sea-faring Malays.

Apparently, the Indians believed that all beings are the same, therefore it is possible for human to become animals and for animals to transform into human. Hence, animals in these stories are capable of speaking and thinking just like humans.

But the truth is that there are stories all around the world where animals became human and vice versa. This makes sense when one considers just how intimately primitive humans lived with animals.

And trickster animals are common throughout the world.

68 - Grandmaster and the Gergasi

Originally from the Hikayat Pelanduk Jenaka.
Many, many versions.

69 - Monkey Business

In the version from "A Chinese Mousedeer goes to Paris"; the lion is defeated by using a wasps' nest.

76 - King Gajah and King Semut: Gajah berperang dengan semut - Elephants fight with ants (Original Title)

Folktales are folktales because people collect them and pass them on i.e., the oral tradition of a people. Unfortunately, by doing so, some things get embellished, and some get left out. The audience generally knows the context in which the stories are told, but in some cases, even this can and has been lost.

There were two questions that baffled me when I read the above story which is believed to be quite old, and its oldest source is the Hikayat Pelanduk Jenaka.

Why was man mentioned?

And why were the weaver ants invited?

Man is the unknown in all the mousedeer's stories. Man does not belong in the rainforest, but he is there nonetheless and so our trickster like the other animals deal with his presence.

King Kancil would have known that if man was present, it would only have been in the capacity of the 'owner' of Gajah. So, man would most likely have been an elephant herder or a rider.

Man would therefore have control over Gajah and man would probably have been suspicious and would have prevented Gajah from taking part in the challenge.

This was precisely what King Semut did not want.

King Semut had one goal – revenge.

This is why he dug a very deep pit, so deep that whoever fell in would be killed instantly. He was willing to kill Gajah in cold blood.

And King Semut knew enough of Gajah to know that on his own Gajah would have charged to his death. Instantly.

So why then did King Semut change his mind and ask the weaver ants to assist?

Weaver ants do not dig. They build.

So, the answer is simply that King Semut did not change his mind. But he knew that King Kancil on seeing the pit would have put two and two together and judged his true intentions.

When King Semut originally asked for seven days – it was all that was needed to dig a lethal pit. But with the entire world of the rainforest looking on, it would have appeared unseemly that Gajah had never been given a chance. This is why King Semut invited the weaver ants. They were to weave a barrier that may have supported Gajah and stopped him from falling to his death.

I say 'may' because no doubt the weaver ants would have been capable of doing so. Provided that they were given sufficient time. But all the ants got were two days.

So why only two days?

Because seven plus two equals nine.

And nine is a lucky number to Malays.

And King Semut wanted that luck for himself.

He wanted to appear benevolent by giving Gajah a chance, but in reality, he really wanted Gajah dead.

And King Kancil knew this.

This is why he ordered the cremation at the end of the challenge and why he was not upset that half of King Semut's people were also burnt to death.

That was King Semut's punishment for seeking revenge, for taking things into his own hands rather than seeking out King Kancil to sort the matter out.

79 - Sang Kancil and his wife the tiger

I have never liked to hear of anything bad happening to a child, much less to hear that it has died.
I have included this story in the interests of completeness.
There are many Asian customs surrounding birth. Here for curiosity's sake are some of them:

Having a bath in the evening may cause an excess of amniotic fluid;

Mistreatment of a bird or fish the month before conception may lead to congenital defects;

A bite from a crab cause the infant to be born with a harelip;
If the pregnant mother is shocked/scared then the baby may have abnormalities;

No eating of lamb. This was one that I was subjected to when pregnant. Or else the baby would have fits;
Defend the pregnant woman from the langsar – the spirit of a woman who has died in childbirth. The physical form of the langsar consists only of the head and entrails.

80 - Harimau's child

Howell 1982 – This was about all that I could find on this story.

83 - A Pelandok Tale (II)

Is it over for the mousedeer in the above story?
I admit that I was gobsmacked when I read of Sang Kancil dying.

This isn't possible, I thought.

This is Sang Kancil after all! Don't the legends date back hundreds of years and doesn't Sang Kancil appear as the victor in all his tales?

But after much reflection, I believe that the ending here is meant to bring us hope. Not despair.

Mousedeer only live for 12 years in the wild. And as these cherished stories are still remembered and retold, I believe that the author of these tales wants us to be encouraged that although the initial mousedeer perished, he still lives on in his offspring as evidenced by the mark of the scroll on each of their backs.

And so, the legend of the Mousedeer Sang Kancil/Akal Pelanduk lives on.

86 - The Victory of the Buffalo

Growing up in Malaysia and Singapore I had always been aware of and admired the special houses of the Minangkarbau and their pointed roofs. I knew vaguely that there was a story of warfare but never knew the actual story, so I am pleased to be able to discover this story in my research.

Glossary

A

Abis = So, then
Achair = Pickled
Ada = Have
Adat= Believed to have originated from the Arabic ʿādāʾt (عادات).
Despite its Arabic origin, the term has been used throughout Maritime Southeast Asia, even in non-Muslim communities. It refers to the rules and customs that regulate conduct within society. It tended to be unwritten.
Akal = Timeless
Aki = grandfather (Iban Malay)
Aku = Me
Aiap = Special term used by a subject to refer to his food to royalty
Alamak = Oh god
Amboi = Hey! Also Wah or Hoi or Hei! (Malay)
Amcham = How (Baba Malay or BBM)
Ampat = Four (BBM)
Anak = Child or Baby
Angin = Air
Angsana = Flowering Tree (Pterocarpus Indicus)
Anjing = Dog
Annam = Old name for Vietnam
Antah berantah = Never Never Land in the middle of Nowhere
Antara = Between
Antu Raya = Ogre or giant. Gergasi. In Burma they devour bad people.
Apa = What
Apa Khabar = What news – a form of saying hello
Apai = Father (Iban Malay or IB)
Arnab = Rabbit
Ari = Day (Baba Malay or BBM)
Arimo = Tiger (BBM)
Atair = On top (BBM)
Atau tanah = Liver of the earth (Iban Malay)

Ati = Heart
Aum = Meeting
Awak = Your or You
Ayam = Chicken

B

Babi = Pig or Wild Boar
Baboy-Ramo = Pig (Tagalog)
Badan = Body
Badak = Rhinoceros
Bagus = Good
Baik = Good
Baju = Clothes or Shirt
Baju Burung = Bird Jacket
Baka = Like or similar to
Balek = Return
Bapak = Father
Bangsat = Trick
Barat = West (Malay)
Bau = Smell
Bawah = Under
Bawak = Bring
Belang = Stripes
Belian = Iron wood. Eusideraoxylon Zwageri
Beliung = Pickaxe
Berfikir = Think
Bergadoh = Fought
Bersama-sama = Together
Bersua = Meet unexpectedly (BBM)
Besai/Besar = Big
Bertapa = Religious penance
Biawak = Monitor Lizard
Bila = When
Buah = Fruit
Buat = Do
Bukit = Hill
Burrit = Anus
Burung = Bird
Berani/Brani = Brave
Berhenti = Stop
Beruang = Bear or Honey Bear

Berburu = Hunting (Malay)
Biasa = Ordinary
Bibek = Mrs, a title given to married women
Binatang = Animal
Bising = Noisy
Bodoh = Stupid
Bohong = Lies
Bolih = Able
Bombola = Hairy
Brani = Brave
Buaya/Buwaya = Crocodile
Bukan = Not
Bungkus = Tie
Burit = Buttock
Busut = Mound

C

Chabot = Fled (BBM)
Chadong = Possibly the quandong fruit. Another favourite of the mousedeer?
Chari = Find/Look
Chelaka = Woe Betide (Swear word)
Chegu = Teacher (composite of Guru and Enche)
Chepat = Quick or hurry
Cherita = Story
Chiku = Sapodilla Fruit
Cherita = Story (Bahasa Malay or BM)
Chrita = Story (BBM)
Chobak = Tried
Choy Sum = Green Leafy vegetable (Brassicaceae)
Crocodile = Crocodilus Porosus
Cucumbers = They are a popular vegetable for Malaysians and Singaporeans, often eaten as part of a dish of satay. They are also sliced and dipped in tomato sauce when eaten with nasi bryani. This is how my grandfather enjoyed them. Or sliced into slivers and served cold with yoghurt.

D

Dalam = In
Dan = And
Darat = Land
Datang = Come
Datok = Grandfather or Good Spirit

Dengair = Heard (BBM)
Dengar = Heard
Dia = He/She
Diampun = Forgive
Diri = Self
Dua = Two
Dudok = Sit
Duku = Langsat Fruit
Dulu = First
Dulu-dulu = Once upon a time
Durian = Fruit (My favourite). The Durian Tree (Durio zibethinus) is native to Borneo and Sumatra.

E

Ekor = Tail
Embuang = Throw
Embui = Give
Empat = Four
Enche/Inche = Sir
Enda = Not
Enggang = Horns

F

Flower named after our hero = Crenata roxb mata pelandok
Folk tales or Folk Literature are stories that have been passed down among the people. It was often oral tradition.

G

Gagak = Crow
Gajah/Gadja = Elephant
Garangkang = Spider
Gasak = Gobble
Gamelan = Orchestra composed of xylophones, gongs, drums and cymbals
Gemok = Fat
Gelap = Dark
Gargasi/Gergasi/Gersang/Gergarsang/Gergahasi/Gasi-gasi/Gĕgasi = Giant. Also sometimes referred to as a demon or Raksasa. Strangely similar to the word gargantuan. See Magic and Beliefs
Gila = Mad or crazy
Gorek = Caesalpinia Jayabo – creeper that produces small hard berries.

Gua = I (BBM)
Gulai = Curry
Gulang = Roll
Gunung = Mountain
Guru = Teacher

H

Halalintar = Electricity (Malay)
Hambah = Slave
Hampus = Get rid of
Harap = Hope
Hari = Day
Harimau = Tiger, also known as Rimau or Arimo (BBM)
Hikayat = A written account in prose
Hikmat = Wisdom
Hilang = Lost
Hilir = Down Stream
Hulubalang = Captain
Hulu = Upstream (In Singapore, if something is far away, we say ulu-ulu.)
Hutan = Rainforest or jungle

I

Ibu = Mother
Ikan = Fish
Indai = Mother
Inggeris = English
Ini = This
Insulindia = archaic geographical term for Maritime Southeast Asia
Isi = Flesh
Isteri = Wife
Itu = That

J

Jackfruit = Nangka. It is the fleshy bulbs inside that is edible portion however, and not the lumpy, bumpy rind which is the barrier to a great feast. Mostly eaten raw, jackfruit can sometimes be found in curries. Today it is often used as a meat substitute. Sweet, succulent, smooth fleshed, jackfruit, however, is notorious for its sticky sap which remains on fingers long after the fruit has been eaten.
Jaga = Guard or Watchman

Jagong = Corn or Maize
Jalai = Path
Jambatan = Bridge
Jambu = Water Apples (Syzygium Aqueum)
Jangan = Don't
Janji = Promise
Jawab = Answered
Jelu = Animal or beast
Jenaka = Many different interpretations. Trickster. Humourous. Young man? Old man? Pure or sacred place? Birth?
From the Hikayat Pelanduk Jenaka mentioned by Werndly as far back as 1736.

K

Ka = You (Malay)
Kali = Times
Kamsiah = Thank you (BBM)
Kancil = Generally means mousedeer although in Achehnese, "kancil" means "crafty" or "wicked."
Kampung/Kampong = Village (BM/BBM). In the old days, villages used to take their names from trees.
Kasi = Give
Kasi Tangan = Gift
Kat = On, In
Kata-kata = Words
Kawan = Friend, kawan-kawan = friends
Kaya = Rich
Keamanan = Peace
Kebaya = Blouse worn by women
Kelapa = Coconut
Keluar = Exit
Keluarga = Family
Kemudian = Then
Kena = Got
Kenyalang = Rhinoceros Hornbill
Kepala = Head
Kera = Ape or Monkey
Kerah = Collar
Kerbau/Karbau = Water Buffalo
Kerosang = Brooch
Kesian = Sad
Ketuai = Leader or head

Keukit = Term used to describe something small
Khabar = News
Khabhair = News (BBM)
Kijang = Barking Deer (Southern Red Muntjac)
Kikura = Terrapin
Kilat = Lightning (Malay)
Kinot = Meaning unknown. Name of the strange beast in the story.
Kisah = Story
Kita = Us, we
Klips-klips = Fireflies
Koran/Quran = Central religious text of Islam
Kosong = Nothing. Zero. Empty.
Koyak = Tore
Kua = Many eyed pheasant
Kueh = Cake
Kuwis = Malaysian flying squirel

L

Labah = Come to nothing (Iban Malay)
Langkau = Shelter, small hut
Lallang = Long sharp bladed grass. Imperata Cylindrica. Also called elephant grass. Maybe because it is so tall that an elephant can hide within.
Lalat = Fly (insect)
Lamah-lamah = Might be the Diospyros Sandwicensis which is a small, slow-growing tree. New leaves are bright pink or red. Possibly a favourite food for mousedeer?
Lama lama lekat = Stories stuck
Landak = Porcupine
Langit = Sky
Lari = Run
Lima = Five
Liok = Look
Lobang = Hole
Lotong = Long-tailed spectacle monkey
Lu = You in Baba Malay
Ludai = Sapium Baccatum. Small deciduous tree

M

Macham = Like
Maharajah = Great Prince or king or emperor
Main = Play

Majapahit = A Hindu dynasty in Southeast Asia

Maka = Then (Malay)

Makan = Eat

Makanan = Food

Makan Angin = Phrase that means to 'take the air' or go on an enjoyable trip

Malair = Lazy (BBM)

Malam = Night

Malik = King of Kings (Arabic)

Mana = Where

Manis = Sweet

Mari = Come

Masok = Enter

Mata-mata = Eyes

Mata Kuching = Fruit known as cat's eyes. Nephelium Malayense

Melanggar = Violate

Melaka Tree = Emblica Officinalis. The Amla tree. Another tree famed for its oil which is supposed to cure baldness. The Indian gooseberry.

Membunoh = Killed

Memerang = Otter. Lutra Sumatrana. On the verge of extinction.

Menarat = Monitor Lizard (Iban Malay)

Menasan = Animal Track

Mendengar = Heard

Mengapa = Why

Menteri = Minister

Merdu = Melodious (Malay)

Mereka = Them

Merunjau = Type of Fruit (Iban Malay)

Merunjau = Exploring (Bahasa Melayu)

Mia = Own

Midge = Tiny flies about the size of a pinhead

Miskin = Poor

Mit = Small

Mo = Want

Moken = Sea dwellers (Austronesian people) who live on boats known as kabang (interestingly the word for boat in Malay is kapal) on the Mergui Archipelago in the Andaman Sea. Only during the monsoon period, between May to October, do they come to land, staying in stilt houses on the eastern coast of these islands. They number only 2,000 to 3,000 people and their sustainable way of life is threatened by loss of habitat.

Interestingly, they predicted the 2004 Tsunami and escaped to higher ground in time.

The stories of the Mokens that are told in this book have all been taken from the Malays according to H. Bernatzik (1897-1953) an Austrian anthropologist.

According to the Moken, Rings of Coral - Moken folktales by Jacques Ivanoff, White Lotus

Press, Bangkok, 2001., the "theme of the mousedeer is a classic of Insulindian oral literature."

Monsoon = Arabic word to refer to the winds that blow from the Southwest in summer and the Northeast in winter.

Monitor Lizard = Menarat or Biawak. Possibly Varanus.

Kabaragoya, the Asian water monitor or Varanus salvator.

Monyet = Monkey

Musang = Fox or Civet Cat

N

Nadai = No (Iban Malay)

Naga = Dragons. In Burma the naga lives underground and on the floor of the sea. They cause earthquakes and whirlpools.

Nama = Name

Nampak = See

Nangka = Jackfruit (Artocarpus Heterophyllus) an evergreen tree

Nangis = Cry

Nanti = Stop

Negeri = State

Nenek = Grandmother

Ng Ko = Big brother or a term of respect for an older man

Ni = This (BBM)

Nonya/Nonja = Young woman. May be a Miss or a Mrs.

Nusantara = Formerly the term for rainforest or jungle. In Indonesian it means Maritime Southeast Asia. Or the Country of the Gaping Mouth.

Nyamai = Nice

Nyumboh = a kind of monkey without a tail (Iban Malay)

O

Oh Nyamai = How nice! (Iban Malay)

Otter = Lutra Vulgaris (Tales from an Eastern Forest) or Memerang (Malay)

P

Pada = On

Pada zaman dahulu = Once upon a time

Padang = Plains or fields

Padi = Rice

Pagi = Morning

Paha = Thigh

Pandanus = Old Mum Mat

Panday = Clever (BBM)
Pangkat = Rank
Pasak = Wedge or bug
Pasair = Because
Para = A shelf above the kitchen (Iban Malay)
Parang = Knife
Paubula = Fable (Filipino word)
Pauk = Lowlands
Paya = Swamp
Pelangi = Stripe (another word for rainbow)
Pelanduk = Mousedeer (Iban Malay)
Pengkalan = Jetty
Perau/Prahu = Boat
Peri = Fairy. Persian origins.
Pilandok = Mousedeer (Tagalog)
Pinjam = Borrow
Pintu = Door
Pekek = Shouted
Pemotong Rotan = Rotan/Cane Cutters
Penghulu = Chief (Malay and Iban Malay)
Pengkalan = Jetty (Iban Malay)
Penglipur Lara = Storyteller. They would have been bards in Celtic tradition. According to Amin Sweeny (Literacy and the Epic in the Malay World) prior to the introduction of print, 'Malay society was a radically oral manuscript culture.'
The Penglipur Lara was the scholar, judge, and protector of Malay culture. But as writing was introduced, his importance diminished, eventually becoming a soother of cares in rural areas where once he had been an important part of the rajah's court. Some story tellers have an elaborate ritual before they can tell stories. They light incense and pass their betel container through the smoke. They chew betelnut, massage the smoke into their limbs and then they tabik (salute) and then story begins.
My grandfather, my penglipur lara, always told me stories at bedtime. This was a ritual that I loved and miss to this day.
Often when telling folktales, the story tellers would change their voices.
Everyone has problems and folktales encourage the people to solve their problems, to be alert to the world around them, not to panic or lie and to ask for aid if necessary. Common sense is important.
How often I remember my mother reminding me to use common sense. I would respond by saying that I had rare sense.
And of course, lastly to make plans.
This is a good strategy. I remember a cartoon series I loved as a child. It had a saying: Motto of the wisest is be prepared for surprises.
I think this is something that Kancil can teach all of us.

In these folktales the animals speak and often act as human.

We have the arrogant or boastful, exemplified by the Bear. Then there are those who are dishonest – Badak the Rhinoceros.

The Deer and the Moth are both described as superior animals while of course the Trickster Kancil (also described as the Joker Moth) to whom intelligence is ascribed.

Cherita Penglipur Lara meant folk romances and were 'tales to comfort your woes.' When the sun set, and the villagers had finished their dinner and relaxed, the penglipur lara began his story.

Firstly, he would, sometimes perform a tabik or greeting.

He spoke until late into the night. If the story was not finished it would be continued on the next night. The storyteller was sometimes illiterate, but he never made mistake. He would have learnt these stories from his father and grandfather. They were also called 'sahibul hikayat' or lords of the story. They were travelling story tellers and the villagers welcomed them and paid them for their stories.

Penunggu Huma = Scarecrow

Perau = Boat (Iban Malay) or prahu (Malay)

Pernah = Ever or at times

Persahabatan = Friendship

Petarakna = Character

Pi = Go

Pikir = Thought or think

Pisang = Banana (Malay and Iban Malay)

Pokok = Tree

Priok = Pot

Punggal = Back Off (B.M.)

Punggal = Friend (IB)

Pungguk = Possibly the Boobook owl.

Puntan = Dead End (Iban Malay)

Punya = Own

Puteh = White

R

Raden = Ruler

Raja = King (Malay) or ruler

Rajah Muda = Crown Prince

Rajawali = Kingfisher

Rajin = Diligent

Raksha/Raksasa = Giant, also a temple watchman. See Gergasi. Female is Raksasi.

Rambai = Fruit resembling the langsat. Yellow-brown skin and white pulp.

Rani = Queen

Rattan = Rotan, a climbing palm whose stems are used for wicker work

Ratu = Queen
Raya = Great or Large
Rendang = Cook by stirring slowly
Rhu Tree = Casuarina tree
Rimba = Primeval jungle
Ringgit = Dollar
Ruai = Veranda
Rusa = Sambhur Deer (Malay and Iban Malay)

S

Sabong = Fight (Malay)
Sakti = Supernatural powers
Salah = Wrong (BBM)
Salaam Aleikam = Peace to You
Salai = Smoked (Malay and Sea Dyak/Iban)
Sang = Revered or Mister
Sama = With or same
Sama-sama = Equally
Sambi = Friendly term of address between animals (Iban Malay)
Samudra = The ocean (From Indonesian)
Sapa = Who (BBM)
Sarong = One rectangular piece or material, often used as a skirt or another piece of clothing. Can be sewn at one end to form a tube. Interestingly, the human body can also be seen as a sarong or a casing in which the soul has its residence.
Satu/Suatu = One
Saudagar = Merchant
Sawah = Rice field
Saya = I
Sebelum = Before
Sedair = Even
Sedap = Delicious
Sekali = Very
Sekarang = Now
Selalu = Always
Selamat = Safe
Sembah = Pray
Semua = All
Semut = Ant (There are two types in Singapore – black and red.)
Serau = Kambing Gurun or Capricornis Sumatraensis
Seraung = A kind of hat (Iban Malay)
Sibau = Fruit like the rambutan (Iban Malay)

Silat = Malay Martial Arts
Silsila = A type of hikayat
Singa = Lion
Sinjakala = Twilight (BBM)
Siput = Snail
Situ = There
Sua = Finished
Suay = Bad luck
Suleiman = Solomon
Sungei = River
Suroh = Instructed
Susah = Hard

T

Tabik = Salute
Tak = Short form of Tidak i.e., Not
Takleh = Did not (BBM)
Tahu = Know
Tau = Understand BBM
Takut = Afraid
Takot = Scared (BBM)
Tapi = But
Tamat = Over
Tanah = Earth (Malay and Iban Malay)
Tanggui = Hat
Tanggui seraung = Type of Hat
Tarok = Put
Tanggui = Hat (Iban Malay)
Tedung = Cobra
Tekura = Tortoise (Iban Malay)
Telingga = Ear
Telomian = Rarest dog breed in the world. The original Kampong Anjing. Able to climb and very adept at using their paws.
Tembusu = Large evergreen tree (Cyrtophyllum Fragrans)
Tempat = Place
Tempu = Time
Tengah = Middle
Tengok = See
Tentang = About
Terima Kaseh = Thank you
Terong/Terung = Solanum Torvum is False eggplant. Real eggplant is the Aubergine or Brinjal

Terperanjat = Scared or shocked
Terung = Eggplant or Aubergine or Brinjal
Tiada = (Short form of) Tidak Ada meaning do not have
Tiba = Arrive
Tidor = Sleep
Tiga = Three
Timor = East (Malay)
Timun = Cucumbers
Tiptibau = Type of Night owl (Lyncornis Temminckii)
Titah = Command (Malay)
Tiung = Mynah Bird
Toddy = Fermented Drink made from the sap of the coconut tree
Tolong = Help
Tu = That (BBM)
Tuan = Master or Sir
Tuai/Tuah/Tua = Chief or Head, basically someone old and wise
Tuba = A poisonous root (Iban Malay) Derris Elliptica
Tuhan = God
Tukak = sharpened bamboo trap (Iban Malay)
Tuliskan = Written
Tumis = Stir fry
Tunggul = Flag
Tupai = Squirrel

U

Uchu = Grandson (Iban Malay) (In Baba Malay grandchild is chuchu)
Umbang = Skin (Iban Malay)
Upih = Spathe (Iban Malay)
Ular = Snake. Ular sawa is the Python Molurus.
Ulat = Caterpillars
Ulu = Interior (Iban Malay)
Unak = Thorn (Iban Malay)

W

Wayang Siam = Malay shadow play

Y

Ya = Yes
Yang = Which

King Solomon and his many names

Charles Bryce, Mousedeer, published by Darling Newspaper Press 2009 refers to him as King Solomon.

King Solomon calls the mousedeer Sir Peace of the Forest. And his chief aide is apparently Noah, also called Old Noah.

Raja Suleiman
King Solomon or Nabi Sleyman
Nabi = Prophet
Raja = King
Solomon = Suleiman or Sleyman

Bibliography

"*Water Chevrotain*," Amazing Animals of the World. (n.d.). Gale Virtual Reference Library.

Amin. (2021, January 17). From Mischief to Hero: Examining Kancil's Role as a Trickster. Retrieved from IMAJI NATION: https://imajiugm.com/from-mischief-to-hero-examining-kancils-role-as-a-trickster/

Andaya, B. (2011). *Distant drums and thunderous cannon: Sounding authority in traditional malay society*. Hawaii: University of Hawaii.

Benjamin Hasbie. (n.d.). *Borneo Literature Bureau - Iban Animal Stories*.

Bro, M. H. (1970). *How the Mouse Deer Became King*. Garden City, New York: Doubleday & Company, Inc.

Bryce, C. (2009). Mousedeer. *Darling Newspaper Press*.

Carpenter, K. (1992). "Kancil: From Mischief to Moral Education.". *Western Folklore, vol. 51, no.2, 27-111*. Retrieved from Western Folklore.

Chew, I. (2020, February 5). *Did Sang Nila Utama really see a lion?* . Retrieved from Kontinentalist: https://kontinentalist.com/stories/singapore-sang-nila-utama-legend

Dehino, P. C., & San Jose, A. E. (2014). THE STORY OF PILANDOK: A POST-COLONIAL READING OF TRICKSTER TALES . *Philippine E-Journals*, 1-113.

Dickens, S. M. (1977). *Kuncil the Wily One - Tales of the Malaysian Mouse-deer*. Thornhill Press.

Gallop, A. (2015, February 10). *The wily Malay mousedeer*. Retrieved from British Library: https://blogs.bl.uk/asian-and-african/2015/02/the-wily-malay-mousedeer.html
Georges, V. (2015). *Tales from the Deep Forest - The very curious adventures of Kancil the Mousedeer*. ITBM.

Husaini Sulaiman. (n.d.). *Borneo Literature Bureau - Mousedeer and the Crocodile.*

Husainin Sulaiman. (n.d.). *Borneo Literature Bureau - Brave Mouse-Deer.*

Ismail. (2016). *The Symbol of Animals in Malay Proverbs.*

Ismail. (2017). *Bird Element Symbolism in Malay Proverbs.*

Ivanoff, J. (2001). *Rings of Coral - Moken folktales.* Bangkok: White Lotus Press.

Karasov, C. (n.d.). *Enviroment/Encyclopedias almanacs transcripts and maps/chevrotains-tragulidae.* Retrieved from Encyclopedia.com: https://www.encyclopedia.com/environment/encyclopedias-almanacs-transcripts-and-maps/chevrotains-tragulidae

Kheong, C. Q. (2019). Sang Kancil as Cultural Artefact: A Comparative Neo-Archetypal Study 2019.

Kuah, K. B. (1972). *Malay customs in relation to childbirth.* Kuala Lumpur: The Clinic, Maternity & Nursing Home, Petaling Jaya.

Loke, V. P., Lim, T., & Arceiz, A. C. (2020). *Hunting practices of the Jahai indigenous community in northern peninsular Malaysia.* Science Direct. Retrieved from https://www.sciencedirect.com/science/article/pii/S2351989419306602

Malay concordance project. (n.d.). Retrieved from MCP: https://mcp.anu.edu.au/Q/info.html#full

Mason, O. J. (1907, June). *Jounral No.48. Journal of the Straits Branch of the Royal Asiatic Society,* 1-107. Retrieved from Biodiversity Heritage Library: https://www.biodiversitylibrary.org/item/130727#page/287/mode/1up

McHugh, S. D. (1977). *Kanchil the Wily One Tales of the Malaysian Mouse-Deer.* Gloucester: Thornhill Press.

Mohammed Sahari. (1964). *Borneo Literature Bureau - entitled Clever Mouse-Deer.*

Mouse deer facts for kids. (2023, October 16). Retrieved from Kiddle: https://kids.kiddle.co/Mouse_deer

Myths Folktales and Legends - About Philippines. (2015, June 9). Retrieved from FLIPHTML5: https://fliphtml5.com/ujqe/vkwc/Print_Page_-_Myths_Folktales_and_Legends_-_About_Philippines/

OConnell, R. (2019, November 13). 9 *Tiny Facts About the Chevrotain.* Retrieved from Mental Floss: https://www.mentalfloss.com/article/64198/9-tiny-facts-about-chevrotain

Peachy Cleo Dehino, A. E. (2014). *THE STORY OF PILANDOK: A POST-COLONIAL READING OF TRICKSTER TALES* . Retrieved from Philippine E-Journals: https://ejournals.ph/article.php?id=12703

Proudfoot, I. (2001). A "Chinese" Mousedeer Goes to Paris. In I. Proudfoot, *Archipel 61* (pp. 69-97). Paris: Perseus.

Proudfoot, I. (2001). In Archipel. In I. Proudfoot, *A "Chinese" Mousedeer Goes to Paris* (pp. 69-97).

Provozin, E. (2023, June 8). *Java Mouse-Deer Breeding in Indonesia.* Retrieved from Rove: https://rove.me/to/indonesia/java-mouse-deer-breeding

Puteh, O., Said, A., Awang, A. J., Salim, A., Minhad, A., Abdullah, A., . . . Hashim, N. (2008). *366 A Collection of Malaysian Folk Tales.* Taman Klang Jaya: YEOHPRINCO SDN. BHD.

Quindoza, L. (2012). THE PILANDOK NARRATIVE IN PHILIPPINE HISTORY AND SOCIETY. *9th International Conference on the Philippines.* Michigan: Michigan State University.

Rahman. (2022). *The Pelanduk Jenaka's Character Strategies In The Power Creation And Soverignty In Hikayay Pelanudk Jenaka.*

Ralls, K., Barasch, C., & Minkowski, K. (1975). *Behavior of captive mouse deer.*

Sang Kancil and Sang Rimau . (2021). *SANG Kancil,* 1-14.

Sellato, B. (2020). Basketry Motifs, Names, and Cultural Referentsin. *Hal Open Science,* 1-19.

Skeat, W. W. (1900). *Malay Magic.*

Strawder, N. (2000). *"Tragulus javanicus"* (On-line). Retrieved from Animal Diversity Web: https://animaldiversity.org/accounts/Tragulus_javanicus/

Tsuji, C. (2023, November 30). trickster tale. *Encyclopedia Britannica.* Retrieved from Britannica, The Editors of Encyclopaedia: https://www.britannica.com/art/trickster-tale

Voisset, G. (n.d.). *TALES FROM THE DEEP FOREST: THE VERY CURIOUS ADVENTURE OF KANCIL THE MOUSE DEER.*

Walter Skeat. (1901). Fables & Folk-Tales from an Eastern Forest. *University Press Cambridge.*

Werndly. (1736). *Hikayat Pelanduk Jenaka.*

Werner, R. (2002). *Malay folklore.* Retrieved from Wikipedia: https://en.wikipedia.org/wiki/Malay_folklore

Winsedtt, R. V. (n.d.). *Some Mousedeer Tales.*

Winstedt, R. O. (1921). Hikayat Hang Tuah. Journal of T*he Straits Branch of The Royal Asiatic Society,* 1-122.

Yokmonceng. (2012, August 8). *Kesusasteraan Melayu Komunikatif (922)* . Retrieved from Blogspot: http://yokmanceng.blogspot.com/2012/08/hikayat-pelanduk-jenaka-syeikh-alam.html

Zain, S. (2013, February 17). *SERJARAH MELAYU LIBRARY.* Retrieved from sabrizain/malaya/library: http://www.sabrizain.org/malaya/library/

Also by Theresa Fuller

LANDS BELOW THE WINDS SERIES

The Girl Who became a Goddess
The Girl Sudan Painted like a Gold Ring

BABA MALAY TODAY SERIES:

Sapa, Apa, Mana or Who, What, Where
Amcham, Apasair, Bila or How, Why, When
Tapi, Abis, Pasair or But, So, Because
Atair, Kat, Bawah or Top, Near, Bottom
Alus, Ka, Kasar or Delicate, Or, Coarse
Chakapan Baba Ati or The Heart of Baba Malay

NEW PERANAKAN TALES SERIES

Gua Pi Keday or I Went to the Shops
Satu Taon Jalan-jalan or A Year of Walks

FOLKTALES

Eating the Liver of the Earth, Mousedeer Tales

OTHER WORKS

Where Cranes Weave and Bamboo Sings

Me and Kun Kun

Author Notes

When I first began this quest, I had planned to collect every single story of the mousedeer but two years later, I must admit that this is virtually impossible. As the author Bro states, new ones are being invented even today, and if one wanted to learn about Kantjil's many adventures and escapades, at least in the Indonesian islands one would have to visit all twenty thousand islands then multiply them by another twenty thousand.

I thus happily admit defeat.

I have enjoyed collecting these stories and trying to write them as close to the original stories as possible, at times going down to the original Malay (Bahasa Melayu) which has changed since the time of these tales. I cannot read Jawi and there were times when I was using translation software to translate Tagalog of which I know nada. Of course, in the interests of heightening enjoyment I have dramatized - which all the penglipur laras of old would have done.

I have particularly enjoyed the memories that these stories have brought back of my late father and late grandfather. And I thank you, the reader, for coming along on this journey with me.

And of course, here is some information about my grandfather – the person I loved most as a child.

My grandfather was Chan Chim Bock.

He always told me, "Theresa, you can do anything."

And thus, so encouraged, I grew up believing that I could do anything.

Isn't it wonderful when a child has someone who believes in them.

I was named after his favourite saint – St Theresa of the Roses.

It was my grandfather's love of storytelling that started me on the road to loving stories and eventually becoming a Penglipur Lara myself.

Kun Kun introduced me to Sang Kancil but his Sang Kancil story was of the mousedeer measuring the crocodiles to see which was the longest. So, as he leapt from back-to-back, he measured their length.

This is where it all started.

And I hope this never ends.

Theresa Fuller
Sydney
4ᵗʰ of January 2024